CHAIN REACTION

CHAIN REACTION

Gillian White

ORION

Copyright © 1997 Gillian White

The right of Gillian White to be identified as the author of
this work has been asserted by her in accordance with
the Copyright, Designs and Patents Act 1988.

First published in Great Britain in 1997 by
Orion
An imprint of Orion Books Ltd
Orion House, 5 Upper St Martin's Lane, London WC2H 9EA

A CIP catalogue record for this book is available
from the British Library

ISBN 0 75280 439 1

Typeset at the Spartan Press Ltd,
Lymington, Hants
Printed in Great Britain by
Clays Ltd, St Ives plc

For Benjamin Hamish Banforth,
with love.

ONE

Flat 1, Albany Buildings, Swallowbridge, Devon

She is not too weak to walk yet, by God. She'll even run if she has to! She has always prided herself on her fibre, on her ability to pull through.

Indeed, there were many times in Irene's middle years when she was comforted by the simple wisdom of Faith Steadfast – the housewives' answer to Rudyard Kipling.

> *If your heart is feeling weary,*
> *Tired of all that burdens you,*
> *Don't give up and don't stop smiling,*
> *Some inner strength will pull you through.*

But hell's bells, she'd never envisaged needing as much blooming inner strength as this.

As she hurries along, Irene Peacock's sense of urgency grows because they are getting crosser and crosser. If they catch her this time they will kill her, she is sure. Either that or they'll suck the juices of any strength she has left out of her for ever.

Getting her tights pulled up was a struggle. She left them on the floor in the end and it felt like leaving fetters behind.

Her fluffy grey hair hangs down to her shoulders, the tresses thin and tangled. Candy-floss hair. The vest they gave her keeps her warm, warm as breath on her chest it is. Gritting her teeth she presses on awkwardly up the hill – the one they used to run up as children on their way to school, skipping along in gingham dresses, calling to each other all of seventy years ago . . . and now those old sounds spin round in her head in a web of spindly voices.

'*House to let, apply within. If you go out,* Irene Mott *comes in!*'

Hah, she was such a good skipper she'd stay in for ages. No matter how fast that rope spun round, they could not trip her up.

Memories as fragile as moths' wings. Her ribbons used to match her dress, tied on hair that was held back in tight, tight plaits which hurt, with an awful parting down the centre wide as a railway track. Spam sandwiches, a handful of cob nuts and home-grown tomatoes in her packed-lunch tin – and ooh, the warm garden taste of it as if it was baked on hot stones. There was such a little crowd of them then, their names she can hardly remember although that doesn't matter because most of them have passed over and their clothes sent off to Save The Children.

Inner strength? Dear Lord. She'd never expected to be left alone like this – ever. Especially when she was married and raising her child, and busy. She thought life would be a continual game of chain tick, everyone pulling hard on the hands of everyone else until the raucous chain collapsed with the force of itself.

Never mind losing the sense of touch, nobody *listens* to her any more; nobody's got respect. She is terrified that her speech will go, like some of them with strokes. She will open her mouth one day and what comes out will be jagged and broken and then she won't be able to shout.

Once they clip you down in those chairs you're lucky if you can walk again.

And on top of this she is constipated, egg-bound, and that doesn't help, being in pain most of the time, nor does the fact that she's taken to sleeping so frequently, gently snoozing in a fireside chair. Do they put something in her Horlicks? It never used to be full of those grainy grey bits at the bottom, nor did she doze away the hours so that sleeping and waking became blurred. She's not sure of anything much. She must be going barmy. Sometimes she can even feel William, so sure, keeping step beside her.

Some of them back there are lying in beds with the sides up, like kiddies' cots with bits of themselves leaking out and farting. She avoids them all as much as she can, fearful of contamination. They'll get her in one of those next if she doesn't watch out – and once you get into that sort of state they touch your body so rudely.

She puts on a good face, tries to keep herself cheerful, remembers Faith Steadfast – her mother-in-law used to give her some of that author's delicately illustrated books for Christmas – remembers some of the encouraging tunes they used to sing in the war. She's clean, always has been. Cold, hard, starchy sheets with the laundry mark, a tattoo blue, looking like a blueberry stain in the corners. Narrow beds too high for comfort. They cut your toenails, they feed you meat and two veg, ice cream and eggs, eggs eggs. A vegetable form of existence. They sit round the Formica tables almost silently like uneasy children playing house, passing the plastic cruets. Bursts of clapping and laughter from the day-room television all night. Eyelids are no protection in there; they are transparent, the images seep through.

She groans when she thinks of all the years when she took so much for granted.

Her back hurts now but fear is the worst thing. She hurries on, a small, bent figure in a powder-blue coat, bedroom slippers, a knitted beret and a crochet bag pulling down one shoulder. Much too hot for the day, of course, but she couldn't button her dress in all the excitement so she left it off and had to wear her coat to keep herself decent. Her walking stick has a hound's head carved upon the handle. It used to be William's – the handle has worn smooth from his hand. Last time they came for her in an ambulance. She had to travel back to Greylands with a red rug over her white-wafer legs as if she was an accident victim, wrapped-up human remains. The shame, oh the disgrace of it. 'You are exhausting everyone's patience, Irene,' they said and you'd think she'd been caught by Interpol, not shopped by the manager of Boots. And their faces were crosser than ever but she felt no remorse. She promised never to do it again but her cheeks sagged with the weight of the lies. 'What d'you want to go and do something like that for?'

Ladybird ladybird fly away home. Do they really not understand?

She passes along the road unnoticed. She doesn't count so they don't count her.

> *When the day's events seem dreary*
> *When life seems pointless, full of woes,*
> *A friendly face, a kind 'Good morning'*
> *Banish all these sorry lows.*

Irene takes a deep breath and hobbles on; she's nearly there now. She must get home again, she must, while she's still got somewhere to call her own, an old wounded fox heading for its familiar lair. Before they diagnose dementia – and then what might they do? Attach an electronic device to her wrist so they know when she gets near the front door? Setting off alarm bells as if she's a burglar breaking into a world she has no God-given right to inhabit. Are they afraid she will steal their air and scuttle off with a bag marked Swag? And Frankie has taken power of attorney, reckons her mother's not 'clear' enough in her head to deal with her bank account any more. 'We don't want you to worry yourself over things like that at your age, Mum.' Said with a kindness that glittered hard. Pound coins, not so nice as the gentler notes, they give her change like pocket money when the newsagent lady comes round. They hide her fags and in three months she hasn't been able to save enough for a bottle of gin.

'Now then, be sensible, dear. *Who will look after you at home?*'

They looked at her searchingly. 'How will you cope with the shopping, cooking, cleaning, dressing and *personal hygiene*, Irene?'

'What if you fell and broke your hip?'

'I've got good neighbours,' said Irene, ignoring the scolding fingers, 'and then there's my daughter, Frankie.'

The eyes that watched her narrowed. 'It would be unfair to lay so much responsibility on their shoulders, surely? There is a limit as to what you can expect neighbours and family to do. And doesn't your daughter work? She's a teacher, isn't she?'

'Yes,' said Irene with pride, to the woman with the martyred expression.

Selfish old woman, they said, their voices whispering in corners about private things like her waterworks and then they devised a test to trap her. Scrambled eggs and drinking chocolate made with milk at the same time. Well, who can cope with those impossible combinations? You'd have to be a chef at the bloody Savoy. To make them properly you need a decent whisk and hers was no good, it was rusty. When she failed they sighed and looked at her sadly as they considered their verdict. That was the first time she'd run away. In the end she sat there in stubborn silence and allowed them to carry her back, unable to resist the inevitable.

But not this time, oh no. Make no bones about that.

Any further would be beyond her. Every step is an effort now but Irene Peacock turns the last corner and there across the main road to the right, is her little one-bedroom flat in a yellow brick block of six, ground floor, with a small entrance garden where sometimes she manages to drag out a chair with a couple of cushions to sit on. She sees it with a kind of radiance, a glow behind a fog.

She rests on her hound's head stick with relief. With a resigned sigh she sees that the little round flower beds need weeding. It's up to the residents to do it, but nobody bothers. They are out at work all day, and people tend not to care about anything communally shared these days. Values have completely changed, although that nice Miss Benson on the first floor is helpful and kind. Irene Peacock takes a deep breath and inches herself and her bulky bag across the busy main road. They'll probably accuse her of stealing because of the milk, the bread and the biscuits she took.

FOR SALE.

In the little communal hall there's a smell of joss sticks and curry.

FOR SALE?

The sign cannot apply to hers, not to number one.

But someone has stuck the sign on her door so it almost obscures the thin letter box like a yashmak hides a smile.

She raises her stick and gives the offending poster a prod.

Is she getting worse? Is she imagining things?

Fishing for her handkerchief, Irene wipes her eyes and blows her nose. Then she turns round, a full circle, and back to face her door again.

A man in a red bobble hat passes by and pauses kindly. 'All right, sweetheart?'

Irene nods so he goes away. She doesn't want sympathy now, it saps energy, but she certainly is *not* all right – no, far from it. Her mouth falls open and she gapes, appalled, as the truth gradually dawns. She must look like a stranded codfish with her mouth drooped like this but she seems temporarily to have lost control. This is her flat, *there is no mistake*. Someone has done this behind her back. Someone is trying to sell her home and that someone has to be Frankie. But what about all her things? There's an acid burst of outrage as her whole world topsy-turvies and twists around her. She is suddenly all the more alone in a roaring cavern of sound.

Inside at dear last (at least they haven't yet changed the lock), with a cup of tea in her trembling hand, Irene Peacock burrows down into her flat, savouring its various textures and smells, the wireless, the armchair, the home-made rugs, everything. Some might call it shabby in here but she can't get enough of it. Everything to be trusted and relied upon, some of these items have accompanied her through the whole of her life . . . the little dog ornament, for example, won at a fair, and the picture of the little blonde girl with the flowers. Her eyes linger lovingly on every detail and yet she had never wanted to come here, had never been keen to leave the bungalow, but as Frankie had said sensibly at the time, 'Now Dad's gone and you've no transport, you'll be far better in town with all the services handy.'

What did she mean by 'services'? – the hospital? The clinic? The off-licence was more relevant, but there was no need for her daughter to know that.

Irene was used to better.

She'd been so damn down then she'd been easily persuaded, but

5

funnily enough Frankie had been right. The bungalow was too full of memories of William. She couldn't bear to stay there, even to cook with the same view from the kitchen window as if she could call him in from the garden when tea was ready and he'd come, easing his boots off at the door. All that sickness. Sweat, wood and lilies and the grey light of so many dawns through bay windows. It took her a while to stop calling out and following men in the street who looked like him.

'You'll be nearer to me and the kids – there's that to consider,' said Frankie.

But Irene didn't approve of the flat. 'Far too pokey,' she'd sniffed. 'What about all my things? And there's no airing cupboard.'

'You don't need all that stuff any more, Mum. Not now. You want somewhere small you can cope with.'

And so she had finally been persuaded – and it had worked very well, she conceded. Although to be honest she didn't see more of Frankie and the kids because the flat was too small for all of them to fit in comfortably. If she saw them it was when she was invited to lunch at their house, or for Christmas or a birthday party. Frankie worked hard, a woman on her own since the divorce. Irene had always been proud of her.

And so, gradually, Irene mended the texture of her life which had been so roughly torn. Lord, it was an uphill struggle.

It worked the same way when she went to Greylands for the first time. She'd had a fall going round the shops, caused by a loose pavement so it wasn't her fault, nothing life-threatening, but she'd broken her leg and needed to be cared for. 'It'll only be for a month or so,' said Frankie encouragingly, 'just till you're back on your pins. You can't manage at home alone, not any more, Mum. You're beginning to forget things, aren't you? And you went calling for tea at Miss Benson's last week when you hadn't been asked. Miss Benson is worried about you. We are *all* worried about you. And look what has happened now . . . you can't even walk with two sticks.'

Irene considered Miss Benson a traitor of the very worst kind.

'Oh God – look at it, Frankie!' Greylands horrified Irene, although it was not unpleasant in appearance – white and lofty, with hedges clipped into tidy shapes, raked gravel paths and wisteria trailing over the door. There was even a full-length conservatory where they propped the old ones out in all weathers along with the geraniums. It was the knowledge of what it was and *what it housed* that upset her.

Even then she felt afraid that once she set foot inside that place, she would never get out again.

6

Inside, in the sleepy heat, it smelled of food and urine and strong arthritis unguents.

Frankie was servile before the matron. Funny, there was something disturbingly similar about them both, apart from the fact that each woman wore an Aran sweater with pockets and wooden buttons.

Afterwards Frankie said, 'Never mind what it smells like. It's only temporary, you'll soon be back home again. Somebody's got to look after you, Mum, and I can't.' Frankie was getting in one of her states and making Irene ashamed of her selfishness. 'You know it's impossible for me to take time off school.'

So it seemed like the only safe thing to do.

It just goes to show: you should always follow your initial instincts, no matter what the odds against you.

Now, back in the beloved safety of her small flat, Irene looks round. She swallows. People have been here while she's been gone, and not just Frankie either. Things are slightly out of line where strangers have pushed past, and someone has piled the post on the windowsill, not the mantelpiece where Frankie usually leaves it. The washing-up bowl has been turned upside down, a sure sign of somebody not coming back. She daren't look in the bedroom drawers in case she finds them empty. She is too frightened to move from her chair for the moment. The flat gave her life a structure, an aim, and now she is loose like a ship on the sea with no rudder and a black storm rushing towards her . . . and it's all very well for Thatcher to say that it all depends on which way you steer.

She is sitting there on the lav of all places when she hears the chink of the front door.

She jumps. *Damn, damn.* Frankie is right – she *is* getting confused, having periods of forgetfulness, else why didn't she think to lock it?

With a thumping heart Irene pushes the toilet door shut with the end of her stick and lies low like Brer Fox.

'Mum? Mum! Are you all right? It's me, Frankie.'

Well, I know it's you, thinks Irene crossly. Who else would call me 'Mother'?

Her daughter's voice has a spiky edge. 'Miss Blennerhasset is with me . . .'

Matron – that unholy cow? The keeper of the keys? She would be! As Irene struggles forward to pull up her knickers, the stick falls against the door. It is William's stick which gives her away.

'Irene, dear,' calls Miss Blennerhasset, and Irene can hear her large sandalled feet squeaking across the kitchen floor. 'What on earth do you think you are doing?'

'Having a pee, since you ask,' snaps Irene, fighting for breath. 'And I would like some privacy – surely that's not too much to ask? You can't get in anyway,' she adds with some triumph. 'The stick has wedged across the door.'

'Then I'll stand out here and wait for you,' says Miss Blennerhasset, rattling the door knob like a bulldog which won't let go, 'while Frankie makes us all a nice cup of tea.'

'You have surpassed yourself this time, Mother. We'll be lucky if they take you back.'

Hopeless to try and hurry. 'There's milk in my bag,' calls Irene, quite forgetting she's stolen it, giving herself away again, asking for trouble. But a question bubbles to the surface of her mind – *Hang on a minute* – it's not her who deserves a good talking to this time, it's them. It's these devious conspirators who have put her flat up for sale behind her back and now they've got to answer to her, the rightful owner. From the kitchen she hears the rattle of crocks, but she's miles away now, thinking about feeding the geese in the park with Frankie when she was little. You try to do something kind with the bits of bread in your paper bag, and how do they react? They overwhelm you, demanding more, pricking at you with their sharp yellow beaks, shrieking and squealing and beating their wings till you wish you'd never come in the first place. Till you vow you'll never feed them again.

Gobble, gobble gobble, the devils. They don't love you after all. They hate you. *They are coming to eat you all up.*

TWO

'Joyvern', 11, The Blagdons, Milton, Devon

Joy is too young to have benefited from the pious verse of Faith Steadfast and anyway, women had ceased endeavouring to be steadfast long before the poet's demise.

All Joy knows is that they are conspiring to drive her mad. Total strangers with fine drizzle on their hair known only by surname and briefly introduced by the agent, come with their swivelling eyes, their cold and greedy eyes, and sometimes their extended families to sneer at Joy's airing cupboard and to take note of the state of her lavatory bowls.

Blue water, pink water, green water . . . out of the colours of the rainbow, Lord which is the most hygienic?

She'll soon close the door on another lot.

They tread mud through on the carpet but still she must be deferential. If they delve hard enough, they might uncover some private life hidden deceitfully from view. Is it through the mirror? Is it under the stairs?

The bathroom glistens and glows and smells like a perpetual garden. It is nobody's smell in particular, Joy has made certain of that. What would it smell like if left to itself – decomposition? Surely not as bad as that! Their lives might have changed for the worse, but they're still alive and in with a chance, aren't they?

If only . . .

'And this is the en suite bathroom,' she gushes. Oh, when did life cease to be fun and turn into one uphill struggle?

And why is Vernon never around when she has to endure this ordeal?

Domestos sits like silk on the water, a layer of hygiene laid across by a loving hand like a sheet over a sleeping child. On guard against germs. Perhaps if the water was black they'd be more impressed? She'd like to do something nasty in it, like drop a fag-end down, a fag-end that shreds and won't flush away. No, she wouldn't. She couldn't bear them to think of her like that.

She doesn't even smoke. Nobody does, these days.

Nobody moves house these days either, not unless they jolly well have to. That's what everyone says, so reasoning otherwise sounds suspicious. You might as well just come clean and admit, 'We've run out of money so we've got to sell or the bank will sell it over our heads.'

As soon as she'd seen them, these latest viewers, these people from Lancashire with their northern accents, she'd quenched a flicker of disappointment, assuming they were not the ones. '*You don't like this house, I can tell you don't like it. You are wasting my time and yours, so why don't you just go away?*'

If only Joy could be honest and say that, instead of playing these mind-games. But rather than be honest that way with anyone, Joy Marsh would bite through her lip, gnash right through it, sharp white enamel through soft pink flesh. Self-mutilation. She'd abuse herself and anyone else if they started being honest like that.

She was brought up as a good woman, not to be honest.

She had crushed a garlic clove in the kitchen the moment she heard the doorbell chime, her shoulders raised in anticipation. Another lie, suggesting she cooks with garlic and herbs although she does, sometimes. Truth be told, she might as well leave out the old frying pan full of Vernon's bacon butty fat. He's taken to bacon butties in the mornings, flying in the face of the health warnings, flying in the face of all sorts of warnings because what does it matter now?

Might as well leave his seat belt off. I mean, it hardly goes round his waist any more, he has put on so much weight. Some people eat when they are depressed. They eat and gorge and grunt grunt grunt. While others starve themselves into shrunken relics. Might as well cut the lawn with the safety catch off the electric mower, might as well leave the door unlocked so that burglars can get in. Oh, it's all so puny, so hopeless these days to do anything COURAGEOUS or CARELESS. You can't ride your horse over dangerous hedges till it drops and breaks its neck and yours, or wage war, or throw down a challenge to Norman Mycroft at the bank, slap his baby face with a glove.

YOU CAN'T FIGHT BACK.

So what does anything matter if you have to go on being meek?

She and Vernon have lost everything, haven't they?

Everything they fought for.

What a good thing the chickens have flown the coop. She couldn't have stood all this humiliation in front of the children.

'And this is the master bedroom,' she smiles, softly leading the way and surreptitiously squeezing the tiny white linen bag full of rose pot pourri – to cover what, the smell of sex? A seasidey, weedy, frondy smell, or is that just the smell of woman? She can hardly remember, it is so long since sex was anything more than a scuffle . . . but she thinks that hot men smell of sex and apples. She knows these people don't like 'Joyvern' but still Joy is anxious to please, keen to impress. She can't help it.

'Master bedroom?' So what is that supposed to mean? That it's owned by the master of the house, or that this bedroom, because of its size, dominates the three others by wielding the stick. A bully bedroom. How absurd is this estate agents' language and how pitiful that she is forced to use it.

A fungal colour? She never thought of it that way when she ordered the Laura Ashley beige, when she considered that beige gloss would offset the bedspread of dusky apricot. The inside of a mushroom? Very tasteful, with bits of burnt bacon rind blazed into the colour of the rug.

Vernon's alarm clock set at seven-thirty, seven-thirty all his life.

Carefully placed books on the two bedside tables are false as the garlic in the kitchen. *Sacred Hunger* – she hopes there is no bedroom message in the title that these – what are their names? – that these Middletons might pick up and misinterpret. They probably won't, for these people clearly have no taste. Joy never managed actually to get into the book although she was guillible enough to buy it when she saw it on special display in Smiths. That's partly why they are in this mess, because of her endless shopping, because she's attracted to display like a dowdy female peacock. Or a jackdaw with a nest to feather. A craving for brightness. For owning things. An illness, some people say. There's counselling groups in America. Wardrobes for His and Hers, only Hers runs along 90 per cent of the wall space while his is a humble single unit filled from Marks & Spencer. On Vernon's side sits a Kingsley Amis which someone gave him one Christmas. It dryly covers a temptingly fat Jilly Cooper.

A tense and nervous woman somewhere in her forties, Mrs Middleton's pink lipstick spiders into the lines round her mouth. 'Not much of a view,' she says from the window, her face gone an unhealthy green from the wet and leafy reflection there.

It creates such a shocking lack of privacy, this showing people round. The bedroom is full of sleeping breath like evening shadows. There must be hidden toenail cuttings splintering over the carpet.

'We get the view in the winter,' says Joy in her most genteel tones, 'when that tree is dead.'

'Hum,' says Mr Middleton, stooping, viewing himself through the dressing-table mirror and smoothing back his hair. That mirror must be shocked, it's so long since it has seen anyone else's reflection but hers, and there was a time just lately when she pressed her lips hard against it, and her nipples, too, squashed and cooled like the blunt, soft noses of puppies. Lips and nipples, both left smudges of cloud on the glass. This was when she was trying to find herself after learning of their financial predicament, so totally disorientated she was trying to rediscover herself physically. Joy is a small, dumpy woman with rounded features and bright blue eyes. Homely, she supposes, homely, nuzzling and familiar. Thousands of women look like Joy, but not many dress with her kind of style. Her haircut is short and sensible with a short and sensible fringe. She's a busy person, only just turning grey at the edges.

'There's no view through there,' Joy would like to remind the usurper, 'unless you enjoy staring at long-nosed men with mean, bad-tempered eyes and thinning brown hair.' That's not fair. Joy knows she is being unfair, but these men are so ruthless with their little bit of power, like everyone else these days in the privileged position to buy. And why doesn't Mrs Middleton tell him that he has a bad case of dandruff?

Joy can't help being spiteful; she doesn't want to sell her house.

The two Middleton teenagers fidget, obviously aware that this house is not to their parents' taste and unprepared to play Let's Pretend like them, nor brave it out. The graceless girl, the older one, dressed from head to toe in black plastic, sits on the edge of the bed as if to test the springs, as if the bed is for sale as well, but Joy will not rise to the bait. Their attitude is a mixture of laughter and scorn. Well, what does anyone expect for the money? This is a perfectly respectable house on a perfectly respectable estate. Some might call it a square box but it's been a good home to Joy and Vernon. These kids have probably been dragged around hundreds of unsuitable houses, poor things, and are bored to death by now. Huh. The Middletons probably haven't even sold theirs yet, it's probably not even on the market. They just enjoy spending their days disturbing other people and conspiring to drive them mad, viewing houses as some folks take to the roads at weekends in order to go deliberately slowly and block everyone else.

Perhaps the Middletons are impostors and don't even have a house to sell.

The agents swore that they vetted their viewers, made sure they were serious contenders before they allowed them loose in their clients' homes. Well, the agents swore many things when first the Marshes went on the market. They promised they would show people round for a start, and that they would advertise widely . . . but so far they haven't turned up once, and there's been no sign of an ad in any of the local papers.

Ah well . . .

'We'd have done better to try and sell it ourselves,' Vernon said morosely after four weeks went by with no response whatsoever. Poor, dear Vernon. Running that shop never worked out; it swallowed all that precious redundancy money for which they'd had such high hopes. Joy is forced to close her eyes against that mocking memory. You would think an electrical engineer would be able to sell electrical appliances, knowing all about them and backing up every sale with a customer-friendly repair deal. Marsh Electronics Ltd, not the most imaginative title, not the most imaginative man. But Vernon was so brave. He is *still* brave. It is she who is the snivelling coward. It's true, heroes are men like Vernon who get up and go to work every single wet morning for the trivial trappings of this world, blind to the views of the universe. Heroes are the lonely people who get through Sundays all alone, not the reckless men who go barging into battle, adrenalin flowing like flags in the wind. It is Vernon and men like him who should be given the medals.

Unfortunately, it had been the wrong time for Marsh Electronics, as well as the wrong place. There're hardly any shops surviving in that arcade now, not since they built the new one beside the harbour. And they can't even fill those – they are still three-quarters empty, and no wonder with the rents they charge! And now he is stuck with the lease to pay and a Sale that goes on endlessly, and unless they can sell the house . . . But that's all water under the bridge. Now Joy must be positive.

'And next there's the roof extension.'

Up they spiral, this forced little party, one by one to the loft conversion Vernon built himself and was once so proud of – the fairy on top of the Christmas tree, this room at the top of the house. When the children left home they had to have somewhere to store the clutter, so of course it was piled up here. In those days they never imagined they would have to sell so soon. Walls of stripped and shiny pine, a window in the roof which floods the little room with light, 'an airy office space,' Vernon called it, 'a quiet room where we can keep the computer or come and read or write letters or even put people up if the spare room is already taken.'

'Isn't this lovely?'

The floorboards are bare but for colourful rugs.

Joy turns to face the Middletons, determined to wrest some positive energy out of these uninspired people. They will not go away disparaging Vernon's important work. 'You can see for miles from here,' she says, standing on tiptoe and gesturing out over the cul-de-sac, seeing a little V of birds fly over. Her washing hangs helplessly out on the line, left in the garden from last night. Rain streaks and tickles down the glass. She sees her own desperate face reflected in the window and it mocks her. Messy wet hair from showing the Middletons round outside. They looked but they *did not see*. And she was the same before she knew she was leaving; she too walked across the cool, green grass, past the cobwebs, the soft mauve flowers, the wonderful wet Michaelmas daisies, the black twigs of the thorn hedge and the dangling swing, abandoned now. All so precious, so familiar, all so taken for granted before.

More like a box room now. Up here the air is acrid from disuse, it smells like skin and the stale warmth of the room is unpleasant. 'On a clear day you can even see the moors.'

'It's not very big,' sniffs the Middletons' oldest child with disappointed eyes.

'No, well it's shrunk since we were forced into using it as a store room,' says Joy with a chilly smile but still determined. 'It is really quite spacious without all these boxes of books.'

'Yes, I'm sure it is,' says Mrs Middleton, fiddling with her handbag strap and keen to renegotiate the spindly stairway, down onto safer ground again. The woman is a bag of nerves, depressed, too, worse than I am, thinks Joy. And she pities her, and wonders what is the matter.

'Look,' she says more cheerfully, 'my husband built a bar behind there. You can just see it if you bend—'

'Very useful,' says Mrs Middleton, looking away. Her little head jerks on a neck like a stem. 'Always nice to have a bar.'

'But you and Dad don't drink,' says the oldest Middleton child.

Cauliflower cheese.

Again.

They eat quietly at the kitchen table but it all feels like an illusion.

This house is for sale, this house is not their home any more, no matter how much she has cared for it and looked after it, and after her latest ordeal Joy isn't hungry, she is quivering and tense. For so long she has seen Vernon as grown up and wise; he is the one who let her feel safe and she experiences a momentary chill, a rebellion against him – for his hurt and his disappointment are also his betrayal.

Its awful, it's mean and unfair to think this way but Vernon has let her down. She has heard of couples married for over thirty years and the man goes off just like that, leaving the woman to wonder whether any of their life was honest. Well, Joy has been married for just twenty-three, and she will never let Vernon know it, but this situation feels rather like that to her . . .

'There's no point in us looking at properties yet, Joy, not until we get an offer which is acceptable. If we did, we would be as bad as them.' And his worried eyes flicker off her.

Cautious and sensible as usual. Chew chew chew. Mastication. She watched a television programme last night which showed you where the food went, the whole digestive process. Liquids and solids. Sensible, solid Vernon like his sensible, solid father before him. Indistinct families moving behind net curtains and voting Tory to maintain the status quo. *Status quo?* She will never vote Tory again. Joy wonders if he can honestly contemplate the mess they are in. Nothing in his life has ever prepared him for this – and how long did he fend off the truth so even she didn't know the true extent of their difficulties? To Vernon, bankruptcy is a crime.

If they sell the house now they will be just in time to prevent it.

Joy argues; she needs to know where they're going. Her home is important to her image. 'But we must get some idea, Vernon. Some idea of size if nothing else so I can sort out the furniture.'

'We can do that by looking in the paper. Simple enough.'

But that's not the same. She has looked in the papers, she is looking all the time, and this is all part of Joy's inner turmoil. She saw a flat this morning, for £45,000. Surely they won't end up living in a grotty flat like a couple of students starting out? She doesn't like to pressurise Vernon any more than he is already. His blood pressure is high. He is on pills from the doctor and he should not eat so much salt. At least they are not caught in this negative equity trap like some; they bought Joyvern too long ago for that. Fifteen years is a long time to live in a house and have to leave it. Still, Joy would quite like to look round other properties all the same. After the debts have been paid they should have enough for somewhere half decent.

What will Vernon do with himself all day?

Tired, sick and fat.

A qualified electrical engineer, fifty-two years old and on the scrapheap. Despite what this government would have us believe, retraining programmes for men of Vernon's age are ridiculous. Who's going to employ a fifty-two-year-old retrained man with no experience when there's kids around in the self-same boat with all their working lives ahead of them? I ask you.

Perhaps he could do some gardening, £3.50 an hour on the side for some cantankerous old woman?

And he'd once been so proud of himself.

They'd even dreamed of a world cruise.

The leaflet said – *Redundancy? Opportunity!*

All is gloom and doom.

Oh, if only they hadn't decided to start that business . . . but their hopes had been dazzling then. If only they had just given up trying and invested the money instead, sold the house around the end of the eighties and moved into a smaller one. Seven years ago, the investments would have doubled by now. Still, you just can't stop and give up like that, somehow it's not right. You have to go on. You *have to give it a whirl*. And it wasn't as if they dived into it cold, either. Oh no, they went on the appropriate courses, did the necessary market research, sent flyers round, advertised in the local papers. And Joy gave up work in the dress shop to keep the books, man the telephone and do the secretarial work. She sent out the bills, too – bills that were seldom paid.

Oh, it's all a great big con. Oh, truly the world is a cruel place and life is nothing but a treacherous bog.

Poor Joy. Waste not want not. Joy will finish the food on her plate. Cauliflower cheese, *such a tired idea*, sums up her present mood to perfection.

THREE

Penmore House, Ribblestone Close, Preston, Lancs

If only they could take time back she would deal with her children so differently. Ah, but it's too late, far too late for that now.

'You don't think she recognised us, do you, Lenny?'

Anyone would think his beleagured wife had a villainous look about her.

Lenny Middleton inwardly groans, concentrates on the road ahead. The traffic is heavy. It's always heavy these days, too many cars, too many people. 'Now why on earth would they recognise us? Come on now, Babs, get with it. We're three hundred miles away from home, nobody's heard of us round here, or of Jody. Come on, pet. This just won't do!'

But Babs cannot relax, instead she plays nervously with her hands on her lap. A tiny, muscular woman with almost a twitch to her lips, she stares through the drizzle, wanting to believe him, wanting so badly to believe him, but her eyes are not focused on anything real; she stares out, but sees nothing. 'I know, love,' she mutters. 'I know I'm daft. It's just that these days I always feel people know who I am and despise me . . .'

'You can never get your mind onto anything else, that's your trouble.' This time her husband is moved to take one hand from the wheel and try to pat her calm with it. 'Don't worry. It's going to be okay. A fresh start, Babs, like we said. A fresh start for all of us. No looking back, pet, not now.'

Babs smiles, but faintly. 'It was just the way that woman looked down her nose at us. As if we're not good enough for her house.'

'She was nothing but a jumped-up snob. What a lot of pretentious nonsense. Glossy white horses with flowing manes – the kind of pictures they hang on the wall in Boots. But the house was grand though. What did you think?'

'I don't really care where we live any more, Len, quite frankly.'

The two girls in the back of the car exchange tired glances before staring blandly out in silence once again. These are uneasy children.

They have heard this discussion so many times of late they don't bother to listen any more. This intense absorption of their parents for one another has turned them into virtual strangers to their kids. Cindy and Dawn Middleton don't care what happens now as long as they escape from Preston, as long as there is a change in their world. Maybe then these endless traumas will cease, and people will stop talking about their brother Jody for once and for all.

I mean. These past few weeks they haven't even been able to go to school. This trip has been a real relief, the chance to get away from it all viewing houses down south. Perhaps, when they get back, there'll be some positive news about their own house. A couple are already interested even though it is only just on the market.

It's not as though they want to move. The fact is, they've been driven out.

'We must try and believe that this hell is nothing but a passage, a pathway we must travel along before we reach something better.'

High-minded, huh. It's fine for Dad to talk like that, he doesn't have to suffer the way they do, because he's a man. And kids are so cruel. At least some adults pretend, the men more so than the women.

Some women seem to thrive on unkindness. Even neighbours, those they'd known since childhood, started shouting obscenities at them. Some shouted, some jeered and some stayed silent. These were the worst. Those silences grew into piercing hisses.

Since the rape they have watched their mother quietly disintegrate before their eyes. She hadn't shouted and sworn like their father had at first, in angry denial. When Jody was arrested it seemed like a kind of death. The house went hushed and gloomy and full of whispers. Even the stairs, normally a space for cheerful communications, turned into the twisting stone steps of a castle, echoing to the whispers of sad ghosts. Nothing good meanders up them any more. It would have been easier for everyone if Jody had merely died, crashed his bike as everyone predicted he would.

Cool to the point of crazy.

RAPE. There's no gentle way of saying it, no way of discriminating between a vicious, violent attack by a stranger in some dark and nightmare alley, and a mistake made by a confused boy and a young woman who is half-witted anyway, according to reports.

'She led him on,' said their father with a little too much emphasis. 'She must have done.'

'Oh yes,' said Mum, eyes red from nights of crying, her small features pinched in her triangle face. Her voice was strengthened by a wild despair, trying to distance herself from her child and even her cardigan was buttoned up wrongly, for Jody was her first love. 'Oh yes, they're going to believe that, Len, aren't they? She led him on and then he thoughtfully left her in an hysterical state in the woods beside the reservoir.'

Real pain. Real pain remembered in the back of a car.

After they heard the unbelievable news of Jody's arrest Dawn sat on the edge of her bed and dialled Alex's number. Alex would help her. Alex would understand. Alex had already heard the news which must have moved like a fuse through the gardens and parks and suburban avenues, 'Oh Alex, we're shattered, nobody knows what to do to help. I left everyone sitting downstairs, Mum is crying, won't you come round?'

'I can't, not just now, actually, Dawn. I've got this essay to do . . .'

'Oh Alex, please. If you only knew . . .' She still didn't get it.

'I'm really sorry, Dawn. There's just no way I can—'

'Jody didn't do it, you know!'

And then she was suddenly, suffocatingly aware that Alex, Jody's lifelong mate and her boyfriend for six months, was trying to extricate himself from everything that had been between them. Too proud to beg, she forced herself to chat on about other, petty things, and finally put down the phone with tears in her eyes and a cheerful, defensive, 'Good night.'

Real pain. Real pain remembered in the back of a car.

On her way to school the following day, how eagerly Cindy had approached her friends. There was Ruth, Martha, Jennie, Carol, all on the corner beside the shop going in for fags and Mini Eggs. 'Hi!' Her step hadn't even faltered. She needed them badly today. She needed their support, their comforting reassurance.

'Hi, Cindy.' A pale response to this, once the most popular member. Nobody's eyes met hers, she saw them flick round with knowing, and lips were bitten and heads went down.

She stopped dead, hands on hips, satchel hanging from her elbow. 'He didn't do it, you know!'

'Yeah.'

'Sure.'

'Right.'

'*He really did not do it.*'

Not one sincere response, from girls who used to fancy him. And the group formed in a ring which was impenetrable. There was a hole in the middle where she ought to be and, for the first time in her whole life, the popular Cindy Middleton walked on to school alone.

It's going to be a long drive back to Preston, mostly through the night. When they were little and going on holiday they used to drive through the night. When they stopped at the Little Chef for breakfast they knew they'd arrived in Cornwall. All silver and dancing ripples awash with colour and images and an oily, salty tang in the air.

Their hearts were so light and happy then, cruising like the seagulls.

Now, as far as Dawn and Cindy are concerned, the future can only be seen as some vague dread.

A homemaker, that's Babs.

And a mother. Three kids. For twenty-seven months of her life, her body was not hers, and for years after that her breasts used to tingle whenever a baby cried.

Some people say it's to do with diet, some say it's a wayward gene, but if that's the case, how come her two girls are so normal while Jody was always hyper-active, up to his tricks, one of the lads, a clown, a lovable, stupid clown. Skiving off school, scrumping apples, writing rude remarks in the church visitors' book and signing them with his own name and address. I ask you. They've been brought up exactly the same, Babs knows that.

She'd been easy on him – too easy? Afraid that too much discipline might knock the stuffing out of this rumbustious, funny and popular kid. Can you blame her? A super character, everyone said, a one-off. Her baby, Jody . . . the first word he spoke, the feel of his lashes against her cheek, the rubbery back of his neck with its talcum-powdery smell.

RAPE.

She liked the house, Joyvern, better than the rest they'd seen. She liked the empty smell of it and the possibilities of putting something new in its place, and when they sit down to talk about it the following day, back in the stifling Close in Preston, Lenny agrees with her.

And it's reasonably priced, too. They will easily be able to manage it.

Can it be that things are working out at last?

'So what must we do next?' Babs asks in dead tones.

She'd never have asked that way once. Lenny tries to hide his irritation, calming her as if she's a jittery horse, as he knows she can't help this new dependency thing. She's so uncertain of everything now she seems to need to ask someone before she gets up out of her chair. Every single thing in her house feels unfamiliar, either that, or, in another minute, full of an overwhelming sense of the past. They have taken her child away unweaned and it's all too late.

'I'll go in tomorrow, love,' says Len. 'Tell them we've decided.'

'You don't think we ought to look at some more? After all, it's a buyers' market.'

'No, Babs, there's no point. We both like that one. That house will suit us fine.'

'If only the Smedleys buy this one. If only they keep their word.'

'She sounded certain when I spoke to her on the phone. We can't ask for more than that. But everything depends on theirs being sold.'

'So should we accept their offer?'

Len would gladly accept any offer, providing it meant they could move out of here. One lucky star shines for them all in this very long and dark night – the company's offer of a job down south, a straight transfer, managing the brand new superstore. 'We'll make an offer for Joyvern first, and if that's accepted, we'll go with the Smedleys.'

'It'll be accepted all right,' says Babs. 'They're desperate.'

Len turns to his wife, surprised at the sudden certainty. 'And how d'you know that?'

Babs gives an ironic smile. 'I don't know, I'm just guessing.' But that is a lie. She knows desperation when she sees it. There's a contact between the desperate in life, like the crackle of electricity passing between two fingers, so how come Len is immune to it?

She knows that her resentment is unfair, but it hasn't been quite so hard for him. He's had his work for a start, every morning somewhere to go and some other subject to concentrate on, people to talk to. *People around him who don't know.* Whereas she resigned her part-time job the minute the monster raised its head. Well, she could hardly continue manning the surgery dealing with local people who viewed her as if she had grown two horns, could she? The doctors didn't ask her to go, but she had to do the decent thing and take the plunge into isolation. Because everyone knows, when these things happen, *it is the mother who is to blame.* Sometimes, Babs Middleton longs to run away, just pack a carrier bag and disappear.

'I'll make some tea, love, if you like. Shall I, Len, are you hungry? A mushroom omelette, perhaps?' She cracks eggs into the bowl and envies the mixture which has more energy about it than her. She's had quite enough of emotion just lately. What she really wants is never to feel another thing. But this will pass, Babs tells herself. Time will pass and one day I will wake up again.

Why didn't he say? If he was innocent, he would have said he'd been with her, *wouldn't he?*

The awful part was the three-day search for Janice Plunket. That's how it started. And naturally everyone was involved. A vulnerable girl aged twenty-three from a special unit gone suddenly missing like that. Her parents appealed on the local TV, there were posters stuck on lamp-posts. You couldn't miss it. You couldn't not know. They searched the river rushes, under boulders where the water whirled deep brown in places, they scoured through the bracken on the hills, the smallest twig, stone, tussock and curled leaf, nothing remained unturned. Naturally it was the talk of the town.

Their dire premonitions buzzed together, formed a cloud overhead.

'She'll be dead by now, poor bairn, mark my words.'

'What a world when a poor little maid like that . . .'

'I'm glad I'm not a mother today. They say it's no different but things aren't the same . . .'

'They'll catch the bastard and he'll get six months.'

'They say she's wandered off before. She's a bit, you know, a bit lardy.'

'But they found her safe that time, didn't they, sitting at the back of the Regal. Apparently she'd been locked in there all night.'

'They should cut their balls off, these men.'

Round and round it went like a dance, a hive of bees buzzing and dancing and Babs joined in, well, of course she did.

'Someone must know who he is,' the police said darkly, and in that small community everyone felt vaguely guilty. *'Someone must know.'*

And so it went on like that, for three whole days and nights. It seems detached now, like a dream. And there was Jody sitting beside her at times as calm as you like, not batting an eyelid, chewing an apple and watching telly. Sometimes having a game of Scrabble and cheating outrageously before he lost.

Should Babs have suspected? Why? What the hell should she have suspected?

And then came the day when Janice Plunket blundered out of the undergrowth beside the reservoir with her lips stained blue with berries, her legs scratched with brambles and wire, and cuckoo spit was not the only frothy white substance stuck to her skirt. An innocent, marching to a different drum. A passing motorist recognised her, picked her up and took her to the police station where they gave her a cup of sweet tea and a couple of custard creams. Her desperate parents rushed to her side. She stuffed her hands down her knickers and sniffed. The flat planes of her fleshy face gave nothing further away. On her father's request the police did an examination, an internal examination.

RAPE, went up the cry!

'We knew it,' came the satisfied public response. 'You can't have a maid missing for three days without her being interfered with.'

'Who did it?' howled the angry chrous. But Janice Plunket did not enlighten them. She turned away, smiled smugly, and fatly crossed her legs upon her secret.

'*Why didn't he say?*' Tell everyone where he had left her? *If he was innocent?*

And Babs Middleton feels her breasts ache now for the eighteen-year-old child in the cell, but the beads of her milk, if any there be outside her own imagination, run uselessly away.

FOUR

The Grange, Dunsop, Nr Clitheroe, Lancs

An interesting fact this, and one that most of his fans don't know, but Jacy Smedley originally intended to be known as JC, Son of God. When he first contacted his agent, the letter that arrived back enclosing that first master tape was addressed to JACY. He studied this for a while, worrying about his image which was, in those early excitements, to include such weird manifestations as stigmata, before deciding that 'Jacy' looked quite nice actually, and was probably less likely to rub the establishment up the wrong way. No matter how wild you intend to be, it is wiser not to upset the establishment. However, in subsequent meetings that same agent advised him to drop the name Smedley altogether, and so it came about that three years later, Colin Smedley found world renown under the single title of Jacy, lead singer for 'Sugarshack'.

His fall from grace he compares with that of Lady Thatcher, for it was around about the same time that he realised things were not as they should be and had not been so for some months. Since that first awful glimpse of reality things have gone downhill fast. But at least Belle is still with him.

Must he really leave his beautiful country house and take up residence in a Close? The double glazing alone had cost him a fortune; he'd replaced all those silly leaded windows, and they'll not recoup that money in a hurry.

Belle, with rings in her nipples, her navel, her nose and another more private place, says yes, he must, he has no choice. It's either that or follow in the steps of some other members of the group she could name, all pride gone, dirty, unshaven, thieving for the dosh they require to fund the habit they all took up when money sprayed over their heads like water, record companies vied for their signatures and women queued up to do virtually anything in order to say they'd been screwed by some Godlike member of Sugarshack.

Colin Smedley was, in fact, to his millions of followers, Jesus Christ incarnate. So much so that he once terrified security by administering Holy Communion to 30,000 fans from the stage at Wembley.

But now. Week after week, and the phone doesn't ring. Nobody wants him, nothing happens, time moves so painfully slowly. Sometimes, even, he wants to die. Now he has become a nocturnal creature, preferring to come out at night with three bottles of wine for comfort, alone in the darkness.

Not only must they move to a Close but they must marry and take up family life, children even, if they've not been rendered infertile by the life of debauchery and abuse they have enjoyed for so long. 'Because that's what it's all about, Jacy. At the end of the day, that's what everyone secretly craves. Grow up, procreate while you still have the capacity for love, grow old and mellow, and bask in the pride of your precious issue.'

Now Jacy has scattered a good deal of his seed around indiscriminately over the years but that's not the point. He doesn't know that *it took*. Even the groupies who still write to him claiming that he is the father of this child or that, even they are probably lying as they all lie in the end. Thirty-five years old and he cannot honestly claim paternity.

Belle, with her long shiny ringlets and pink cheeks, says that she's even made an offer on this house in the Close. She seems to have taken over completely. Jacy half hopes they'll turn it down. 'There's nothing wrong with the house, Jacy. You should come and see for yourself. It's a solid, friendly Victorian house with large rooms and a decent garden . . .'

Decent garden? Christsake. Jacy, with a furry tongue, a glass of wine and a cigarette, looks out over his fifty acres and shudders. His eyes focus and shift to the enormous gilt mirror that dominates his marble fireplace and there is his peering face, the flesh of his cheeks hanging haggardly, dark lines engraved from his nose to the corners of his mouth and bags under his eyes.

'What are the good times without the bad?' says Belle.

Where have they all gone, his hopes, his dreams – the looks and the self-respect? Look at him now. There are tell-tale nicks of a clumsy shave on his neck and chin. He is forced to admit it, hell's bells, he could be mistaken for fifty.

A surprisingly short man as stars often are, he paces the thick, gold carpet, no longer noticing the priceless curtains in a paper-thin silk, silver moons against midnight blue. Beyond the sliding plate-glass windows, outside on the terrace the geraniums in the jardinières are headless and dead. Azaleas and rhododendrons hedge the length of his driveway. The only shade on the daisied lawns comes from a scattering of three-hundred-year-old oaks. The swimming pool he installed is now only a deep black pit with frogs and eels living in the soupy dregs at the bottom.

Jacy inhales a long fern of smoke. What will the press say when they learn he has gone to live in a Close? What about a barge, or a gypsy caravan? Something with style, please, *please!* But Belle's not having any of it; she lost her awe of him years ago. Give her her due, she has stuck by him through thick and thin – the fights, the jealousies and the chaos – and she loves him in spite of the fact that he treats her like muck.

The real thing!

But poor Jacy does not feel loved.

He is surprised by the strength in her voice. 'Those sadists can't be crueller than they've been already. Let them say what they like. I would feel proud to live in a Close. What's the matter with you anyway – snob?'

But it's not snobbery, it's image; Belle ought to understand that by now. Ah, and the press *can* be crueller, yes they can, and Jacy gives a derisive snort.

But before all that, oh those were the days.

Pure gold flooded him.

Muscles burning, lungs exploding, he was saturated by the intensity of the whole wild show. With blood pulsing through every part of him Jacy was suffused, engorged by it all, his ego ballooned by one exhilarating sensation after another, kids screaming, lights blazing, music thrashing, power, wonder, his mind a blur, and now it has vanished and is only a woman with a broom sweeping between the seats.

The sadness of an empty theatre.

And can you blame him for being unable to recover from any of this? It is only by rubbing his eyes with his fists like a child, keeping the pressure there, that he can still conjure up the shimmering bubble of foaming colours, the magnetic pull into that black hole . . .

Jacy is in mourning. In mourning for sensations as brilliant as all eternity; no man-made substance can touch it, no, not even the juice of the poppy. It fizzed his veins. Like a desperate, passionate fuck that he thought would go on endlessly.

Real life was nothing but a bothersome scratch on his mind.

In those days.

But suddenly his business head, the head that made and helped him spend over five million dollars in five years, takes over. He runs his hands through his shock of black hair. 'Why are they selling this house?' he asks Belle suspiciously. 'Nobody sells these days unless there's something up. What's wrong with it? Dry rot? Or it's probably subsiding, knowing our luck.'

'No, slaphead, nothing like that,' says Belle, who makes a point of never reading the papers. 'The bloke's moving jobs, that's all.' She crosses the room to give him a nuzzle and makes her little fretting sound. 'Now is the time to be positive, Jacy. The agent says it's a snip. There's hope for us yet, you'll see. And anyway, we have no option. You know that.'

The sickening thing is that she is right. 'But they'll find out . . .'

'No, Jacy, no one knows you.'

'People might recognise . . .'

Belle puts her arms round her man and tells him gently, 'No, Jacy, *not any more.*'

Pig-ignorant! 'For God's sake,' and he pushes her away. She can be so cruel, so unthinking sometimes, but with an uncanny knowledge of where to aim, what will hurt the most. Christ, he could do with a joint. He might have changed superficially but he's still the same charismatic and talented man underneath. Worry and stress have conspired to age him before his time, but give him some peace and normality and he'll get his old looks back again. Women will fancy him again as his intense brown eyes wreak their charms on the fresh young things, and when he has rested, who knows, he might even get back on the circuit again, do some jamming with a few old buddies . . . there must be some still around who are sane. No, Jacy suspects that Belle is making the most of his present misfortunes, weakening him, trying to smother him so that she feels less threatened. That's understandable, he supposes, but it's not quite as easy as that. She might be a clever jailer but he is an unwilling prisoner.

Jacy's not finished yet.

'You've just lost your centre, that's all – the part that holds you together,' Belle says with an almost satisfied tone to her voice. 'But it's only temporary, you'll see. It's this intense absorption with yourself that's doing it. Perhaps you should get some counselling.'

What am I now? thinks Jacy sadly. Just a fading figure in the world's imagination?

Sometimes he looks through the windows of the houses he passes, at all the flickering televisions, families sitting, babies crying, children playing, cats and old people dozing, but try as he might he can no longer identify with the human race on their side of the curtain. Secretly he wishes he could, but success takes normality away. His restlessness and his yearning make him separate, some other species never to be engulfed by the mediocre rest. Sometimes he used to flinch and feel nauseous when they reached out imploringly to touch him, so afraid they might pull him down into their own dreary, subordinate worlds. When he felt like this, his minders used to push them away and hurry him out the back of the stadium. Those immortal words: *Ladies and gentlemen, Elvis has left the building.* Their lives are bleak and grey and cold. Sometimes he pities Belle's ordinariness, at other, more realistic times, he envies her.

Jacy purses his lips.

He can hear the Hoover coming towards him.

His staff left months ago as he was unable to pay their wages and now Belle goes round the eight-bedroomed house like a head-scarfed slag with a fag hanging between her lips and her fluffy slippers clacking, pushing the groaning Hoover. Round and round in an ashy circle. The house has developed a tatty, unkempt look, the window-sills spattered with dead flies and wasps, dirt-engrained soaps in the basins, dark, hairy rims round the baths and mottled stains round the skirting boards. He has to shop for stuff like Vim. She flails her hands. 'I can't be expected to cope with all this, Jacy. The least you could do would be to cut the grass. When people come viewing they must be allowed to see the potential.'

There's a gleam of something in her eye, Christ, her bullying makes him nervous.

From the squashy white leather sofa Jacy waves his arm a fraction and turns up the thudding CD. *February Rain*, his last real hit.

He lets out a long moaning breath of anguish as he disappears into his own music. The ride-along mowers, a novelty when they first bought them (he and Jip the drummer used to race the two machines over the flat and glossy acres) are boring now and nothing but a chore. One is dead on its feet and the other's a hell of a job to start. He can't afford to get the blasted things mended. The villagers around here were never too accommodating; even when he was in his prime they viewed him with suspicion although he did his best to support the local shops and small businesses. He and his entourage chased round the lanes and villages on low-rider trikes, still piled up in the garage somewhere, not working. They'd had the nerve to get up a petition when they heard he was buying the Grange. The press lapped that one up and Jacy pretended not to be hurt. Well, they'll have a good laugh now, won't they, at his expense, now they know the place is up for sale. He is shunned by everybody; even if he had the dosh, no one round here would work for him. Everyone said he was mad to buy up north where the people are so barbaric and primitive, and they were dead right, no matter what Belle said. He should have chosen Surrey. And as for the grass . . . 'They'll think we're just encouraging the wildlife,' he said lazily. 'It's more natural like this, more laid back.'

Since the gardeners left, even the fountains are all blocked up.

Jacy smiles faintly. He turns his cigarette in his fingers.

The snooty prat from the agents shows the viewers round, the upper-middle classes with their flowing names, their braying voices, their dogs and their long noses. On these humiliating occasions Jacy and Belle make a point of being out, or they hide in the grounds like guilty children discovering places on the estate they never knew existed, and hidey-holes. Because the Grange is for sale Belle refuses to allow any of Jacy's old mates to visit. They're a bad influence on him, she says, they are messy and they cost money. Not that there's many requests these days and so they are living like recluses. Jacy refuses to go and look at the house in the Close; he doesn't think he could stand it. What a dump. 'The Middletons are terribly odd,' says Belle, not helping. 'Jumpy and peculiar. And funnily enough the last time I went to measure for carpets and curtains I got the oddest feeling that hundreds of eyes were watching me.'

She's measured already? The nerve of the woman. She must be fairly certain he is prepared to go along with her plan. 'What eyes?'

'Eyes behind curtains. Perhaps I'm getting a complex, like you. But they are desperate to go. I imagine he wants to start his new job soon as poss. The woman hardly speaks a word, leaves it all to him and those unwholesome kids with their deadpan eyes. Probably some sort of promotion. And there's no photographs anywhere. Don't you think that's pretty weird?'

Is she suggesting that Jacy himself finds a job, an ordinary nine-to-five job in insurance or something like that? Or selling second-hand cars on a forecourt? How mean can she get? What is she trying to do to him – sapping his strength, tormenting his mind, sapping his bodily juices. '*I* work,' she likes to remind him whenever she gets the chance. 'There's nothing wrong with work.'

She is so transparent. He would like to perceive her as weak, clinging and needy, but she's not. Her beauty is the only valuable currency they have left. Belle still works as a model for the exclusive mail-order magazine *Elegance*, gallivanting off to sumptuous places where seas glimmer like pewter behind her stretching, sand-kissed body and silver horizons circle her waist. A silver woman with a silver smile. His smile, slow and long, was once described as the smile of a wolf. He liked that. He still likes that. Hers is the only money that's still coming in, and that's what they are planning to live on. 'Some people would consider it perfectly adequate,' says Belle.

He is sure they would.

There's no talk about moving south now. It's too late – the great divide, house prices, forbid it and because of his financial position Jacy is forced to sell the Grange at a 'realistic price'. Realistic my foot. It's the cheapest house in *Country Life*. His heart clenches and unclenches like a fist wanting to hit somebody, anybody, punish the world for failing to love him. Perhaps he should have done himself in like The King, and left his audience while in his prime. But no, it looks as if they'll have to endure a few more years in Lancashire until Jacy's star rises once more in the heavens.

As it will, one day. As it will . . .

FIVE

No fixed abode

The purchase of the house near Clitheroe is a tricky and sensitive issue, dealt with by a succession of trusted professionals trained in the ways of The Family. Despite the fact that the private secretary, Sir Hugh Mountjoy, is by now well used to pouring oil on the troubled waters of his superior master, James Henry Albert, this is one of the most delicate matters to which he has been forced to put his great mind.

There is nothing that pleases Sir Hugh more than the generalship of a major operation, a trait no doubt passed down by his highly decorated fighting forefathers. If only the young fellow would listen and ditch that attention-seeking and ludicrously conspicuous Packard Convertible and run a Vauxhall Corsa instead.

Damn the fellow. So persistent, so enthusiastic.

The young lady must be bought off. The official engagement is imminent and in Sir Hugh's opinion the thing should have been done long ago. Bed companions come two a penny, so why oh why couldn't young Jamie, twenty-three but still very much an adolescent at heart, have stuck to his own kind – the sort of docile, respectful young woman who would keep her mouth shut, stay out of the limelight and take care of 'that side of things'.

Arabella Brightly-Smythe, known to her friends as Peaches, was and is the gravest of errors. Knowledge of her existence was dropped upon him light as a hint by the Prince, at first, but since then the weight of her being has grown with a steady and fearful importance, as her own body is destined to grow for the next six months. Unfortunately.

The northern climate might cool her down. Remove her from the social circuit for a good while anyway. That has to be part of the bargain.

The house in Clitheroe is perfect for the job. They found it in *Country Life* and originally considered the purchase for Civil Servants recovering from stress and requiring peace and privacy for the painting of egg boxes and the weaving of baskets. Unfashionable area. Suitable for security. Off the beaten track. And going for a song as the present incumbent is desperate.

So far, more by luck than judgement, the national newspapers have been kept at bay and the regal heads of The First Family need not be bothered with the scandal. They've had enough on their plates just lately, poor things, and this could prove the last straw – the scandal of scandals designed to rock the Crown at its roots. Luckily, this most unfortunate business is in the very safest of hands.

When this whole ghastly nightmare is over Sir Hugh, with his cool eye on promotion, will make it his business to drop a few hints to the Monarch. Nothing wrong with getting a few well-earned Brownie points, nothing wrong with smoothing your path to the top. But many a slip 'twixt cup and lip; there are so many pitfalls along the way.

They have certainly not heard the last of this.

The imperious and elegant Sir Hugh gazes out of his office windows, elbows resting on his gigantic desk, suit jacket hung on the knob of his chair, the same chair on which his illustrious father started his career with The Family. A bit like a baby's training potty. His father ended up as Lord Chamberlain before his sudden, frightful accident. Now he's a virtual cabbage, stuck in a wheelchair on his estate. Sweet fragrances waft into the room, resting on the warmth of the air. The tall, smooth man compresses his lips. There's Jamie's friends for a start, if you can call them that. A pack of louts would be a fairer description, monied young men, debased and wretched, with not a brain between them, but alas, poor Jamie has ever been attracted by the seamier side of life. A rebel without a cause – bah! Sir Hugh has always stood out contemptuously against this nonsensical business of a 'normal' education. Rubbing shoulders with God knows who in the infernal undergrowth of the outside world. There was a time when the great public schools were populated by those who knew better – the sons of the gentry. He himself was educated at Eton and Trinity, followed by a stint in the Foreign Office to finish him off. He has already accompanied the Prince on official visits to Canada, the States and Kenya (do they still call it Kenya?). But everything's changed in that respect; money and the power it brings have seen to that. Far better when these high-born folk were educated amongst their own in their nurseries with their gillies and their governesses and their riding masters. After all, they require a wholly different education from the masses, have educational needs which experience and wisdom alone, handed down through the generations, should be quite sufficient to fulfil. For theirs is a destiny unlike any other. Theirs is a higher purpose.

'The woman is obsessed,' reported young Dougal Rathbone, aide to Sir Hugh, son of Lord Rathbone and the man picked to deal directly with the hapless young person in question. Sir Hugh's revered name must not be mentioned in any discussions which might take place, there must be no suggestions of any of The Household being involved in this disreputable affair. 'She won't listen to reason.' Dougal ran a frustrated hand through his sleek, black hair. 'He loves her and she loves him and the fact he denies that now is because he is running scared.'

Jamie? *Running scared?*

Sir Hugh, middle-aged and handsome but for a certain look, a look that has hardened over the years until it has become his whole self, his attitude and his bearing, clicked his tongue in annoyance.

'And you saw her . . . ?'

'. . . in her flat in Queensway, as arranged. Arabella was on her own. I don't think anyone saw me arrive or leave.'

Why the hell doesn't the fellow get to the point? 'And you put the proposition to her?'

Dougal nodded. 'As a friend of Jamie's, as we agreed. I think she trusted me, after some initial hysteria. She seemed to be most upset because Jamie hadn't called himself. She needs to talk to him – she kept telling me she must talk to him. Of course she understands that he is in Scotland with The Family at the moment, but as she points out – that never stopped him before.'

'And her own family?' interrupted Sir Hugh.

'They don't know yet but they soon will. The young lady is already leaning backwards on her heels like a duck and she's only ten weeks—'

'Good God, man!' This is the kind of sordid detail Sir Hugh does not wish to hear. It's the hard facts which interest him. Her family pose an uncertain threat. City people, made it under Thatcher, no form, only a whiff of class and certainly not enthusiastic supporters of the Crown, according to reports. 'And she's still maintaining the child is his?'

'Naturally,' said Dougal, adjusting his very white, crisp cuffs, fiddling with elaborate cufflinks of gold. 'She is sticking to that and I am afraid it sounds as though she is telling the truth. And anyway, these days a DNA test would prove—'

'Let's hope it never comes to that,' snapped Sir Hugh, irritated by the prideful preening of his equerry. He lowered his voice for the next question. 'And no fresh evidence from Lovette?'

'No, Sir Hugh. Lovette himself telephoned me yesterday. His men have discovered nothing new. She did have a slight reputation – she let her hair down when she first came to London, but not since she started seeing Jamie. According to her friends it was true love after that. That's why she came off the pill.'

'Damn fool,' cried Sir Hugh, slapping his fist into his hand. 'Silly, stupid little fool. What on earth did she think would happen?'

'She is not the most intelligent of mortals,' Dougal explained with a wry, handsome smile. 'Not according to old school reports.'

'None of them are,' snorted Sir Hugh. 'Sex mad, probably. But in the very lowliest of life-forms one expects to find some sense of natural preservation.'

'But I don't think she perceived any threat,' Dougal went on, far too complacently for his superior's liking, in his Brasenose College accent. 'She's just not very worldly-wise. She actually believed he would marry her and she's only just recovering now from his thoughtless advice to abort the child. When she saw him on television attending church last Sunday, hand in hand with Frances Loughborough she went into an immediate decline. She told me she couldn't believe it. Lord knows what her reaction is going to be when their engagement is announced.'

'Oh my God,' moaned Sir Hugh, briefly closing his cold blue eyes. 'What are we dealing with here? We must get a settlement before then, signed and sealed. And the Grange – you put that suggestion to her?'

The charming Dougal hesitated, wondering how he could soften the blow. 'Her initial reaction is that she doesn't want to live up north.' He ignored Sir Hugh's heightening colour. 'She says she doesn't know anyone up there.'

This time the private secretary slammed his fist on the desk. 'But you took her the brochure?'

Dougal nodded. 'Oh, she liked the house well enough. It was just the isolated location and the idea that she should live there without Jamie. I think she was pretty taken aback. I pointed out that of course she would have staff to see to her every whim, and visitors, too, naturally. She just sat there with her arms wrapped round herself and listened with her mouth gaping open. Didn't really seem to take it in, if you know what I mean?'

'Perhaps this little madam is more cunning than we take her for.'

'It didn't seem that way to me.'

'Pushing for more . . .'

'She is not that kind of girl.'

'*What?*' Sir Hugh rounded on Dougal with scorn. 'Don't tell me you are enamoured of her as well.'

'Absolutely not,' said Dougal, fidgeting uneasily. Surely Sir Hugh knew all about his closet preferences. He'd been screened, hadn't he? He hurried on, 'But I do see what Jamie saw in her.'

Thank God he is not the firstborn.

She might not be that sort of girl but James Henry Albert, third and last son of the Sovereign, knows exactly what he is doing, the disgraceful bounder. He is as eager to sort this business out as everyone else involved. Sir Hugh had been deliberately hard on him, playing the strong father figure, last time they talked. Well, someone had to get through to the idiot before he ballsed everything up.

Since he cocked up at university, quitting after a year and a half to the great consternation of the tabloids, the boy has been treading water. Gadding off round the world disgracing himself while the country falls deeper and deeper into recession. Turning over luxury yachts, bungee-jumping off aircraft from the Queen's Own Flight, motorbike-scrambling on sensitive mountains, intent on destruction. Well, hell, he has almost succeeded. His public rating is nil at the moment, let alone if this unfortunate business comes out. Refusing to go into the Services, refusing to throw himself into Good Causes, living in easy affluence, the only option left is for him to marry and procreate and thank God the virginal Frances is available and willing.

The traffic below was a steady grey noise, the rhythm of ordinary mortals. Little people. Sir Hugh closed the window.

'I don't consider your attitude to this as responsible as it might be,' he stated firmly, raising a charcoal eyebrow.

'She'll get over it,' said Jamie lightly, his easy, honeyed voice making everything sound so simple, his overlong curls half concealing the supercilious look in his eye. 'And anyway, I'll still see her.'

Sir Hugh felt like moaning aloud. 'Oh no, you won't, young fellow, that's exactly what you won't do!'

Instantly Sir Hugh sensed the tension. There was that hostile glance again, that challenging stare that has always been Jamie's since early childhood as if to say 'You can't *make* me!' The press used to love that look, considered it endearingly boyish. 'Right little rough-neck,' said the *Sun*, but fondly when he was six years old. He used to clench his little fists while his face contorted to hold back the tears. And then

35

came the tantrums. Sometimes Sir Hugh, ever the realist, wonders about the boy's IQ. Jolly good thing it was never tested.

'I have the strongest impression, sir, that you don't fully appreciate the extent of the scandal, should any of this come out into the public domain.'

Jamie smiles, a weak-faced man with his hands in his pockets, barely pubescent in a strange sort of unshaven way. But his eyes are extraordinarily bright, with flecks of amber round the pupils that spark whenever frustration hits him. 'Do stop fussing, Sir Hugh. Peaches is a biddable wench, she'll do whatever I ask her.'

'I sincerely hope you are right,' said his secretary, holding tight to his anger. 'We are having to go to a good deal of trouble, let alone expense.'

'Whose expense?'

'Your expense, who else's?'

'You have never discussed this with me.' Jamie's shoulders tensed, his face seemed suddenly hot.

'A girl is carrying your child!'

'She's not the first.'

'No, indeed, but despite what you say she is not prepared to fade decently away into the background.'

'I'll see her . . .'

'No! No, you must not! You must not be seen anywhere in her vicinity. The press—'

'Bother the press!' And then, as suddenly as he had flared up, James Henry Albert calmed down and bent his long, lean athletic body over the majestic desk and glanced with interest at the brochure from Jackson Stopps & Staff.

There was silence for a moment.

'It is an ideal retreat,' explained Sir Hugh. 'Perfect in all respects. High-walled, to keep out the press, security gates and alarms sprinkled everywhere. Owned by one Colin Smedley, otherwise known as Jacy from the popular group Sugarshack, of whom I am certain you will have heard.' This last was said down the thin, aristocratic nose of Sir Hugh with a fair amount of disdain.

'Perhaps,' the young Prince hesitated, 'perhaps if I were to take her there myself, introduce her to a few characters, a house party perhaps . . .'

'No! Sir, if I might speak frankly, it is crucial that Arabella should understand that this affair is over. It is essential she be made aware that whatever her behaviour, she will never, ever see you again. We are far too close to your engagement announcement to take the slightest risk. If Lady Frances should ever discover . . .'

'Lady Frances is quite happy to turn a blind eye.'

'Excuse me, sir, but I do not believe one can predict a woman's reaction after that ring slides on her finger. There's likely to be a complete change of attitude, if you'll pardon me for pointing this out.' My God, in spite of his dubious experience, the silly ass is so damn naive. Did Sir Hugh have to spell it out? Was he totally unaware of the dangers implicit in all this?

'How much is this Clitheroe place? How much am I coughing up for Arabella's silence?'

Playing the selfless Civil Servant, Sir Hugh attempted to hide his disgust but all the same his sensibilities flinched. Money is something he would far rather not discuss. He spoke wearily, well prepared for a negative reaction. 'Half a million, I'm afraid, sir, and much work to be done on it yet.'

'And where is this money to come from? I'm so skint at the moment I have to borrow the dough for taxis.'

Blast the idiot! He knows full well he should never travel by taxi. His security guards are at their wits' end, so much so that it's proving difficult to keep them. Sir Hugh decided to ignore the gaffe. 'The money will come from your grandfather's trust, an early release. The trustees have looked into the matter. We can wangle it.'

'You can find the money for this little tart and yet I have to wait till I'm twenty-five!'

Sir Hugh stared at him warily. 'And an income for herself and the child for life . . .'

'This is outrageous!'

'We have little choice, sir, in the circumstances. We can hardly approach the Queen.'

'Well, dammit, can't we marry her off to somebody else? How about young Dougal?'

What an absurd remark. What sort of world does the fellow inhabit? Certainly not the real one. 'She vows she is in love with you, sir, and that is the nub of the matter.' Sir Hugh was suddenly aware that his words of counsel were falling on stony ground. James Henry Albert barely recognised his presence; his mind was already somewhere else, dwelling in pleasanter pastures. The older man sighed as he raised the other important matter of the moment. 'And before you leave, sir, I must pass on a message from your mother. Would you please get your hair seen to – *pronto*.'

SIX

Flat 1, Albany Buildings, Swallowbridge, Devon

Mother has the gall to suggest she is going to write to the Queen. It really is quite pathetic. She honestly believes that the Queen would write back. She can hardly see to write anyway and is constantly sitting on her ill-fitting spectacles. She looks wild, older and more shrivelled than usual with her hair down like this, grey rats' tails, pinned down by the weight of her years.

Returned to her little room once again, back safely among the aproned professionals, Irene Peacock refuses to accept that it is County Council policy to force their senior citizens to sell their homes when they need permanent care.

'But how can that be, Frankie? *I have paid.* Me and William have contributed towards our old age every week of our lives, in his pay packet. That's what those taxes were all about, surely – health care, pensions, roads, hard times . . .'

Frankie attempts to quell her own annoyance. It stems from a sense of guilt, of course, and she is well aware of that. She can still hear her own strident voice, 'You have surpassed yourself this time, Mother,' when they discovered the fugitive hiding in her flat, and Frankie's teacher training doesn't help her naturally imperious manner. It's too easy to slip into the classroom role. 'I know that, Mum, but back then no one envisaged the rise in the elderly population and the few people left at work to pay for the care of those in residential homes.'

'Rubbish, Frankie. You sound like one of their forms, the way you speak. We have already paid and anyway, *I do not need care.* I hate it here, waiting to leave in a box with a spray of flowers on top. I'd be perfectly safe in the flat now and you know that very well. They hide my cigarettes. And anyway, how is it that nobody needs my consent?'

Frankie sighs, noticing how trembly-nervous her poor mother is. Many more adventures like this and they'll kill her. She sits stiffly on the edge of the bedside chair, the bad daughter, the infected seed, and she can see what this situation would look like to a stranger. 'That is because I took power of attorney over your legal affairs and I did that, if you remember, Mum, because you were getting very confused, forgetting to pay your bills, going about wearing odd shoes, leaving your purse lying around and giving money to beggars as if you had any to spare!'

Mother's bony face takes on that rigid, stubborn look. 'I only did it the once and just because old mother Blennerhasset happened to be passing by, and that toffee-nosed little nurse Jenkins, they jumped to the conclusion that I was always at it. But that does not mean you can sell my flat over my head without my permission.'

'Well yes, it does, I'm afraid . . .'

'William would turn in his grave.'

'There's no need to bring Dad into it. Anyone would think it was me going to benefit from this sale. In fact, the opposite is the case.' A legacy of £45,000 some time in the future would have come in incredibly handy, helped to relieve the stress and go towards setting the children up. But by the time Mother dies this will all be gone.

'Bullying me like this! My mind is crumbling by the hour and I don't need you scolding me as if I'm a retarded child. This is the last time I will listen to you and your silly advice, Frankie. *You have no right* . . . and I want my own bedroom back!'

And on she goes, berating her daughter and blaming her for every single thing that ever went wrong in her life, and now they seem to be lurching from one petty crisis to the next, with Mother's behaviour worsening all the time.

'A Garibaldi or a Rich Tea, dear?' asks an assistant, popping her head round the door.

'Oh, go away and leave me alone,' snaps Mother. 'They have lost my mirror with the cross-stitch pattern on the back.' And then she gets into tolerance and how, in her day, when Swallowbridge was but a village and not an ugly, expanding suburb of Plymouth, the old and the odd were accepted as part of the rustic scene. 'That's why you're all turning into clones nowadays,' says Irene testily. 'Terrified to be different. All wearing the same clothes with the same disgruntled looks on your faces. Why, I remember the days when old Warty Nosworthy would jump out at us from the bushes and everyone just accepted him . . .'

Frankie tries to kiss her but is pushed angrily away.

In Matron's office . . .

From the smell you could tell there was steamed fish for tea.

Matron's Vauxhall Astra was scented by a vanilla tree. It swung

39

beside the driving mirror along with the miniature lucky pixie. Picking up the odd absconding resident, frightened and in distress, perhaps Matron needed an over-riding perfume to cover a multitude of sins. The large bathrooms at Greylands are sanctified by cleanliness and the smell of pine disinfectant. They are hung about with tortured hoists and sparkling metallic rails. The bathroom mats are fluffy and clean as if they have never been used.

'Mrs Rendell,' says Miss Blennerhasset, while Mother is being bathed and changed into her nightie, 'I think it is time your mother was put on something to calm her down, because, as I warned you last time this happened, we are a residential home not a hospital trained to cope with the demands of the demented.'

Frankie flinches and widens her eyes. Her chestnut hair hangs neat and straight to her shoulders. She wears jeans and a black sweater with marigolds emblazoned upon it. Matron is in her plaid skirt with a white blouse under her stiffly over-washed Aran. It is essential that Frankie remain solicitous and agreeable; she is more than grateful that Greylands have agreed to take Irene back. God knows where she would have to go if they expelled her, but Frankie is trained to remain calm and reasonable under difficult circumstances when you think what sort of parents she has to deal with at school. 'Calm her down?'

'For her own sake, Mrs Rendell, as well as for everyone else's. We can help her be more at peace with herself. Less dazed. We haven't the staff to keep watch on your mother twenty-four hours a day, especially as she seems to be so determined to leave us.'

Of course Frankie can understand why her mother hates it here; she is not entirely insensitive. Some of the residents have given up and gaze into space waiting for death, but Irene is nowhere near ready for death. 'She hasn't settled yet,' she says, defending the cross old woman upstairs. 'I mean, she's only been here for three months and that's no time at all.'

'You could well say that,' says Miss Blennerhasset, 'but I can only report to you that her attitude towards the staff is at best surly, at worst downright rude. This does not endear her to anyone.'

You have to be liked to survive, thinks Frankie. When you are old and vulnerable, or sick, or smelly, or just lonely. Most of us learn that, but Mother, at seventy-five, is too old to learn anything and those rules have never applied before in her sheltered existence. The only real relationship in her life has been with William. Her reason for living has been William and since his death she has gradually mentally evaporated.

Sinking sinking sunk.

Seeing this, observing this from as far back as she can remember prevented Frankie from following her mother's example when she married Michael Rendell twenty years ago. She felt lucky to have escaped her childhood whole and functional. Her mother's subservient behaviour made Frankie feel sick. Irene even cut the tops off her father's boiled eggs. She kept house compulsively, made friends with no one. She was always jumping at sounds, waiting for Father's key in the door, or the phone which might be him. And Frankie was brought up as a second devoted fan of the man until she grew old enough to understand and detest the calculated way in which William allowed Irene to adore him.

He was her love, her treasure.

She was his spare rib and contented with that.

A human being should not be at her happiest when thinking of somebody else, should she?

Frankie asked her mother once, 'What would you do if Daddy left home?' Irene reached forward and slapped her daughter's face.

Mother tried to discuss his work. She responded over-eagerly to his long and distracted stories. She laughed over-loudly at his jokes. Oh, he was nothing special, a skinny, tall, glaring man with a bald head and a bristly moustache. He invariably wore a beige anorak and spent his whole life in the competitive world of insurance.

'We'll have lamb chops with new potatoes tonight, Frankie, seeing as how it's your father's favourite.'

'We are having a golfing holiday this year. Now don't look so grumpy, dear, it's your father who needs the rest, not you.'

'Not that chair, Frankie, Daddy will be home in a minute. Hop on to the stool, there's a good girl.'

'No, dear, no, you are quite wrong. I don't think the green looks so good. William hates green, the blue suits me far better.'

'We will stop at the services when your father feels ready to stop and not before. Stop scratching.'

And, 'Smile for Daddy, Frankie, smile!'

When Frankie got into university it was, 'Oh Frankie, your father will be so proud.'

A good woman and look where it got her. Irene was not a victim, she was a fool. Her long and patient subservience should have received some lasting pay-off, but look what happened. William turned up his toes one morning and left her.

It was unforgivable of him to die first.

And now Irene is enraged and turning her anger on everyone else.

41

But drugs?

Frankie knows very well that in days gone by she would have had her mother at home with her. That was the accepted behaviour until a generation ago. She wonders what communal understanding suddenly changed that noble concept.

Of course the very idea is right out of the question. Poppy and Angus would not tolerate that notion for a second – and rightly so. They are studying hard at the moment. Poppy, a troublesome adolescent, is struggling with her A levels and Angus is at the new university training to be a computer technician. They have their own rooms. They need their own rooms and Frankie certainly needs hers. They also all need their space, and peace and quiet in order to get on with their lives. Mother, with her demands and her confusion, would soon put paid to all that. Poppy and Angus were both taught from an early age never to disturb their grandfather, to tidy up after themselves whenever they went to Granny's house, not to make a fuss if the sport was on all afternoon or when Grandpa told them to keep off his precious lawn. No, no, she cannot come home, there'd be no one around to look after her. Frankie's first responsibility, especially now Michael has left them, is to her children.

Matron is right: it will have to be drugs.

'But nothing too rigorous, Matron, please. Nothing that might change my mother's personality.'

'But of course not, Mrs Rendell,' says Miss Blennerhasset sensibly.

They have drugged her and they have taken away her shoes.

Frankie is going to have to press on with the sale of the wretched flat. She has no option. So far there's been little interest, although the agent tells her this will take time. On top of her other responsibilities Frankie has to pop round occasionally to give the place the once over, to make sure it is spick and span for any viewers. Life is such a rush these days. Her eyes turn in on her problems as she fights for a parking space, bumps into people along the High Street dodging between parked vans and buses and even missing a turning in her haste. She has thirty essays to mark tonight and she doesn't get enough sleep as it is, thinking of Michael and his moll. Twenty years and it's suddenly over, the destruction of love, a wilderness complete. But she was the one who demanded separate lives, separate holidays, separate interests, separate friends – well, she is certainly separate now all right. She dusts. She hoovers. She wipes the surfaces over and sprays a little fresh air. All her mother owns in the world, these precious, pitiable things. How little they matter in the end. Disposables. They will have to sell them when the flat goes, or get the Council to take them away. Funny how flies like to congregate in deserted places. Where do they all come from? Do they make nests in the winter?

'How is Mrs Peacock, Mrs Rendell?'

Frankie starts and turns. But it's all right. The head round the door is drab and benign with a genuine enquiry into her mother's condition.

'Not good, I'm afraid, Miss Benson. She came back here again yesterday.'

'Oh dear, not again,' says Miss Benson with feeling, stepping into the room, a tall young woman with fly-away, pale brown hair. She looks as if she works in a bank. Nervously she clears her throat. 'I am so sorry. It must be such a worry for you, and with the main road, too.'

'It *is* a worry,' admits Frankie, stretching upright while kneading her back, glad of a rest, glad of an opportunity to discuss this pressing problem with an impartial stranger. 'And my mother is very angry with me.'

'She is bound to be,' says Miss Benson, dismayed to hear it. 'It is all very sad. She was just getting used to life here, too, after the move.' And can those be tears in Miss Benson's eyes? Surely not! 'I wondered if a visit from me might help to cheer her a little.'

'Oh, would you do that? Would you really?'

Miss Benson seems like a lonely soul, at home most evenings, according to Mother, always time for a chat, even inviting Irene in for tea and a piece of Marks & Spencer angel cake at her first-floor flat on occasion – unusual in a young person these days, unusual to bother like that. 'But of course. In a funny way I miss Mrs Peacock. You really would think there would be a way that society could look after her at home. I mean, she's not—'

Gaga? Miss Benson shrinks from the word and leaves an empty space while fiddling with the shoulder strap on her cheap black bag. 'Well, there isn't, I'm afraid,' says Frankie. 'We have been through all that. Apparently that sort of care would cost more than Greylands.' Frankie looks suddenly doubtful. Will Mother be rude to Miss Benson, too, upsetting the woman, perhaps, with her tall stories of conspiracy and unkindness? She is now convinced that someone is stealing her things. Probably not. Miss Benson, so mild, so obviously kind and good, is nothing to do with Mother's present predicament. She might even be able to talk some sense into Irene, make out she is on Mother's side.

'I will go on Friday evening, if you don't mind then,' says Miss Benson with pity in her voice. And then the rather surprising addition, because she doesn't look the type to offer such sinful gifts: 'And I'll take her some cigarettes along while I'm at it.'

43

SEVEN

'Joyvern', 11, The Blagdons, Milton, Devon

And now Joy is insisting that Vernon take her out to look at some suitable properties. She can't wait to leave Joyvern, for someone to come along and buy it so she can pick up her dusters and flee. All this is too much for Joy and losing face is the worst of it, losing face in front of her friends and neighbours. She has always been needy of other people's approval; she used to enjoy showing people around her new house, her decorated house, her extended house, her newly carpeted house, always something to show them. But not like this, oh no, not now she is leaving and forced to give it up.

Vernon and Joy were one of the first residents of this brand-new estate. They were given a bottle of champagne and a bouquet of flowers by the builders. Prideful people, they set the standard as it were, first to put up hanging baskets and their little red mail box beside the gate started a colourful trend. They moved in when the garden was little more than a shape scraped out of the muddy earth by a digger. Those were spindly saplings, now grown into sturdy standard cherries. The road that led to the cul-de-sac was hardly passable in those days, what with the builders' mess and the asphalt wagons and the dangerous piled-up mountains of paving.

But during all their fifteen years on the estate, Joy suffered a perpetual worry that someone else would move into the cul-de-sac who was more affluent, more sophisticated than they, forever afraid of embarrassment in front of other people, or of one of her family committing some social gaffe. Vernon is the only one in the world to know how much she suffered. Spend spend spend seemed to be the only answer. Joy's magazines tell her that this is an illness but Vernon would disagree with this. *Joy spent with a purpose.* She had to keep in front. The kitchen shines with its new yellow tiles, begonias in the window, bright blue plates, all matching, not cheap. Decorating the whole house every couple of years and then came the roof extension. She wanted to get the builders in but Vernon insisted on doing it himself. 'Money doesn't grow on trees, Joy, you really must try to remember that.' The lists run on and on, ever changing – the small conservatory at the back, greenhouse, gazebo and pergola, the patio and the bathroom jacuzzi. A sensible navy Ford for Vernon and a neat little Mini in a daffodil hue for Joy. Holidays in Greece, Corsica and Turkey, Benidorm is not for the Marshes. They held barbecues and At Homes on Christmas Eve, and Tupperware parties when they were in vogue and they were the first to join the new Neighbourhood Watch scheme. Suzie and Tom, five and eight when they moved here from Joy's mother's house, were well-kept, well-behaved children with green-shampoo-shiny hair and scrubbed and rosy English faces. They played in the garden, not out in the road like they tend to do nowadays. They never had sweets stuck round their faces. They did well at school, went riding, played tennis, joined the Scouts and the Guides and went on to further education and are now living with their partners. Tom is already married with a baby of his own.

Suzie swears she will soon be engaged and that *everyone* lives together nowadays. She's got a good job as a Clinique beautician and as Joy says, you can't get a more reputable brand than that.

Nothing to shame Joy there.

As a mother she has a great deal to be proud of.

Then, seven years ago and out of the blue, Vernon was made redundant.

He had wanted to search for another job, difficult though that might be, at least it would be safe, but Joy said no, this is your chance to use that money and those brains of yours to become self-employed – 'your own man' were the actual words she used as if, up until then, Vernon had been somebody else's. 'Your own man at last!'

They were already in debt. Oh, not the dangerous, embarrassing kind – more like Access, Visa, Joy's accounts at M&S, Laura Ashley, the loan for the second car, for example. Vernon knows now that that precious redundancy money should have been used to pay these off, but we would all be millionaires with hindsight, wouldn't we?

He has let Joy down with the failure of Marsh Electronics Ltd, the tatty shop where he goes every day trying to get rid of the bits and pieces, hopelessly picking the mail off the mat without ever needing to read the demands that spiral monthly like weeds in a garden.

He has never been the kind of man to make a success on his own. He lacks the drive, the energy needed for that sort of lonesome enterprise. Now Joy would probably have done better, being more ambitious than he. She might have made a success of a dress shop – that's if she hadn't smuggled out all the stock.

She tries to make out she does not blame him, that she believes he did his best, but she doesn't honestly mean that, not deep down. Deep down she thinks that Vernon, her man and protector, has let her down badly. Oh yes, he knows his wife well enough by now. He is a fat, flatulent failure and there's not a damn thing he can do about it.

Joy – you might well imagine some frivolous blonde but she's not like that, not at all. Five foot four and firmly built, she doesn't go in for glamour but taste, the navy-and-white-spotted styles of sailing folk. Underplayed, but just as costly as if you were dressing in silks. Timberland coats and Timberland shoes. Bridge handbags, or Emmy. Beautifully tailored mock-riding jackets, hand-knitted, chunky sweaters that somehow cost hundreds, leather jerkins from Jaeger while Vernon shops for his suits from Marks and feels fine in them.

That rich, bronze tone in her dark brown hair does not come off a Superdrug shelf. She might wear her hair short in a sensible style but that cut and that loose perm cost an arm and a leg every time she goes to the salon.

'Well, you want to be proud of me, Vernon,' says Joy when she senses his disapproval. 'You don't want me to look like just any old thing.' And she smuggles in her purchases and tells him she's had them for years, it's just that he is too lazy to notice.

He dreads going round to view houses. He imagines what sort of property they will find for £45,000, and that is taking a risk by the time the bills are paid off. He can imagine the look of pain on Joy's bravest face as she turns and smiles and says, *This will do nicely, Vernon.* She has put her name on several mailing lists and already picked out some which might suit, but the last place she wants to end up is some pebble-dashed, terraced, former council house at the wrong end of town.

And the other morning she told him with horror that she'd dreamed of a mobile home.

'It won't come to that, dear,' Vernon said.

'Promise me.'

'I promise you.'

From the kitchen window she heard him discussing their affairs with Bob Pritchard next-door-but-one.

She called him in. She shouted that the phone was ringing.

Hands on hips she scolded, 'Vernon, what in heaven's name do you think you are doing?'

'Just putting the world right there with old Bob.'

'You were not putting the world right! I heard you! I heard you saying that things had reached crisis point. What's that got to do with Bob? Angela has been longing to find out what's going on round here, and now you've spilled the beans it'll be everywhere tomorrow. Why do you never listen? *We are moving because the children have gone and we want somewhere smaller . . .*'

'Don't be silly, Joy. Everyone knows—'

'Excuse me, but no, they do not! Or they didn't until you put your oar in. Sometimes you can be so insensitive, Vernon,' and she fled upstairs in floods of tears.

She had told everyone they sold the Mini because she was finding driving so stressful.

Oh, why can't she be honest? Life would be so much simpler. Honest with herself if no one else. There is no shame in what they are doing – thousands of others are in the same boat. There certainly would be shame if they went creeping deeper and deeper into debt until everything was beyond redemption, as some people do. But Vernon isn't that sort of man. Vernon is a good man; he intends to pay everyone back and still end up with a place to live in.

'This can't possibly be it, Vernon.'

They draw up outside the house in the highly polished blue Ford. Vernon might be in a mess financially but he still cleans and polishes the car on a Sunday. A man of habits, sometimes just lately he thinks it is the habits that have been keeping him sane.

Vernon glances at the brochure again. The place is in the middle of nowhere, fields to front and back. He strains to read the name on the broken gate. '*Hacienda*. It is, I'm afraid.'

Joy fidgets, peering out. 'Well, at least it's a house on its own, with a garden and a name.'

'But look at it, love! It's nothing but a heap of ruins. It can't have been lived in for years. Come on, let's go.'

'Hang on, Vernon. Hang on. It could be made nice.'

Vernon senses trouble brewing. 'It could be made nice, yes, if you had a spare fifty grand to spend.' And he rests his case, firmly folding his arms on the subject.

She won't have it. 'But we might have one day, who knows?' says Joy hopefully, suddenly drawing strength from the notion that she *could after all* have a detached house with a garden and a decent-sounding address. This when he has spent hours trying to convince her that they really have got to make a sensible choice.

The gate is not attached to the post. They walk up the weedy garden path and push open the shabby front door, avoiding the nettles that grow amongst the feelers of ivy. 'It could be a charming little cottage. I can see exactly how it could be in my mind's eye,' calls Joy, cheering. 'And look, what a cosy little sitting room this must have been. We could sit in front of the fire in the winter and—'

'*Joy!* The ceiling is caving in with the damp. None of the doors fit. The chimney is running with water.' Vernon wanders round the room in a gathering state of gloom, and out into the small kitchen beyond. There's an old stone sink, flagstone floors, rotting shelves hanging off the bulging walls. He sniffs. There is something dead and decaying behind the alcove. He wishes he could share his wife's optimism but he can't. She is resorting to fantasy because she cannot bear the truth.

'We could put a Rayburn in here and cook on it and heat the water. And what a wonderful, overgrown garden, Vernon. A secret garden! We could even keep chickens. We could grow all our own food, eat our own eggs and sell the surplus, and we could have open fires instead of that costly central heating. This house is even small enough to light with oil lamps, they're in all the shops again now.' She is suddenly gleeful after months of depression. 'Oh, Vernon, think. Just think of the money we'd save!'

He will normally say anything to avoid confrontation. 'Joy! Stop it!'

'But Vernon . . .'

'It's just no good.'

'But Vernon, listen to me.' Her restless hands are washing each other over the cracked and dirty sink. Seeing this makes him want to cry, Joy is so unhappy.

But he makes himself answer her patiently. 'I don't need to listen to you. My own common sense tells me that this sort of property is right out of the question. We couldn't begin to live like this . . .'

'Oh, we could, we could! Don't you see? I could go out to work and you could stay at home all day on the dole and grow things and do the place up . . .'

'Joy, just listen to me for a change. You can't even pull the giblets out of a blessed chicken and there's nowhere for a washing machine. Think about that for a moment. And the plaster is falling off the walls – look.'

She is pleading with him and he just can't bear it, walking through this house like walking through her own day dreams. He loves his wife dearly, he loves her little ways, he wants to give her what she wants, he has always enjoyed providing for her up until now. She is scuffing round the garden among the thorns and brambles. She gushes on, 'And there's a well somewhere under all this. We could have our own water and generate our own electricity. I read all about it, Vernon, in *Take a Break*. There was this down-and-out family—'

'Joy! We are not down-and-out!'

She is losing patience with him now. 'Well, it feels as if we are, thanks to you,' she cries bitterly.

'Stop it!'

'When we married I never imagined—'

'I know, Joy.'

Rage and fear are making her cruel. 'If my mother could see me now! When I think what that woman sacrificed—'

'Stop it, Joy, please!'

'And now you won't even try to make things up to me. You never had much imagination, Vern. You were never one to see the possibilities, you always have to be led.'

But Vernon is on his way back to the car, head bowed and sighing. He has to convince her that he simply cannot undertake another dangerous venture and risk certain failure. These hopes of hers are just a glimpse of old pain, they were energised like this before he started the business. He does not want their happiness to depend on him, ever again. Vernon is exhausted. He knows she will sulk in the car for the rest of the afternoon and automatically dislike anything else they look at.

Her attitude just isn't fair! All right, she has suffered, showing people round the house, making excuses to the neighbours, facing a move she never wanted to make. But so has he. Begging for money from this bank and that, made to wait in carpeted foyers, treated like a scrounger, trying to make things right with angry customers. One way and another his humiliation has been complete.

Joy slams the car door behind her. 'If you're going to take this negative attitude towards everything we see then there's not much point in me coming with you, is there, Vernon?' she snaps. 'You might as well just drop me off at home and be done with it.'

Joy merely shrugs her shoulders when they are shown round the sensible Swallowbridge flat. She is car sick, she says, from having to read the map.

'It is lovely and clean,' Vernon says to the eager woman who shows them round, a professional person no doubt, carefully made up and in her forties; maybe Joy will be humoured by that but she will despise the net curtains. He finds his wife's silence embarrassing because there's not much to say about such a small property and normally Joy would fill in the gaps. But now she merely picks at invisible threads on her sleeve. She might as well have stayed in the car.

'It's my mother's flat really,' says this Mrs Rendell with a warm smile. 'She has only lived here for two years and now even this is too much for her. Unfortunately she has had to move into a residential home so I am showing people round in her place.'

'Oh?' says Vernon, unsure how to respond. 'I do admire your colour scheme.' He suspects that this daughter has chosen it, blues and whites and pale greens. It is most relaxing.

The only response that Joy seems prepared to make is that aggravating little noise in her throat.

'Cool in summer and warm in winter. As you see, the double glazing stops the noise from the main road and there's economy heating. The cooker is built in, and it's all very cheap and easy to run,' says Mrs Rendell, a highly competent speaker. Could be a teacher. 'And yes, that's a heated towel rail but there's no airing cupboard, I'm afraid. My mother uses a clothes horse. She stands it round the cistern and finds that just as effective.'

'I'm sure,' says Vernon uneasily. Ought he to mention that his wife is ill, explain her ill-tempered behaviour?

'And there's double locks on all the windows. My mother was . . . is . . . very safety conscious.'

'You have to be, these days, unfortunately,' agrees Vernon.

This is a far more sensible option than any of the other places they have looked at this afternoon. One terrible estate where they hadn't even stopped, one ugly, tattered house with broken cars in the garden, and one converted flat in a large fifties house, not enough room to swing a cat. But he and Joy could live here very cheaply. It would meet all their basic needs and they might be able to knock the vendor down £5,000 or so, bearing the climate in mind.

'Well, what did you think about that?' he asks her when they have thanked Mrs Rendell and are back on the noisy pavement again.

She doesn't even bother to answer. Joy just stalks off towards the car park, turning her back on Vernon.

She is clinging on to her old life with her nails and with her teeth. And he is the one who must finally pull her down off the mountain.

EIGHT

Penmore House, Ribblestone Close, Preston, Lancs

Jody Middleton buries his face in his pillow, perhaps to rediscover the innocent smell of himself, and is amazed, on raising his head, to see the kind of slobber there he associates with childhood sleeping.

He thinks of the Turin Shroud; perhaps Jesus was doing this when He made that famous impression . . . He feels a spurt of yearning for that younger boy he once was, and his freedom, and a longing for that overwhelming sea of the past.

Look at him now.

Waiting for rescue.

British justice, my foot.

He has already been tried, convicted and condemned. He is only on remand but there's no one around Preston who doesn't hate him. His nails are bitten down to the quick. The eyes that stare at him through the slot in the steel grey door are cold eyes, mean eyes, like your own eyes are if you cover the rest of your face and stretch them chinky in the mirror. You can frighten yourself like that. The light is sunk in the ceiling so you can't hitch yourself up and smash the bulb to use as a weapon against yourself or one of the screws. The brick walls are painted pale grey. He'll stay in a cell on his own until after the trial, they say, like he can wear his own clothes until then and have visitors and letters every day. He's allowed to wear his earrings, too. That's daft – if he wanted to, he could pull them out and carve right through the veins on his wrist.

He stares at the scratches on the frame of the bed. What other poor kid put them there and where did he come from? Was he just as homesick? Jody thinks of his mum, Babs, and what she must be going through now.

Everyone hates him and his mum and dad and Dawn and Cindy – that is why they are going away and leaving him here all alone. He can't imagine what sort of hell their lives must be like now. He wants to call out and stop them from going, to shout, 'Wait for me!' and to follow them out into some bright and fantasy afternoon, and be little again.

But Jody is tainted with the darkness of sin and has no voice any more. He is served pale food, as if anything colourful might excite him to riot or rebellion. White, grey, brown, so as not to bombard the senses. He stares everyone out if he can, trying to be cool, not wanting them to see that he doesn't dare catch their eyes, that he wishes he could shrink back, backtrack through time out of this excruciating place.

He feels the flush of shame again. The word RAPE disgusts him deeply and will certainly disgust his mates. There's nothing big or macho about it, and why on earth would anyone choose to do it to poor Janice Plunket? Everyone thinks he's a sad misfit with something sexually wrong with him, and he has to see the shrink every week so she can get reports together.

His heart is skittering in his chest. They call him a pervert. But he's done nothing wrong, nothing *really* wrong.

Jody Middleton, aged eighteen and three months, lets out a long sad sigh to the night.

But the time is going. That's the good thing about time, it does pass. It will go on passing and one day he will be out of here in a place of real voices and faces.

It was Mum who broke the news when they visited yesterday. She kept her arms folded as if she was protecting herself. Dad just looked away, embarrassed, and rasped his long hands together.

'You already knew about Dad's new job and the fact that he was considering it seriously. In the circumstances.' Mum hesitated and look at him nervously. 'Well, now we've definitely decided to move, Jody, for our sakes as much as for Dawn and Cindy's. We saw somewhere we liked last week and Dad's going to make an offer soon. We felt you should know.'

They say that Dawn and Cindy are not allowed to visit but Jody knows they wouldn't come if they could. They're ashamed to have him as a brother, to be related to such an alleged disgusting pervert, and he bets they're suffering as much as he. Gone is the closeness, the friendship they shared for so long, the laughter and the teasing and the sledge-races on the landing.

And now it has come to this.

He has taken up smoking since he has been on remand. It's something to do, something to bargain with and it depresses the appetite, not that Jody's got much of one anyway. Jody squeezed out the end of his rollie, burning his fingers deliberately while keeping his face quite calm. Why should he care? He knew they'd been away to look at places down south but Jody could not really believe they'd do anything about it. After all, he was born in the Close, he's known no other home, no other territory, no other mates and neither have they. Boots in the kitchen, toys all over the floor, jigsaw puzzles and photographs because Mum was always proud of her family, it was always a warm, messy place. He used to be able to wind Mum round his little finger. He knows he is a good-looking boy, tall and slim and athletic, he once had acne but has grown out of that now. But his skin has already taken on that unhealthy prison pallor thanks to bad air, no exercise, bad food and worry. Where will he go when they let him out?

What Mum said made him want to scream. It made him want to sob like a child. If none of this had happened they'd never have considered moving. Even if Dad had been offered promotion he reckons he would have turned it down because they were all so happy where they were.

He was struck by a new and sickening feeling, the knowledge that now he was out of control, they were coming together like an army closing ranks against him. For the first time in his life, he is powerless.

'When you come out,' said Mum, careful not to venture a date – she believes that he's guilty, too, and likely to face a pretty long stretch – 'when you come out you can come and visit.'

Not LIVE, you notice, just VISIT. So has he forfeited his home as well as his reputation and freedom?

How could she do this to him when he's done nothing wrong?

She blames herself. She believes she should have been firmer, she believes he would do better away from her influence, that independence would curb his high-spirits.

Mum went wittering on, anything to avoid talking about the reality of the situation. 'Dawn and Cindy both think the house is rather small, and compared with the Close I suppose it is.' She even laughed, though warily, and Jody hasn't seen her do that for ages. 'Goodness knows where all our things are going to go.'

'Well, you can chuck out all my stuff,' said Jody provocatively, seeing himself riding off across a foggy plain all alone. He whined a little as he sat there across the peeling table. 'My bed, my chest of drawers, my wardrobe, my telly – that's if you haven't given them away already. I won't be needing them again. I won't have anywhere to put them.'

'Oh Jody love,' Mum exclaimed as he'd known she would. 'Don't talk so soft. You'll find somewhere, pet – a nice flat. You could share with a friend and maybe one day you'll find a girl . . .' Mum tailed off, embarrassed.

'Give over, Mum.' He wished he was out of here on a horse riding across the sands through the sea-spray as they had on holiday once. Free. Free. And as light as a bird, almost non-existent, so light had he felt. Or dancing with the music loud, lost in a kindly wave of sensation.

He considered his mum and dad from this new position of helplessness and found that he had great difficulty in speaking to them from here at all. He could hardly make the words he wanted come out of his mouth. All the blood inside him was rising to his head so his brain felt as if it was bubbling. This sort of rage was new to Jody.

They'd never asked him if he'd done it. They kind of looked away from the crime like they looked away from him then, wishing they weren't there visiting at all, wishing he wasn't their son any more.

But he deserves to be believed, doesn't he – by the people who love him, at least! He wanted so badly to be believed but all Mum said was, 'Why didn't you tell me you'd been with her during all that time when they were searching? You just sat there and said nothing!'

What he said sounded so weak. 'Because I did have sex with her, and I did leave her alone at the reservoir, and I felt guilty about that, but I never imagined they'd call it rape.' And then the very worst part of all. 'And I was embarrassed that everyone would know I'd had sex with Janice Plunket. But it wasn't rape, Mum. Honest to God it was nothing like that.'

'Well, what was it, Jody, with a girl too subnormal to know what she was doing?'

'It wasn't like that, Mum. It wasn't like that at all.' But the more he tried to protest the worse it sounded, so it seemed much better, in the end, to say nothing. A kind of weary fatalism.

Janice Plunket noticed him, not in the nudging, giggly way of most of the girls round here. Jody has never been short of girlfriends; he is just the kind of exciting boy the girls have always been drawn to; his personality as well as his looks made him one of the lads. Jody lost his virginity at the ripe age of fifteen. He had no need to rape anyone. But Janice was always following him around to his great consternation and the amusement of his mates. She had what they call a crush on him, always staring at him out of those strangely slanty eyes, giving that goofy grin she thought was sexy. If he didn't watch his back she'd creep up behind him and hug him. Jeez!

'You're all right tonight then, Jody.'

'Gross!'

But they had no need to be as cruel as they were to Janice Plunket. They teased her, specially Kurt and Stew, made her dance to their rap music, gave her E one day for a laugh, took her on a ride on the back of Stew's bike and didn't let her off until she was sick. Her dad would have a fit if he knew all the stuff they did.

Jody never took part in that. He only stood by and watched; if he could, he walked away. He would never do those things for a laugh, not for any reason at all. They were acting like big kids. There was more fun to be had with the real birds outside the arcade. He wished she'd stay away from them and not walk straight into the trap every time, on legs like two hefty pillars. She never seemed to learn! Her head must be like a garden cluttered with weeds and no one knew how to stop them growing.

Janice Plunket had pale, fuzzy hair like a baby and soft brown eyes. They shouldn't let her out on her own so much, Jody thought. And that if only they'd get her out of those old women's clothes and dress her in something decent, she'd even be quite pretty in her own way.

But Janice was not the innocent child everyone liked to make out she was.

What Jody did wasn't half as bad as what Kurt and Stew had done. She'd wanted it, too – that was the crazy part. She'd been determined to get it and that's what the police refused to see, the fact that she was normal enough to enjoy it.

She was standing there, flatfooted as usual, in the car park, staring at him again so he asked her if she wanted a ride. Well, no one else was about and he wasn't ready to go home yet. *God – what had made him ask her?* Jody implores the heavens. If only Jody could take time back. He was standing beside his green Datsun, a present from Mum and Dad for his eighteenth birthday, not much of a car, he supposes, but Jody was over the moon with it and you didn't need much of a car to impress Janice Plunket. He loved driving, he loved to have a good reason to drive. She fed him roasted peanuts as they sped out of town towards the moors and the wide open spaces. This, and all the vast loneliness, was where Jody really loved to drive.

The moors were quite silent apart from a pair of ravens high in the upper sky leaving their hoarse calls behind them. Far away across the valley lay the ribbon of road. They parked on a hill overlooking the reservoir scented by bracken and heather and the car was quite hidden among the sleeping rocks and boulders. He found some seashells in the glove compartment and gave them to Janice who beamed as if they were diamonds.

'Won't your father be worried about you?'

'Nah,' said Janice nasally. 'Anyway, I don't live at home any more. I live at the Centre. I can do what I like, I can. I'm allowed.'

He watched her, staring intently, as she tried to behave like a grown-up woman just as he always seemed to be pretending to be a grown-up man, but failing. She brought a lipstick out of her old woman's bag with the silver clip and pushed it round her mouth, pouting into the passenger mirror. He was surprised – it was a nice ladylike pink shade. She had a nursery-rhyme type of face, the kind you see in old picture books. Little Miss Muffet.

Jody opened the door and got out, walked past a solitary sheep and made for the wood round the lower slopes. Janice Plunket could do what she liked, he didn't care. He wasn't responsible for her; she'd had her bit of excitement and Jody wanted to stretch his legs. He knew she was following because of the heavy treads in the undergrowth behind him, but she could please herself where she went. He would take her back safe and sound in a little while.

He sat down between two boulders overlooking the lake. Thinking. The wind rippled the water below and sent shivers all the way down his spine as if the two were connected. The soft ground squelched and water bubbled up over his boots. He heard her puffing and groaning beside him as she started to sit down. He said nothing, just looked away over the water pretending that he was all on his own.

He wondered what her skin felt like and realised she would let him find out if he wanted. She would let him do anything he wanted, she wouldn't stop him. He was surprised and curious when he felt his erection, that sharp ache between his thighs and his breath caught in his chest.

He was getting excited. It was daft, but he had to speak. 'I could kiss you if I wanted.'

She turned her face upwards and moved with her lips towards him. She puckered her newly painted mouth and edged her great body closer, abandoning all decency, heavy, sprawling and available. With a look of half-frightened desperation he lunged forward and kissed her, and then he was kissing her seriously and hard, his tongue parting her lips, his chest and his hips straining against her.

She was harder bodied than he'd imagined, and better muscled too.

Janice Plunket made a start. She began to take off her clothes. She took off her knickers and her old woman's bra and she was eventually lying there like a pink blancmange in that kind of broken Christmas-tree shape; she was lying there with her legs apart, ready for him.

Now he stared at her with confusion. Janice Plunket . . . why? Half of him wanted to laugh but the other half felt sad for her lying there, waiting for him, and he had started it all off with his casual remarks. He was responsible for this. Her boobs were huge and dangly and he touched her flanks and her hips, moving his hand up her thighs and parting the warmth and wetness there. Janice thrust up from the ground, ready and willing, offering him all she'd got. Raw feelings of power engulfed him. Ashamed of his feelings, he thought this must be what incest felt like, when you knew you shouldn't, when you knew what other people would say. She allowed him to touch her all over her body and inspect every part of it, something he had wanted to do with lots of the girls he screwed but had felt silly about asking.

He did not feel the sword of destiny poised over his life. He had no premonition that this was an action he was going to remember for ever. He no longer felt disgust or guilt or a sense of immorality. Jody felt none of these things.

Not then.

Because she was a girl and he was a boy.

He climbed on top of her, grasping her hard, mumbling, whispering, 'Are you sure?'

It didn't take long and he rolled off her abruptly, gradually easing himself further away, not wanting to stay with her or be part of her any longer. Feelings of guilt began to return, as if he had done something vaguely bad, and he put them down to her being different. He was suddenly overcome with the urge to cry, to have a shower, but Jody often felt this way after sex. He stood up, arms dangling uselessly at his side, unsure what to do next. Still on the ground and naked, not even attempting to cover her nakedness, Janice stared up at him blankly but neither of them spoke a word as he zipped up his jeans and left her, resolutely starting off up the hill.

She wanted more but he couldn't give it. She wanted him to stay and love her but he didn't know how.

He called out a vague, 'Come on,' but she didn't answer and he wanted, very badly, to leave her. 'Come on, Janice, or I'll leave you behind and you'll have to walk!'

RAPE.

It's not fair! It did not occur to Jody that Janice would be unable to find her way home. Any crime there was, he considers angrily, lay in that disgusted rejection and now look – here he is, confused and cold, and Mum and Dad are doing exactly the same thing to him.

NINE

The Grange, Dunsop, Nr Clitheroe, Lancs

It doesn't seem that long ago, certainly not six years.

Together they watched the fall of Thatcher with a morbid fascination, thrilling to the horror of every toe-curling moment, the sense of a gang of powerful men meeting in posh London Squares, an icon brought low by secret revolution, an institution ground underfoot when it became too downright embarrassing for its own good.

Total mortification. If only the woman would acknowledge defeat, just go away and lick her wounds. If only she would stop fighting.

And Belle would have liked to remind Jacy of that when the messages started to seep through. His buddy and his agent, Curt Wendel, came to the hotel for a chat and Jacy, so totally self-absorbed, didn't get the message, but straight away Belle noticed the change in the fat man's attitude.

'Trouble,' wheezed Curt, coughing, following the route of his long cigar and taking the leather swing chair, unconsciously placing himself on a higher level than the group members who were sprawling over the sofa and chairs in the altogether, re-playing the video of the gig last night.

Jip the drummer was still in the clinic, right out of his head, they said on the phone. So that left five plus Belle; you couldn't count the groupies who came and went to order like the bottles of champagne in the ice buckets.

'Shuddup and have a drink,' slurred Rab, the keyboard player, still guzzling beer, his boozed eyes sliding back to the giant screen on the wall. 'Gedda look at this.'

But contrary to tradition Curt declined the drink and only Belle bothered to notice, and the tired look he had, like a pair of frameless shades round his gimlet eyes.

Continuing with the video, they came to the hilarious part where Jacy fell off the stage to the joy of the crowd and the guys carried on

58

without him, Deek stepping forward and taking his place at the microphone, plugging in his own guitar. The pace of the thing took off from that moment. The very ground of the Superbowl began to shake.

Something was wrong. Curt wasn't bothering to watch. He concentrated on his ash instead, rolling it round the glass ashtray, prodding it till it broke. You could tell where you were in the film because of the screaming punters. 'You behaved like an arsehole last night, Jacy. You could've scuppered the whole darn thing.'

'Get lost, Curt.' And Jacy, his sleek black hair pulled back into a pony tail, reached out a lazy hand to pat the kid asleep on the floor below him. He moved like a diffident prince. On his stomach were balanced french fries and a tub of coleslaw. Belle stayed in the background; with Jacy it was a choice between having something or nothing. She had no desire to be pissed or high like the others. While they were touring the States Belle made sure to pay for herself, sometimes earning thousands of dollars for a day's work, just posing for photographs. She sometimes acted as social worker to the runaways, the waifs and strays and under-age kids who prised themselves into their idols' beds. Some were upset, broken-hearted to find themselves on the pavement in the morning along with the trash; some even tearfully begged her for reasons.

She sipped a small glass of cognac and watched, her blue eyes passing over those in the room. She wished she could care less for him, wished she could simply dismiss Jacy from her mind and get on with her own life. Her friends called her crazy. But she was used to living like this by now, all the upheavals, physical and emotional. If she'd left him he wouldn't have cared.

'You could've got yourself killed. Torn to pieces by the mob. What is it you want, boy, immortality?'

Jacy was dangerously tired as usual. Belle was scared for him. He lived in another world these days, he thought he was invincible and that his fame and fortune would last for ever no matter what he did. But recently his outlandish behaviour was causing all sorts of problems. He wasn't even amusing although he believed that he was, making an ass of himself on talk shows, pretending to drop off to sleep and last time pissing at the camera. People were getting cheesed off with it. He'd made it, for Christsake, he didn't *need* to do that kind of shit any more. People were saying he'd lost it. Even the real, dedicated fans, Belle sensed a change in their passion; it had sour edges about it now like cream beginning to turn. The group's last album never made it past six in the charts, unheard of for Sugarshack and Jacy just laughed when he discovered Deek had been tempted by an offer from Elektra to do an informal session at the studios as lead singer. Jacy's name didn't feature. Rumours had it they'd been advised to dump him.

He would not discuss his work with anyone, he refused adamantly to do so. The press had called him a genius and he'd taken that to heart years ago. Nobody tells a genius what to do. Jacy was immensely powerful and recklessly arrogant. Composer and lead singer, yeah, Jacy was up there flashing in all the bright lights with the gods.

Like lottery winners and film stars Jacy had lost his ability to judge other people, surrounding himself with scroungers and flatterers who were clearly only after what they could get. He was into compulsive spending. A crack-head now, like the rest of them, it was up to Belle to protect him; he'd never have lasted so long without her to bail him out of scrape after scrape. In the last small disaster Jacy had flown over the heads of his financial advisers as usual and allowed his name to be used by some textile company in exchange for a massive sum. They were later revealed to be part of an unscrupulous child-slave racket, and to keep his name out of the limelight cost him thousands. Belle hung on in there, reserved and careful, answering his calls when he was in no condition to do so, reassuring him always by making out she was softer and simpler than she was.

Jacy was a gambler, too. He loved the horses and the roulette tables.

And so it went on . . . and on . . . He studiously ignored all the warnings.

Curt snapped his fingers and said, 'We've got to talk, Jacy.'

But Jacy waved a disinterested hand.

'And I mean soon, son.'

'Don't call me son, Fatman, I don't need this hassle.'

Success and acclaim were not enough for him any more. Spoiled rotten, it seemed that Jacy needed to push to the outer limits in order to feel anything at all. He ignored Curt altogether, still believing the guy wouldn't dare upset the lead singer of Sugarshack. No matter how big or influential, no agency could risk losing a hot property like them.

Curt groaned. Knowing otherwise.

When Belle tried to warn Jacy, he would curse and swear and glare at her. He was looking awful these days; the pace of life was telling on his beauty. 'And you, don't be so judgmental. Get a life, why don't you? The earth could blow up tomorrow; we could all die on the nearest freeway.'

It featured in a magazine and Belle fell in love with it at once.

It was Belle who persuaded him to buy the Grange. Property prices were still rising and it seemed you couldn't go wrong with an investment like that. She loved the permanent look of the place, the sunny rooms and the elegance. She could see it filled with baking smells, children, dogs, everybody home. Dream on. Carefully, as only she could, she steered Jacy away from the ranch in Texas, the partnership in the Vegas casino, the Hydro complex in California and the cable station in Virginia.

Mostly she just listened to him with a passionate, honed attention and gave him whatever he seemed to want. He had got to thinking she would put up with anything regardless. But this time she ventured much further, into what could have been dangerous waters. She broached the subject with some apprehension. 'What you really need is a base, somewhere you could go to recharge your batteries every so often, somewhere which is just yours and yours alone.'

'Stables . . .'

Belle nodded wearily but she must follow his lead. 'Well yes, stables certainly, if that's what you think.'

'Honey, I could turn the place into the best goddamn racing stables . . .'

'Of course you could, Jacy. Of course you could.'

'I could hire interior decorators, dump most of the crap.'

It took time, but Belle was quietly persistent and finally got him back home for a week and it wasn't long after that that the bid for the Grange was accepted and of course the press, the local press in particular, were in their element, interviewing all the old crusties who had lived around Dunsop all their lives.

Even in those days Belle rarely read the papers and in this particular case the quotes were so predictable as they clicked and clacked their sour disapproval:

'It'll be AIDS next, mark my words.'

'It's all those raves that worry me.'

'The drugs, think of the effect of those drugs on our local youngsters.'

'How sad that a grand house like the Grange has ended up in such circumstances. He'll ruin it, a man like that. He will ruin that poor house.'

'This young man does not sound like a suitable addition to our little community. Dunsop has always been such a quiet, respectable place.'

The locals decided to protest, led by a neighbour, Mrs Julia Farquhar – a tall, tweedy northern woman with fierce bosoms and a ferret's face who made dainty sandwiches and put out bowls of nuts for the meetings. A petition bearing 500 names was handed in to the Council but what could they do? The Grange was on the open market. Preventing a pop star from making his home there was way beyond their remit.

Belle found it all rather amusing, but to her surprise Jacy was furious. How dare they? It made him all the more determined to fulfil the locals' every fear, if he could.

He did. He surpassed himself. Because he was so hurt.

And now, after six dreadful years here, it is up to Belle to persuade Jacy to move again.

'So you are happy to let me phone the agents with a firm offer this afternoon?'

'Suit yourself . . .' he started to say.

'Now I don't want you coming on strong afterwards and backing out and saying you knew nothing about it and it was all my idea.'

Jacy stares at her warily. The silence between them stretches taut and hums like a live wire. 'But it is your idea, Belle, nothing to do with me.'

She is only just back from the launderette, a good six miles there and back, biting her lips all the way in case the bright red Jeep, the only vehicle they have left, failed to get her there and back, and in no mood to put up with his sulks. Of course there is a large industrial machine in the basement but that doesn't work and nobody seems to be willing to mend it. It is obsolete, apparently, gone out of production since Jacy bought it. And what's he been doing while she's been away? There is one simple answer to that – nothing! Or drinking wine.

Belle turns on Jacy, the golden ringlets piled up on her head bobbing about with righteous rage. Before she speaks she makes an attempt to control her voice. She'd love to slap that smirk off his face because there's nothing that suits Jacy more these days than riling Belle, and she knows it.

'You're a middle-aged man, dammit, going grey, with the start of a paunch and you behave like a bloody great spoilt kid and wonder why everyone laughs at you . . .'

'You're sick.'

But Belle can't stop. She has reached breaking point. 'There's not a madly excited market out there ready to pay the kinds of prices you're expecting, dickhead. We'll be lucky if this solicitor guy follows through on behalf of his mysterious clients who seem so interested in this . . .'

'I thought you understood my needs.'

Her voice, so carefully modulated for so long, rises to a manic scream. 'Your needs, Jacy! *Your boring needs!* Don't talk to me about your needs, I'm up to here with them, I've had years of them and they're boring, BORING, BORING! I am sick of hearing you pouring out your anguish, blaming everyone else for your own miserable plight, waiting for some belated apology from a world that isn't even out there any more! You're a broken has-been, Jacy. Since you, life has moved on!'

'For God's sake, Belle.' His voice is thick and urgent and his mouth twists in a sour grimace.

All she ever wanted to do was get married and live happily ever after. Is that too much to ask? She could have had anyone and yet she hung around waiting for this pitiful bastard. All those years. Belle begins to shake, like her voice, hardly coherent. 'OK, you went to all the great parties and head waiters called you by name. Money grew on trees, then – you only had to click your fingers and women prostrated themselves at your feet. But you messed up, didn't you, Jacy, and how! And it's a real downer. Real life is hell, it's bloody hell for most of us but we don't just sit on our arses boozing ourselves to death, you gutless bastard!'

'You hysterical slag! Get out!'

'Make me!'

He has to silence her somehow, or break down at her feet and cry. Short and quick, Jacy charges forwards and grabs hold of her shoulders hard so her neck whips back. His eyes are bulging, his lips drawn thin and white when he slaps her across the face with the bony back of his hand. She takes the full force of the blow and falls against the wall. Belle tastes blood. Disbelief, fear and anger chase each other across her face; she cannot believe he is capable of this! She crouches down on the floor, crawling crab-like towards the door.

'Get out, you whore! Before I kill you!'

'You're mad!' she whispers so he can only just hear her. 'My God, Jacy, you have finally lost your mind completely!'

With his eyes fixed firmly on her he approaches maliciously once again and his grin is horrible. Reduced to all fours now, Belle scuttles across the slippery wooden floor in the hall. His voice is a snarl between his teeth. 'If it hadn't been for you . . .'

'For me?' Even in her red-hot pain Belle can feel astonishment. She can hardly recognise his face any more it is so transfixed with rage. *'For me?'*

'Yes – *you!* You resented the fact that I was the star, making millions while all you could do was strip in sordid basements for grubby magazines.'

'But Jacy . . .'

'Oh, don't think I didn't know!' He hates to hurt her, he hates to hurt her. He shakes his head like an animal attacked, as if attempting to clear some buzzing sounds from his ears. 'Don't think I wasn't aware of your nasty little game! Screwing with everyone else, you bitch! Between you all you pulled me down, you deliberately conspired to bring me to this!'

She stumbles and almost falls at the door. 'But I've never even kissed another man . . .'

'Get out, get out!' Oh God forgive me!

Later, when he comes to find her and she cuddles in close, she can feel the shudder where his sobs have been. He does need her. *He really does!*

TEN

No fixed abode

Princess-in-waiting. The silver choker round her slender neck makes her look almost regal.

'Jamie doesn't know about any of this, be honest with me, does he? It's Them who are doing this to me, isn't it – sending me off into exile?'

So Dougal Rathbone protests, 'I'm afraid that Jamie *does* know, Arabella, and is a hundred per cent behind the course we are taking. "They", as you refer to them, don't know a thing about it.'

'Well, I won't believe that till I see Jamie and he tells me himself.'

Dougal shakes his head dubiously. Powerful behind the wheel of his gold Mercedes convertible, he has finally persuaded Arabella to accompany him to the wilds of Lancashire to view the property in question. The bribe, if you like. He knows what he would do if he was offered such a property – he'd jump at it. The potential of the place is enormous. The girl beside him is pretty and sweet-smelling like an English rose, dressed quite simply in dainty florals. Her silver-blonde hair, drawn back from her peachy face with two combs, curls naturally to her shoulders. Even if Dougal were straight it would be hard to view her in a sexual way because of the innocence about her. During the journey this sophisticated and worldly young man is stunned to realise exactly how naive this mother-to-be appears. She started off in her childish voice by relating her morning's horoscope: 'Keep your counsel today, it will pay you off in the end for it is to and from this day that all future rivers will flow.' She turned to Dougal. 'Weird! Really spooky. So what do you think about that?'

'You believe that sort of rubbish?'

She is glad to leave the hot grey dust of London behind her. 'Naturally,' she says, drawing clean air into her lungs. 'I thought everyone did, at heart. They might pretend they don't but they do really.'

And another shock to the system came when she suddenly

exclaimed, clasping her bangled hands together, 'Oh, wouldn't it be nice if everyone was just allowed to love each other?'

Oh God! Barbara Cartland. Dougal stared intently at the road and found himself unable to answer. Was she subnormal or what? He must have a long and realistic discussion with this young lady tonight.

Peaches has been over-protected. Mummy and Daddy live in a gorgeous Georgian house fronting the road in Epping. Apparently Arabella has no relatives up north, has never been there and seems to regard it in the context of the historical romances she reads, all moorlands and russet skies, revolting rabbles in clogs and braces and broken factories peeping out from sooty, cobblestoned towns.

'Well, you are going to be pleasantly surprised,' Dougal reassures her, searching for a decent hotel where they can have a leisurely lunch, and if he can get a fair quantity of wine down her pretty little throat perhaps her perceptions will be lightened further. Tonight they are staying in a country hotel before attempting the return journey in the morning.

Dougal is a nice kind man, thinks Arabella, the sort of person she imagines Jamie might be close to, not the loud assortment of young men he was with when they were first introduced. He is the sort of brotherly type she feels she could confide in, but his attitude surprises her. Perhaps the fun-loving Jamie is playing some game, luring her to a secret love-nest to surprise her on her arrival. She wouldn't put anything past him, knowing him as she does. He's a joker. Posing as a motorbike freak on his precious Harley Davidson, that's how he always approached his Little Venice hideaway, his neighbours on the river never saw him without his helmet and goggles. It is perfectly ghastly how her sweet, sensitive young lover is misrepresented by the press. Anyone would think they were conducting a private vendetta against him. But he's so brave, he merely laughs and says they know no better. If they attacked Arabella like that, following her round, quizzing her friends, setting her up with their intrusive lenses, if they treated her as meanly as that she would be completely destroyed.

But look at her now. She has to admit that all this is rather exciting. Arabella Brightly-Smythe had lived a quiet and protected life carefully monitored by a loving family until she started sharing the flat in Queensway with her two school chums, Charlie and Mags. 'You will be all right now, darling, won't you,' asked Mummy, kissing her goodbye and looking worried. Arabella was launched into the big wide world on the day she unpacked her bags and laid her old brown teddy bear, Beppo, on the frilly pillow in her room. At first she couldn't quite believe it, all the excitement, the glamour, the places to go, the friends they knew. She felt a sense of rebirth. She went a little bit dotty at first, she supposes, but then she met Jamie and has never looked back.

She hasn't seen him for two weeks now and there's no point going to the houseboat. It's kept locked and chained with a watch on it at all times. Oh, the overwhelming pain of this love and the terrible joy of it.

'Perhaps I ought to be swathed in veils,' she says to Dougal lightly, 'like poor Mrs Simpson.'

She daren't tell Mummy and Daddy about the baby, not until she has at least an engagement ring on her finger; they would be so disappointed in their only daughter. Nor dare she confess to Charlie or Mags. They would be on Jamie's side and try to persuade her to have an abortion. Neither of her flatmates sees Jamie through her own loving eyes; both of them have tried hard to warn her against him. They don't try any more because the only result is that poor Arabella flies weeping to her bedroom and refuses to come out.

'I wish you wouldn't say these terrible unkind things, not when you don't know him!'

She has to admit that Jamie disappointed her with his response to her pregnancy, something that filled her with joy and delight, a condition she has looked forward to since childhood, to be a mother and a wife. But when he saw how disturbed she was he became his old gentle self again. 'Come on, old thing, dry your eyes. If you want the baby of course you should have it, only it is going to be frightfully tricky in the circs.'

'In the circs?'

'Bearing in mind who I am, silly.'

'But you are my Prince and you love me, don't you?'

Jamie gave a half-smile. He ruffled her hair and climbed out of the messy bed. She couldn't see his expression, or hear what he was saying to himself over the noise of the shower in the bathroom. She thought he was probably singing. The fact that they met on his sacred houseboat said something about how important she had become to him.

'I do hope it's a girl,' she called. 'Mummy is going to be terribly thrilled.'

He can't have heard her because he didn't shout back a reply.

He came back smelling of an exotic manhood. Expensive. Sultry, of deserts and temples. His chest was broad and shiny with a few blond hairs wisping out of the centre in a sweet soft line that led down to his pubes. He was clean, golden and soft-spoken; his towel-damp curls hung over his forehead forcing him to peer through with his soft brown amber-flecked eyes. With a gesture both lordly and casual he flicked it back and kissed her.

She wanted to be one with him, man and wife made flesh.

He stroked her forehead with his finger, moving it meticulously around her face and over her eyelids so she felt hypnotised by the sensation. 'Fact of the matter is, old fruit, that it's not going to be quite as straightforward as you seem to think.'

'Love will conquer all,' moaned Arabella softly, 'and I really believe that, Jamie, don't you? Isn't it a miracle that we found one another out of all the millions and billions of people in the world, isn't it wonderful?' And she stretched out in all her nakedness, flooded with perfect happiness.

Some people would say that Arabella has led a charmed life and she would have to agree with them. I mean, Mr and Mrs Brightly-Smythe are still together, not even separated like most of the middle-aged people she knows. Her two young brothers, Garth and Cedric, are bright and healthy and doing well at school, specially at games. Both sets of grandparents are still alive. Sometimes she worries that it's all been rather too charming and that one day something really awful will happen, someone will die or get ill, or they'll lose all their money or the house might burn down and take all their magical childhood things with it. But then she reassures herself, because although you are always reading about the terrible things that happen, they do tend to happen to other people, *a certain type of person*, and in her heart of hearts she wonders whether some people don't actually attract these disasters.

'I suppose they have someone special lined up for you already,' Arabella joked to Jamie as he sat admiring her on the side of the bed.

'That would seem to be the case, yes.'

'Oh Jamie! You are a fool! Even I know that whoever you are these days, you are allowed to choose your own partner. It's no longer the Dark Ages. You're not poor Princess Margaret. Nor are you first in line to the throne and your parents seem to be frightfully nice . . .'

Jamie's laughter interrupted her gregarious flow. 'How the hell would you know?'

'Well, of course I know, silly. I can read, can't I? I watch television. I was even invited to a garden party once, with Mummy. You should have seen our marvellous hats. But I must admit I didn't see Her, although we were told She was there.'

His smile was crooked, only half his mouth moved into it. 'I don't believe you. I truly don't believe you. You are just too much!'

'I'm not sure I know what you mean, Jamie.'

'Oh, never mind. Forget it.'

He rarely talked about his older brothers, George, the heir to the throne, grave and shy, just married to a Princess of Denmark, and Rupert the sporty one two years younger. She sometimes wondered whether he was actually happy at home, wherever home really was, they moved about so often. They didn't seem to have much family life but then it's so difficult for Them, isn't it? Always in the limelight. After all, their bond is probably stronger than blood alone. So many disguises. Sometimes it's dark glasses and a wig. He always gives a false name if he is ever asked and says he is of no fixed abode, like a tramp, poor thing.

Everyone at school had a crush on James Henry Albert, by far the most attractive of the Queen's three children. If it wasn't Agassi pinned on the wall above the bed in the dorm it was him, decked out on a horse in all his splendour, or striding across the moors in a deer-stalker with a gun over his manly shoulder. Arabella longs to tell her secret to some of those old friends of hers; she keeps in touch with most of them by letter or meeting in town occasionally for a coffee or a salad to chew over the good old days. She longs to see their reaction, those Janets and Jillies and Judies with whom she shared so many windy hours on the lacrosse pitch, or down by the tennis courts dreaming and gossiping. Gosh. How they will envy her when they know! And he's so much sweeter than any of them had imagined.

When she first met him at the wine bar in Maida Vale he told her his name was Wayne.

And what is more – she believed him. Called him Wayne for a week and talked about motorbikes until it slowly dawned on her that the young travel agent in the hornrimmed glasses who so resembled the Prince was actually Him Himself. Their eyes were the first physical parts to meet, meaningfully, across the proverbial crowded room, causing Peaches to come close to swooning. It only took one week for the rest of themselves to be introduced, and yes, yes, everything about him is as powerful as his eyes were then.

'So when are you going to tell Them?' she asked, cuddling into him like a fluffy toy. She loved the way he wrapped himself around her.

'You'll have to give me time, old horse,' he told her seriously. 'This is a grave matter.'

'Oh yes, it is grave,' said Arabella pouting. She didn't like the word 'grave'; it reminded her too much of death.

'They might be rather taken aback.'

'Because I'm just a commoner?'

'Yes, probably.'

'They'll have to look into my background, I suppose. All that takes time. And what about the love affair I had before I met you?' Arabella flushed and started to panic. 'What if that counts against me?'

'Well,' Jamie said slowly, 'that is a possibility.'

'But it didn't mean a thing, honestly, Jamie!'

'Well, I know that. But I am supposed to marry a virgin so that nobody can tell tales, and Tom was a bit of a playboy . . .'

'Yes, I know, Mummy warned me. She didn't approve of him at all. Thought he was leading me into temptation but he was always perfectly sweet to me.'

'I'm sure he was,' mused Jamie, 'but your relationship with him is certainly a factor they would want to take into account.'

'Perhaps I should give up my job, go into purdah so I don't offend anyone before it all starts to happen?'

'No, no, don't do that.' Jamie was most insistent that she go on with her life just as if nothing had happened. 'There's loads of time for that, old bean. You won't start showing for weeks, and people might get suspicious.'

'You are quite right, of course.' And secretly Arabella was glad. She loves her job at Habitat, enjoys the companionship and the stuff they sell and the fun of unpacking a new delivery, and everyone likes her. And what would she do if she did give up work? She cannot imagine hiding away in the flat all day, and it would be rather premature to move into the Palace.

So when Dougal Rathbone came round with the brochure on the Grange she was startled at first, undermined, wondering whatever was happening. I mean, *Clitheroe* – what sort of a place was that? However, a second meeting made her see that there was something afoot. Jamie was trying to smooth the pathway so the big announcement would be easier. After all, if she stayed in London she would be a prisoner hounded by the press and They would probably want the wedding to take place as quickly as possible.

It wouldn't look too good, would it, if she had to heave herself down the aisle heavily pregnant, clutching her back and unable to kneel without toppling over. Giving up the job, she supposed, as Dougal was now suggesting, was unfortunate but just the first of the many sacrifices one must be prepared to make when marrying a Royal. Arabella would just have to accept it.

Thank goodness she's over her morning sickness.

'I hate lying to Charlie and Mags,' she confides to Dougal when they set off on the second leg of the journey, having wined and dined in a glorious setting in an hotel among the trees beside a lake. She shouldn't have drunk quite so much. She is not used to drinking at lunchtime but Dougal was so persuasive and the wine was delicious. He didn't touch a drop, she noticed with relief. That was the trouble with Jamie. He thought he could drink and drive and he was so fast and reckless, she hated travelling anywhere with him, always ended up feeling sick. 'They have been such super friends to me. I told them we were visiting some relatives of yours in the Lake District. They were surprised. They keep asking about Jamie, of course, and it's terribly difficult to deceive them. After all, they, of all people, know how I feel about him.'

They are cruising along in companionable silence through a landscape browned by the sun. A silver tremor runs over the hills like a happy little sigh which matches her mood. She thinks she can hear the birds singing, and even the cows munching in the distance make a chewy sound in her ears. She is in love and in tune with the whole wide world. In a few hours she will see Jamie! Arabella glances at Dougal but his expression is giving nothing away, not so she can notice. How long will he carry on the deception? Is he going to tell her about the surprise waiting at the end of the journey, or will Jamie show her himself? This is all so terribly exciting!

'I even practise my wave,' she confesses, smiling and feeling silly but Dougal is the sort of person you feel you can trust with anything, 'in front of the mirror! Don't laugh. I know it's just playing with a dream but this dream is about to come true. And a gracious smile, whatever that might be. I want to get everything exactly right.'

Dougal compresses his lips. The little fool. She's going to take one hell of a tumble. 'Arabella, I think you are being a trifle over-romantic about all this . . .'

'Oh, you don't need to tell me!' cries Arabella, her voice rising dramatically. 'I know the job isn't all romance and flowers. I know it involves sacrifices and hardships. I understand what a strain it must be, I have thought a great deal about it.'

'I am sure you have,' says Dougal, now decidedly uneasy.

She must control her vivid imagination. She must not be so selfish. Perhaps poor Jamie won't be there, after all. Perhaps he couldn't get away or feels it is too dangerous, even here, in this bleak and windswept part of the world, to break cover and reveal too much to his mother's unsuspecting subjects. Waiting eyes, sun glinting on long-distance lenses. Well, she'll put a brave face on it and be patient. She will go along with all this and give her opinion on the Grange which is what is expected of her today; she won't make things any more complicated for Them than they already are. This is the least she can do, after all, for her future husband, for the man she loves more than life itself.

ELEVEN

Flat 1, Albany Buildings, Swallowbridge, Devon

M iss Benson is not even slightly shocked when she first sets
foot in Greylands because the home where her own mother
died not three years ago was depressingly similar. Funny
how you're upset by things that threaten you most . . . It's like those
women who shriek outside the courts – they are the ones who most
nearly batter their kids, or the anti-abortion campaigners who are the
ones least likely to sympathise with fallen women.

Generally speaking, thinks Miss Benson, of course. Everything is
generally speaking.

Greylands. Anyone can come in or out – burglars, rapists, swindlers
– security is nil. She goes to the office at the side of the hall with the
door marked: *Matron – Miss Blennerhasset* – and an impressive list of
nursing qualifications set out below her name. Miss Benson, smart in
her crisp white blouse this evening, her pale brown hair having flown
into a kind of halo over her head in the wind, ignores the list and
knocks politely.

'Come!'

Miss Benson's timid head edges round the door. Everything in the
room looks pink because of the subdued lighting, even the budgie
which chirps from an elaborate cage. 'Excuse me, I am looking for a
Mrs Irene Peacock.'

You can tell by Matron's expression that Mrs Peacock is not her
favourite resident.

'Are you a relative?'

'No, I am just a neighbour.'

'I don't think we've seen you here before.'

The use of the royal 'we' does not phase Miss Benson, whose voice is
naturally apprehensive. 'I would have come before, but not being
family I was worried about imposing. But now I have cleared it with
Mrs Peacock's daughter.'

'Come in, come further in,' says Matron, leaning back in her chair, putting her supper tray aside, and sensing an ally. 'And take a seat.' Matron considers what to say next, ever cautious. Visitors, in her experience, can be easily upset and troublesome. 'I don't know how much of Mrs Peacock's circumstances you are aware of, Mrs . . . ?'

'Miss, and it's Benson.'

Miss Benson takes the soft chair offered, situated beside the unlit gas fire in Matron's cosy office. On the glass coffee table lies an assortment of gardening magazines and one copy of *The Lady*. The remains on Matron's plate are of egg and cheese pie; she has pushed the hard-boiled and blackening yolk to one side. The handmade rug has obviously been done by one of the more able residents and so has the embroidered cushion of a seagull coming in to land on which she settles.

Miss Blennerhasset's long-fingered hands are actively independent, picking up objects from her little footstool like a ball of wool, a pen, a diary, turning them over and over to examine them as she speaks. 'Unfortunately, Mrs Peacock has found it hard to settle here, and we are quite concerned about her at the moment. It is important that both staff and visitors adopt an encouraging attitude, not too much impractical sympathy, if you follow my meaning. Listen by all means to what she has to say, but a gentle yet firm reaction is the best one to take.'

'Poor Mrs Peacock,' sighs Miss Benson unthinkingly, her memories going to her own mother's plight.

'There is nothing poor about her,' Matron contradicts with a look of sad reproach, and Miss Benson wonders what it is about nurses that make them so unimaginative, what makes them so convinced that suffering must be endured regardless? Miss Blennerhasset, hunched a little in her easy chair (back trouble probably) does not look like an unkind woman. Indeed, her long, rather ponderous face and her broad forehead give the impression of a thoughtful person, but she is a woman without animation, someone who has, maybe, been sat on in childhood so she would always speak without inflection or raising her voice. Miss Benson sniffs, and over the scents of cheese and egg pie she can definitely smell mice.

'No, of course not,' backtracks the constantly apprehensive Miss Benson, eager to avoid the slightest confrontation.

'She is in comparatively good health, has her eyesight and her hearing and a family who care about her,' Matron goes on in-dignantly. 'It is just that her mind is becoming a little enfeebled so it is all the more important not to put any ideas in her head.'

Miss Benson has heard all this before. 'So I believe.'

'And unfortunately her recent behaviour is causing some nuisance not only to ourselves and her daughter but to the police and the ambulance service who have more to do with their time than rush around finding confused old ladies who are intent on making trouble.'

Now Miss Benson is fond of Irene Peacock. She has known her for two years, since she arrived at Albany Buildings and moved into the flat below her looking rather dazed and bewildered. Cautiously, Miss Benson looked out over the road and watched the daughter, Frankie, a hard, bossy creature, and the grandchildren, Angus and Poppy, carting Irene's bits and pieces from the hired van, across the pavement and up the steps into the foyer. No man then.

She tried to concentrate on *Wildlife on One* but could not get the newcomer's face out of her mind – there was something so tragic about it all. After everyone had gone there was such a silence from the flat underneath her that Miss Benson, not normally one to push herself forward, went downstairs in some trepidation and rang Mrs Peacock's bell. She still doesn't know what impelled her to do this, something so way out of character. She took a packet of Earl Grey tea and some M&S shortcake biscuits.

Miss Benson knows what it's like to be frightened and lonely, and early evening is the part of the day she hates most. Early evening, and Sundays. You could talk about this with people and they would say they understood but they didn't, not really, not unless they'd been through it themselves.

After a longish pause during which Miss Benson wondered if the newcomer might be deaf, there was a nervous rattle of locks and a sobbing, a muttering under breath.

'Yes?' The red-veined cheeks hung loosely from the bones of a face which must have been pretty once, the shape was still there. The eyes that fixed on Miss Benson's were bright and incredibly blue and wisps of grey hair escaped from the hairnet round the base of the old woman's neck.

Miss Benson looked doubtful. 'My name is Miss Benson and I live directly upstairs. I watched you move in today and I thought I'd pop down and introduce myself. I know what it's like—'

'I don't hold with neighbours. Never have.' All the aggressiveness of the insecure.

'I understand, but perhaps you would accept this little gift . . .'

A scrawny hand shot out and took the tea and the biscuits. The old body took time to straighten. 'I have all I need. My daughter makes sure that my cupboard is well stocked, though it's going to be difficult without a pantry. I always had a pantry before, and an airing cupboard.'

Miss Benson, flushed after a few more futile attempts at conversation, remembered how words like 'loony' and 'old crone' had been flung at her mother when she found herself toothless and living alone behind locked doors in the village where she grew up. She'd been driven into a home in the end, by lack of Social Services and a shortage of good neighbours. Nobody knew her any more; the entire population had changed in one generation. Constantly alarmed by reports of high crime levels and police dramas on the TV, the old woman was firmly convinced that someone was out to get her. She refused to open her door. She was starving slowly to death. They took her away in the end. They did not contact Miss Benson because nobody knew her address and there was nothing to be found in the cottage that might reveal her whereabouts. Later it was discovered that old Mrs Benson had deliberately disposed of any clue to her daughter's existence, so convinced in her mind was she that these imaginary villains would threaten her, too, if they only knew where Emily was. Emily hadn't known for months. When she finally tracked her mother down she discovered her unable to walk and rendered incontinent and totally senile by the sterile regime at The Cedars. The mother no longer recognised the daughter. But standing there on the landing, facing a silent Mrs Peacock, Miss Benson couldn't for the life of her think of anything useful to say. She wasn't going to be invited in, she had done her best so she added lamely, 'Well, I'm just upstairs if you need anything. Don't be afraid to call me.'

Mrs Peacock cast a grim look at the cold concrete stairs leading up from the hall and huffed before closing the door, and the echoing sound of the locks and chains shooting home was definite and terrible like fear. Oh yes, Miss Benson recognised Mrs Peacock and the calls for help she had not heard as an undutiful daughter only a few years before.

Today Miss Benson goes upstairs nervously and opens Mrs Peacock's door with a fair degree of anxiety.

To her relief the room is fresh and sweet-smelling. Mrs Peacock sits in a flowered nightie with her bag clutched in her lap and her head bowed but she fumbles impatiently with the new packet of cigarettes she is offered and lights one happily before she starts to grumble. 'So this is what it's come to now, Miss Benson, I'm afraid. Look! Look at this! They say they have no option but to sell my flat to pay the fees for keeping me here, but I'm not an invalid, I was coping until I broke my leg and now that's mended I just don't know what makes them think they need to keep me here locked up like a prisoner. I can get along quite well with only one stick.'

'There must be a social worker who would listen to you and help you . . .' starts Miss Benson, appalled to see her neighbour here in this little room, like a child's, with a single bed along one wall and a fitted wardrobe along the other, hardly room to take a full stride before you bang into one or the other. The floral nightie they have put her in, communal, Miss Benson is sure, reveals the chickeny skin of her throat. She sits on her day clothes that seem to have been thrown down in a careless heap, and the old lady was always so fussy about her clothes. Remembering Matron's warnings, Miss Benson attempts to be positive. 'The view from the window is lovely. The garden looks nice.'

'Matron's a keen gardener. The social workers are the worst of all,' snaps Mrs Peacock impatiently. 'Left-wing do-gooders, just out of college with filthy hair and sandals and silly ideas. And anyway, I've never needed the services of a social worker in my life and I don't intend to start now. They sent me a man with a beard.' The eyes that lift towards her are opaque and dull – a look she has never seen in Mrs Peacock before. She reminds Miss Benson of her mother. Have they put her on drugs?

Mrs Peacock is sitting in her bedside chair, the visitor has to sit on the bed. 'At least they let you have a few of your own personal things, I see.'

'Yes, everything else I own will be sold when they get rid of my flat.' And then she adds musingly, 'I thought you'd have come to see me before, Miss Benson. I've been stuck here for three months now.'

'I just didn't know if I should. I worried about your daughter. I don't want her to think I am interfering.'

Mrs Peacock stubs out her cigarette into a floral-shaped soap dish. Then she wraps it up in a tissue, riffles through a drawer and hides the last sign of her habit in a carrier bag before dropping it into the wastepaper basket. With fierce blue eyes she glares at her visitor. 'Whose side are you on anyway, Miss Benson? I thought you were *my* friend, not my daughter's.'

'Oh, it's not a matter of taking sides, it's a matter of doing the best for you.'

Mrs Peacock snorts and says nothing.

'Perhaps you should see a solicitor?'

'And pay him with what – moth balls? And anyway, they have taken out power of attorney over me. I no longer count as a person. You can't even choose what you watch on TV. They probably won't even let me vote although I could still play a pretty fair hand of Canasta or Rummy.'

This is awful, for what can Miss Benson do? She feels guilty as if this is her fault which is very silly because this really is no business of hers. She wishes, now, that she had brought Mrs Peacock gin as well as cigarettes. If she visits again she will make up a hamper and fill it with various little treats.

She tries to lighten the conversation by bringing up the subject of Frankie, but she should have remembered that this is one topic very likely to distress Mrs Peacock. In earlier confidences the old woman admitted how her daughter always came second after William. 'And she's never forgiven me for that – with reason, I suppose. It is fashionable today to condemn your mother or your father. Sometimes I feel that Frankie would have been happier if she'd been abused, something firm to get a grip on. She was always a sulky child. And demanding. Is that bad, is that wicked, Miss Benson, to love your husband better than your child? And I've always come out straight and admitted it.'

Miss Benson, who had been slightly shocked to hear this at the time, had to confess that she just didn't know, never having been married herself, and of course the *last* thing she wanted to be was judgmental. 'I'm sure Frankie didn't even realise,' she'd suggested comfortingly. 'As long as a child is happy and loved, she's unlikely to feel jealousy because her parents adore one another.'

There was a long pause before the answer. 'You don't know Frankie,' said Mrs Peacock grimly. 'She even blames me for the failure of her own marriage.'

So now she moans on. Mentioning Frankie's name when Mrs Peacock is so upset was a fatal mistake, opening up a whole new can of worms. The old woman's eyes keep shutting as if she is already exhausted but it's not yet eight o'clock. 'And they never invite me out of here to go to Frankie's house. You'd think I was incontinent already. They lead such busy lives, you see, Frankie, Angus and Poppy, so full of other people. You should see their notice board in the kitchen, little flags on every day, a different colour for each of them. Frankie is such a capable, organising person. Well, she's a teacher, isn't she? But there's no room for me any more.'

Miss Benson knows all about this from sad and worrying personal experience. 'It's easy, sometimes, to pretend to ourselves that everything is all right, especially when we feel powerless to change things. I'm sure Frankie would like you at home, I'm sure she worries about you terribly in here, but it seems that her lifestyle makes this impossible. Especially with no man to support her.'

Mrs Peacock's wedding picture stands beside her bed. Next to William she looks tiny but oh so blissfully happy. 'Huh, I should know,' she says dryly, lighting her second cigarette. She notices how Miss Benson is staring at the picture. 'I loved him, you know, and I still miss him.'

'I know,' says Miss Benson.

'So let that be a warning. Never get married, Miss Benson. Never depend on somebody else, it's just too painful when it ends. And I can't even read any more because I've sat on another pair of glasses.'

Back safe to Albany Buildings at last.

She has promised Mrs Peacock that she will visit again next week. She has also promised her a day out at her flat. Miss Benson will pick her up in her car and take her for a little outing, maybe a meal out at a pub before they return to Albany Buildings. These promises were the only things that seemed to cheer Mrs Peacock up. Somehow Miss Benson couldn't leave her in the same despairing state in which she had found her. She just couldn't bear it. But perhaps Miss Benson should have cleared all this with Matron first, or her daughter, Frankie Rendell. The last thing she wants is to cause trouble and make poor Mrs Peacock's situation even worse. I mean, perhaps the old lady is ill and they are keeping it from her. There could be all sorts of reasons why it might be considered inappropriate for her to leave Greylands.

'I think we have sold the flat,' says a pleased-looking Frankie when Miss Benson meets her in the hall, on her way out with a bucket of cleaning things. 'The agents seem to think there's this couple who are very interested. Fingers crossed,' she smiles at Miss Benson and then thinks to ask, 'Oh, how was Mother this evening?'

'Pretty depressed, I'm afraid.'

Frankie Rendell removes her Marigold gloves and sighs. 'I hate to visit, she's always so unhappy. And there's nothing anyone can do! We have to sell the flat in order to pay the fees and that's that.'

She might as well grasp the nettle. 'Oh, Mrs Rendell, I hope I haven't gone and put my foot in it, but your mother was so low I suggested I might take her out for the day, give her an airing, bring her back here for a cup of tea . . .'

'That would be very good of you, Miss Benson,' but Frankie's voice is cold, she senses some blame in Miss Benson's suggestion. She can't be bothered to take her own mother out herself and yet here is this neighbour . . .

The over-sensitive Miss Benson sees and hurries to put this right. 'You see, I have no responsibilities like you have. My social life is very routine, I'm afraid. I spend most weekends either cleaning my flat or walking, if it's fine, and if you think your mother might benefit from a few hours away from Greylands it really would be no trouble. She seemed so thrilled . . .'

'I am quite sure she did. My mother can be a difficult woman, Miss Benson.'

'Yes, I realise that.'

'Not many people warm to her.'

'No, I suppose they don't.'

'She is also manipulative and vengeful. And I wouldn't be at all surprised if she tries to work one of her dramas again. She's there all day with nothing to do but to plot and plan.'

'She is old, Mrs Rendell. And she has broken her glasses.'

That was definitely the wrong attitude to take. 'Well, if you think you have more rapport with her than her own daughter . . .'

Miss Benson rushes to her own defence. 'Oh really, it was just the same with my own mother, Mrs Rendell. We found things difficult as she grew older and I remember thinking that most of the nurses managed to communicate with my mother better than I did. She was senile, by then, and unable to recognise me but I still feel I should have got through. Somehow. It's this mother and daughter relationship which can be so severely tested when age turns the relationship the wrong way round. I don't see this as anyone's fault . . .'

'Well, I *am* glad to hear that,' says Frankie coldly, rattling the Jiffy mop in the plastic bucket. She brings her own mop when she comes to the Buildings to clean the flat because Mrs Peacock only has a squeegee and they are too much hard work. 'For a moment there I thought I was in for another telling off and I'm getting a bit pissed off with the image of grabbing, greedy, selfish daughter at the moment, I can tell you. At least Matron understands.'

'I expect she is well used to it,' smiles Miss Benson. 'Difficult old people.'

'Unpleasant, cantankerous old people.'

'Yes, well, I expect she is used to them.'

'And I *would* be grateful, Miss Benson, if you would refrain from mentioning the latest interest in the flat to my mother. There is no point in distressing her further.'

'Certainly not. Of course I wouldn't dream of it,' says Miss Benson, gratefully gripping the iron stair-rail leading up to the first floor because she senses this difficult exchange is over. Mrs Peacock is right, Mrs Rendell *is* a difficult woman – although perhaps she does have reasons for treating her mother in such an unsympathetic manner. Miss Benson might be a timid soul but she is also stubborn; how often these two personal traits accompany each other. So it's in a firmer frame of mind, not slightly intimidated now, that Miss Benson, with a banging heart because she cannot bear confrontations, lets herself into her flat at last, absolutely determined to overcome any obstacles in order to give her poor old neighbour a treat she will remember.

TWELVE

'Joyvern', 11, The Blagdons, Milton, Devon

'Well, Vernon, do we accept the Middletons' offer or do we not?'

Vernon tries to curb his impatience. 'Joy, we have no alternative.'

'But it's ten thousand less than we're asking.'

'We are lucky to get an offer at all.'

'We won't have enough left over to pay the bills.'

'We will if we're careful and if we don't immediately start wasting money on new carpets and curtains in the flat. Remember, if they accept our offer of forty we'll be getting a bargain, too.'

'But will they accept it?'

'I am sure they will. The old lady's in a home anyway. They won't want it left empty.'

'No, not in that area they won't. Oh God, that grotty little flat.'

Vernon sighs. 'There's nothing wrong with that area, Joy. Anyone would think we were moving into some inner city tenement.'

'Well, sometimes it feels like that. I mean, I never thought we'd be sharing a flat, like a couple of students, not like a middle-aged married couple. D'you realise, Vernon, that the adverts for cruises and Estée Lauder make-up and private hospital care, all these luxury items are aimed at people like us with their children gone, couples who are supposed to be able to sit back at our age and relax and enjoy their savings. But we don't have any savings . . .'

'Well, I realise that, Joy. I do realise that.'

And ten minutes later. 'So we're accepting the Middletons' offer, are we? Funny really, I could have sworn they didn't like it and they only came round the once. A strange family, giving nothing away.'

'Too right we are,' says he, turning on her with a worried frown. Worry is ageing him prematurely, he is already too fat, he smokes and now he fears he is going bald. The top of his head seems more bare and shiny than usual. When he washed his hair this morning, amongst the green seaweedy shampoo there clung some mysterious weed which refused to go down the plughole. Further investigation showed the weed to be strands of his own hair come unattached in the rubbing motion. Soon he will be one of those men who place odd strands across their heads. His body is warning him this can't go on.

'And we're going to put up with that flat and live in it exactly how it is now, is that it, Vernon? No new lino, no fresh paint, no decent cushion covers and it stinks of smoke . . . that old woman must have been quite disgusting with her habit.'

'Yes, Joy, I'm afraid that it is. Anyway, I liked the colours. Calming pastels. They seemed perfectly acceptable to me.'

Damn, damn, damn. Poor Joy does not know if she can endure. If only Vernon was more assertive they could have bid for that lovely old ruin and told everyone they saw it as a challenge, a perfect country cottage for two with a vegetable plot and an ancient well, just right for his retirement. They'd be the envy of their friends, they'd be buying a brand new lifestyle.

Watching for clues, as soon as the SOLD sign goes up the neighbours will come round asking for the latest news. They are bound to. She knows they will. Their questions pain her already; already she has taken to peering out of the front bedroom window to make sure if it's friend or foe before she opens the door. Gets her story ready.

Already Joy is in danger of being snared in the web of her own lies. 'This place is too big for the two of us now,' she is so weary of saying. 'Three big bedrooms and all that wasted space in the roof. No, it's only fair we move on and a younger family take the place on. And we'd really prefer somewhere quieter, you know, off the beaten track a bit.'

Wait till everyone hears they are outcasts going to live in the middle of Swallowbridge, that ugly and godforsaken suburb right on a big main road. *Nobody must know.* She must make sure Vernon keeps his mouth shut, lies if necessary. After all, there's no need to see any of these people again. They can make new friends, can't they, although what sort of people might befriend the residents of Albany Buildings it is difficult to imagine. Certainly not the sort of people Vernon and Joy are used to – middle class, middle of the road, middle management, middle minded.

'Mrs Rendell was a perfectly polite, nice person when she showed us round,' argues Vernon. 'And you can't deny that, Joy. For goodness sake, what are you so afraid of? I'm not worried about moving at all.

83

All I will feel is an enormous relief. Freedom from stress at dear last.'

And he does deserve freedom from stress. Vernon has been so brave, battling on like he has week after week. She is so worried about his health. Perhaps he will lose some weight now. Well, what *is* Joy so afraid of? Is it fear that makes her heart ache so? Or is it loss of face?

If only she had a family who might come along and bail her out.

If only they could win the lottery.

But two days later, watching from her window with a sinking heart, Joy sees the man from the agents come to stick the SOLD sign over the old FOR SALE, like offending litter in the tidy front garden of the sanctuary which used to be her house. She watches from the shelter of her bedroom like a tight knot, rigid. And what will Suzie and Tom say when they find out where their parents are going?

'I don't know, it's all so terribly complicated,' she explains evasively when Adele Mason from The Arches, yes, that opinionated creature, comes snooping around that very morning. Typical, the first of the sharks to taste the blood of the Marshes' mortification. Didn't she have better things to do than harass an already over-harassed woman? 'We are having to rent this awful flat while Vernon renovates the cottage, but it'll be well worth the inconvenience in the end, I'm sure. We've always wanted a cottage in the country and this will be a real picture postcard when it's done! Vernon is so excited about it, like a little boy with a box of Lego for Christmas, you should hear his ideas!'

Oh dear, she has probably said too much when all she intended was to be interestingly vague. But here is Joy, stranded upstream in the shallow tributaries of human existence, floundering but still trying. She will never give up. She just prays that Vernon will go along with her little white lie. Perhaps he will if she begs him.

But instead of sitting back satisfied, Adele slyly presses for details.

Joy is driven to fetch the brochure from the drawer in the kitchen.

'This is it. What do you think?'

The brochure is more than flattering. You wouldn't recognise the ruinous building from the carefully rose-coloured picture put out by the agents, and luckily there is no price on the cover so Joy ups it to £90,000.

'A little gem!' Adele reads out loud, glancing sideways at Joy, cool and provocative as usual and smelling of olive oil, garlic and crushed sweet herbs from her kitchen. This woman touches too much; an invader of space, she is forever leaning over somebody's shoulder so they can smell what a good cook she is. 'With a well and old beams and a twisting staircase and a bread oven in the fireplace! My word, Joy, it sounds absolutely marvellous, if that is the sort of thing you are into. Although to be honest Ted wouldn't want to have to start coping with a white elephant like that. The Blagdons houses are so easy to run, so convenient, so in demand. Well look, everyone reckoned you wouldn't sell but you did, and in this sort of market. It's amazing really when you think.'

Has she backed herself into a corner?

No doubt, as a result of Vernon's earlier blabbing Angela and Bob have been spreading the dirt.

They might have been able to cling on at The Blagdons if Joy had kept her job at the boutique, although Vernon says that's nonsense. When he ventured into the world of small business it seemed as if he'd need a secretary, someone to answer the phone and do the letters and keep the books, and Joy couldn't wait to stop work and stay at home surrounded by beautiful things all day. A fatal mistake, of course, just another mistake among hundreds. When you are young you can make thousands of silly mistakes and survive, but the older you get the more effect they seem to have.

Terrified by their impending plight she'd tried to get her old job back, but without success. She'd then applied for countless others, but they all wanted somebody young and cheap.

'Stressful or not, you'll need a car, Joy, being so far off the beaten track.' And Adele polishes her sunglasses if you please, then twiddles them round her finger. So fake. Such a poseur. Intent on the titbits of life like Joy picks up crumbs and tissues and matches and coasters, but whereas Joy clears them all up, Adele thrives on the sight of them. 'No regular public transport any more like here.'

'Now that Vernon is able to retire early we think we might buy one of those Jeeps, you know. I must say that Frontiera looks very nice,' says Joy shortly.

'That's another thing,' says Adele and her hair is as hard as her inquisitive eyes. 'I never did understand why you didn't sell that thriving business of Vernon's as an on-going concern, instead of letting it run down like that. Surely you could have made a bomb.'

Joy waves a haughty arm. Her voice is super-rational. 'Oh, it's all to do with tax avoidance. I don't really understand, but we think it is probably sensible to follow our accountant's advice, wouldn't you, dear, in our position?' And she cannot hold herself back from adding this extraordinary remark, 'There is such a thing as too much money, you know.'

Neat is the code round here, which is why the red-haired Adele with her dangly earrings, her creamy silk blouse under that cashmere cardigan – obviously new – has never truly managed to assimilate no matter how superior she might consider herself to be. And she's been caught making eyes at other people's husbands. Today she wears large square-cut earrings of amethyst, much too big for her face. She and her husband Ted imagine they are top of the tree but you don't get accepted by folk at The Blagdons by wearing sexy sunglasses and calling them shades or revving up your sports car when you're just off to the shops for an hour. And when all's said and done, that's only a Triumph with the roof down. He's only got a job laying cables and she is a massage therapist whatever that might mean. You don't need a dog that looks like an ornament with a pretentious name like a Borzoi. At Christmas-times, Adele and Ted overdo the decorations and the hospitality in a most inappropriate manner – their house was a Disneylike fantasy of blue and silver last year – you don't need gold-plated chalices from the Reader's Digest to drink from, nor do you need a tree in the garden with lights on when you've got one in the hall. There was far too much food, what a waste. The mulled wine was far too spicy. Common, is what Joy calls them and common, therefore, is how they are perceived by everyone else in the cul-de-sac. Of course, with her limited imagination the buck-toothed Adele would not appreciate the subtleties of a cottage in the country. It is impossible to make such an uncultured person envious of Joy's new lifestyle.

And anyway, why should Joy bother?

But she decides she must go out for the day before somebody else comes poking and prying.

Joy stands and frets at the bus stop lest somebody sees her.

Glass, glitter, glamour and soft music plays. Joy is not in a hurry. Some people eat, some smoke, some buy clothes and some have habits that are far more dangerous, you read about them in the *People*. At least shopping will be easier once the house sale is complete. Joy can't help herself browsing through the boutiques and stores in the city's main precinct even though she knows she is not able to buy, not yet. Soon, she thinks with an aching relief, soon she can get out her magic chequebook again. But at this stage she daren't even try anything on for fear of that old compulsive need. She might find herself on the pavement with a carrier bag on her arm.

But, oh dear, how dowdy she looks when she catches a glimpse of herself in a mirror. How dowdy and old and cowed by restraint. She backtracks and returns to the mirror, stands there staring at herself, sauntering, posing, even unconsciously pouting. Something new . . . doesn't she deserve a present to celebrate their unexpected good fortune, after all she has suffered over the months and years even, worrying about Vernon and Marsh Electronics?

There. She seems to be breathing more easily.

She has been a good wife and mother, hasn't she?

A brand-new outfit is like being born again, turning into a brand-new self with a whole set of new chances. Approval. A gold star. And nosy neighbours will notice her new self-assurance. A positive image at this most critical time. If she uses her Access card, Vernon won't know for over a month and by that time they will probably have the Middletons' deposit. She will have no need to face that hurt, disappointed look in his eye. He might even smile and understand. But even if they haven't, the bank will know they have sold 'Joyvern' and will be happy to accommodate a temporarily increased overdraft.

Until then, Vernon's not likely to search through her drawers. Hell, he's not that sort of man.

I'm not dead yet, thinks Joy.

Once she starts she feels herself shaking like a dipso and it's almost impossible to stop. She hurries down Gandy Street, nearly tripping over the cobbles in her new and energetic haste. One garment naturally leads to another – she must have a good coat for this winter and those long flowing black ones are clearly the rage. She speeds up, moving frantically in and out of the shops and pecking about like a crazed hen after grain. Jaeger have an attractive selection, and that suede waistcoat, she'll have a look at that while she's at it, and she hasn't any suitable boots, she needs long ones in black, preferably Italian, and how about gloves for when she's in town? She likes to be flattered and admired by all the grovelling assistants, and told how attractive she looks. She's taken in by all the sham, she knows it is sham but she falls for it every time, it boosts her fragile underpinnings. However briefly, however dementedly, she is back in control again. She snatches up designer scarves, pieces of glittering jewellery from Liberty, she grabs them before anyone else can have them, she wants to shout MINE, ALL MINE.

She is not a fussy shopper. She does not dilly-dally, or need confirmation that she's made the right choice. Joy Marsh knows what she likes. She knows what she needs and at this moment, intoxicated still, she needs a few more items of make-up. She is still going when the shops start to close at five-thirty, still savagely defying the world.

Crawling determinedly on for she knows that good clothes make a woman visible.

She has to queue to get on a bus, she climbs awkwardly on, top-heavy with her purchases. The man beside her rubs his beard and frowns at her as she struggles with her bags – does he know? Does his wife do this to him, too? It's like being unfaithful. If he was a gentleman he wouldn't look so damn sanctimonious, he would get up and give her a hand. But by now she feels sick, bloated, satiated, worn out with the gorging and weak with the worry. Her spirit moves in an infinite waste. What if the house purchase falls through? Lost, now, and frightened by her own reckless behaviour, Joy tastes despair like the bitterest bile in her throat as she huddles there under her baggage trying to make herself as small as possible. All that terrible urgency's over. She shakes with a nervous reaction. She's landed herself in real trouble now. There's no fun any more and she might as well throw all her precious buyings straight out of the window for all the pleasure they give her now. What would Vernon say if he knew? She'd better have sex with him tonight, good sex, to make it up.

The Ford is in the drive. Just as she fears, Vernon is home before she is.

So Joy creeps round to the back and sneaks her purchases into the cedar gazebo before she lets herself in the door.

Just to see him there is a reprimand. He is sitting at the kitchen table with his head in his hands. But a man's face in repose is *meant* to be serious, isn't it? When he sees her he looks up and tries to smile.

'All right?' she asks, dreading the worse, the latest worst.

Vernon nods. 'I'm a little tired,' he says wearily. 'Just sorting through the essential bills that have to be paid. The electric. The gas. And I think the car clutch sounds as if it's going . . . God knows if Norman Mycroft is going to honour these cheques.' He looks up at her sadly as if this is all her fault. 'We'll just have to risk it – we don't have any choice.'

'We don't seem to have any choice over anything at all any more,' snaps Joy, sick with guilt. He is punishing her for crimes he is unaware of and that's just not fair. She directs her nervous eyes to the chequebook. 'And I'm cheesed off with it.'

'You and me both,' says Vernon, shaking his head heavily, as if he knows very well that she has just taken the kind of steps which could lead him, at fifty-two years old, into the world of the cold and hungry, the unwashed, the lame, the sick and the terrified homeless. Maybe Joy should attempt to torch the house. At least, if Vernon has kept the insurance payments going, they might receive more than the wretched Middletons are offering to pay.

What is she doing to him?

She sits down gingerly in the chair directly opposite. 'I've brought you some liver from Marks,' she says. 'Liver and onion with gravy, and summer pudding and cream to follow.'

The wrong response. Vernon looks worried, keeps pushing his brown-framed glasses back on his head. Why couldn't his wife stay home and cook something cheap and sensible? Why does she have to go over the top? She knows what the situation is, doesn't she? You only buy food from Marks when you're really flush. They used to joke, Joy and Vernon, that when the children left home not only would they go on that cruise but they'd either dine out or buy Marks' food every day. It was a dream. Where's it gone now? I mean, one packet of lamb's liver and poor Vernon's blood pressure soars through the roof.

But Joy needs him desperately; she loves him and she hates to hurt him. It's all so perverse because why is her behaviour so bad? She looks at him with a warm glow of love. Thank the merciful heavens she's got him, he is too fine a man to succeed in a vulgar world. Vernon is far steadier than her; Joy knows this and depends upon that fact. While she is like a tuft of down, blowing along with her moody and peevish emotions, Vernon's a deeply-rooted tree. Defeated yet not disgraced, he bends but he does not break.

At least he hasn't done so far. Phew.

THIRTEEN

Penmore House, Ribblestone Close, Preston, Lancs

The sacrifice of his son. His only son, Jody, has been taken to the mountain, and just as Abraham offered his own son to God, so Len Middleton feels he is offering Jody to the God of this screaming decade – the Mob.

Jody is definitely innocent of the crime for which he has been accused. From what the boy tells him, and Len is used to believing a son who was rarely a liar, there was no force involved. Janice Plunket sacrificed her virginity quite willingly, and it's not fair the State suggesting that Jody took wicked advantage of a woman with the mental age of a six year old. That's not the point. She was battered and bruised and scratched all over, yes, but that happened as she struggled to find her way back home.

If only Janice would stand up and tell the truth instead of repeating over and over that she cannot remember.

One way or other, Jody has hurt her; perhaps he ought to be facing a charge of neglect. But *rape* – good heavens, never!

Yet the Middletons have been hounded out, and much as Len would like to turn his back to the wall and fight, he has his wife and two daughters to consider. Cindy and Dawn can no longer attend school because of the bullying there.

They have written off his son's life.

Lenny loathes visiting Jody on remand, in a building that seems to have been designed precisely to magnify sound – doors clanging, scuffling, banging, someone crying, someone moaning. And the place stinks. It is dirty, ugly and noisy and it smells of despair. They are forced to talk to their son in that dreary room sitting round those terrible tables supervised by a bored official as they try to wring some sort of intimacy out of the couple of feet between them. Hopeless. *Hopeless.* Babs ends up weeping, trying to understand what she did wrong, and Jody terrified and negative, making things worse.

Shocked to the very core of himself, Lenny Middleton has taken to going for long walks alone, seeking the time for contemplation. And while Babs, guilt-ridden and withdrawn, has taken up the role of insecure child-woman, after his initial anger Lenny has sunk into a cold, unfeeling lethargy, the only way he can take the strain. It started with dog mess pushed through the letter box. You read about things like this and you tend to assume that the victims in question must have done something to deserve their plight . . . why else would such malicious attention be focused on one particular party? But it doesn't work that way. There're background forces which stir the ever-simmering soup of crowd malevolence. It's the way the police spokespeople handle it, the way the press describe it, the gossip that suddenly oozes from nowhere like a leak in a sewer, smearing everything with filthy insinuation.

Oh yes. Shit sticks.

Even to a kid who was once the most popular lad round here.

Oh, they have been lucky parents. The less fortunate, of which there are many, occasionally used to confide, 'I don't know where we went wrong. Look at you, look at your three. If only . . .' Babs and Lenny would feel so self-righteous it makes him cringe to think of that now. 'It's so simple to produce well-adjusted, contented children,' they used to compliment each other with pleasure. 'It's all in the way you love them. You show them they're loved, you praise them, you discipline them and you lead by example.' OK, Jody could be difficult, that's natural after all. During adolescence the Middletons went through the normal traumas, but they talked them through sensitively and carefully, and Jody always knew where to come if he was unhappy or in trouble. Ever a popular boy, his close friendships helped boost him at any difficult times, as did his sport, his football and cricket. Was he too easy-going? Too good-natured? A kindly lad, a natural leader, he was bright, he was fun, and now look, Lenny is thinking of him as if he is gone for ever. There's such an emptiness since they took him away.

The hair that was once a shock of gold is limp, now, and without lustre. The prison seems to have stolen his colours and Jody was such an attractive child with those deep blue eyes and that healthy skin. His body was rigid under Lenny's hand last time he tried a reassuring squeeze to the shoulder, and the boy would not meet his gaze when he told him he loved him.

'Talking' was always their answer to everything. Talking and working things through. They didn't need experts to tell them that. The boy had everything to look forward to, including a conditional place at Birmingham to read Law in October.

Where were the slums, the bleak poverty, the drug gangs and the loud house music? Everyone is nonplussed by the fact that Jody comes from a 'normal family', parents still married, homeowners, respectable middle-class people with two daughters to be proud of, never the slightest problem with either Dawn or Cindy. It's not right that those sweet girls should suffer so. They have suffered enough already.

'There's people outside the house, Dad, I can hear them.' Dawn woke Lenny soon after the nightmare started. It must have been gone midnight; he was sleepily befuddled while she was sobbing with fear.

'What? What people?'

'I dunno, I *dunno*, Dad, but they're outside in the garden.'

This was the terrible night after Jody had been arrested. They were all dazed and confused.

Armed with a golf club, all the lights in the house blazing and his womenfolk huddled behind locked doors upstairs, Lenny was about to open the back door when a brick came crashing through the kitchen window and a slurred voice yelled, 'Bastards!'

'Who's that?' called Lenny, limbs shaking, heart playing tricks. He was too old and cowardly for this sort of thing.

'Fuck off, you wankers! Shit's too good for you. You'll suffer for this . . .'

Len could not speak. His eyes burned. He breathed deeply, quickly, as if an overdose of oxygen would calm him. The violence in the obscene voice was worse than the shattering force of the brick. Shaking and vulnerable in his dressing gown and pyjamas, Lenny dare not open the door, and when he looked out into the darkness he could make out shapes but no faces. That was the most unnerving thing. He thought of the Ku Klux Klan and its cunning use of masks: it's the faces that make a crowd human. When you have no faces, you have only a baying tide of violence and hostility.

'RAPE, RAPE, RAPE' chanted the faceless mob.

The following day a wreath was delivered to the door. Cindy answered.

Babs was hounded by anonymous phone calls. She'd had to give up working at the surgery straight away, just as Len stopped going to the golf club. Nobody said anything, but sometimes you just know when you're not wanted. When Babs answered the phone, there was just silence, or sometimes abuse, even threats against her life and the life of the girls. The police could do nothing, they said, unless they had proof, or a name. There was no point pushing it, you could see you'd get no sympathy there.

At work, those who did not visibly recoil were a bit *too* nice, going out of their way to speak to Len, avoiding all references to children, family, home life, finding sanctuary instead in sales figures, office gossip, new and interesting brands, conferences and the incredible behaviour of upper management. He wanted to hold out his hands and beg them to be natural. Whatever natural was. He has already forgotten. It is disconcerting and uncomfortable to say the least and he was weak with relief, quite overcome by the man's understanding when his immediate superior had him in and suggested he move to the West-Country branch.

Len is finding it hard to be loving and tender these days, although he knows it is desperately required of him at this time. After all, his tranquillised wife isn't to blame – or is she? She was the mother after all, the one who brought the children up while Len made perfunctory gestures at helping. *Jody should never have touched Janice Plunket.* What made his boy do something like that? Babs loved Jody deeply, she still does. Did she spoil him, pamper him, reward him for the wrong behaviour, give Jody too much attention? His sisters were often jealous. The lad had certainly been given most things he wanted – most kids are these days, but then Jody frequently helped in the house and the garden without being asked. The Middletons used simply to feel glad that they had the resources to be benevolent like that.

So what a blessed relief it was when the agents phoned yesterday with the offer from the Smedleys in Clitheroe, of £98,000. Up until then it had been unofficial, but it meant they, in turn, could make an offer for the house in Milton and their offer was immediately accepted. No attempt to push them up, and Len would have been perfectly happy to pay another £10,000, even £20,000, to escape from here.

He prays that the Smedleys do not find out about the notoriety of the place, or that if they do, this odious taint will not put them off. After all, they are not talking about murder here, it's not like the West house in Gloucester with bodies under the floorboards although, from the local reaction, you would have to believe it was equally sinister. No crime has been committed on these premises. Perhaps the settling in to a new lifestyle, the organising of a new home will be the healing of Babs who, contrary to his reaction, loathes being alone these days having nothing to do but think.

But today the house he comes home to is unnaturally quiet, no whir of the mixer, no hum of the Hoover. The television is seldom on nowadays. Babs just sits and frets and loses weight, or gardens compulsively. She won't be leaving friends behind, not after this. You soon learn who your friends are when you are struck by this sort of disaster.

They haven't had sex since the day they took Jody away. If Len tries to approach her Babs looks disgusted, and he, in turn, feels ashamed that he should require this basic animal satisfaction when their only son is in jail. He feels the same when he finds himself inadvertently laughing. Will they ever laugh naturally together again?

'Sometimes I wish he had died,' Babs sobbed to him, 'or been the victim instead of the criminal. I would so love to have all that sympathy, and it does feel as if Jody has died and yet everybody hates us. You think I'm awful for saying that, don't you?'

No. Comforting her was easy, for there are times when Len wishes this himself. Particularly when the girls are involved. At school they've been sent to Coventry, not invited to the homes of their friends any more, excluded from the usual social roundabout so essential in a teenage world. No longer do they sit on the stairs hugging the phone and giggling. They daren't go out any more in case they bump into someone they know, and their former companions have started crossing to the other side of the road when they see Dawn and Cindy approaching. Cindy has had her satchel snatched. Dawn found her PE gear in the swimming pool; there was a brand-new badminton racket with it. It is all so terribly cruel. Len never knew the world could behave so callously towards the innocent. He should have known, he supposes. After all, he reads the papers, he watches the news.

If this move goes well, they will make new friends, build new lives, and all without Jody's unjust notoriety to cast a shadow over everything and everywhere they go. The trial itself is bound to be awful but there is still hope, and it's hope that keeps them going, hope that Janice Plunket will tell the truth – if she knows it. Hope that before the trial, Jody's story will be believed by somebody other than his closest family. Hope that the highly-respected barrister who is representing Jody will manage to convince the jury . . .

But it's all out of his hands now. Len cannot protect his beloved son any longer.

Len heads for the chocolate fingers. The womenfolk must have gone into Preston together, shopping most likely. There's security in numbers. Yes, they are shopping – the basket's missing from the back of the door.

When the phone rings Len regards it with apprehension before

94

bending to pick it up. Friends rarely ring any more. He is ready with a vitriolic response to whoever might be there, getting sick kicks from hounding the Middletons.

'Dad?'

'Jody?' Len shifts gears. This is a surprise. He has never rung them from prison before.

'Dad, I have to be quick. Are you on your own?'

'Yes, I am. The others must have gone shopping. What's the matter, son? What's happened?'

Jody's voice is puffy, his breath harsh, short. Len can almost taste the fear. 'Dad, I can't speak for long in case they're already monitoring your calls. *I'm out . . .*'

'Out?' Len's eyes widen.

'I'm on the run. Me and two others went over the wall this afternoon.'

'But Jody, wait! Listen, you can't—'

'It's done, Dad, and I'm out, but I desperately need some money.'

Lenny's mouth goes tighter. 'Jody, wait a minute, listen to me!'

There's a sob in the lad's voice this time. 'Don't shout, there's no point. Just tell me, Dad – can you help me?'

Stupidly, in his confusion, Len pats his pocket as if it's Dawn or Cindy asking for a sub. 'I don't think I've got any on me right now, son.'

'But you could get it – out of the wall?'

Hesitation. 'Well, yes, I could get it, but—'

'I haven't got long, Dad.' He is galvanised, talking faster. 'And I can't stay here in the phone box. I'm sorry, but I've got to go. Listen, get me some money, please, please, and be at the park in half an hour, the bench nearest the café – you know. The old wooden café where we used to go with the boats. I've got to go now. Bye, Dad. See you . . .'

Dear God, this is all they need. Len stares, mesmerised, at the silent phone while his body shakes and his brow moistens. It's all so absurd and melodramatic. It's the shock! Not only the shock of hearing Jody so out of the blue like that, but the awful realisation that his son has done something so appallingly foolish. He has played right into the hands of his enemies and now Lenny has the choice of either aiding and abetting him in this reckless behaviour, or handing him over to the law in the kind of betrayal that might result in his being imprisoned for the rest of his young life.

He raises a tortured, anxious face, listening for his wife's car. What would Babs' reaction be? What is his own reaction?

At the moment he only feels numb, sick and confused. Sometimes, when the family were watching *Crimewatch* together they used to ask each other what they would do if they suspected someone they loved to be guilty of one of the crimes featured on the programme. Would they give them up to the law, or would they protect them, guilty or not?

Should he feel pleased that his son is free? After all, a fair trial for Jody, after this publicity, will be out of the question. But if Len is pleased, then what is this heavy weight that presses against his heart? Running away is never the answer and yet, if he had been in Jody's position with a chance of escaping that dismal place and that terrifying future, what would Len have done?

Jody can't stay in hiding for ever. They'll catch him and his mates in the end and there'll be worse trouble.

The boy is innocent. Innocent of the charge he faces. So perhaps Len should attempt to use the next lot of publicity – oh, those awful headlines again, shouted from street corners! – to try to convince the public of this. But how should he do this, and when? Len is so out of his depth – they all are.

High-shouldered beneath his umbrella, Len slips out of the house and into the rain. The note he leaves on the kitchen table says, quite truthfully, that he's gone to get some money from the hole in the wall. What if he's seen? He holds the umbrella well down. He could lose his job. He could lose his home. By the time he sets off towards the park the rain is in full force. The damp penetrates his knees and shins and trickles down his arm. A patrolling policeman passes by and Len is moved to glance at his watch, considering this a gesture of innocence. But he is a guilty man, going about bad business. Does he look as furtive as he feels? Other people pass him, ordinary people, going about the simple business of their lives. With a gasp of relief he reaches the park and lowers his umbrella when he's under the shelter of the trees. He heads speedily for the café, his eyes watering from the strain of staring, his body shivering as his summer trousers blow against his legs.

And there is Jody, half-hiding, standing nervously beside the wall of the dilapidated café, closed at five-thirty, of course. He looks so young and frightened as he sees his father and raises a hand. That, and an incomplete smile, is the only acknowledgment of his father's arrival.

No more hugs. No more slaps on the back. Just, 'Thanks a lot, Dad,' as Len hands over the five £20 notes. 'I owe you.'

Len is nervous, twitchy. 'Where are the others?'

'Back there somewhere.'

'Where will you go after this?'

'There's a place.'

'A safe place?'

'Safe enough, they say.'

'They're going to find you, Jody.'

'What else could I do?'

'Mum's going to be so worried.'

'Better than being inside.'

'But Jody, this is never the answer.'

'Dad. I've got to go. I'll come home if I can. Tell Mum—'

'Jody, no! They'll be watching. That's exactly where they'll expect you to be.'

'Or the last place.'

They both lift hands defensively as a way of saying goodbye without touching.

On his way home, trying to decide how to tell his wife – *'it'll be all right, Babs, it'll be all right'* – Leonard Middleton nervously purchases a newspaper. He opens it with dread in his hands.

FOURTEEN

The Grange, Dunsop, Nr Clitheroe, Lancs

It's all such a muddled mess. From now and into the foreseeable future, all Jacy's royalties must go to pay back taxes. After Capital Gains Tax, any profit he might make from the sale of his house must go towards the legal fees he is still paying for a defamation-of-character case which was settled out of court. He called Deek the guitarist 'a fixer' – not the most startling abuse, and far weaker language than he has used towards his former buddy in friendly banter in happier times. Jacy was referring to Deek's shady negotiations with the recording company, Elektra, which ended with him being dumped on, and how. The papers took it to mean that Deek was an addict, which he was, but they made such a fuss about it, and the hostile publicity was so intense, that Jacy was forced to pay up and shut up.

And then there is that sorry business when he was done for drunken driving. He is still paying for that.

When the small Lancashire estate is wound up, Jacy will be left owing a little money, a petty sum hardly worth bothering about. However, in order to sort his finances out and to his great humiliation, he was dragged to court with Belle like some loser to explain humbly how he will manage to pay his debts over the next few years.

A wicked blow to his ego.

Belle's irregular but impressive income, which she will use towards these liabilities, especially after they marry, went a long way to satisfy that uppity judge.

And now it looks as if they might be on the brink of selling The Grange.

'Time to tie the knot,' says Belle firmly. 'Or have you changed your mind since your shockingly violent outbreak?' She holds that incident over his head like a bucket of cold water. She will not leave it alone.

'Leave it out,' pleads Jacy, desperately wondering what marriage might do to his image. It won't necessarily taint it, especially when you think he is marrying a top model. In fact, the publicity – if they can swing any positive publicity after all the flack they've taken from the press – might do his flagging career some good.

But the problem with publicity at the moment is his shameful move to Ribblestone Close. The last thing he wants is for his adoring public, who are still out there somewhere he's certain, to discover he has sunk so low in the credibility stakes. Any publicity is *not* good publicity, not in Jacy's experience. Naturally, there has never been a FOR SALE sign up at The Grange, so there's still a chance they could call in the press, announce their marriage, and make out they are living together happily in impressive circumstances. That's if the nosy locals can keep their mouths shut.

Belle is not immediately opposed to his idea – amazing! – but she does worry about the state of the house and how they could get it spruced up in time for any romantic announcement. 'And then we must consider the real possibility that nobody will be interested . . .'

'We could even get married here at The Grange,' says Jacy with hope in his heart, ignoring her undermining remarks. He colours angrily but says nothing. Sometimes he thinks he's going crazy with anger and no way to speak it out loud. The last time he tried, Belle ended up with a black eye and he's never hit a woman before. Believe it – he was as shocked as she was. What is happening to him these days? Where has the old Jacy gone? 'We could get a licence.'

'We might,' says Belle reluctantly, still only half-convinced. 'It would cost an arm and a leg to get a firm of cleaners in, and then there's the tatty grounds to think about. We would have to know that people were interested before we coughed up that sort of money.'

Tight as a duck's arse as ever. Oh dear God. But all is not yet lost, thinks Jacy to himself.

'Of course the whole idea would work much better around some positive information – say, if you were to start up another group, for instance, or if Deek and you and Rab were reconciled, or if Jip took up religion. All hypotheticals which don't stand a hope in hell, of course.'

Belle will do anything, go through anything, shell out any amount in order to marry him. This is a dream coming true for her, and Jacy considers that he is doing her a magnanimous favour. It is right and proper that he should get something in return. 'I wonder if any of the old group could be persuaded to join in a publicity session . . .' she muses.

Jacy doesn't need to think any further. No is the answer to that; no, they would not – and the thought is an uncomfortable one. After all, those three who are making it with the new band don't need to, and

Darcy and Cyd are coke-heads living in squalor in London squats, last time he heard anything. Darcy had been beaten up, mugged if you please and quite seriously injured according to reports, poor guy. There but for the grace of God . . . And anyway, Jacy would get far more pleasure from publicity created for himself alone. Christ, how his enemies would hate that . . . the thought of Jacy getting back on his feet again.

In those far-off and balmy days, people who hated him felt impelled to tolerate him. Not any more. Most had taken advantage of his downfall and been quite unnecessarily outspoken. 'The main trouble with Jacy,' said his old friend Jip, 'is that he doesn't love his work enough not to put money first. Now I can't help it, but I'm totally different. I don't happen to be one who regards money as the first and only thing in the world.'

Sanctimonious pig.

Jip love his work? That was the first time Jacy had ever heard him say that. He'd grumbled enough about it at the time.

'It would work much better if the press thought they had dug something up by themselves,' he says. 'If only we could swing it. That way they'd be far more likely to turn up in numbers.' But what might they dig up? All Jacy's skeletons were long ago let out of the cupboard and there's nothing interesting about him left. He does nothing. He goes nowhere. The rake has even turned monogamous and has been for almost six long, boring years. No, there's nothing about Colin Smedley that anyone out there would want to know.

The idol has been eliminated and left with this hollow feeling of loss.

And it's all Belle's fault, with her two-edged love like a sword. But he will not allow his last wisps of hope to be taken away, not by her, dear God. Not by anyone.

They have to hide in the grounds today. For once it isn't raining; the climate in this godless part of the world is always ten degrees lower than it is down south and it takes some time to adjust.

Some hairy-jacketed jerk came round last week and seemed pretty interested. Apparently he was 'acting for clients', or some such ridiculous notion. Today somebody even more important is coming. The agents aren't showing them round, some solicitor from Sheffield is. It all sounds a mite shady to Jacy, who doesn't give a damn as long as the offer is confirmed.

Four o'clock they said, so after Belle has finished the Hoovering and washed up the dishes from three days ago, the two of them set off with

Jacy's old metal detector to the quarry which Belle reckons must hide some interesting Roman remains. Jacy is always on the lookout for treasure; this is just about the only outdoor activity which he finds acceptable.

Funny how this battered old thing is still going after so many years when the expensive, luxury goods have mostly packed up and been chucked out. Jacy and his two younger brothers used to spend hours searching the beach at Bishop's Head when they lived outside Swansea as kids. Never found anything save for the odd loose change. But you always had this burning hope, it was more like a firm belief, that one day you'd come home puffing and struggling over the dunes with a casket full of gold. You were far more likely to step on a mine but kids don't think that way . . .

Even in those days Jacy went everywhere with that plastic guitar his mum got him out of her catalogue.

Belle is convinced that his working-class roots make him bitter, most of it directed at her with her 'prattish' middle-class background. To annoy him, and only for that reason, she has always gone on about meeting his family. As a child Jacy had struggled to better himself, always been determined to make it. His Mam had ambitions for him, too, and dragged him in front of his first audience when he was twelve years old, some corny seaside competition to discover the entertainer of the year. Being twelve and small for his age helped. He called himself Little Devil because of the peak of dark hair at his forehead. He came tenth out of over 1000 contestants with an Elvis Presley number and won a racing bike which was too small so he gave it to his brother, Jack.

For as long as he can remember, he has alternated between an almost unbearable impatience and a demoralising panic. Since then every single rejection has felt like a lash across the face of a very hungry man.

Only Jacy knows this, and he would never share this information with another soul, least of all Belle who might use it against him. Even when he was at the top he expected people to see through his bluff and laugh at him. He did, honestly. He feared mockery more than death. No amount of success took his terrors away or made him feel more secure. He always believed that he was somehow putting something over on everybody underneath all that acclaim and worship.

An expert con man. Unlike Jip who really knows about music.

Not for the first time he wonders what his life might have been like if nothing had ever happened to him, if he'd stayed stuck at home, that gloomy semi full of bric-à-brac, embroidered Biblical texts and odd pieces of furniture. He used to hear from his family now and again, mostly hinting broadly for money or warning him about sin among the savage peoples of the earth. He did not reply – well, he was too busy on the road to fame and fortune to write letters or spend hours on the telephone sympathising with his mother's stomach condition. And she is a commonplace little woman with a bag of mending on her lap and a bag of second-hand morals stuffed in her head. Luckily his enemies in the tabloids never dug her up. Jeez, that would have been ghastly. She has never abandoned her peasant respect for gentility and money, while new riches are sinful and, as an atonement, ought to be shared. A real pain. *Mam. Mam.* He says the familiar word in his mind but it means nothing. Jacy feels a tightness in his throat. They probably all still live around Swansea, he supposes . . .

Beep, goes the metal detector. Jacy pauses in his tracks, and it is Belle who squats down with the trowel to do the dirty work for him.

If Jacy did find a fortune down there in this hard stony ground, would he share it with Belle, as she is now proposing to share all her worldly goods with him? He doubts it. He never has shared his wealth with her, but only because she always insisted on paying her own way. 'I don't want that hurled back in my face one day,' she used to say, knowing him so well, *and accepting him* with his childish swiftly changing moods and his broken attachments. But my God, every single thing he does in future he is going to insure by iron-clad contracts that are quite impossible to wriggle out of.

If Jacy or Belle could be spotted from a distance, nobody would assume that either of them were the owners of a grand house like The Grange. They are both in shabby jeans and T-shirts, more like gardeners than gentry. 'Nothing,' says Belle, getting up off her knees, wiping off an old bit of glass. Nothing but litter. 'Come on. Carry on.'

Jacy dreams on while making the necessary circular movements, just about all the expendable energy he can muster these days. He'd been frightened of his little fierce father, a short and pot-bellied man, not that he was unkind or a bully, just that he was vain, full of dreams for himself and moody and peevish when anxieties beset him. Tee-total, of course. He was master of the house, a man of ideas and fixed opinions, a part-time preacher and his talents were wasted in Wales. Jacy must have inherited all his ambitions from him.

'Here they come . . . car's not bad.'

Jacy shades his eyes and glares. The gold Mercedes looks in keeping as it rolls sedately up the drive among the deep blue-headed rhododendrons and azaleas, dead on time. Spurts of golden gravel fly up behind the heavy wheels. Behind them comes the Range Rover probably bearing the legal beagle, though what a solicitor from Sheffield has to do with the sale of The Grange is impossible to fathom. Still, the agents seemed to accept the rather odd situation.

The resonant upper-class voice of the driver echoes a greeting across the still summer air and the two men shake hands.

'It's all so mysterious. I wonder who they are,' muses Belle. 'I wonder if they are local.'

'She's a bit of all right,' says Jacy predictably, but to his chagrin he knows that this remark won't bother Belle. Since she was a baby she has always been pretty and therefore takes her looks for granted. She never considers another woman as a threat, that is the size of her confidence. She rarely flirts with anyone. Even when he was into screwing every bird he could lay his hands on, Belle turned a blind eye or pretended to do so, he is still not quite sure which, and time has not yet nibbled away at her looks. In her trade they know how to take care of themselves. Jacy says, 'That interfering bag Julia Farquhar is bound to find out, we'll hear about it on the grapevine soon enough. You can't fart around here without that old sow knowing about it.'

'I doubt we'll hear a thing,' says Belle, 'seeing as nobody round here speaks to us any more.'

'Swine,' grunts Jacy, a natural response to almost everyone these days.

'There's money about,' says Belle, still staring at the car.

'There used to be money about here.'

'Yes, until you went and threw it all away.'

'*Touché*,' says Jacy. But his thoughts are bitter.

After being ushered from the car, the female passenger stands oddly motionless in the drive, inhaling and exhaling deep breaths that Jacy and Belle can see from here. What is she doing, staring around with one hand on her hat as if she'd expected to be met, or photographed? And eventually the posh little party of three disappear through the front door.

'Wow,' jokes Belle, 'what an entrance! What a couple of swells!'

'No better than you and me,' snaps Jacy, swinging the silent machine over the barren earth till it meets with a bush and damages it.

Suddenly—

'Tusker!' screams the elegant stranger. 'My God. Tusker! Is that really you?'

Belle starts, taken aback, far too engrossed in her digging to have noticed the little party of three moving in their direction.

'Peaches!' Belle screams back eventually, having focused her eyes on the approaching blonde and recognising that unmistakable face, those eyes, that absurdly wiggling walk, the image of Goldie Hawn.

Belle hardly hears the alarmed *pssst* which shoots from between Jacy's snarling lips as he stands half-hiding behind her. *'Get them away from here, they'll recognise me in a minute . . . get them away, Belle, go on, quick . . .'*

So just as old Peaches is about to raise an enquiring eyebrow in Jacy's direction, Belle flings her arms round her old chum and hurries her in the opposite direction.

'Darling Tusker, what on earth are you doing here?'

'I live here,' says Belle, amused to hear that old nickname rising from the fathoms of the past like a shipwrecked relic washed up from the sea.

'But why are you hiding away down here?'

'We're not hiding actually, we are metal-detecting. Searching for treasure.'

Peaches looks fresh and appealing as ever. She has not lost that adorable lisp that everyone once tried to copy. 'Oh, how absolutely wonderful! You always were so exciting. And who is the Adonis?'

'Just a friend.'

'Ah. So we're not going to be introduced?'

'No, actually,' says Belle with a wink. 'Come on, come indoors and have a drink. Normally we can't bear to be in the house when there's viewers round, but of course this is totally different.'

Peaches peers forward and stares, bringing her velvet skin disconcertingly right up to Belle's own. She lowers her voice to a husky whisper. *'The brace worked, then?'*

For a moment Belle can't figure it out but then she remembers and displays her teeth with great pride. 'Yep, after all those painful years of looking like Jaws, my incisors have gone back into place and as you see, I am no longer a tusker but a perfect example of what the best dental surgery can do!'

'They were never that bad, darling,' giggles Peaches. Even her laugh is as frivolous as ever, it's hard to take her seriously. 'We were terribly cruel to give you that nickname. I think it was because you were so horribly perfect everywhere else.'

'It's better than some I can think of.'

'How true. I see your pictures wherever I go these days, Tusker, half-naked down in the Tube, sometimes a leg, sometimes a boob. You must be doing incredibly well for yourself – no wonder you've got a dream pad like this, quite marvellous, and look at the daisies.'

The two are so excited by this incredible meeting that they seem to have forgotten there are others about. 'Excuse me,' says the authoritative young man at Peaches' side. 'Might I be permitted to butt in here?'

'Oh, sorry, so sorry, Dougal darling,' and Peaches is all ruffled up like the petticoat that shows just an inch under her pretty-as-a picture floral dress. 'This is Tusker, an old, old friend. *Do you see any of the old gang?* I would love to hear. There's so much to catch up on . . .'

'I think we ought to be going, Arabella, really,' smiles the amazingly groomed and attractive young man, long and slight and superior. But he seems unaccountably nervous. 'Much as I hate to interrupt this highly emotional meeting.'

'Are you married, Arabella? Is Dougal your—'

She blushes sweetly, just like the old days. 'Oh, no. Nothing like that.'

'Arabella and I are hoping to become engaged soon,' says Dougal with quite unnecessary forcefulness. Poor Arabella looks quite startled. And no wonder, thinks Belle. Doesn't she know he's as queer as a coot? My God, the poor thing is in for a shock unless Belle has all her messages wrong. What on earth is all this about? 'And we have a pressing appointment later this evening.'

'No, we do not, Dougal,' says Arabella airily. 'We're booked into an hotel and we don't have to be there till we want to. You told me that, I remember.'

Dougal looks even more uneasy. 'I think you are forgetting, my dear . . .'

There's a tension now that Peaches, of course, is too thick to notice, but Belle, who lives with tension every minute of her day, picks up on it straight away. She decides to speak for her friend. 'Well, if you can't come in now, perhaps we could make arrangements. I mean, I want to know why you are interested in The Grange, what is going on in your life, what has been happening since I last saw you. Honestly Peaches, I'm so excited . . .'

'We liked the house very much, didn't we, Arabella?' Her young man seems to be trying to persuade her.

'I think you can leave that side of everything to me,' puts in the white-haired solicitor from Sheffield whose old-fashioned gentlemanly ways remind Belle of her own father.

'So you're going to confirm the offer?' Belle knows she has to ask. It will be the first thing Jacy wants to know. He has disappeared completely now, slunk like a ferret into the undergrowth leaving nothing tangible or visible behind. And Peaches has done this, all on her own. She has magicked him away!

'Of course we are, especially now that I know it is you,' laughs Peaches, always so naive and trusting but not half as empty-headed as she likes to make out. Once a temporary teacher told Arabella she had a stagnant mind. She cried for a week and the whole school went on strike. 'Oh, my God, my God. Just *wait* until I tell Charlie and Mags who I've seen.'

This is incredible. The best thing that's happened all year. 'You're still in touch with them?'

'I share a flat with them!'

Oh, how wonderful! 'Next time I'm in London . . .'

'You must, Tusker. Oh, you absolutely must! I have so much to tell you, so many wonderful secrets. Here,' and Peaches fumbles in her hopeless bag, more like a G-string dotted with pearls. 'Here's my address. Mummy had these cards specially printed and this is the first chance I've had to use them. It's quite embarrassing. I mean, who uses cards these days?'

Belle stands at the doorway of The Grange and watches as the small cavalcade disappears up the drive. After the shrieking of Peaches everything is suddenly very silent round here. She feels shaken. The visit has left her cold and lonely like waking up from a dream and the duvet has slipped off the bed. She certainly didn't approve of the way poor Peaches seemed to be manipulated by that aloof young man, almost as if she wasn't sure where she was supposed to be going – far worse than her normal bewildered, dizzy self. She was so easily squashed, her sweet nature so often taken for granted. And what on earth was that relationship meant to be all about? There must be some simple explanation. It's such a relief for Belle to discover an outside world actually still exists, together with a past that excludes the all-pervasive Jacy . . . So there *was* another life, once – playful and affectionate. It might seem like a dreamtime now, but there was one, and a happy one it had been, too.

Funny how you fall into things – relationships, situations. Nothing that matters is ever planned but then it's the same trying to grope your way out. Sometimes you're stuck fast like a cow in a mire and you have to wait for someone to free you.

'Who the hell was that? asks Jacy, sliding back into view, smoking nervously.

'Nobody much,' Belle assures him, aware that he will dig at her if she seems too thrilled by the meeting. His is a perverse kind of jealousy which she's never been able to fathom. She plays it down. 'Just an old schoolfriend we were all very fond of.'

'She certainly seemed to adore you!' says Jacy with contempt in his voice. 'Didn't want to go, by the look of it. Highly emotional, hysterical, from where I stood. The old alma mater must specialise in those sorts of types.'

Belle turns round and looks him straight in the eye. 'From where you stand, Jacy, I'm afraid you can't see anything at all except for your own bum.'

FIFTEEN

No fixed abode

'It is beginning to look as if the Clitheroe project is becoming too perilous to proceed with any further.'

If so, it's a damn shame. The Grange makes an ideal retreat stuck up there among the native hordes, surrounded by security, and even the floozie herself is gracious enough to give her approval –although not, it would seem, to live there without her Prince.

'The time has come to be firm, Dougal,' says Sir Hugh Mountjoy, gazing over the mellow Palace lawns, steepling his fingers as he rests his head against the tall back of his leather-lined chair just as his father did before him. 'This nonsense cannot be allowed to continue further. Time, after all, is moving on.'

Dougal Rathbone feels like a boy at school again confronting a cynical headmaster. He thoroughly enjoys the feeling although he knows that Sir Hugh is a respectable married man, straight as a die; his wife, Constance, is the daughter of a Count. Dougal pulls himself upright in an attempt to calm his fantasy. 'It was the most remarkable coincidence . . .'

'Quite a shock.'

'Indeed, Sir Hugh.'

'Although, of course, Miss Brightly-Smythe is just as likely to blab to any of her other friends, luckily this little reunion seems to have been nipped in the bud. But it's the fact that the owners of The Grange now believe they know the identity of the purchaser . . .'

'Which they would have done sooner or later,' Dougal reminds him.

'And the fact that the two young ladies seemed to be so close.'

'But that is the nature of these old school friendships,' says Dougal, who knows a thing or two about boarding-school relationships. 'Personally I don't see, at this stage, that any lasting damage has been done.'

'You could be right,' muses Sir Hugh. 'And the girl did approve of the place.'

'Very much so; she is a most effusive character and easily influenced. All she wants before she makes a final decision, and she is like a dog at a bone with this one, is an opportunity to talk to the Prince.'

'Out of the question.'

'That's what I told her.'

'Absolutely impossible at this delicate stage.'

'She thinks about him constantly. She has given in her notice at Habitat as I advised her to do. The fewer people she meets at this stage, the better. But she is getting rather fractious.'

'Let her. Let Miss Cutie stew in her own juice.'

'Perhaps if you spoke to her, sir.'

'Heavens! Have you lost your senses, Dougal?'

'What harm would a meeting with you do? You of all people, with your experience, would be most likely to influence the young lady. A fatherly influence, if you like.'

A silence now, as Sir Hugh moves into a deeper state of contemplation. And then, 'It couldn't be here. She mustn't be allowed to set foot in the Palace.'

'Naturally. I was thinking more in terms of a neutral rendezvous.'

'London is far too dangerous.'

'Actually, I was thinking of Brighton. I have an aunt who runs tea rooms there with a friend.'

'A tea shop on the coast? Run by two old dykes?' He has heard about Dougal's eccentric family.

'They are wonderfully discreet, Sir Hugh. I have had occasion to trust them with my own reputation more than once.'

'I don't doubt you have,' says Sir Hugh, frowning. Time is not on Sir Hugh's side. In under a week the announcement of the engagement of James Henry Albert, third son of the Monarch, to Lady Frances Loughborough, oldest daughter of the Earl and Countess of Weir, is to take place. All the relevant screening has been done, the in-depth probing into health, antecedents, reputation . . . The only surprising fact to emerge from all this research is that the Princess-to-be has the reputation for rather a foul mouth. Well, that can soon be curbed. The bride of a Prince must consider herself as a vessel, no more, no less. And in this particular situation a spare vessel, twice-removed, like a vase which will come out only if the first two smash. At the moment there are no heirs and troublemakers are suggesting that George, recently hitched to Princess Gunhilda, can't get it up at all. What's more, rumours are spreading from Denmark that Gunhilda is not remotely interested anyway. All frightfully worrying.

The second son, Rupert, a sprinter over 400 metres, is at the moment more interested in his athletics career than the lineage. The Palace recently had to deal with that nasty little publicity snarl-up when Rupert was caught in practice dropping the baton *again*. I mean, as the press pointed out, anyone else who kept constantly dropping the baton would have been sacked from the Olympic team by now . . . Fatal to be royal and involved in anything slightly competitive.

The Earl and Countess of Weir are suitably thrilled, as is Lady Frances herself. The Countess is an old friend of the Queen's and holds tremendously successful charity balls at Portland Square. They have booked their daughter into their own private villa on the Island of Mustique for a month after the news comes out to avoid too much press harassment. The life of James Henry Albert must carry steadily on; he will be busy shooting grouse with his Mother in Scotland. Nobody can afford an hysterical reaction from the wretched Peaches. The great British Public is already fed up with forking out for the super-privileged, and there's a dangerous air of Republicanism abroad in the land. Perhaps Dougal is right and Sir Hugh *should* see the hussy himself – warn her off for the last time, give her a taste of the Establishment's most severe disapproval.

And so this is how Sir Hugh finds himself sitting waiting at a window table at the Blue Bird café, fiddling with the slender glass vase containing a small bunch of sweet peas, the centrepiece on the pristine cloth. The stone walls are covered in brasses, particularly those beside the chimney, along with bedpans, jugs, saucepans and horsebrasses; a little brass bell is perched on every table. The tea he ordered arrives in a metal pot which drips and the handle burns his fingers.

'Oh, do let me be Mother!'

Great heavens above! Sir Hugh starts as the pretty young thing with the small clean hands introduces herself. 'Call me Peaches – and you must be the dragon, Sir Hugh!' She pours his tea with a casual style and sits herself down on the blue-painted Lloyd Loom chair directly opposite.

This is not a propitious way to start. She seems to have taken over completely as Sir Hugh is reduced to blowing desperately upon his smarting skin. 'Butter,' she cries with glee, and passes it over.

He'd felt foolish enough before Arabella arrived, sitting there reading the *Telegraph*, garbed like a spy in the navy Guernsey with the patches on the elbows recommended by Dougal as the sort of camouflage he would need to fit into his present role *incognito*. To cap it all, he is wearing a stylish pair of pumps. Suits predominate in Sir

Hugh's London wardrobe. He rarely has cause to slip into anything casual and his wife, Lady Constance, is far too busy with her social life in London to spend much time in the country. He was forced to allow young Dougal to go and choose him some suitable clothes for this most important expedition.

'You don't want to frighten her off,' said Dougal. 'You don't want her clamming up on you.'

Sir Hugh rather thought that intimidation would be a good move, but Dougal argued otherwise. 'She wants to be able to consider you as a friend,' he insisted. 'She wants to be able to trust you.'

It occurs to Sir Hugh that they are all bending rather too far backwards in order to accommodate this little madam.

Dougal drove him down to Brighton in the Merc, an unnecessarily hair-raising experience, and is at this moment in a car park nearby, tuned in to Radio Five, waiting to hear how Sir Hugh gets on.

'Leave it now, please, I am perfectly all right,' Sir Hugh insists, withdrawing his injured hand. 'What would you like me to order for you? Tea? Coca Cola? A slice of chocolate gâteau?' In this imperious manner a man can regain control. He looks around. 'Damn. I don't believe the Blue Bird is licensed. How was the train journey?'

Arabella Brightly-Smythe, the thorn in the Establishment's side who looks more like a rose this afternoon, considers the flowery hand-painted menu. 'I think I would like a cream tea,' she says, smiling timidly, 'if that is all right with you.'

What on earth is the matter with him? He can't take his eyes from her stomach. Does the little foetus growing inside realise what an almighty explosion its birth would be likely to cause? Ripples around the world? They exchange some small talk, and then at last the food arrives. He is forced to sit back and watch her spreading the thick layers of cream and jam, wasting valuable time. He could murder a gin and tonic.

Sir Hugh launches himself when he believes she has finally finished. 'I hear you approved of The Grange, Arabella.'

'I told you to call me Peaches. Please do. And did I hear you mention chocolate gâteau?'

He has no intention of calling her Peaches. Can this be the helpless, waif-like creature that Dougal has described? She looks perfectly self-assured, not a worry in the world. She must be even more backward than she is given credit for.

Sir Hugh leans forward, and lowers his grey and ponderous

eyebrows. His voice follows and becomes almost intimate. 'You do understand, don't you, Arabella, that your relationship with James has to finish.'

Arabella raises her delicate eyebrows. 'I am waiting for Jamie to tell me that. I am not prepared to believe these things you are telling me. I know how the world manipulates poor Jamie and says things about him that are just not true. Why should I believe you or Dougal are any different?'

'Because, my dear girl, we have his well-being at heart.'

She smiles at him thinly. 'But how am I to know that? I only know what Jamie tells me, and he says that he loves me. He promised me he loved me. Even the last time I saw him, before you took him away from me!'

Drat the fellow and his abominable behaviour. 'And I am sure he means it. But there are many variations on the theme of love, and love doesn't always mean that those involved can be together. Jamie, as you know, is not free to pick and choose like any commoner.'

She is tucking into her chocolate cake, ignoring the polite little fork provided, as if she is on the point of starving. Does she always gulp her food like this?

'When am I going to see him?'

'My dear child, you are not going to see him.'

'But I am carrying his child.'

'So you say.'

'I am not a liar.'

'Look here, Arabella, in these circumstances it does not matter a jot whose child you carry. Jamie is aware of your predicament and is sorry if it is causing you grief. He gave his advice to you when you first informed him that you were pregnant. He now wants to end the relationship, and is only prepared to support the child from a distance provided you accept a home at The Grange and are prepared to say nothing to a soul regarding the paternity of your baby.'

Her answer is simple and straightforward. 'I don't believe you.'

'It is my job, my dear, to act as spokesman for those who are not free to speak for themselves. I am sitting here this afternoon representing James.'

Her voice is soft, he has to lean forward to hear her. 'Well, whose baby should I say it is?'

Aha, Sir Hugh is finally breaking through. He dabs his mouth with his napkin in a gesture of quiet satisfaction although it is quite clean. 'That is entirely up to you.'

'What, make somebody up?'

'If that would be the simplest answer.'

'And the baby would never know who she really was?'

'Naturally. That would be the gravest mistake and not fair on the child.'

'And Jamie would never want to see it, his own offspring?'

'Jamie will go on to have other children, Royal children, children with a destiny to fulfil.'

'And my child is to have no destiny?'

'Not within the Royal Family, no.'

'And there's nothing I can do about this?'

'My dear girl, don't make it sound so dramatic. You knew who he was when you agreed to have intercourse with him. Presumably you also chose to take no contraceptive precautions. You made informed choices and must be prepared to accept the consequences. We all of us have to obey the rules; without rules the whole structure of society collapses. You wouldn't like to live in a drab Republic, would you? You wouldn't like to see our sense of history cut out of our lives like a core from an apple? Or our—'

'I wouldn't mind,' says Arabella. 'Why should I mind? The people in other countries seem quite happy without a Royal Family. I don't notice them suffering particularly.'

'Aha,' says Sir Hugh with a mean smile. 'Now we have it. Quite a little revolutionary at heart, aren't we? So that is what this is all about. As I understand it, your parents are not particularly avid supporters of The Crown.'

'I don't understand what you are insinuating. I don't think they care much either way, and neither did I until all this started.'

Damn. Damn. He has upset her! He sends a bright white handkerchief across the top of the table, scrunches it up in her hand and lets go. 'Now then, now then. Come on, it's not as bad as all that now, is it?'

Arabella sobs on. 'You don't know what you are saying! How do you expect me to behave faced with banishment to a strange house away from everyone I love and never to see my baby's father again?' Tears are streaming down her pretty face. 'Don't you realise, Jamie would be perfectly happy to give up all that rigmarole just to be with me. He's not interested in The Family, why should he be? He's never going to be King so why should he suffer so?'

He decides to be blunt, to be cruel to be kind. 'Jamie is not suffering. Jamie has sensibly accepted the situation. He has sent me to see you today in order to tell you so.'

'I refuse to listen to you any more.'

Sir Hugh struggles on. 'But you don't want to bring shame and disgrace upon your family . . .'

Arabella sniffs, no longer quite so daintily. 'Shame and disgrace?'

'You are unmarried, and soon to become a mother. A single parent giving birth to a fatherless child.'

Now it's her turn to fiddle with the vase. Her hand is sticky and wet with her tears. 'Only because you are making me! How can you be so horrid?'

'It will get a lot worse than this, Arabella, if you continue with this futile resistance, and it is not I, dear child, whom you should blame. It is the whole unfortunate situation. You must try to be adult about this. You must acknowledge the fact that you are nothing but an embarrassment to Jamie and if, as you say, you truly love him, you should be prepared to release him and even, in time, forgive him.'

To Sir Hugh's horror, Arabella bursts into a fresh flood of tears, attracting the attention of several customers and the watching management.

'Is this man upsetting you?'

A giant of a woman, dressed all in black and with arms like hambones, stamps across to their table causing the fragile crockery to rattle. This must be Dougal's aunt or Dougal's aunt's friend.

'It's all right,' cries Arabella, cowering, blushing brightly.

'Well, it certainly doesn't seem all right to *me*!' The Gorgon in black turns violently upon Sir Hugh, her moustached lip quivering with anger. 'You should be ashamed of yourself, a man your age!'

Sir Hugh leaps up boldly. 'I say . . .'

'I think an apology is in order.'

'No, no, it's all right, really,' sobs Arabella.

'I will not put up with this sort of behaviour on my premises. My friend and I have a reputation to keep up here and it's just not in order.' Like a fishwife she shouts at Sir Hugh, arms akimbo. In a straight fight he would stand no chance.

'Madam,' says Sir Hugh, getting a grip on himself and rising to his true imposing height. 'I apologise for causing a disturbance, quite unintentional I assure you, but I absolutely insist that this young lady and I have no relationship other than a formal acquaintance.'

The woman remains steadfast. 'Then why is she sitting there crying her heart out? You tell me that!'

'Because, I'm afraid, I am the bearer of bad news.'

'You look as if you are,' shouts the overweight harridan. 'Coming in here and carrying on with your airs and graces. I'd rather you'd picked some other place to break it.'

'So do I,' agrees Sir Hugh, picking up his copy of the *Telegraph* and whatever shreds of pride he can muster while trying to coax an hysterical Arabella towards the tea-room door. All eyes are now turned in their direction. This is a dreadful scene, the worst scenario the discreet Sir Hugh could possibly have imagined. He should never have agreed to Dougal's suggestion. He should never have come here at all . . .

'Well?' enquires Dougal, turning down the car radio. 'How was it?'

Sir Hugh gets in, still bristling with shame. 'Not good.'

'You failed to convince her?'

'I failed. Just leave it at that. I failed. We are going to have to come up with some other strategy. There is no way of getting through. I am beginning to feel that the only person who will convince Miss Brightly-Smythe is James himself, much as that prospect distresses me.'

'But the engagement . . .'

'I know, Dougal, I realise that.'

'Did you mention the engagement to Frances?'

Sir Hugh slumps further down in the car, squeaking the soft leather passenger seat. He clears his throat. 'No. I am afraid I did not.'

'So she still doesn't know! Why didn't you mention it? I thought that was one of the main purposes of the meeting.'

'No need to go on, Dougal, there didn't seem an appropriate moment, that's all. I was about to bring the subject up when all hell was let loose, and to tell you the truth, I am lucky to get out of that establishment with my life.' He turns to Dougal enquiring, 'Which one is your aunt?'

'My aunt?'

'I met a lady . . .'

'My aunt's no lady.'

'Then it must have been her.'

'Nobody's ever been entirely certain of her sex, but if she was dressed all in black . . .'

'She was. I think I upset her.'

'Oh,' says Dougal, driving speedily out of town, heading for the motorway. 'Perhaps I should have warned you. She's a darling when you get to know her, but she's got a temper. So what are we going to do next?'

'We are going to stop at the next public house and order me a double gin and tonic while we consider our options,' says Sir Hugh, washed out, grey and exhausted.

SIXTEEN

Flat 1, Albany Buildings, Swallowbridge, Devon

Emily Benson is a woman of her word.

She did not need telling that it would be courting disaster to bring Mrs Peacock back to Albany Buildings after their pleasant day out. An offer has been accepted on number one and it is felt by all concerned that the wisest course is to steer Mrs Peacock well away from that sensitive area, for her own peace of mind.

But Mrs Peacock would not be denied what she called, 'my very last chance to see my last home.'

'There is no question of you going inside,' said Miss Benson, concerned at the force behind Mrs Peacock's request. 'If we went to Albany Buildings we would go and have tea in my flat. Apart from your daughter's very firm instructions, you have no key to number one.'

It has been arranged that Frankie Rendell will take her mother back to her flat in order to sort out her belongings nearer the completion date.

Until this little argument started, the two women had spent a most enjoyable day at one of the popular attractions close by, the Shire Horse Centre. In spite of the crowds they had managed to find a shaded outdoor table for lunch, and ate a pasty (cheese and onion for the vegetarian Miss Benson), washed down by a lethally-named local cider. They went round the grounds on a wagon ride, ignoring the noisy children, bought ice creams and Mrs Peacock purchased small packets of fudge for a couple of the Greylands' residents. Miss Benson bought a hand-painted slate of the largest shire horse in the land, *Dapple*, to hang on her lounge wall under the mirror. The sun shone in a Wedgwood sky, the birds chirped and the smell of horse and manure and fresh hay exhilarated the primitive senses in the same way that woodsmoke does. 'Reminds me of the good old days,' said Mrs Peacock dreamily, blowing up the nostrils of a giant beast with hooves the size of dinner plates. 'They love that,' she said as the horse tossed its great mane and snorted, dangerously in Miss Benson's eyes. 'It comforts them. I wish there was such an easy equivalent in the human world.'

But they did not dwell on unpleasant issues, they were not here for that and it had all gone so well that Miss Benson had already decided to make these outings a regular treat if Mrs Peacock's daughter, Frankie, would agree. Give her something to look forward to. Mrs Peacock was fascinated by the fine display of ancient rustic implements. 'I remember most of them being used,' she said, 'and then they were lying around for two-a-penny in grass verges all over the place. I bet they're worth a fortune now, done-up and painted all shiny like that.'

She looked so much better today. The outside air and all the excitement had put a colour wash in her papery cheeks. Someone had done her hair and it was tidily hidden under the net, and her dress was a faded blue sprinkled with daisies. They went slowly. They didn't walk very far, of course, and the old lady leaned heavily on her stick at times to watch the fowls and water-birds on the pond, to rest and get her breath back. She carried around a little pillow to sit on. A favourite granny, Miss Benson mused fondly, with those alert blue eyes, now frowning at some private thought or recollection. What a pity she wasn't.

Miss Benson took care to avoid mentioning home or family, subjects which were likely to cause Mrs Peacock serious distress. This was a complete U-turn from the proud and benevolent attitude Irene had shown when first she arrived at Albany Buildings two years ago. In those days she never had a bad word to say about any of her family. No, at that time Mrs Peacock was far more worried about living on her own and being burgled – an attitude Mrs Rendell treated far too lightly, in her opinion. Many times the old lady asked her daughter to send a man round. 'I am shredding under the stress,' she complained, 'and being on the ground floor I can't sleep at night, waiting for a hand to come groping through my window. I lie and listen to passing footsteps.' She grew very nervous. Nothing happened and nothing happened. 'Well, Frankie is a busy person, teaching all day and marking most of the night, looking after those two children as well,' said Miss Benson comfortingly. 'I am sure she'll get round to it when she has the time.' Now she looks back, she senses that it was this small blot which first started Mrs Peacock feeling she was not being cared about sufficiently.

When Miss Benson finally screwed up her courage and mentioned the matter to Frankie, the younger woman had been understandably indignant at being taken to task by a neighbour, and was sharper-faced than ever.

It was like being late. Frankie Rendell and her children would do better not to give a time at all if they couldn't keep to it. Once Mrs Peacock was expecting them, she stood at the window as if magnetised to it, looking out with one eye on the clock and one on the boiling kettle, unable to relax until they arrived and by then she was so tensed up she gave them an earful. It had been the same with Miss Benson's mother. These elderly people with their reinforced attitudes, she became a stickler for punctuality too.

And, oh dear, what a fuss if Irene was invited to her daughter's house! It became an ordeal in the end – for both parties, Miss Benson is sure. These outings never lived up to their promises. 'Angus's birthday and I don't remember seeing him more than once!' moaned Mrs Peacock when she got home. 'They stayed upstairs with their loud music and when they came down I only saw the backs of their heads, playing some silly computer game with bleeps and flashes and irritating music. He only just managed to thank me for my five-pound note.'

'I know,' said Miss Benson, not knowing at all. 'It's their age.'

'You can go on saying that about people all their lives,' snapped Mrs Peacock grudgingly. 'Or "it's a phase", that's another cliché to make rude behaviour sound more acceptable. I wouldn't have it if I was Frankie. I'd never have accepted that sort of behaviour from her. And Frankie wore herself out doing all that food, and the lovely party decorations. I don't think those lads even noticed, let alone appreciated it.'

Oh dear oh dear. She was so hurt. It sounded like such a dismal time.

'And what young Poppy looks like these days I don't know.'

'They think they look nice,' humoured Miss Benson, 'following the fashion.' She smiled. 'I'm sure you did it in your day.'

'There wasn't such a thing as fashion in my day and we didn't have the money to throw around like they do now.'

'True,' agreed Miss Benson mildly.

The trick was to listen and sympathise.

'Those two children are so spoilt. They never volunteer to help round the house. They seem to feel that food is going to appear magically when they feel hungry and that it is quite acceptable to throw dirty clothes all over the floors. I feel as if everyone is dissolving around me,' said Mrs Peacock. 'Everyone and everything. Do you think I am going mad, my dear?'

But she wasn't, not then. That came later.

Invitations home became fewer and fewer.

As their happy day wore on Mrs Peacock became more fractious, like a boarding-school child not wanting to be returned after a day of precious freedom. She started dragging her feet. There was nothing more to do, they had exhausted the Shire Horse Centre's attractions and it wasn't four o'clock yet.

'You can't get tea out like you get it at home,' said Mrs Peacock pointedly. 'Or cake. Not nice and tasting home-made.' She was referring to Miss Benson's Marks & Spencer angel cake, a firm favourite of hers. 'And I thought we were going to have a meal in a pub. You did mention . . .'

'But we had a nice lunch here, Mrs Peacock.'

'I know we had a nice lunch here, but what about an evening meal? Where are we going to have that?'

Miss Benson was embarrassed. 'I can't keep you out too late, not the first time. We don't want to upset Miss Blennerhasset, do we?'

But the older woman continued to push for a way out. 'Why don't we go back to your flat now, watch *Coronation Street* together like we used to and then go round the corner to the Monk's Retreat? They do a lovely steak and kidney pie there, or they did the last time Frankie took me there. You could have the mushroom pasta. That,' said Mrs Peacock with a manipulative sigh, 'would finish the day off *perfectly*.'

Emily could see from the firm set of her face that Mrs Peacock was prepared to be difficult. Fearing this, and taking the necessary precautions, Miss Benson had purchased a large bottle of Booths gin as a pacifier to be given on the point of departure, but sadly she now realised the gin was not an appropriate substitute. If Mrs Peacock did not get her way they were heading for a scene and when all's said and done, what harm could there possibly be in allowing an elderly lady a perfectly harmless visit to a friend's flat for a piece of cake and a half hour in front of the telly?

After her uncomfortable sojourn at Greylands she probably longed to spend some time in an ordinary private home, and who is the timid Miss Benson to deprive her of that?

So here they are.

Mrs Peacock expresses an unusual interest in Miss Benson's flat, wandering round looking at things while Miss Benson is preparing the tea, staring restlessly out of the windows and she spends an inordinate amount of time in the bathroom 'freshening up'.

'You always keep it so nice in here.'

'Your flat was cosy, too, Mrs Peacock.'

'Yes,' she agrees, 'it was. Dunno what it's like down there now though, all those nosy parkers prodding and poking about.'

'Well, it doesn't matter really, does it? Nothing but bricks and mortar when you boil it down. Home is where the heart is, after all, so they say. You can make your home anywhere if you are determined enough.'

'You might be able to do that, Miss Benson. I can't.'

'No. Of course. Everyone's different.'

There is a pause as Mrs Peacock fidgets and looks about her. 'I might go and have a wander round in a minute.'

'But I thought you wanted to watch *Coronation Street*?'

'Not particularly. I feel that I need to stretch my legs. Cramp, you know. At my age always a hazard. You wouldn't know.'

'After the day we've had? You must be joking! I, for one, am exhausted.' Miss Benson feels a buzz of alarm. 'Where will you go?'

'Oh, just to the stationer's and back.'

'They'll be closed.'

'Do stop quizzing me, Miss Benson. May I remind you that you are not my keeper.'

Now Miss Benson is genuinely worried. What if Mrs Peacock does another of her runners? She might harm herself or get knocked over or end up in the canal. She comes hurrying from the kitchen, shrugging off her spotted apron. 'Wait! I'll come with you.'

'Miss Benson! For the last time, I am warning you. Don't you dare start treating me like some mutinous child! Others might feel it necessary to do that, but I would have expected better from you.'

'But where are you going?'

'I am going, Miss Benson, into my flat!'

Emily Benson is wringing her hands. 'But you can't, Mrs Peacock. It's against the rules.'

'Whose rules, I'd like to know?'

'And you haven't got a key.'

With a look of extraordinary cunning Mrs Peacock delves into her plastic holdall and brings out a key, holding it aloft triumphantly. 'Hah! They never took my key away,' she snorts. 'Naturally, nobody asked how many there were. And so, Miss Benson, I am going to let myself into my flat, quite legally, as the sale is not yet completed, and I will sit and watch *Coronation Street* there with my own bits and pieces about me. After that I will accompany you down the road to the Monk's Retreat for a tasty slice of steak and kidney.'

And with that Mrs Peacock turns her back on her friend, opens the door to Miss Benson's flat and marches off firmly down the cold concrete staircase. 'Come and ring when you're ready,' she calls back over her shoulder like an echo. 'I'll have my hat and coat on waiting.'

At last! At dear last! She is so glad to be home although the flat feels unlived in, and the dust is finally settling in the empty rooms.

She sits back in her chair for a while; her ankles are quite badly swollen after such an active day. To carry out her plan successfully she is going to have to persuade Miss Benson to help her. The art of persuading Miss Benson is to make her feel so overwhelmed with pity that she'll do anything to come to the rescue – look how she had behaved over those poor little veal calves. There was no stopping her then, you'd never believe you were dealing with such a timid, inoffensive little person. She'd strutted about with banners, she had laid herself selflessly down in front of lorries. Irene had watched her on the local news, marvelling at her tenacity. Yes, Irene is going to have to bring those ready tears to Miss Benson's soft brown eyes.

But *how*? How to induce such missionary zeal? The dream of one spectacular deed?

Pity, she reminds herself. Pity and anger – a heady cocktail.

Irene must play the victim. Good Lord, it's not hard, when you think about her predicament.

Irene's only got half an hour. Best not waste any more time.

A tiny rehearsal of the plan yet to come.

So, with enormous effort, she sets about gathering all her favourite personal belongings around her – the ornaments, the pictures, the photographs, the diaries, the books – everything which makes her separate from any other soul on this earth. She scuffles her way round like some small predatory animal, touching everything, endeavouring to choose. A vase with cats on which William gave her, her two special candle-holders, the embroidered pillow cases with their initials on, her favourite casserole dish, the gravy boat from the dinner service, the felt dressing gown with the hood, the wooden horse Frankie had when she was small, her Confirmation prayerbook, the bits of jewellery . . . what a mess she is making! What a terrible mess – like a jackdaw's nest. She doesn't take the pills they give her at Greylands. She pretends to, then pours them away when they're not looking. If she took those she'd have no energy at all; certainly she could never do this. She gathers her favourite bits and pieces round her on the floor and sits within the ring of possessions as if they are talismen against the devils without. And then, hardly able to see without her glasses, she starts to compose her letter.

Your Majesty, she starts in large, spidery writing covering half the first page on the pad. She must try to sound as pathetic as she can. She uses one of the set of pens Angus gave her last Christmas, all colours and thicknesses. She considers a red one most appropriate, red for royalty, red for emergency, red for instant attention.

Perhaps she should put her best dress on.

She has never tried writing to anyone famous before.

Please help me, your humble subject, she writes with cramped fingers and shaking hands; it's harder when you're on the floor with nothing decent to press on. *I am a woman of seventy-five, living alone since my husband died nearly three years ago. I tried very hard to pick up the pieces of my life after the tragedy of William's death and I know that so many people of my age are suffering just like me. I am not alone. Nor am I very brave. But now I find that not only am I a widow, but homeless, too, as my little flat, my refuge, is being taken away from me to pay my fees in a residential home where they are trying to put me against my will. Please don't think I am being mean and difficult, my husband fought in the war, but I realise that after a long and useful life I have now become a burden on my fellows. All I ask is that I be allowed to remain in my humble home for the few years I have left, with my things around me, comforting me. I can manage, I know I can.*

She has never written such a passionate letter. *What is happening to me now is so very frightening. I am all alone in the world. I knew that I could appeal to you and that you would understand.*
Yours most respectfully,
Irene Peacock. Mrs.

'Come on in,' she calls, when she hears Miss Benson's expectant ring. Irene remains seated there on the floor, head bowed, circled by her possessions and the image is so bleakly despairing, so intensely painful that poor Miss Benson rushes over.

'Oh, my dear Mrs Peacock! Oh, my dear. Have you fallen?'

Irene clutches her little bits to her. 'No, I'm just looking at everything, gathering my old friends around me one last time.'

'Oh, you mustn't—'

'After this I will never see them again.'

'Don't say that . . .'

'Why not? It's true. I have to accept it.'

'You've been writing . . . ?'

'To the Queen.'

'To the Queen?'

'I know that she will understand.'

Miss Benson glances quickly down at the letter. 'No one will understand this, Mrs Peacock. I'm afraid it is barely legible.'

Irene's voice is no more than a whisper. 'I can only do my best.'

'Here, let me help you . . .'

'No, no, I don't want you to involve yourself. I don't want to impose on you, make things embarrassing for you . . .'

'Mrs Peacock,' and Miss Benson bends and attempts to help her up. 'Do try and push up, let's at least get you up on the sofa. And if I want to help you write your letters that is no concern of anyone else's.'

'Oh, would you help me? I feel so alone!'

It could be her own mother speaking, God rest her soul. Miss Benson is touched in a very raw place. 'Of course I will help you. I wouldn't be human if I didn't,' says Miss Benson, revealing that stubborn streak, her pity aroused to the full. 'Not after seeing you so unhappy. But I have to say I don't hold out much hope. The Queen will pass this on to the local MP to deal with. I doubt she ever becomes directly involved herself. If she did, she'd never have time to turn round.'

Irene lifts a tired head and gives a courageous smile. This is all going just as she'd hoped. 'But I'd feel at least I had tried.'

'I know, I know,' says Miss Benson, laying a soothing hand on her arm and nodding her head in approval. 'And I will do all I can to help you.'

'Will you give me a copy for me to keep?'

This is merely the start of Irene Peacock's clawing for independence. It is much too early to reveal the whole plan. Poor Miss Benson has no idea of the lengths that will be required of her. But one thing will soon become manifest out of all this mess . . .

Irene Peacock might well be dotty, but she's not dead yet.

SEVENTEEN

Joyvern, 11, The Blagdons, Milton, Devon

Picture it. Imagine how you would feel if you worked here.

This arcade, once so full of promise, opened with pomp and ceremony by the Lord Mayor himself, is empty but for a group of kids obviously truanting from school. They lurk with their cigarettes beside the coffee machine, scattering stubs on the floor with the streaked marble effect.

Vernon keeps his shop door open, believing that by doing this, would-be customers are more likely to perceive it as consumer-friendly and enter. But who but the manically-depressed would be fool enough to cross this threshold? You can see by looking in the window that there's nothing there you would want to buy. You can see it is mostly tat, and electronic tat at that – all plastics and blacks, novelty telephones and travel hairdryers, surely nothing less tempting. How lucky are those, thinks Vernon, whose leases have already run out and who have hurriedly packed up and gone leaving behind them cavernous retail spaces scattered with packaging and litter. If only he could do the same. But he's worked it out, as long as the sale of the house goes through they can pay off what is left on the lease, cancel their debts and buy the flat at Albany Buildings.

Just.

It is as tight as that.

And that's what Vernon's got to hang onto.

His nearest neighbour, Mrs Toolie, who runs the gift shop four doors along, is readying herself to abandon ship next week. She has moved most of the junk she had left by going to car-boot sales, as she told him, 'Better get a few pence than nothing at all.'

'Absolutely,' Vernon agreed. But who's going to rifle through light bulbs, leads, plugs, a few cheap Walkmans and Hoover parts in some muddy field in the rain?

After she's gone that will leave him and the wallpaper shop, the clairvoyant, Madam Dulcie, who is hardly ever here anyway, and the card shop whose wares have gone damp and floppy from being displayed for so long. Hardly the sort of attractive package to attract the punters his way. He does not envy those hopeful few who took on premises in the new arcade. He suspects it won't be long before his own fate overtakes them. Some developer will build or convert somewhere new and better and more glittering, and so the vicious circle will continue.

Most of the time Vernon spends sorting out his papers, already sorted a hundred times, composing letters to hold off the bailiffs, and cleaning and dusting his listless-looking stock. Any repair jobs that come his way he undertakes of an evening. He turns nothing down, but still these repair deals that he made when his hopes were high cost him more than he earns. He takes sandwiches to eat at lunchtime but dare not leave and close the shop even for a half-hour in case a customer should come in.

So he is trapped; his failure has formed bars around him like the caged bird who failed to get away. His brain is working, always working, round and round the old questions: how much would they need to come out clear, how much would they make on the house, how much of the bits and pieces of stock will he be able to off-load at the end? He is making himself ill with worry, his doctor tells him that every time he goes for a prescription for more of his blood-pressure pills. And he must lose weight or he'll die. Until the house sold this week, despair blocked his every route of escape but now there is hope at last. *Is it possible that all might be well in only a matter of months?* These dark times put behind him and even, one day, forgotten? Sometimes when he thinks about this his hands, normally so steady, actually begin to shake at the prospect of this tiny glow on the horizon. He tries to dismiss it from his mind, fearing that too much hope might put out the precarious flame.

Joy confided in him last night but he was not in the mood to be big-hearted. 'I know you'll laugh and tell me I'm hopeless, but I have let it drop to that awful Adele Mason that we are merely renting the Swallowbridge flat while we do up that cottage we saw,' she said, going on to explain with her usual maddening logic. Vernon sat down in his chair heavily and tried to hide behind the paper. 'I did it for the children's sake . . . no need to look at me like that! The idea just slipped out and by then it was too late to retreat.'

Vernon sighed. Once he might have laughed and sympathised with his wife's little idiosyncrasies, like always taking five years off her age. After all, they make her what she is. 'I am not looking at you, Joy. I am trying to read the paper.'

'She believed me, of course.' She looked at him with exaggerated straightness so as to give some sincerity to her ludicrous words.

'Of course.'

'So I would be grateful if you could try to remember to keep to that little white lie whenever you happen to be out there putting the world to rights with Bob.'

She must invent a drama. She must never allow another soul to see her as she really is; even old and well-worn clothes might give some sense of herself away. She cannot abide decay or disintegration. Everything has to be new, artificial and strained and quite without flaw. Better still if everything and everyone was kept under cellophane wrapping. Vernon seems to be seeing much further into his wife since their downfall, and into himself too, no longer contented with the superficial stuff that oils so many old relationships. He has never forced her into giving away what she couldn't. But this time he was saddened by the glimpse of the real Joy, as disappointed, and probably as wistful as he. When she was young she had loved her mother, but as she grew up she had developed selfishness, and selfishness destroys the power to love. Oh, it's his fault, Vernon knows that. No monster is created without somebody sustaining the embryo.

It has always been so easy to give way to Joy, especially when your temperament is as easy-going as Vernon's. Theatrical and manipulative, it has always seemed natural to try not to 'burden her' and he'd wanted her to feel cherished. But there are so many fraught and important issues firing his brain at the moment that it seemed quite bizarre to Vernon that his wife should still be worrying over such insignificant matters as image.

'Will you do that for me, Vernon? Will you remember?'

Vernon groaned; he rattled the paper. She has so much more pride than he. 'If it's important to you, Joy, I will certainly try.' But her present suffering is pitiable. He can't help but see it as an exasperating betrayal.

Why is she so afraid of somebody finding out?

'Because they'll all enjoy seeing our downfall.'

Bemused, Vernon argued, 'Why would they? We wouldn't enjoy seeing theirs!' The moment he'd spoken he'd known he was wrong. She *would* enjoy it; she would derive some sense of achievement to see somebody else come to grief. Somehow she would feel that she had succeeded in keeping everything clean and sweet while they themselves had failed. That's why she is always so interested in gossip, in rumour, in fanning the flames of scandal. In finding comfort from the disasters of others.

'Well, I just hope you know what you're doing.'

'It's all so depressing. Vernon, we must keep them all from figuring it out. It's no good, I can't begin to be as brave as you.'

Brave? Vernon's not brave, just a sticker. But last night he couldn't be bothered to argue with her. If she wanted him to support her lie then he would, he supposed – if he remembered. For the sake of peace and quiet if nothing else. But she'll be hoist by her own petard in the end. The truth will come out and then she will look a greater fool than she's ever looked before.

It is after lunch when Norman Mycroft phones from the bank. Vernon has just finished his cheese and tomato sandwiches. Since the start of this financial nightmare he has never heard the phone ring without a shot of trepidation, ever prepared to deal with an angry voice, a supplier demanding payment. The awful thing is that Norman Mycroft's voice is never angry, it is always menacingly balanced.

'Mr Marsh?'

'Ah yes, Mr Mycroft. Good afternoon.' But inside he winces. This phone call alone will take him over his extended overdraft limit.

'I am slightly concerned about a number of withdrawals made on the Tuesday of this week, passed on to me by my colleague, Miss Grear, withdrawals pertaining to your credit card. As you no doubt remember, last time we met we agreed that those facilities were no longer available to you.'

What's this? He can hardly believe it. Vernon gives his immediate reaction. 'There must be some mistake.'

'That's what I thought,' says Mr Mycroft, slyly affable as he prepares to unload his bombshell, 'and so I made enquiries this end and double-checked, and I am afraid there is no mistake. Therefore I would be grateful, Mr Marsh, if you could make an appointment at my office as soon as possible, as this matter is now one of some urgency. Might I suggest tomorrow morning at ten?'

Is there no pity, no imagination anywhere?

Certainly not at the bank.

A moment of still horror. It is true when they say your heart sinks, but it is not Vernon's alone that now sinks into his bowels, but his throat, his lungs, his gizzard, the very hair on top of his head until he is nothing but a melted mass of glutinous terror standing there in his sad little shop.

It takes all his courage to make the necessary enquiry. 'Might I ask how much these recent withdrawals amount to?'

There is a pause while Mr Mycroft pretends not to know, draws out the agony as he peruses his heartless computer screen and lies back in his swivel chair, no doubt rubbing his managerial hands. 'The withdrawals to which I refer amount to one thousand six hundred and eighty-nine pounds.'

Vernon's face goes grey. 'But that cannot be right.'

The voice on the phone grates with a mild irritation. He has more to do in his busy day than waste time with wastrels and doubters. 'I assure you it is, Mr Marsh. We have the counterfoils to prove it.'

'To whom were these payments made?'

'I can't go into the details right now – I have a customer waiting, I'm afraid. But I thought I should let you know so that we can meet and discuss this soonest.'

Vernon lets the last heavy breath hiss out of his body. There is nothing to add but, 'Thank you, Mr Mycroft.'

'Right, I will see you tomorrow. Good afternoon, Mr Marsh.'

The phone goes down of its own accord, Vernon is too shocked to take any such positive action. If it's not a mistake then it has to be Joy. Joy, who is as well aware of the circumstances as he, who is in this trouble up to her neck just as he is, who is even more concerned about a reasonable future than he is. But she wouldn't! It is quite unimaginable that Joy, his wife of twenty-three years, would go out deliberately and spend money on God knows what when she knows full well what the consequences will be. God, he didn't bother to tell her that their Access card could no longer be used. He didn't want to worry her further and he never dreamed she would go out and attempt to use it, not at this precarious stage.

Vernon remembers . . . She was out on Tuesday when he got home. He had taken the opportunity to sort out some more bills, write a few more letters while she was absent because he knows how much the very sight of such awkward correspondence upsets her. She commented on it in so many words, when she got in, he remembers. She had said she was cheesed off with it all, and he had told her that he was, too.

Had he asked her where she had been?

No, he imagined she'd been over the road chewing the cud with Adele or that other so-called friend of hers, Bob's wife Angela. Having a companionable sherry or two with the neighbours, the very people she'd come back and vilify for hours on end. If Vernon ever asked why she bothered with people she so disliked, people who were so obviously inferior, she would answer, 'Who else is there around here to talk to? Since I gave up my job to work at home I am hardly the centre of a social whirl. I can't afford to choose any more, Vernon. I have to take what's on offer.'

Vernon sits down, feeling sick. He is hardly thinking, mostly staring. His head shakes from side to side as he holds back the tears. His eyes are wide with despair. He is dumb, empty and exhausted, for the most wasting emotion of all is fear. Joy! But why? Perhaps he should have shown more enthusiasm when she took such an interest in *Hacienda*, that ruined cottage. Perhaps they should have talked about it more. Vernon should have taken the proper time to explain just how much money it would require to make the place habitable, let alone bring up to the sort of standard demanded by Joy . . . gingham curtains fluttering at the windows, patchwork quilts on the pine beds, polished wooden floors covered with tasteful rugs, laundry room, en-suite bathroom, blue jugs filled with flowers and cushions scattered on the window seats . . . Hopeless to try and explain to her that the people who dwelt in such rustic cottages never lived like that, that her concept was as much of a dream as the very idea that the Marshes might be able to afford *Hacienda* at all.

Is Joy's shopping a way of exacting revenge?

No, that doesn't make sense either. This way she is punishing herself!

It is she who finds the prospect of homelessness intolerable, dreaming about mobile homes and the like. It is she who is already appalled by the thought of moving into that small flat.

Vernon is going to have to close the shop and go home although he knows that a shop closed early is the simplest way to announce to the world that here is a business about to pack up. Any customers will just have to lump it although he has to admit that a customer on a Thursday afternoon would be an unlikely phenomenon anyway.

Home, when he gets there, is empty. Joy, who frequently moans that she has nothing to do, has obviously found something, or somewhere to go, probably elaborating on the plans they have for the renovation of a cottage that does not exist beyond the confusion of her own sick mind.

Wearily Vernon mounts the stairs, unemotionally, deliberately, like a policeman on the prowl. How can he play the strong protector?

He moves across the bedroom towards Joy's wardrobe, turns the key and slides it back. There, still with the tags, with the labels, are some of the purchases Joy must have made on Tuesday. They are pressed in tightly, amongst the racks of other clothes, rank after rank of them. 'Never anything decent to wear, well, never anything suitable,' she always says.

Vernon catches his breath, swallows, and runs his finger inside his collar. Then he moves on to her chest of drawers, slowly, like an aged man. Going through his wife's things feels so wrong and distasteful; he is no better than a pervert rifling through women's washing on garden lines. But he has to do this. He can't turn back now; there is no other answer. Everything is neatly folded and smells of some sort of soap she stores in the drawers to keep her beloved garments fresh. He tries to do it delicately and with a measure of respect but his eyes do not want to look. Nothing can ever be the same again, and there, as he expected, hidden away under the slightly older jumpers, blouses, underwear and nightwear, are the carrier bags full of Tuesday's treachery, of tissue paper, of new wools and silks and cottons and lace and his own white unhappy fingers feeling.

He can't bear to face her jewellery box; there's a premonition of too much pain. He feels like a man who's expecting a shot in the back.

And he'd wanted to fight the world for her sake.

When Joy returns half an hour later, Vernon is downstairs in the kitchen smoking a cigarette.

'What on earth?' she starts. 'Where did you get those from? You haven't touched one of those for five years!'

'Where were you on Tuesday, Joy?'

'I am disappointed in you, Vernon. Honestly, what with your obsession with bacon and fried bread and chips with everything, what do you think the doctor would say if he knew you'd taken up smoking again? Nobody smokes these days. Everyone knows that it is disgusting.'

'Where were you on Tuesday?'

'I thought we'd have stew tonight. They were giving away braised beef at Dawsons so I popped some in the oven to braise at lunch-time.'

'Where were you on Tuesday, Joy?'

Her frightened eyes fix on him.

Vernon pours it all out in a broken and passionate stream, all the arguments, stresses and mortifications he has been putting up with for months, all the hopes this new move gave him, working up to a desperate rage.

She listens, scared, silent and staring. The old defiance sparkles for a second in her eyes, 'Can you blame me?' she pounces back contemptuously, attempting to claim the drama of the moment. 'After all I've been through . . .'

Her words are like stones that blind him. Damn her! Damn her with all her ridiculous blush and stutter, with her hundred punishing sentences already rehearsed and ready! Her eyes are hard, blaming and unloving. The shiver which he hardly noticed a few minutes ago now shakes and worries his body and his limbs. With the hurt passion of a child tortured for too long he hurls himself towards her. 'Am I never to get free of all this?' And he raises the only weapon at hand, the steam iron on the draining board.

'I'm left on my own nine hours a day, sometimes ten, while you're away at that nasty little shop and now you decide to come back early and have the nerve to go rooting—'

His eyes glare. His voice rises. '*What have you done? In God's name, Joy, what have you done?*' His eyes look like a madman's eyes and she is forced to recoil from them, and from his uplifted arm. His temples beat, his limbs shake, his heart plays tricks and he no longer sees, hears or feels anything around him. And then, as he hammers the iron down again and again, he feels his brain give way.

EIGHTEEN

Penmore House, Ribblestone Close, Preston, Lancs

Jody is home again, thank God. But it's a mixed blessing and he can't stay long.

The Middleton family once again feel like hostages in their own house.

He arrived under cover of darkness last night, two days after Len's nerve-racking visit to the park to give his son the money he'd asked for. When, on that evening, he broke the news of Jody's escape to a white-faced Babs and showed her the tabloid reaction, she acted as though she had just been given the news of a holy birth, prepared to travel 1000 miles with only a star to guide her.

'Where is he, Len? I must see him at once!'

'Babs, I honestly don't know where he is. He's with two friends as far as I gathered and I presume he is hiding out somewhere with them. Let's face it, dear, they'll catch them. Jody's case is the most notorious to come up round here for decades. He's the lead player and the public are baying for justice, so they're bound to pull out all the stops to put him back inside again.'

Babs scoffed scornfully, 'Inside – where he belongs, I suppose. Well, just let them try!'

Len hesitated, braced himself. 'I did wonder, for his own good, if we ought to turn him in.'

She snarled at him then like a she-wolf protecting an injured cub. 'Don't you ever say that again! You know how unjustly he has been treated and all because that cretinous girl won't tell the truth – attention-seeking, no doubt, making up all sorts of mischievous stories.'

'Babs, there's been no suggestion of that.'

'No, but I'm fairly certain that's what is going on. They wouldn't tell us, would they? We'd be the last people to get to hear about that.'

Len tried to take his wife's hand but she shook him off impatiently. 'For his own sake, pet, it would be better if he had never absconded . . .'

'He's out of that hell-hole, Lenny, and neither you or I are about to put him back in there again. Over my dead body!'

Telling the girls was a stressful exercise. But they had to be told before they saw the evening papers.

Cindy rushed upstairs in tears and Dawn just sat on the sofa sighing, rolling her eyes in disbelief, 'Wait till everyone hears about this! Oh no, oh no, so it's all blowing up again. No sleep for us, tears from Mum all the time, screaming headlines, abuse in the street . . . Why the hell did he have to do this to us?' She rocked herself backwards and forwards hugging a cushion as if she was racked by stomach cramps. 'Hasn't he already done enough? *I hate him! I hate him!* And you . . . you could have turned him in, Dad. You just don't see, do you? Both of you are as bad. *You just refuse to see . . .*'

And then she leapt up and followed her sister, slamming her bedroom door behind her.

Wearily, Len shook his head. 'They're too young for this, Babs. You mustn't blame them, they've been to hell and back.'

'And hasn't Jody? Don't you think he's been there, too? Sometimes I honestly have to wonder if any of you ever really did love that boy.'

'Stop it, love, stop it!' She poured out the cruellest words she could find in order to justify herself. Off we go again, thought Len, the same old arguments and tensions as before. Living on edge all the time as they tore themselves apart to discover where they'd gone wrong. Shouting, crying, blaming, blaming. At least, since the house was half-sold, Babs was a broken-hearted wreck but there was a sense of lightness, the chance of a new tomorrow, clearing the debris of the past. His wife would get better eventually; her pain would ease and there was hope of Jody's acquittal. But now with all the uncertainty again, with new life pulsing through her again – well, now she's back to the start.

She was instantly worried that the police would pick Jody up and deliberately manhandle him out of revenge. She feared he would be cold, frightened, alone – you'd think the lad was still a baby – and end up in more trouble at the end of the day, caught breaking and entering for money. She hurled her accusations at Len. 'You should have given him more! Only a hundred pounds? How could you be so stingy?'

Len was torn between upsetting his wife more, and sheer common sense. 'For his own sake I think I was probably wrong to give him anything at all.'

'How can you speak like this about your own child! If it was one of the girls you wouldn't think twice.'

'Jody's circumstances are vastly different . . .'

'And whose fault is that?'

'I really don't know, Babs, I really don't know. Perhaps, after all, it is nobody's fault, nobody's but Jody's.'

'Well, now we will just have to hope and pray that Dawn and Cindy keep quiet about you two meeting. They'll be questioned, of course?'

'We will all be questioned.'

'And are you going to tell the police that you saw him?'

He had neither the courage nor the cruelty to deny her. 'No, pet. No, I'm not.'

'Well, I'm glad to hear that!'

When the morning paper came out, the news of the 'dramatic' escape was plastered all over the front page. The focus of their hatred was Jody; the two other lads who'd escaped with him were on remand for far lesser crimes, dangerous driving and inflicting bodily harm. They called Jody a fiend in so many words, tried and condemned by the innocent words, 'charged with the rape of a twenty-three-year-old handicapped woman'.

And that seemed to say it all.

A police car was stationed outside the house. The Middleton family was questioned, but all denied having seen or heard from Jody. Their phone was bugged, their mail was opened; they felt like cornered animals. There were long silences in the house and much straying of uneasy eyes. Len stayed home from work in case there was a repeat of the attacks they had suffered after Jody's arrest.

The police were up to their eyes in it, dealing with the public's fury that a man accused of such a crime could just walk out of jail when he pleased. An enquiry was demanded. In fact, Jody and his mates had escaped from the local hospital, having first inflicted wounds upon themselves and then deliberately infected them. Easily done when you think of the primitive sanitary provisions in most of the country's jails. In the hospital lavatory they had overcome their accompanying officer and that poor man, suddenly a hero, was now in hospital suffering from severe concussion.

'But Jody wouldn't harm a fly. Is he badly hurt?' cried Babs, overwrought.

'There didn't seem to be anything wrong with him when I saw him,' said Lenny.

'Would you have noticed?' she asked sarcastically.

'I think I would have mentioned something if he'd been limping,' Len suggested quietly. He wanted to say, 'He's my boy, too.'

But Babs snatched the paper off him. 'Where were their wounds? Does it say?'

'I think you'll find the press more concerned with the prison officer they attacked.'

'More concerned with him than three boys who are meant to be innocent until proved guilty.'

He tried to make his voice sound kind. 'Well, that's the way of the world, pet. And you know that.'

'I certainly ought to by now,' said Babs.

It was that same night that Jody came home. Still an athletic lad in spite of prison conditions, he approached through the unlit garden, climbing onto the garage roof and from there in through the bathroom window. He secretly, sadly spent that night sleeping in his own room for fear of disturbing them, as if they could sleep anyway. It was in the morning, soon after dawn, that he crept into his parents' bedroom and woke them up.

Like a child having nightmares.

At first they were too alarmed to make out what was happening. 'It's OK!' With a finger to his lips Jody countered the fear on their haunted faces. 'This is the last place they'll think to look. They had someone watching all night out the front and I still got past them.'

'Are you on your own?' In the premature daylight Len shivered. Anxiety like a deadening bruise was a lead weight in his head. Deep within him love and fear struggled for supremacy. He stared into his son's bright eyes and saw no shame in them, only his own, reflected there.

'I'm alone, Dad. I left the others.'

'You're hurt, love,' Babs cried, homing in on the one thing she thought she could cure. 'The papers said you were hurt. Come here.'

'It's nothing, Mum.'

'Let me see,' she fussed.

Jody, this boy who still needed them both, lifted his T-shirt. The jagged knife-wound there was painfully inflamed, but only superficial. His mouth twisted slightly. 'I've given it a clean-up as best I could.'

'Come here, come into the bathroom with me and we'll do a proper job on it.' Horrified by the sight of his injury, Babs was happy now she could fuss over him. Anything physical she could handle, just like when he was little.

Lenny sat on the edge of the bed and heard the sink filling with water and the First-Aid tin being brought down from the shelf. The sound of gentle commiserations flooded into the bedroom with the shard of cold fluorescent light. 'How on earth did you do this, Jody?'

'It was easy, Mum. We had to make it seem like we'd had a fight, you know, to make it convincing.'

'But it looks like a knife. It must have hurt so much! What were you doing with a knife?'

'There's more knives and drugs in there than there are on the outside.'

'Oh Jody, love. You really need a doctor.'

'Daren't do that.'

Babs has lost a stone in weight since Jody was arrested and the marks of her recent experience – shock, shame, guilt, bereavement – linger for all to see beneath her pallid skin.

Len wanted to ask his son how long he intended to stay. Was he merely passing through or was this an open-ended visit? But he held his tongue. He dropped his head in his hands. He wished he could discuss these matters sensibly with Babs but where Jody was concerned she could no longer act in a rational manner. Nontheless, in this intolerable situation she must be made to see the detrimental effect Jody's presence here would have on his sisters. It was too much to ask of Dawn or Cindy, already so miserable and confused. Len, scared out of his wits to think that his son had spent one night here with nobody knowing, wanted to ask what would happen next, what was demanded of him and how he was expected to cope, as a father, with this new crisis.

Jody couldn't stay here in Ribblestone Close, not with the hue and cry at its peak. The police, with a heavier presence than normal would soon seek him out. Good grief, they'd see him moving about the house through the windows, it was as simple as that.

Len wanted Jody to go before the girls woke up and saw him.

In his dressing gown and slippers he followed his wife and son downstairs to the kitchen where the curtains were still drawn against the new day. Babs started a fry-up, Jody, his chest now expertly bandaged, tucked into cornflakes while Len put the kettle on.

Babs kept her voice low and conspiratorial. 'You can't stay here, love. You know that, don't you?'

Thank God it was Babs who said it, not him.

'I could spend the days up in the attic and come downstairs at night.'

Babs shook her head while Jody watched her anxiously.

'But I have to stay here, Mum,' he protested. 'Where else would I go?'

Babs concentrated on cracking the eggs one by one into the pan. She started to push them round roughly. 'You can't stay here because of Dawn and Cindy. They are already too badly disturbed. If it was just your father and me, of course it would be different.'

'The girls don't need to know where I am.'

Babs pushed aside the already browned bacon, leaving more room for the eggs. 'Jody, don't be silly. For your own sake you mustn't stay here.'

Scarcely noticing his mother's firm answer Jody went on like the child he still was. 'I've got it all worked out.'

'They are likely to burst in here any moment and search this house.'

'But I *have* to stay here. There's nowhere else.'

'We'll make sure you've got all the money you need and suitable clothes in a rucksack.'

Neither was listening to the other. There were two separate conversations going on in the room. 'Mum, they'll catch me the minute I step out of here. Please, please . . .'

'And we can always arrange to meet you . . .'

'How, Mum? How, when they'll probably bug the phone?'

Hot smoke from the pan formed a fragile dome around her. She dished out the eggs one by one. She spoke in a tired monotone as if she was alone in the room, as if she was talking only to herself. 'We can't have Dawn and Cindy drawn into this any further. We can't risk being accused of aiding and abetting.'

He pleaded then, for the last time, and Len felt his own heart breaking. 'I know how hard this is for them but it's me whose future's been wiped out, it's me they are telling lies about, and you know I won't get justice, the way everyone thinks about me . . .'

Babs raised her blue eyes to his identical ones. She fetched him the mayonnaise from the cupboard. 'But you can't stay here. You know very well you can't.' She lifted her shoulders as she finally sat down and pushed his breakfast towards him. Only Len knew how much this decision was hurting her. 'It's no good Jody, you'll just have to go.'

'But where, Mum, where?'

And Len, surprised, even touched by Bab's overwhelming concern for her daughters, turned away from them both and felt like weeping at his own helplessness.

*

He stayed in the house for the rest of that day, hidden away in the attic, and the following night after the girls were in bed asleep, Len let him out.

Nearly six o'clock. On the early morning radio news they announce the capture of Jody's two mates – Jody swears he never told them where he was going. They give out another description of Jody – tall, blond, freshly shaven, two earrings in his left ear – and warn the public not to approach him. If that's not defamation of character, what is? Janice Plunket's father is furious that his daughter's attacker is on the loose. There is talk of him suing the Home Office. Len is praying that Babs won't have weakened in the twenty-four hours she has had to think things over. Watching her nervous movements, listening to Jody's pleas, he has several moments of sickening doubt.

'I can't stand it in there any longer, Mum. They'll catch me and do me over and when they've finished I'll never get out of there again. They've stitched me up, that's what they've done.'

Her frightened eyes fix on her son. 'I know, Jody, we all know that. That's why you can't stay here, that's why you have to stay free.'

'*How*, Mum? If you turn me away I don't stand a chance,' moans Jody so full of misery.

She sympathises. She touches his hand. That awful indecision from which she has suffered of late has miraculously left her. She is back to her old, competent self again and it took Jody in need to work the magic. 'If we keep you here they'll find you. Believe me, Jody, this is the only way.' Her nerve is breaking, she is half-sobbing now and pleading with him as if it's her own life she is trying to save. 'Get out of Preston. Go somewhere nobody knows you – go down south. We'll be down there in six weeks' time if all goes well, and maybe then we can take you in or—'

'Babs!' Lenny warns her. 'Don't make promises you might not be able to keep.'

At last she is moving, doing something! She paces up and down the kitchen like a General on a winning campaign. 'It's summertime, Jody. The West Country is flooded with visitors. Take the tent and your mountain bike, and your dad's fishing gear. Keep your head down, keep out of their way and I'll give you our new address, but whatever happens, Jody, don't contact us here. Just wait till we get there and don't give up hope.'

With a gathering anger against the injustice that threatens to take his sanity away, Len steps forward and hugs his son as if he can protect him like that, as if he could weave magic round him and render him invisible. Babs joins in, clinging hard, reduced to tears of pain and frustration. How did their lives come to this? And where will it end now that it's started? It seems they can't go deeper than this, for this is a fathomless despair. Jody stiffens, sways, and steadies himself with the back of a chair. He turns quickly away but cannot hide his watering eyes, or his dismay. His mother's white-knuckled hand rests on the table, taking her weight, it's as if she can go no further.

And one and a half hours later, when Jody leaves the house with his rucksack packed and his bike by his side and money in his pocket, she hasn't the heart to close the back door till he's down the lane and out of sight. The same way she acted when she was his mother and he was her child going to school.

NINETEEN

The Grange, Dunsop, Nr Clitheroe, Lancs

Soon now, maybe in six weeks or even a month, soon they will be gone from here.

After six years of concerted effort Jacy believes that time will heal them. Time has certainly not healed Darcy and Cyd although they, too, took advantage of the expertise on offer at Wideacre House when Belle made a block booking six years earlier. The place has an excellent reputation.

Jacy has not even lapsed back into smoking pot since that whole torturous experience. Perhaps he lacked their courage, perhaps he was too afraid of death, of coming face to face with a power even greater than himself. Against all the rules, and under threat of immediate expulsion, both Darcy and Cyd made moonlit trips into town, sneaking out through the french windows to pick up the crack they craved. Jacy ached to go with them but his super-ego held him back.

They were dismissed in the end with a do-not-darken-our-doors-again warning, part of the strict discipline which is the linchpin of the therapy there. Self-discipline. Every expulsion had a salutary effect on the remaining wretched residents. Jacy, for one, felt inwardly strengthened by the experience; their ignoble departure gave him the fortitude to go on. He was being good and they were not. There were thousands on the waiting list ready to take their places.

Oh no! No!

Two men with cases and a tatty guitar. Lean, wolf-lean with skin as pale as cigarette-papers. They arrive at The Grange in the morning – filthy, long-haired disreputable-looking cases. By merely passing through the village they must have raised a few worried eyebrows. By chance Belle sees them first. They come staggering down the drive like poor Ashley arriving back from the wars to Tara and Melanie. However, Belle's reaction to the men in the driveway is markedly different from Scarlett's. *Snip snip snip* go her ferocious garden shears.

'Get lost,' says she, recognising them instantly. 'You know you're not to come here. I don't want you anywhere near here, or Jacy.' She lays down her shears and glances nervously towards the front door. Perhaps she can get them to leave before he spots them.

Heat and anger combine to itch her hair. The grass around the house is tall and unkempt, the bugs chirp from the beds of brambles and the sun sits hotly in the midday sky. 'Ah, Belle, wonderful Belle, bells on my fingers and bells on my toes.'

'Shut up and drop dead, Cyd,' says Belle with her hot fists clenched.

They are laughing at her. 'Now now! What sort of welcome is this?'

'No welcome at all,' snaps Belle, releasing the skirt that's been tucked in her knickers, walking towards them with the kind of haughty look on her face she wears for her most dramatic photographs. 'Go on! Right now! Turn round and GO!'

'You can tell who wears the trousers round here.'

'Too bleedin' right,' says Darcy, hands in his pockets, the limp he picked up in the streets of London along with other and various unseen handicaps, many of a sexual nature, becoming more pronounced as he saunters towards her insolently. 'Where's Jacy?'

Belle spreads her body size like a very pink sea-going creature under attack, she would change colour, too, if she could, placing her hands on her hips and standing square with her legs planted apart. 'Jacy, as you can plainly see, is not here.'

'Then we'll wait,' says Darcy, his smile wide, his stained teeth clamped together round the bent stem of a cigarette. Circling Belle, he wanders up to the steps of The Grange, dumps his Salvation Army suitcase and sits there prepared for a long wait, elbows on his knees. 'M'darlin',' he says, 'you know you have the breasts of a virgin . . .'

'Piss off.'

'He is not a well man,' smiles Cyd in his Liverpool accent, apologising for his friend while taking the space beside him. His long fingers start plucking at the guitar strings. He throws back his head as if to sing and calls out, 'JACY, WHERE ARE YOU?' sounding like a wolf lamenting.

'I'll call the police.'

'Oh yeah?'

'I'll go straight in and call them now. No doubt you've got enough dope on you to warrant a few years inside.'

'*What the hell?* Hey, guys! What's with you?' Too late! Damn, damn, damn! Jacy runs down the steps of his house with his arms outstretched to greet his old buddies, garbed in his tight denim jeans and his white shirt unbuttoned to the waist. Round his neck is a moonstone pendant. 'Hey, Jeez, I thought you two tossers were dead.'

'They smell as if they are,' snorts Belle. 'Offer them a couple of quid and they'll probably go.'

'Gee, Jacy, you look great, man!'

'I feel great!' He cannot swap the compliment; even Jacy is sensitive enough not to try. 'Hey, how are things?'

'Things are bad, man. Real bad.'

They do the old hand greeting act, clap, clap, smack, slap slap . . . and it's like some secret communication of brethren. They are back at school again, just little boys, in league with one another. Belle, watching anxiously from above, looks away, sighing heavily. Perhaps they will just have a meal and go. Perhaps they are merely passing through. But try as she might she cannot convince herself of this, she knows these losers too well of old. The next thing will be the old days . . . Well, they can hardly cheer themselves up by talking about life as it is today. None of them can do that.

'Ah God, Jace, we were real, we were there, *we were it.*'

Cyd rolls his sleazy eyes to the sky; the chords he strums automatically change from major to minor. 'Jeez, the ace life, the birds, the hash, the good days . . .'

'Never forget it, man, not any of it.' Darcy slurs his words and passes wind grotesquely.

'Not so good now, though, is it?' interrupts Belle.

'She's a nasty bitch, always was. Why do you take her along?' asks Darcy.

'She just won't go away,' laughs Jacy, winking at Belle to cover his mocking disloyalty.

'So hey, what's the score, man? You're still here in the old cool pad . . .'

'Not for long,' snaps Belle. 'We've just sold it.'

'Ah no, whaddayamean, sold it?'

'We are moving,' Belle enlightens them with what dignity she can find. She passes a cool hand over her forehead and that's not because of the heat. 'We are moving to smaller, more sensible premises, miles away from here.'

'Just down the road, actually,' says Jacy to her absolute fury.

'Smaller? Oh yeah! We believe you,' mocks Cyd. 'What is it this time – a castle?'

'With a bloody great stinking moat,' laughs Darcy. 'You'd like that, wouldn't you, Belle? You could operate the drawbridge – sit in the snooty gatehouse with your finger hovering over the button all day long.'

'Oh, get lost, Darcy. Why don't you just get lost.'

'And when you saw us come up the road you could wrench it up, chains 'n all. Cackling like an old witch and that'd be nothing new.' He roars with laughter at his own idiotic words.

'With boiling oil,' shouts Cyd, strumming more loudly now and stamping his delighted feet on the step below him.

'At least we'd be offered the boiling oil. Hey Jacy, we come to visit an old buddy and we're not even given a drink. That doesn't say much for your two best mates from the good old days, does it?'

'Oh, come in.' Jacy makes to ruffle Cyd's hair but pulls back just in time. Perhaps he sees something moving there; he claps him on the shoulder instead. 'Come on, what are we doing sitting out here when there's cupboards full of booze.'

They are drifting from one unrecoverable minute to the next. Belle clenches her teeth, she can hear her own breath rising and falling. 'No, there isn't,' she tells them with a fair amount of glee. 'I had to give what was left back to the merchants and they certainly won't deliver again. We owe them too much money. Jacy, why don't you tell these good ol' boys the truth and perhaps they'll do you a favour and leave when they know there's nothing here for them. The merchants won't deliver because we owe them like we owe almost everyone else around here.' She stands at the door as if to prevent anyone crossing the threshold, because in all honesty this house is all Jacy has left and if they get inside they will defile even that, put it at risk like its owner. She wants to thump them and push them and scream at them so they leave Jacy alone. 'That's why we're leaving – tell them, Jacy, tell them how it really is! The great Jacy is still slipping and on his way down, down, down, but not down to your depths, you losers, not if I can sodding well help it.'

'Oh shut up, Belle, and get out of the way. It's too hot out here and there's bound to be something—'

Belle's voice shakes with anger. 'Yeah, Jacy, wine smuggled in by you with the money I give you to go round Safeways!' Oh, what is happening to her hopes of fulfilment?

Indoors, in the cool of the library which is Jacy's favourite place because he can lean right back in his chair and put his feet up on the desk, his two unsavoury friends loll on the leather Chesterfield with their shoes off, looking ridiculous dressed in rags and smoking the outrageous cigars Jacy gives them. The stench of sweat and old socks wafts from their direction, gradually overtaking the rich essences of leather and cigar.

Apparently, and pathetically, they are interested in hitting the big time again. This is their excuse for coming here today. Up until now they have always had the decency to ring first, giving Belle the opportunity of putting them off with various plausible excuses. They have never pitched up unannounced before, probably because they knew damn well they'd be turned away. But this time, before Belle can work on them seriously, Cyd announces the portentous news, unwrapping it slowly like a precious parcel long awaited. 'It was this friend of a friend who knew this guy who was looking for old acts gone out of style. He reckons it's the old groups the kids want to hear – they're fed up with all the contrived stuff that's around at the moment, this rave hype. Well, Darcy was in hospital with his leg but I went round to see him at this place in Putney, a garden party with canapés and beautiful people swilling buckets of Chardonnay.'

'Wow. I bet they were thrilled when *you* arrived,' scorns Belle, from the brown-buttoned, brown-leather armchair, bristling with defences designed to repel any possible inroads. Her head is propped up on a tapestry cushion which itches her skin. 'Made their evening, I don't think. Or p'raps they felt sorry for you, thinking you were the local tramp.'

'So here's this guy holding court on some kind of stone throne under this wicked arbour of roses, could've been Caesar, with his big white knees bulging under his Scout shorts and these young birds in flowing dresses with rings in their noses and bangles round their ankles, dead cool, with jugs of booze with mint and cucumber floating about giving you the eye.'

'Get to the point, Cyd,' groans Darcy, fiddling with Cyd's guitar. 'For God's sake.' He holds up his empty glass. 'Woman!' he calls. 'Any more Scotch?'

'Get it yourself,' snaps Belle, still furious that Jacy had somehow managed to stash a ruddy great bottle of Glenfiddich in one of the desk drawers when she'd had such a raging argument with the merchant, swearing they'd never even had it. It's wasted on these two dickheads.

'Well, I told the bloke about us.'

'You must have been having a good night for him to bother.'

'Lay off, Belle,' says Jacy with a glint of hope in his eye. 'What did he say?'

'He was interested – particularly in you. Said he thought you were dead or something. I told him no, you were just resting. Waiting for the right moment to make a comeback.'

'So?'

Cyd lowers his voice. 'So he wants us to go round there. He wants us to put something together and he'll hear us.'

'You're bull-shitting,' says Jacy, spitting out shreds of wet cigar, wiping his lips with the back of his hand but never moving his eyes off Cyd.

'I'm not, cretin, why would I bother?'

'What's this guy's name?'

'Walter Mathews. You can read about him in any of the pop magazines of your Sunday supplements. He's right there, man, right at the top with his finger on the button, King Midas.'

Jacy kicks back from the desk and leans his body forward over it. 'You didn't make out we were desperate!'

'Nah. Course not. Anyway, I wasn't to know that you were, was I? From what we get from Belle it's "leave him alone, he's OK, he doesn't want to speak to you, he's getting his head straightened out, go boil your own." Even when poor old Darcy was dying there in the hospital Belle said you wouldn't want to know . . . speaking for you as if she's your full-blown wife or something.'

'So it's three cheers for good ol' Walt,' scoffs Belle, staring at Cyd with a harsh derisive pity. She wears a full-length lacy dress and granny boots, her cheeks are delicately rouged. Sitting there, slumped in her chair with her head back against the cushion she looks like the professional model she is, elegant even in her anger. 'Jesus, *I don't believe this!* Here you are, after all that's gone on, taking what this sad idiot tells you to heart. Think about it, Jacy, for God's sake. Why, oh why in this world would some talent scout with money behind him take a second look at this scum at some weird garden party . . . It doesn't make sense. I mean, look at him, Jacy! Just open your dozy eyes and look at the brain-damaged fruitcake.'

'It's true, you bag,' Cyd protest indignantly, his right eye twitching and jumping with irritation.

There he sits, this loser, this crack-head, this mental cripple, sounding for all the world as though he's made an impression on some bigwig in the music world, this unshaven, scruffy, stinking drifter from the gutter who couldn't even take a fortnight of cold turkey, this jumped-up, opinionated has-been.

'I know you don't like me, Belle . . .'

'Too dead right.'

'You never have, jealous whore with your acid tongue.'

'Jealous?' Belle throws her head back and laughs bitterly. 'Of what?'

His lips are drawn tight in a bloodless snarl. 'Because Jacy needs us.'

'Needs you? *Needs you!* Like a bullet in the head.' She directs her venom at Darcy and Jacy. On her face is that old expression, a defensive mask, almost motherly, of kindliness, self-righteousness and patience sorely tried. 'And have any of you given a thought to how you three are going to get any sort of act together?'

Jacy looks pained. She is aiming at the sorest, most vulnerable spot, like she always does. The last thing Belle wants is for him to take off again, not now she's so close to taming him, tying the knot, castrating him. His voice is desperate but determined. 'We could play around with a few old numbers, the ones that never made it. We could give them a face-lift, do some work on them. There's a grand piano in the conservatory—'

'Not yet paid for,' she reminds him gleefully.

Jacy picks up his paper-knife and fiddles with it casually. He is sprawled back in his swivel chair with a dreamer's smile playing round his mouth, a silent whistle on his lips. He stands on the threshold of some new world, a world where he was once indomitable, all-powerful. He turns his slow, hypnotic eyes upon his partner-to-be, cold eyes, all traces of amiability gone. 'Belle, go and get us some ice!' When she fails to respond to his demand he strikes the desk with his elegant, still-manicured hand, as if the wood is human flesh. 'We need some ice for the Scotch, Belle. Please will you go and get it.'

Their eyes meet. Her heart is thumping. And she thought she'd ridden out all the bad times.

She loves him. She loves him. The revolutionary spark of energy suddenly dies within her and gives way to that old lethargic apathy. The nervous smile and the shrug are stricken as she prepares to get up and go, to minister to the needs of the powerful as some women seem destined to do. Shaken, oh yes, but still expecting and deserving abuse, loud and reproachful. Jacy loves her, yes he does, or he wouldn't bother to treat her like this. It has been getting more hopeful for so many months and now suddenly it isn't. Hope fades when she looks at his eyes, she feels lost and lonely, her heels click on the hardwood floor and slowly she closes the door behind her.

Belle's tragedy is as simple as this . . . after all these years, if she loses him now she is left with nothing.

TWENTY

No fixed abode

Her encounter with Sir Hugh Mountjoy at the Brighton tea rooms upset Peaches terribly. It was unkind of Dougal to lure her into that sort of trap, with such a conceited, overbearing person. If these were the sorts of insensitive types that Jamie had to deal with, then who could blame him for proceeding with caution?

But who can poor Peaches talk to? Where can she go to find the comfort she craves? Jamie either can't see her, or is being prevented from doing so. Mags and Charlie are too prejudiced against him and Mummy and Daddy would be frightfully upset to discover their precious little girl was with child.

What began as such an exciting adventure has turned into something too awful. Peaches thinks of the opening scenes of *Oliver Twist* – the unmarried mother staggering towards the workhouse through the lashing storm, her limp and wasted body too feeble to survive the trauma of birth, her child a little orphan cast upon the winds of destiny. And it's even more macabre today, she considers, staring into her mirror to see if pain has altered her, to try and discover if there is something physical there, a hump, a scar, a withered ear, to differentiate herself from others as one who has suffered, indeed, is suffering still. Unmarried mothers are the scourge of society, in their squalid high-rise flats with their rampant, violent offspring setting fire to shabby estates and stoning the police. Not that she would suffer this fate; probably Mummy and Daddy would forgive her and support her, but she'd rather do penance than live off their pity. If Arabella cannot live with the father of her child then she honestly does not care what ghastly fate befalls her, she tells herself dramatically.

However, the indignity of banishment to some godless northern outpost, no matter how acceptable the house and grounds, abandoned and forgotten by her Prince – that has to be the worst scenario of all. They might as well just lock her up in the Tower.

It's bad enough going to the clinic alone, National Health of course, in that big, impersonal London hospital. James would take pity on her if he only knew. She has to get through to him somehow, she absolutely *has* to.

Charlie and Mags, to whom she was reluctantly forced to confess her condition, constantly demand to know what's going on. 'You're in a hell of a strong position, you know, Peaches, carrying a royal child, hell, and discarded by the father, left on the scrap-heap like a used condom.'

'That is not how it is, not at all,' fumed Arabella. 'You just don't understand. They are stopping me from seeing James, that's what the problem is, and as far as I know they have told him all sorts of lies. They might even have told him I've had an abortion, or that I never want to see him again.'

'If you played this right you could be set up for the rest of your life,' smiled Charlie in her silk pyjamas, sitting before the mirror and brushing her pewter-blonde hair a hundred times just as Nanny ordered. Every now and again she tops up the glass on her dressing table with a light Beaujolais. Peaches was sipping Ribena. She daren't touch alcohol because of the baby (her hotel lunch with Dougal was an exception, she needed extra courage that day), or buy sandwiches for lunch from Marks, or eat cottage cheese, or steak, or soft-boiled eggs. Oh, these are frightened times, and no wonder, when one woman in five miscarries before the three-months threshold. 'Or you could ball the whole thing up and end up a bitter, resentful woman with a problem child. From where I stand, you're balling it up, Peaches.' Charlie laid down her brush and came to put her arm round her friend's shoulders. Fresh from the bath, she smelled of silky, sensuous soaps and minted toothpaste. All around her messy bedroom, clothes lay in piles on the floor like the little white mole-hills on the moon. 'Come on, sweetie, threaten the swine. Tell them you're going to go to the papers. Christ, the sky's the limit. Tell her, Mags, someone's got to get through.'

'I don't want to be known as a fallen woman.'

'You are nothing like a fallen woman, dear heart,' said Mags, still in her curlers and her old Magic Roundabout dressing gown. 'You are a blooming, beautiful, healthy mother-to-be.'

'Don't be disgusting, Mags,' said Charlie. 'There's nothing beautiful about it. It's a hideous condition that ends in the sort of pain that's normally associated with terminal cancer. But that's not the point. The point is, darling, that you have been well and truly dumped on. You should have had an abortion. You should have listened to us.'

'She's not the first.'

'No, but she's the first one prepared to "out" the bugger.'

'I am not prepared to *out* anyone! I truly love James. And he loves me.'

Charlie and Mags exchanged rolling glances. At school Arabella's errant stupidity had a certain charm about it; she was never unkind, never too busy to stop what she was doing and listen to somebody's adolescent miseries, never too greedy to share her tuck, her money, her bike, her clothes, her shampoo – and she would have shared her homework except that nobody would want to copy such rubbish and end up with a D. She would never have made a prefect, house captain or head girl, she was just too silly and forgiving, ever aware of the plight of those less blessed than herself.

'She wouldn't cope with the publicity,' said Mags, holding out her party dress, balancing against the bed in an attempt to step inside it. She wobbled the words, 'It would kill her.'

'Yes, but you don't stay and face it, do you? You go abroad. They pay for you to go abroad, you lie low till the furore is over, and anyway, the whole point is that once Peaches has blackmailed them there'd be no need for the press to be told – they'd give her whatever she asked for. Oh Peaches, do think about it seriously! It would be killing. Imagine – a fugitive in hiding! We could come with you . . .'

'But all I want is James.'

'You are pathetic and childish and not worth anyone's serious concern,' snapped Mags, still struggling to insert herself into the wispy dress of silver slippery tulle. Strewn over the bed were puffs of cotton wool like dandelion seeds smeared with nail-varnish and lipstick. 'Anyway, you'll have to do something soon. It's showing already, soon it will be monstrous. Mummy and Daddy will have to be told. You can't hide it from them for ever.'

Peaches shrugged. She had learned to be patient with their attitudes. How could she explain to these, her best and favourite friends, that she had already been offered a house in the wilds of Lancashire, staff to run it, and an income for life . . . how much, she doesn't yet know. How could she tell them that the pressure was building each day as Dougal Rathbone became more insistent that she make up her mind for once and for all. If she confessed all this, their indignation on her behalf would know no bounds. Peaches was afraid they might decide to take some action of their own, in her interests, and upset poor Jamie needlessly. Arabella is still convinced that all she needs to sort out this mess is to see him.

If only she didn't live so far away.

If only he'd given her a number.

Funny how it was always Jamie who contacted her in the past.

She is secretly relentless in her pursuit. She has tried to get in touch with him on numerous occasions. The first hurdle she encountered was trying to get the number of The Family's Scottish retreat from Directory Enquiries. In a strange, conspiratorial manner she was treated like some sort of nutter; she felt she was going on record somewhere as a possible future terrorist. Saying she was a friend of The Family, using as innocent an air as she could assume, only made matters worse. She has written a dozen notes, careful in tone, but has received no reply whatsoever.

Still, she mustn't give up. At this very moment in time, Jamie is probably fighting to convince those in high places that Arabella Brightly-Smythe is the right woman for him.

This thought envelops her with overwhelming tenderness.

She is going to stay in tonight, again. She has not told her friends, but tomorrow she has agreed to go with Dougal to visit a doctor in an expensive private London clinic, 'because whatever happens in the future, it is essential that this baby be properly looked after, and, as you say, while the National Health Service is perfectly adequate for some people, it is hardly appropriate for the mother of a Prince.'

Arabella sits on the sofa with her knees up and her arms round a cushion. Perhaps she ought to have told Mags and Charlie, then they might realise the extent of Jamie's true concern. She sighs with a little flutter of pleasure. Thinking of that loyal and lonely figure she overflows with gratitude and love. She senses Jamie's caring hand in this latest development. Of course he would be concerned about her and the child, it has probably taken him ages to persuade his attendants of the necessity of excellent pre-natal care. Of course he would be concerned that his own creation should be no less than perfect. When she asked Dougal about the visit, he told her it would probably be the same old tests she'd already had, 'But you're not afraid of a few little pricks in the arm, are you, Peaches?'

She'll probably ring Mummy and Daddy later. Her hand itches to try James again but she knows there's no point.

Doors slam, followed by calls, chattering, laughter and curses as Charlie and Mags eventually manage to leave the flat, knowing that to persuade Arabella to go with them is useless.

'You'll be all right, though, darling, won't you?' Charlie reminds her of her mother. 'I do hate to leave you all on your own like this, and nothing on the telly.' Her quick eyes search her friend's face for a clue to likely unhappiness.

'I'll be just fine.'

'Change your mind! Come with us.'

'Honestly, Mags, I am perfectly happy to stay in.'

'And dream of the elusive Jamie.'

Peaches merely smiles. She loves their cheerfulness and their positiveness. They are so full of joy and life, and she's always wished she could be more like them, not so shy, not so serious, taking everything in life to heart. When they were young and at school Arabella used to think how sad it would be when they all grew up and lost this closeness by pairing off with men. What a shame it was, she thought then, that friends couldn't just stay together and live in communes and have fun. She used to worry a lot about this. She couldn't understand, in those days, what it was about men that attracted them. Boys were disgusting. Boys were rude and unkind. She hated it, she cringed, she felt personally wounded as, one by one, her school friends fell by the wayside. Tusker, of course, was the first skittle to fall but Tusker was unlike the others – deeper, darker somehow, forever searching, aggressively ambitious, competitive to a fault; she always argued the call at tennis and got banned in the end, for rudeness and lack of fair play. Belinda, she calls herself Belle these days, oh yes, she was first, with all her beauty in spite of the brace on her teeth. She was expelled in the end. How marvellous it had been to see her again, at The Grange of all places. It's such a small world. She hopes Tusker will look her up next time she's in London.

But Peaches was sure no one would ever choose her, although everyone said she was pretty, and the fear was like not being picked for a team in games, or picked last because you were the only one left. Peaches never excelled at athletic pursuits, she did not excel at anything. She was more of a dreamer, a poet, a lover of nature and quietness, a loather of competitive sport. But she knows now, she understands now how it happens, how men come to mean so much. Thomas the Tank was her first boyfriend apart from innocent childhood loves. She was amazed to be made so much of when she first came to London. Mags says the whole experience went to her head, but with Tom it didn't go to her head, it went to a more delicate part. She gets tired of being treated as a wide-eyed witless creature – OK, so she's not so bright, but she's always managed to get by. She loves her friends and yet their concern does tend to get overpowering at times, and their raucous jestings, their chattering night and day, yes, she looks forward to a night in the flat on her own and yes, she might well do nothing but put on some music and dream of Jamie, dreaming about what his baby will look like. She might even cry a little.

There's nothing on, but she turns on the TV all the same, just has it quietly there in the corner. It takes the place of a comforting fire, crackling away there in the background. She cannot concentrate on her book, so decides to play some music in a minute even though she knows that this will upset her. She is too emotionally raw for music or poetry at the moment.

After the news at nine she will ring Mummy and Daddy in Epping; she knows better than to disturb them between nine and half past. Daddy watches or listens to every news from eight o'clock in the morning onwards. All her memories are of being woken up by the bleeps on Radio Four, the shipping forecast with the volume at full blast and the wonderful aroma of bacon, coffee and toast from downstairs.

'A small crowd assembled outside the gates of Buckingham Palace this evening after the news of the engagement of Prince James was announced. The Prince's fiancée is twenty-one-year-old Lady Frances Loughborough, daughter of the Earl and Countess of Loughborough. Both sets of parents are said to be delighted.'

The conversational tones of the newscaster penetrate the dreams of Arabella as she lies on the sofa with her arms round her cushion – or her baby? – in a state of semi-wakefulness. Is this a dream? Her tired eyes focus on the screen in the corner, first to see the familiar sights of the people outside the Palace gates, more wandering around, lost, it would seem, than grouping together to form an actual motivated crowd, but now the picture moves to the hills of Scotland and there, calm and smiling in an open-neck shirt and a kilt with a sporran is James Henry Albert himself with his arm round the waist of a woman in white.

She appears to be carrying a basket of berries. Frances Loughborough? *Lady Frances Loughborough?* Arabella sits stiller than stone.

'How do you feel on this happy day, Lady Frances?'

'Thrilled! Absolutely thrilled to bits. Naturally. Don't we, James?'

A fuzz of loudspeakers thrust towards him. 'Of course we do.'

'How long d'you think before the marriage?' shout the excited press.

'A Christmas wedding, we hope,' says jaunty Lady Frances with her horsy teeth pushing out her smiling upper lip. 'Wouldn't that be nice?'

'Very romantic!' chortle the men and women of the press.

She licks her very dry lips. Watching, riveted to the TV, Peaches turns white. Her fingers twist and pull at her hair. She is the only inhabitant left in a dry, burnt-out world. All she can hear is a panting sound and it's her, a figure crouched round herself, pressed in agony against the back of the sofa as if shielding her body from more twists of the merciless knife.

'So how long have you known each other?'

'What is it, darling? One year? Two?'

'It must be two by now,' smiles the Prince. 'Didn't we meet at one of your mother's charity balls?'

Peaches doesn't know how much longer she can keep from being sick. Why is he doing this to me? she wonders weakly. I am prettier than her. She looks silly in that flimsy white dress, much too feminine for such a stocky figure, and look at the size of those breasts! There's a terrible hardness about her features and a preoccupation with herself. Arabella crosses the room to turn down the TV. The air in this confined space threatens terror and madness. She feels ready to choke, to beat her fists against the door. Her eyes circle the room wildly but they are so full of tears they see nothing. Damn! Damn! Where is Dougal's phone number? Somewhere there on the table. *I love him*, she screams to herself silently. *I love him and he is breaking my heart! Please, please God let this not be true. Make it some mistake . . .* She looks up at the screen again and sees James and Frances laughing.

She tries to dial, stabbing at the phone so it falls off the table and she has to start all over again. Dougal will have the answer, she tells her trembling hands. Dougal is a kind, gentle man, he would not see her treated this way. Hasn't he promised to take care of her future, even bothering to accompany her to the hospital tomorrow? 'Bitch!' she cries feebly, uttering that profanity for the first time in her life. 'The bitch!' she screams, beating her head with her fists, but it still doesn't help.

Wait, a voice warns her. *Wait. Do nothing you might regret. Sit down quietly and think.* Dulled, defeated and blunted like an edgeless knife, she puts down the phone and sits back on the sofa sobbing, her elbows on her knees and her hands clasped tightly. She must try and collect herself before she speaks to Dougal. Upset like this, she won't be able to make herself heard. It's funny, isn't it? This morning she had woken up feeling nothing but hope and joy that this might be the day when Jamie came to claim her. Tonight she will toss and turn unable to sleep for this blinding desolation where no one can reach her, where the comfort of friends won't even help her. And there'd been no premonition, no sign, not the slightest warning that today would be the very worst day of her life.

Did Dougal know this was going to happen? Did he? Could he? And not tell her? Or has he been trying to warn her and is it she who refused to listen? Now, somehow, reduced to this poor, defeated creature, she must either end it all or carry on with her life . . . the clinic tomorrow . . . facing friends and family . . . that lonely big house in Lancashire . . .

The clinic! Arabella sits up straight. Why are They planning to pay exorbitant prices to take her to a clinic when Jamie isn't remotely interested in the welfare of her, or her child? She's been getting medical attention from the start of her pregnancy, on the National Health. She has her own midwife to contact whenever she needs her. They have taken any number of specimens and samples and tests, her weight has been checked, the baby scanned. There can be no possible reason for any further involvement, unless . . . unless . . .

No! She is going mad! All this must be driving her mad. How could she even think such things, even They wouldn't dare, not in this day and age. They wouldn't find a doctor who was willing to . . .

. . . To do what? Abort the child – or drive her mad? Or both. So she ends up in some asylum drugged out of her mind. And if they are prepared to do this, what else might they be prepared to do?

Flight? Why not – it need not be difficult. The more she puts her mind to flight, the more the ache inside her subsides. She could lose herself somewhere in the city until the child was born. If she gets away, all might be well. If she stays and does nothing, if she goes obediently along with Them, her worst fears might come true. She could spend the rest of her life regretting that she had missed this chance. The more she thinks about it, the more inevitable it seems until it becomes a longing, a longing to escape, to get away, even if she has to take this pain with her. For her baby's sake she must flee.

She is mad with grief.

In turmoil Arabella paces the floor, one hand rubbing her back. She'd be a fool to hesitate; she should leave before the others come back. They would insist that she went to the press and that would make her even more frightened. It is essential she keep her mind on this and not the other matter, that of James' betrayal. She is better keeping moving, doing something. And she need not disappear into some dire hotel, she could quite easily go to Tusker at The Grange. Tusker would have her, Tusker would understand and look after her and help her to fight them all for the life of her child and whatever else They might be threatening. She won't ring up, she'll just appear. She'll hurry straight to the station and ring Tusker when she gets there. Yes, yes, this is what she must do . . . and Arabella Brightly-Smythe peers fearfully out of the window, for out there in the darkness, one of the Queen's Men could even be watching her now.

TWENTY-ONE

Flat 1, Albany Buildings, Swallowbridge, Devon

It's weird. Mother is behaving very strangely indeed. No more sulks or sobbings, no moans or protests or accusations of theft or abuse. She's even taken to saying a cheery good morning to Miss Blennerhasset and Nurse Mason, the little redhead she hates most. It is such a relief because visits pass so much more quickly when they can sit and chat about old times. 'Well, there's not a lot you can say about the present,' was the only jaded remark Mum made on Frankie's last visit and Frankie is grateful.

Miss Benson's steady involvement is obviously paying off. She has a calming influence; just to be with her sometimes, merely to listen to her voice with its Psalm-like modulations, can send you into the kind of myopic state you have to pay for through the nose if you visit a hypnotist. And Frankie knows all about the prices of alternative therapies. Since Michael left her two years ago she has been through the bloody lot. Seaweed massage. Reflexology. Shiatsu. Group and drama therapy and psycho-therapy at £40 an hour while you talk yourself to sleep with boredom. A load of rubbish. No one can really help you when you've finally gone down that slippery slope. It's no good shouting for help; nobody's got a rope that long – you have to scramble out yourself.

It was pride, of course. Pride was at the heart of it. As it usually is.

Anyway, she's over all that now and she hears about Michael's turbulent new relationship from friends with a satisfactory glow. The more miserable that unlikely couple – she could be his daughter – the stronger Frankie feels. If he thinks he's going to come back someday, cap in hand, expecting to find all sweetness and light then he's got another think coming.

Frankie was surprised to discover that Miss Benson was an animal nurse. She didn't expect anything that interesting; she was convinced the shy, inoffensive young woman worked in a bank or a building society. She has a building society face with features like an audit book, sensible, calm and organised. She could look into her driving mirror and not be phased out by her own starting eyes. She would never pick her nose while driving, or talk to herself, or wear yesterday's knickers because she'd forgotten to put the machine on. The only subjects on which Miss Benson gives vent to her feelings are her own mother's demise and the export of live animals.

In the short time she has known her, Frankie has gathered that Miss Benson was unusually close to her mother. They lived together for some years in a village in the Dales, until Miss Benson came south to take a job with a vet in Swallowbridge. 'I should never have done it, of course, I know now,' Miss Benson said, 'but at that time I felt I ought to be more independent. I didn't want to be, you understand, I just read modern novels and magazines for the new young woman and I felt that I *shouldn't* be living at home. They suggest there's something odd about you if you're still at home by the time you are thirty.'

'I know what you mean,' said Frankie, lulled by Miss Benson's voice, sitting in her plain, utilitarian flat with the shire-horse slate nailed above the fireplace, having a quick cup of tea before she left with a few more bags of Mother's belongings.

'Same as getting married,' Miss Benson droned on, not a crease in her starched cotton dress, not a line on her face, but a few beads of sweat slowly appeared over her top lip as her words gathered pace. 'They say you don't have to these days, but the message is still that you ought to. I mean, who wants to grow old alone, having to visit friends' houses at Christmas just because they feel sorry for you, and send birthday cards to other people's children? Who really wants to do that?'

'I think you're making it sound much worse than it is,' said Frankie, who was beginning to value life without Michael and his finicky food fads, his awful sporting pretensions and his overbearing manner. OK so he was a lecturer and she a mere secondary-school teacher, but anyone would think he was the mega-intellectual Dean of some University, the way he gave voice in public. 'Lots of women don't marry these days and if they do and it doesn't work, at least they have the sense to get out, not like in Mother's day.'

'But your mother had a happy marriage.'

Frankie turned down the Rich Tea finger. Miss Benson was dunking hers. She raised her eyebrows. 'She would call it happy. I would call it a life of slavery and hero-worship. Not an adult relationship at all.'

'But if she believes it was happy . . .'

'The tortured can be reduced to idolising their torturers in that twisted emotional wilderness . . . it's incredible what the mind can do. She was numbed into submission by that appalling poetry – a woman called Faith Steadfast. It is only lately I've realised that was not the woman's own name.'

Sitting here and chatting about nothing induced a companionable sort of intimacy between these two unlikely women. 'But poor Mrs Peacock wasn't tortured!'

'No, no, of course she wasn't actually tortured, but I do think she tortured herself, and that can't be right.'

'She talks about William with nothing but love.'

'I wonder,' said Frankie after a pause. Miss Benson should really open a window. The sun was streaming through so that Frankie's cheeks were burning and she felt sweat pricking her hands. 'If she was honest, she would say she loathed him for dying and leaving her. She hasn't got anything else, you see, not even me and the children. We were never important. There was only ever Father. Mother deliberately denied herself, like a nun entering an enclosed order. I've always considered that a fishy business.'

'Oh, I thought about taking the veil myself once.'

'Don't we all when we're little and being dramatic?'

Miss Benson hesitated before admitting, 'I wasn't little and I am never dramatic. I thought of going into a convent after my own mother died.'

'Well, there you are, that proves my point,' said Frankie, like a teacher slamming down a book on her point. 'It was cowardice that motivated you. You couldn't face reality so you wanted to find a sanctuary. That's understandable, if not very admirable. Certainly nothing to do with the selfless ideal of those supposedly called by God.'

Miss Benson's voice suddenly rose a notch. It broke towards the end of her speech. 'You don't understand. She was driven out of her home, driven into care by fear, by the programmes she watched on television, and the News she would never miss, and *Crimewatch*, her favourite programme. By the end she truly believed there were people with criminal intent surrounding her cottage. She didn't even dare write to me in case her letters were being intercepted. Her neighbours, people who had known her for years, were gone, there were only newcomers in the village. Yes, she was driven into that awful Home and she died there of a broken heart.'

'Surely not,' cried Frankie, appalled. 'Where were the Social Services?' How terrible for poor Miss Benson. No wonder she wears such a wounded look; what a shocking burden of guilt she must carry.

Miss Benson closed her eyes for the next bit. Her words hung in the quiet room like slicks of fog over water. 'Nobody knew it was happening until it was too late.'

'You didn't visit home?'

'Not for a whole nine months.' Miss Benson's voice was choked with shame. You could tell she hadn't shared this knowledge with many people, and it was obviously too great a burden to carry alone for long, festering in her mind. Frankie was glad that the shy young woman felt she could confide in her.

'I had an affair, you see.' Miss Benson smiled sadly. 'Oh, it was nothing, but I thought that it was. He filled my whole life. My every waking hour was given entirely to him, if I wasn't with him I was thinking of him, if I was asleep I was dreaming of him, and I really believed we would marry one day and I'd have him beside me for ever.' She looked away and closed her eyes, 'And there was Mother all alone and going mad with fear. And she never wrote, and she never said, and I never knew. You see, she believed that I ought to be independent, too, and she knew I'd come straight home at once if I realised what was happening. I rang her up every night, you know, I never missed, not once, but she thought that her phone was bugged.'

Frankie, such a practical person, found it hard to understand. 'Couldn't she have moved house?' she enquired bluntly.

Miss Benson seemed amazed to have to go on to explain. 'She couldn't cope with that sort of thing, not without my help. And anyway, the problem was all in her mind. If she'd moved house it would have moved with her.'

What a sad tale. And how guilty Miss Benson must feel. 'It's easy, when you're in love, to forget there's anything else in life.'

Miss Benson turned away. 'It wasn't just love, it was an obsession. I was a woman possessed and in the end it was my obsessive behaviour that ruined the whole relationship. Martin found somebody else. That was more absorbing even than the love had been. I nearly took my own life: I never realised such pain could exist.' She lifted her head and breathed in deeply through her pinched-looking nose. 'If I'd only visited my mother I would have known instantly that something was going very wrong and I would have moved back to the cottage with her, and taken care of her, and protected her. Mother used to love that village. She'd lived there all her life.' She lowered her voice to a sad murmur, her breath catching on the edge of her tears. 'She was found by the police, driven almost witless and suffering from hypothermia, hiding in a copse on the ridge above the village. It was winter, you see. She didn't know me when I arrived to see her. She never recognised me again, not before she died. And I blame myself. It just shows you what can happen when a frightened, impressionable old woman is left all alone with only the TV for company. And how easy it is to become a victim if you're alone and afraid.'

'It must have been a living nightmare.' Frankie looked down at Miss Benson's bowed head and fancied that she could see pieces of broken shell lying around her feet. 'Where were the Social Services, where were the neighbours, the church, the charities?'

'It's no good, I can't blame anyone else. It was my fault and it is me who should suffer the consequences,' said the undemonstrative Miss Benson. 'It's a crime, of course, but some would call it society's crime, the way we treat elderly people today.'

'I know I would want revenge on someone,' said Frankie. 'I couldn't rest until someone was punished for what was clearly a case of neglect.' She thought of Michael and how, for so long, she had wished for revenge, the bastard. After all she had done for him, cared for him, made love to him, worked and shared the family expenses, feeding him, respecting him, and then what does the swine go and do? Takes off with a sly little whore with breasts too large for her body and nothing between the ears but acne, someone so moronic it would be easy to impress her. And that's what Michael craved more than anything, the appropriate awe for his gigantic brain.

Revenge. Once it was the only emotion which allowed her to sleep at nights, and the sweet dreams of accomplishing it. How utterly weary she was in those first awful weeks after he left her. And for months her conversation was nothing short of a monologue of venom. Her friends grew weary of hearing it. They started to leave their answerphones on when she knew damn well they were in.

Eventually, of course, the rage burned down enough to live with, especially when tempered by juicy gossip about their present plight . . . The bitch is never in, apparently, and Michael has to do the cooking! According to welcome reports, their flat looks like a Persian slum, hung with ethnic curtains and beads and hairy mats coming unwoven.

Oh yes, revenge, when it comes, is a sweet soothing balm, but hers came a little late, unfortunately, for total satisfaction.

'Yes,' said Miss Benson piously, back to her old gentle self again. 'It is a question of values. I not only blame myself but this callous world we live in.' The strain showed in her face and in the muscles of her neck and her rigid bearing. There was something alarming in anguish so carefully checked, as if, under that mild and gentle exterior, whatever festered there was intensified to the utmost.

And Miss Benson is a woman of action, Mother told Frankie that. She demonstrates and protests quite fiercely over live animal exports and vivisection. So is Miss Benson really the best person to befriend Frankie's angry, bewildered mother?

Because of Mother's improved behaviour Matron is more amenable to her outings with Miss Benson. She is always back at Greylands before nine o'clock, in time for her bath and bed. She is less frosty with the staff and even exchanges little jokes, helps to lay the tables, to dust the mantelpiece, things like that.

'She is settling in at last, Mrs Rendell,' Matron told her when last she visited. 'It does take some more time than others. In your mother's case it was longer than usual but I'm sure the drugs are helping. They invariably do, you know.'

'Is there any chance my mother could be taken off them now?'

'Best not,' said Miss Blennerhasset, with a professional smile. 'Not yet.'

'And she seems to have accepted the sale of her flat. She doesn't talk about it much, of course, not to me. I wondered if she had mentioned anything . . . ?'

'I think that's where Miss Benson comes in,' said Matron confidentially. 'Mrs Peacock seems to have taken to sharing her little problems with her young friend, and that's no reflection on you, Mrs Rendell. We all know how much easier it often is to confide in those who are uninvolved. And Miss Benson does seem to have a wonderful way with the elderly. I did wonder if she might be interested in working in that capacity, there are so few people around these days with the patience. I myself find it hard to attract the right kind of staff. Old people in general are not particularly appealing.'

'Miss Benson works with sick animals.'

'Aha,' said Miss Blennerhasset profoundly. 'That would explain it, then.'

There's an underlying smell of gin in the room but Frankie decides to ignore it. 'You seem much happier, Mother, though I hesitate to say it. You're bound to contradict me.'

To Frankie's disgust Mother lights another of Miss Benson's cigarettes. 'Oh no, Frankie dear, you are quite right, I *do* feel more relaxed. It is probably the medication Matron gives me. It seems to suit me. I feel much better.'

Do Mother's eyes look slightly shifty as she sits here so much more perky than usual on the chair by the bed in her day clothes? Is she up to something?

'And you are enjoying your little outings with Miss Benson?'

'I certainly am,' says Mother, prodding the floor with her stick.

'Angus and Poppy asked when you were next coming to have tea with us.' This is a lie. Angus and Poppy rarely, if ever, ask about their grandmother. She has never been their favourite person. But there's no harm in pretending if it might make Mother feel better, and once the flat is gone Frankie feels she owes her mother more consideration, more attention. 'I told them I'd ask you.'

'Well, when would be convenient with you, dear?'

Frankie crosses her arms and her legs. 'Not this week, this week is out because of the German student staying with Poppy. We feel we ought to take her out somewhere new and interesting every day, you know. Next week would be better, but not Mondays, Wednesdays or Fridays because that's when I do the Play Reading Society.' Frankie frowns when she suddenly realises just how absurd her invitation sounds. 'The week after that, say two weeks' time on a Tuesday would be easier. Do you think you could make it then?' She will force the children to stay in despite their groans and protestations. After all, this is their own grandmother.

'I should think so, my diary is not especially full these days,' said Mother, puffing out a mouthful of smoke, but apparently without irony. She doesn't seem at all upset by Frankie's unintentional slight. She considers Frankie thoughtless anyhow. When Michael left home Frankie knew that Mother thought she was lucky to have kept him so long. 'You youngsters think that you can just go your own ways, but it's give and take that make a marriage, Frankie.'

'*Give and take*? What, you mean one gives, like you did, and one takes, like Dad. That's one way of living your life, I suppose.'

Mother's frail hand gripped the hound's head handle. 'The difference is, Frankie, that I enjoyed looking after your father. Doing things for him didn't feel like a chore to me. The more I could do for him the more pleased I was. And I had no idea how much you, as a child, resented that.'

'Well, it's not like that these days, Mum.'

'Then it's no wonder there's so many drift apart through lack of trying.'

'What did Dad ever do for you? Even when you were ill the neighbours came in to change your sheets and make your dinner. He never put himself out one iota. He never washed up, I doubt if he even knew how to butter a slice of bread, let alone boil an egg.'

'He had no need to because I was there to do it for him.'

'Yes, but Mum, what sort of a life is that, merely being a servant for somebody else? I had to work, remember. It was different for me.'

'But I kept William till the end,' said Mother severely.

'You make it sound as if he was a trophy awarded annually for good behaviour!'

'We will always disagree over this, Frankie, so there's absolutely no point in talking about it any further.'

But you could see Mother was gratified when Michael walked out. She didn't say so, of course, but her face closed up in that satisfied way as if she had finally proved her point.

And is Frankie satisfied, in some disgraceful way, to see her mother here like this? Is this Frankie's revenge? Surely not. No, that's an absurd suggestion, right out of the question.

So they decide upon tea on Tuesday the week after next. 'I am going to Miss Benson's again tomorrow,' says Mother with pleasure, changing the subject. 'It's become quite a regular little outing.'

'Miss Benson is very good to bother like this,' says Frankie, unthinkingly because it is just so hard to see Mother as a pleasant and chatty companion.

'I think it might be because she likes me,' says Mother smoothly, that old closed look filming her eyes once again. The effect of the drugs? Probably.

'Well, yes, of course, she must do.'

'It is possible, Frankie, you know. I am not a waste product. William liked me too, when he was alive. He loved me till the day he died, if you remember.'

She sounds quite triumphant, not herself at all! *What is Mother up to?* Frankie leaves Greylands this evening slightly perturbed and properly chastened.

TWENTY-TWO

Joyvern, 11, The Blagdons, Milton, Devon

It took a while for the thundery crashes to cease vibrating inside Vernon's head. What staggered him most was the speed of his violence, when he was normally a man of such a gentle and serious demeanour. He looked down at his feet, at what he had done. There, on Joy's ultra-clean kitchen floor, the scarlet had splashed on the new yellow tiles, keeping colour with the window begonias and a streak of the bloody gore had stuck to the shining photograph, the smiling childhood of Tom and Suzie.

He stood with the fingers of one hand in the fist of the other, both trembling. Sometimes they jerked spasmodically as if they wanted to carry on wielding the weapon and bringing it down and down again. *He is one of those men who kill their wives.* You read about them. You wonder about them. You imagine they've been beating their spouses up every night for years. Not cherishing them, protecting them, as it says you must in the marriage service; with my body, I thee worship . . . *with my body I thee bludgeon to death with a steam iron.* God help me.

It was the pressure, of course, and the unendurable stress Vernon had been under for the last two years, struggling to keep Marsh Electronics afloat and to make sure that Joy was looked after according to the standards she craved. The last straw, that last flash of horror, was the phone call from Norman Mycroft and the discovery of Joy's enormous deceits – rail upon rail of them in her wardrobe, pile upon pile in her chest of drawers – and all so useless, so unnecessary, so *pathetic*, those needs that had driven her to the shops on that fatal Tuesday to spend spend spend as if there was no tomorrow.

What sort of tomorrow will there be now? Vernon gazed down at his wife's battered head with dropped jaw and beaten eyes. How she would hate to be seen like this, with that expensive haircut all over the place – literally, as half of it had seemed to travel of its own accord and lodge like a sleeping cat under the kitchen table. She was wearing an expensive top and smart summer sandals. They couldn't be ordinary sandals, the sort some people pick up from beach shops – oh no, Joy's were expensive thonged white leather, Italian, from her last London excursion. One of them has come off and is waiting there by the bit bin.

And Vernon is a peaceable man.

Vernon sat down heavily at the kitchen table, removed his glasses and wept, and trembled, and longed for time to go back just ten minutes. Let her make her entrance again, let him be reasonable this time, reasonable as he had been for twenty-three years over Joy's little idiosyncrasies, knowing them to add up to the sum of the woman he loved, still loves, will always love. With shaking hands he lit a cigarette and inhaled deeply. Had she gone yet? Or was her spirit hovering somewhere in this room even now, beside the vases on top of the dresser? And what would she say to him now if her mouth was still a mouth and not just a gash of brutalised flesh in a face white, staring and horrified? *Vernon, how could you do such a thing. What will people say? Clean it up, clean it up straight away and use the Dettol in the left-hand cupboard because there's nothing worse than decomposition for germs, and flies will soon be laying their nasty eggs. And don't just put the cloth back after you, throw it away when you've finished.*

He sat in his chair as if chained there by terror. His heart went dead, it had to. His arms would never enfold her again.

If there was capital punishment he would be hanged for first-degree murder.

His heart started palpitating like a beast's in a trap. He would wait in the condemned cell with a few carefully picked jailers watching the hands of the clock go round, wondering when the hangman would peer through the slot to get a look at his neck and measure him up for the drop. Everyone in the whole wide world, the great, the washed and the consecrated righteous, would be indifferent to his death. His Queen and his country would not want him to be alive any more; not even his children would be able to forgive this unspeakable crime.

His head stunned, his thoughts a racing disorderly mob, his feet alone commanding his movements, he edged towards the cupboard under the sink for the roll of black rubbish bags. He won't use the dishcloth, that would be wasting money. He would use the decorating rags he had carefully cut up and stored for future use. He'd never imagined in his wildest dreams that these innocent rags would do anything more than wipe the dust off skirting boards, or dab up a little smeared gloss paint. Oh God God God, his body blundered on, wiping around his fallen wife, rubbing at the spatters and the streaks and the bits that looked like grey mince. Some of the jelly was stuck to his shoe. It took ten cloths to finish the job properly so that Joy would have approved of the cleanliness in her kitchen. While he was at it he also wiped the crumbs away from underneath the toaster.

The evening was warm, even hot. The air was heavy with garden scents, and the crushed smell of cut grass; children were playing somewhere outside. Soft, early television sounds could just be heard on the evening air. Extraordinarily, Vernon longed to go straight into the lounge, change into his slippers and turn on his own TV, have a glass of sherry perhaps and glance at the evening paper. How lucky were those who were doing just that this evening, moaning because they were bored with nothing better to do. He longed to assure them how lucky they were. He desperately wanted life to go on as usual. In spite of the murder, his appointment with Normam Mycroft tomorrow still loomed large in his mind, almost too large to cope with. He had annihilated his wife but not managed to avoid the confrontation that he knew must come. Menace was everywhere. Almost, he would prefer to give himself up to the police so that he would be in custody when Norman Mycroft sat back in his office tomorrow and pressed the bell for Vernon to enter. Anyone would think the two events, his wife's murder and a meeting at the bank, were equal in terms of total horror. The idea of suicide drew him close, for very lovely seemed the white emptiness, the forgetful sleep that lay beyond death, where Joy had already gone. But Vernon reached for the brandy bottle and poured out half a glass while trying to decide what to do next.

He twirled his glass and stared morosely through it. He must think of the children, Suzie and Tom. They must be his first priority.

He must get his finances straight.

He must continue with the sale of the house.

He must do something with the body on the kitchen floor.

The cavernous chambers of his brain slowly flooded with the golden liquid, soothing first, calming his grim meditations down and eventually, as he poured a second, and then a third, lit his senses brilliantly until he felt briefly equal to anything. By now Vernon's conscience was oddly fuddled and confused; only furtiveness and a desire for self-preservation were left.

Could Vernon pretend that some violent villain had broken in and battered his wife to death sometime during the afternoon while he was at work? He thought about that for a while. There were bound to be witnesses who had seen him locking up his shop to come home, and others who had noticed the car passing by and him parking it in the drive. These days it is easy for the police to find the most minuscule clues. No matter what he did with his clothes or his hands or his hair they would find traces of his crime somewhere about his person. Anyway, why would a thief break into Joyvern and be prepared to commit such a heinous crime? Their bits and pieces might have been very dear to Joy's possessive heart, but they were hardly worth a fortune. No, Vernon cannot pass the murder off and blame it on somebody else. That just wouldn't work.

What if he put her in the car and drove to some remote cliff top – he knows the very place – and sent the car crashing down onto the rocks below? He could tell with hysterical horror how he jumped clear at the very last moment. If he filled the petrol tank first, the blue Ford would probably burst into flames and there'd be little of Joy left for the forensic people to examine, would there? But to set up such a stunt would take some doing. He'd just have to hope that nobody was around to notice his nefarious antics. But even at night there are lovers, especially in places where there's a dramatic view of the sea, and wouldn't there be clues left on the grass . . . footprints, tyre-tracks – and what would the Marshes be doing so close to the edge of the cliff anyway? Vernon took another swig out of his third glass; the liquid ran hot and comforting through his nervous body. As it permeated his being he felt more and more hopeful, enlarged, sanguine, even grandiose. As the glow of assurance brightened, the old timorous caution faded so that he wondered how he had ever been at its mercy and the idea came to him in the distance, coming closer as he concentrated harder like one of those Magic Eye pictures you have to stare at to make sense of. And there it was, suddenly, standing out as clear as day as if some jumbled kaleidoscope had been given the correct turn.

Joy had wanted the ruined cottage, *Hacienda*, to be her final home. He sat and considered the place, what he remembered of it, and then went to fetch the brochure from the cupboard. He studied it as well as he could through his boozy eyes. There was nothing much about the well in the garden, no measurements to describe its depth, whether it was dry, or broken, or functioning, or contaminated over the years. But Vernon knew it was most unlikely that anyone would bother to use it as a well, not in these days of intensive hygiene, washing machines and dish-washers that require gallons at a time. People are very particular about the water they drink these days.

Should he declare Joy missing?

At what point should he declare it?

Wouldn't it be reasonable for Joy to move first in order to prepare the temporary flat she'd told everyone about, while Vernon stayed behind in the house until the contracts were signed, until it was finally time to move out?

In certain circumstances some people do that, don't they?

Nothing in his life had prepared him for anything like this. A humane and sensitive man, Vernon was not a fan of medical dramas, or war films. Even the violence in some of the soaps upset him and his own family life was free of loud disagreements, old-fashioned if you like, certainly mundane and so he could never bear to confront Joy at her worst extremes, with her penchant for social drama and shopping, preferring to bend with the wind and wait till her moods were over. The Invisible Man, he supposed.

Vernon was consumed with a desire to sleep, but the first thing he had to do was run the car into the garage. *He must stick to his usual habits.*

Then, while Joy was still free of rigor mortis, he must get her through the door that led directly from the kitchen into the garage, and bundle her into the passenger seat. Hurry, hurry, before anyone called or the phone went and caught him speechless.

Joy was lying relaxed, legs apart, arms above her mangled head as a small child sleeps. The wetness that spread over Vernon's face in his efforts to move her was not just sweat; there were tears there too, for he was a harmless man. He tried a gentle approach so as not to wound her further. He must block her away from his senses, this woman who was not Joy any more. After the black rubbish bag he must wrap her in a blanket. He fetched the rug from the car and rolled her over onto the bright red tartan. He dragged his gory burden through to the garage, opened the passenger door and struggled to lift her inside. She was a small woman, but heavy and hard to manoeuvre. He could not believe this was real life. These are things which happen to other people, never to oneself. With tautened hearing he listened for the slightest sound. If someone stumbled upon him now about his sinister business he would give himself up straight away and confess to everything. Such an action would almost be a relief. He felt boxed in, in the garage – entombed, already cut off from ordinary life, the birdsong, the sigh of the wind, the falling of sunset down the sky and the visits of the stars. He slipped the bin bag and the blanket down so the top of her body was exposed. Then he arranged her but she, slack and untidy in death, flopped against the seat belt, but ended up as though she was naturally searching for something in the glove compartment.

That would have to do for now.

Vernon bathed and put his clothes in the washing machine.

He heated up some beans and took a pork pie out of the fridge. He had it with bread and butter and pepper and great dunks of piccalilli. After his meal he washed up the plate and the pan and then, with the passing of time, the terrible passing of time and four cups of black coffee, he readied himself to lie to his children.

It was essential that he did not stutter or fumble; as it was he was forced to pause in order to clear his throat. 'Mum's gone to the flat already. There's so much to be done and you know what she's like.'

'Why on earth didn't she ring me herself and say goodbye?' asked Suzie.

'Because it all happened in rather a rush. The old lady who lived there is already in a Home and the daughter said she was worried about the flat standing there empty. She'd let us move in early, she said, and it seemed the most sensible course to take.'

Suzie sounded doubtful. 'But will Mum be all right on her own, without you?'

'It was her idea,' said Vernon, fighting to justify his words. 'I think she feels pretty restless, moving out of Joyvern after so long. The strain of waiting was beginning to tell. It's probably better that she's gone early.'

'I still don't know why you decided to make that move. It seems crazy,' said Suzie. 'I mean, lots of people live in houses that are too big, but they don't have to move somewhere smaller for no other reason. Mum loves that house . . .'

Damn Joy's lies. Vernon bit at a nail and noticed a fleck of blood underneath the skin. Oh dear God. His or Joy's? 'I know, but to tell you the truth I think Mum was beginning to find the work too much.'

Suzie's voice took on an anxious edge. 'She is all right, isn't she, Dad? I mean, first she gives up driving the car because it's getting too stressful, and now she's decided to move out of the house she loves. And then you say you're retiring before you have to. I really don't understand what's going on.'

'It's silly to work when you don't need to,' said Vernon, going along with another of Joy's silly lies. He gave his voice a studied carelessness, a very far cry from his true feelings. 'But more important than that I feel I want to be around to look after your mother.'

'You've always looked after her. She depends on you totally. Why the sudden intense concern?'

Vernon paused for effect. He took another gulp of brandy. Wonderful how easily his part slipped over him. 'Joy has been having some problems lately.'

'What problems?'

'Oh, nothing much,' said Vernon lightly, puffing hard on his cigarette. 'Just the kind of mild depressions that come on in middle age, nothing serious, nothing for you to worry about, but I feel I could help by being around and taking her out and about during the day. Create a few pleasant diversions. Why not, after all?'

'Well, you've certainly earned it, Dad. But I hope Mum's OK. Perhaps I should come down . . .'

'Not while we're in this mess, Suzie. You know how your mother needs to create a perfect front. Wait till the flat's all sorted out and we're both settled into our new way of life. By then she'll be much more cheerful, I'm sure.'

'But Dad, should she be alone, feeling low like you say?'

The muscles tightened in Vernon's face as he battled to hold his own. 'She won't be, most of the time. I'll see her most days and we'll spend most evenings over there. What she needs are diversions, and the flat will give her lots of leeway, preparing it all, curtains and wallpapers and colour schemes – you know the sort of thing she's always been so good at. And it's much closer to the shops than it is here. She can hop on a bus and be there in five minutes.'

'Well, I suppose it sounds like the sensible thing. Perhaps you two should go on holiday when all this is over, take that cruise you promised yourselves. But keep in touch, Dad, let me know how she's going on. I'll write to her. What's the new address?'

'Send it here and I'll see she gets it. It would be too confusing for the Post Office until we're officially over there.'

'Fine. Fine. I'll do that. Take care, Dad, and it's nice to hear you again.'

Vernon had much the same kind of standard conversation with Tom, except Tom was less interested, too immersed in his new wife and baby, and his career was taking up most of his time. No, Vernon hadn't been half as worried about Tom's reaction as he'd been about Suzie's.

A sleepless night, pacing the floor, wandering round or standing still while he bit at a nail or pulled at a finger, his face drawn, his hands

shaking and sheer fright in his eyes. The effects of the brandy had long
worn off leaving him weaker, worse than before to deal with the time
on his hands. Once he dropped off for a moment, and woke, forgetting
what had happened, believing this was an ordinary night until one
heartbeat later he remembered with awful realisation where he was
and what he had done. Only five minutes gone since last he glanced at
his watch. He couldn't open the garage door, he couldn't even walk
near it yet. Tomorrow he would have to get in beside Joy, wave
breezily at the neighbours and drive her away from Joyvern for ever as,
with one lifeless hand, she grovelled in the glove compartment for a
sweet which wasn't there.

TWENTY-THREE

Penmore House, Ribblestone Close, Preston, Lancs

His untidy hair hung in his eyes – already it was itching, he'd left his comb at home – when he heard the car arrive about nine-thirty this morning. When Jody Middleton, fugitive from the law, Lancashire's most wanted man, homeless drifter, when Jody saw what this guy was up to he nearly shouted out loud.

He'd come upon the old ruin last night after he left the station at Plymouth and started heading for the vast outdoors, the wild and lonely ranges of Dartmoor. Different from the last time he was down this way, on holiday with the family, all excited with buckets and spades and eager to get to the big white house at Marazion. Jody liked to spend his holiday money on the first day, on plastic boats and buckets and spades and flags and cars he could run through the tracks he dug and not worry if they got lost. Dawn, the youngest, saved hers and went home with more than she came with, and Cindy, just two years younger than he, spent the whole lot on dolls and dolls' clothes.

Incredible, he was so unfit. A few months' incarceration really takes it out of you. Sweat rolled off him as he pedalled along on his mountain bike, feeling like a fugitive decked out in the pair of Dad's khaki shorts Mum made him put on before he left the Close, because, she said, khaki made him look more like anyone else in this weather. She made him leave his own gaudy cycle shorts behind.

They'd never been critical of the clothes he wore and the friends he made and the music he loved. They were the world's best parents. Other kids used to envy him and it was always his house they went to when he and his friends had a choice. There were the difficult times, of course, like the day when he'd stripped a pear tree, risking life and limb so he could share the fruit with his two sisters. The farmer caught him at it and Dad forced him to go round and apologise, red-faced with humiliation. He'd hated Dad then, really hated him. It wasn't until much later that he saw that Lenny was only being fair.

But sometimes Jody wished he could live up to his mother's high opinion of him. Why couldn't he? Was there something wrong with his head? Well, he's finished with all that childish stuff now, hasn't he. The shrinks will probably find out he's mad.

Aching in every limb, weakened by his spell inside and the grey diet of tasteless food, he knew he must stop or he'd never be able to get up tomorrow. He turned down a lane which looked pretty convenient, grass growing up the centre, wild brambles and other green rubbish double-decker high on either side, dark already, hardly the sort of welcoming place any tourist would turn down, even by accident. Half a mile on and he found this ruin, more of a spindly silhouette than a building of substance and bang in the middle of nowhere, rough brown fields tilted away on all sides, rising steadily and merging in shadows until they met a rocky horizon.

He liked this sort of scenery. He'd always loved the moors at home, feeling so small standing against them – sometimes he leaned and the wind held him up. They told him how little he mattered, that he'd be dead and gone long before he could understand what they were saying. He liked that feeling. He'd heard that scientists had sent up whale sounds in the satellite headed beyond our galaxy, believing that whale language was the most likely of all to be understood by aliens. Jody was greatly moved by this; he thought he might understand it, too, better than he understands some of the batty things people say. When he thinks about this he reckons some of his music is trying to talk about ideas like this.

He fell off his bike with relief – his bum felt raw, his sweltering back was a sea of sweat. He couldn't imagine himself travelling much further in his new role of lone student, or birdwatcher – this was really one of Mum's more way-out suggestions. She believes in him, she really does; she's always gone round telling everyone that Jody is university material, that he's so good-looking he'll cop it some day, and won't his dad be proud of him when he gets to play football for England. Jody wouldn't have minded if just one of her dreams was even halfway to coming true. University – yes, he managed that one all right, or nearly did until he gave Janice Plunket a lift. That part was easy. But some of Mum's dreams he wasn't so sure of. Jody loved his football and cricket and he was good, he *excelled*, at both, but as far as playing for England went, he would have to disappoint her, and to disappoint Mum upset him terribly. Look at him now, he couldn't have done a worse job, could he?

She was so OTT. She came to everything they put on at school; even when Jody had a walk-on part he could hear her cheering in the audience. Later, however he'd done it, she would call him talented. He lied once, and said he'd lost three recorders just because he couldn't play *Greensleeves*. Sometimes he wanted to yell at her, to stop and ask her – *what if he was just ordinary?* What would she honestly think of him then? Cindy and Dawn were far more likely to make the grade than Jody was.

'You've just got to have more confidence in yourself, Jody,' Mum used to tell him. 'Like I have.'

He wheeled his way up the tangled path, crossing a broken FOR SALE sign stripped of its colour by the sun and the wind. No chance. No one would risk their arm by throwing good money into this place.

Jody, alone and forlorn, had taken the risk of travelling by train from Preston to Plymouth. They'd put his bike in the luggage van along with the mail and the travelling animals. If they'd known who he was he'd have been crated up like those poor creatures. He'd been so upset when he got on the train he'd thrown caution to the winds. They might as well catch him and get it over and done with. I mean, even Mum was against him now. 'For his own good,' she'd said, she'd sent him away from the only place of safety he had. 'Because we love you, son,' said Dad.

When he thought about Dad, he wanted to cry, remembering some of the stupid old things they had done together, father and son. Like eating hot chips out of paper in the car on a freezing cold day, like when Dad ran behind him mile after mile when Jody got his first bicycle – he fell off laughing at the sound of Lenny's puffing – like when Dad broke the model Jody had half-completed, just trying to join in and be helpful, like when Dad sat all day waiting with him for his broken arm to be set at the hospital . . . And now Jody's let him down. He has let Dad down although he is innocent of the crime. He has let him down anyhow. The accusation is enough.

The thought of his two mates being arrested so quickly made Jody's blood run cold. The police seemed to be everywhere. He added up his own chances because his only relief was to play with hope. He pretended to sleep most of the way with his face nearly stuck to the grimy window of the Inter-City train. He supposed it made sense to abandon his old haunts, to hide out down here until Mum and Dad made their move. It might only be four or five weeks, and if this warm weather held out he'd be OK. He'd manage somehow even if it meant living constantly on his wits. Lucky it wasn't mid-winter – you could easily die out here. He'd got their new address somewhere in Cindy's rucksack; he'd go and see if he could find it tomorrow, just for something to do. He supposed they blamed him for having to move –

and they're right. It *is* his fault, isn't it? He should never have touched Janice Plunket.

So he'd found this abandoned shack, its name, *Hacienda*, hung on the half-rotten frame of the door, he'd eaten a couple of apples and broken into Mum's coffee cake, not particularly hungry though because he'd had a bacon roll on the train, and he'd burnt his lip on bits of red-hot hanging tomato. He sat slouched against the dusty walls of what must once have been a kitchen watching the shadows form in the first presage of the dark. He was exhausted. With his head uncomfortably propped on the rucksack he sank into a death-like sleep, more of a coma because the next thing he knew it was bright daylight. What time was it? He dragged his aching body into a sitting position. Thirst constricted his throat; he needed a drink badly. He'd just pulled the cap off a can of Coke, about to be overwhelmed by gloom, no fried breakfast for him then, when he heard the engine. He froze. He'd left his mountain bike in the overgrown back garden, hadn't he, idiot – but how had the law tracked him down so quickly?

There was no escape from here. Maybe he should have considered that and staked the place out before he settled. There was no cover as far as the eye could see in any direction; it reminded him of the moors of home. Once he'd bolted from his hiding place he'd stand out like a telegraph pole.

Jody, wide-awake with fright now, scrambled up the broken staircase, brushed the rubble and old distemper that crumbled and clattered as he touched the walls and trusted his luck to the buckling floorboards. What a dump. Who would ever want to live out here? The bedroom window was missing, it was positioned so low in the bulging wall that as he crouched there on the floor he had a view of the garden. He couldn't see his bike from here, he'd thrown it down without thinking and it must have been gobbled up in the nettles.

He heard the strange guy come in, heard him walking around downstairs with a slow, steady tread, heard him light a cigarette as he stood there silently – listening? Jody could almost hear the guy thinking. He held his breath. And then the man went back down the front path to his car again. Jody heard the car door open, and then there was this dragging sound coming towards the cottage. He lifted his body slightly so he could get a better view of the garden and saw the stranger struggling with something that must have weighed a ton, wrapped up in a red tartan rug. And it wasn't a bag of spuds.

Jody shivered. Just some ordinary old guy, half bald, with specs and a summer blazer, should've been off to work, not grunting around in some pig-sty on the moor up to God knows what.

The bundle was dumped in the back garden just outside the kitchen door while the man beat a pathway towards the far right-hand corner. He seemed to know where he was going. Just about daring to lift his eyes, Jody watched as the fellow stood there peering down, then he searched the undergrowth, and picked up a broken slate. He seemed to brace himself and let the slate drop . . . getting down on his haunches, staring and listening for something with a dull, glum interest.

The stranger wiped his hands before returning to his burden, dragging it the last few yards and then kneeling to unwrap his weighty parcel. Jody saw an arm, you can't mistake an arm, before he saw the shape of the woman, still with her clothes on. He couldn't catch sight of the face, as the head was kind of flopped back. She seemed to be in a reclining position, reminding Jody of when butchers' lorries delivered in the High Street and you had to look away because death was just too real and awful and it stank of sawdust and rusty blood. Jody flinched as if from a physical blow. He saw a white and dangling leg. It took a great deal of effort for the guy to get the body in position while insects buzzed and birds sang, and then, needing every ounce of his strength to drag the whole sagging lump up against him, he dropped it, and Jody, watching intently from above, fought the first choking sobs in his throat. At first the guy appeared to fall with it. He flopped, and sat there among the briars and brambles looking totally beaten and defeated like someone begging forgiveness in church, wiping his face with a handkerchief, even removing his glasses and wiping them too. They were probably fugged up 'cos you wouldn't believe the effort it took.

For a second Jody got a look at his face. Without the glasses it seemed vulnerable, the eyes tired and sad. Then the man sat back on his heels meditatively and gratefully.

The British Rail bacon roll was churning away inside him. By now Jody was terrified, trapped up here with a murderer not yards away, a desperate man, mad as a hatter, probably prepared to do anything, anything it took to cover his dastardly tracks. Jody knew the feeling, but he'd done nothing compared to this. Compared to this, Jody's 'crime' was like telling nursery stories to kids. Slowly, excruciatingly slowly, Jody eased himself over to a half-broken beam and picked up the piece of withered timber to use as a club if it came to it. He'd have to fight for his life, and he would, if necessary. The whole world, including his mum, might believe that Jody's life wasn't worth a light but that suddenly wasn't Jody's opinion.

He was innocent. *He was innocent.*

After ten whole minutes of silence, but for the birds and the breeze and some distant sheep, the man in mourning rose to his feet and drove away.

OK, so what is Jody supposed to do about this? He can hardly go to the police without getting himself promptly caught, an anonymous phone call is not Jody's style, and anyway, who is he to say that the guy is guilty of anything? They call Jody guilty when he's not, so how can you say for sure that this guy has bumped off some woman? Jody knows what evil tongues can do. But then again, and this is a chilling thought, what if this is some serial killer coming to his burial grounds! How many more bodies might be hidden down there in the brambles?

Understandably, it's a good half-hour later before Jody dares to leave his cobwebby hiding place and venture into the overgrown garden to take a look. Some of the brambles are almost impenetrable; it's not a place to venture in shorts. He reaches the spot where the body seemed to mysteriously disappear – and steps back just in time. He sees the black hole which drops to nowhere – is it an old mining shaft? Or a disused well? Jody copies the interloper and drops a small stone down . . . Was that a sound? Hard to tell. Whatever, the bottom is some way down. A suitable place to hide a body or anything else for that matter, so long as you never wanted it back.

So what does he do now? He can't get in touch with Mum or Dad because the phones are probably bugged. He's no intention of going to the law and getting himself locked up again. He would like to try and contact Janice, and he would if he was *The Fugitive*. He'd give her a ring if he knew she wasn't so crazy. All she needs to do is tell the police the truth, tell them she wanted it and that it wasn't him who hurt her. She's scared of her dad, that's what's the matter with her. Even though she's moved out and lives on her own in the Centre, she's still terrified of the bully. Even Jody's solicitor can't interview Janice on her own because she is legally classified as a minor. A minor! Her dad's in there with her, isn't he, every time someone tries to get at the truth. And she'll never tell what really happened with Mr Plunket in there listening.

He can't blame Janice totally for the fact that they came to get him. She never uttered a word, she never accused him of anything, just sat there looking smug. No, it was his old friend, Stew, who went and said he'd seen them leaving the car park together in the Datsun, Stew who'd told on him on the day they found Janice Plunket all cut and bruised and with sperm on her dress. Jody had to admit it when they confronted him. Jody knows about DNA, and nobody else would have been mad enough to go near her, like he was.

Jody would never have betrayed Stew like that. Stew the hero – is that why he did it? Stew the crawler, more like. Some friend. And just for a moment of public praise – he loved to be liked. Well, Jody hoped Stew enjoyed the novel feeling.

After that, no amount of explaining to the police in that hot and headachey-room would convince them. His smile might have been part of his downfall, his wide and confident smile as he tried to tell them in the fewest possible words how ridiculous the whole stupid idea was. Underneath, he had felt sick with shame because he *had* been with Janice Plunket and now everyone in the world would know.

His mum said tearfully, 'I know Jody, and my son is not capable of such an act.' They ignored her. They yawned and examined their fingernails.

No, Jody Middleton was a rapist as far as they were concerned, and that was that.

A roar of hate and a spray of hisses and stones thrown by the idle and the curious had followed the van after his first appearance in court. The vengeance of the masses.

And now he has witnessed a murderer about his gruesome business, but there's no one to talk to, no one who'll listen, no one who is as afraid and lonely as Jody Middleton, fugitive, aged eighteen and a half years old.

TWENTY-FOUR

The Grange, Dunsop, Nr Clitheroe, Lancs

'How very different it is when we're dealing with one of *your* friends,' sneers Jacy when Belle comes white-faced off the phone. 'A totally different ballgame.'

Belle gasps at the nerve of the man. 'Poor Peaches is nothing like your friends! She's never in trouble of any kind, not for as long as I've known her, and she doesn't deal in mindless drama and hysteria as a way of life. If Peaches says she's in danger then she's in danger, so I won't come to London with you today, but if you want a lift hurry up because I want to leave right away to pick her up from the station. As it is she's hiding in the Ladies'. She says she thinks people are after her. It's crazy, completely crazy! Why on earth would anyone be stalking Peaches with evil intent?'

But Jacy, caught up with his own immediate and highly important agenda, hasn't the time to stop and chat for it is this morning he sets off for London with Cyd and Darcy, to the studios in Shepherd's Bush owned and run by the great, the worshipful Walter Mathews with his garden parties beside the Thames. Today Jacy's fate will be decided. And Belle's, too, though he's sure she doesn't know it yet.

'Probably some sort of breakdown,' he says. 'We don't want her here. Not now. Not just when everything is about to take off. We don't want the press coming around and finding some woman weeping in the flower beds.'

'You selfish fool, Jacy! You're telling me the press would be more appalled to find an unhappy Peaches, than your two mindless cretins snorting God knows what in the greenhouse. Pack it in. Peaches needs me, and I've already promised her she can stay with me for as long as she likes.'

'Whose house is it? That's what I'd like to know.'

Jacy is in the bedroom getting prepared for his big day. If he takes much longer he will miss the train and Belle's not going to hang around and wait all morning. Peaches is waiting, hiding in the Ladies', and

Belle is impatient to be off. 'Stop preening. Do take that moronic look off your face, you look fine, just fine. And don't disturb your hair again, it's great as it is.'

Jacy has done his best but if only he'd stop moistening his lips and screwing up his eyes. He's wearing silk this morning – a buttermilk silk shirt with flouncy sleeves and a tight pair of black leather jeans with an Indian-style jerkin and an excess of Indian jewellery round his neck, on his fingers, round his waist and through his ears. The Big Chief turned civilised? Belle thought twice about telling him he looked like a cloned Gary Glitter. That would only throw him into total disarray and hold them up for another half-hour. He'd gone out and bought male make-up, and coloured hair gel for men, and she'd had to stop him laying it on too thickly so he was left with an orange ring round his neck as though he hadn't washed for weeks. Still, some of the lines on his face are less prominent, and he's almost erased the bags beneath his eyes. He does look better, if slightly powdery. And that old sparkle is back in his eyes.

'Does it really matter what you look like?' she asks. 'Surely it's the sound you make they're going to be interested in.'

'You know naff all about it.'

For everyone's sake Belle hopes this highly risky exercise proves worthwhile. It does seem an extraordinarily lucky break, but only based on Cyd's word. Perhaps this Mathews guy mentioned the matter in passing, hoping to get Cyd off his back and out of his garden, not expecting to be taken seriously for one moment. Misreading the signals – that would be typical of Cyd.

Give them their due, they've worked at it single-mindedly since the day Cyd and Darcy arrived. They are all as desperate as each other to find fame and fortune again, and why not? Belle was excluded as she'd known she would be, the coffee-maker, the washer-upper, while the talented trio went through their paces. She was supposed to sit and listen, but only allowed to give praise, no negative criticism. They worked all night sometimes, in order to have enough material prepared for a serious recording session. There was such a short amount of time; they'd been so hastily summoned. Belle is torn between hoping for the best for Jacy's sake, or the worst, for her own. She has begun to worry that she might not be able to cope with another six years of Jacy hell-bent on self-destruction.

'I'm scared,' he confessed last night, back from the loo for a third time. 'Really shit-scared.'

'You're bound to be frightened with so much at stake. But just remember, I love you whatever happens. It makes no difference to me what you do. It's you I care about, and I swear I always will.'

Was that honestly true, or habit, she's so used to saying it? She held him, she rocked him like a baby until he finally slept.

All she wants to do is marry Jacy, live in a cosy house and raise a family. She's done everything else, so has he, been there, got the T-shirt, and it wasn't much of a place. Another bout of wild living like the last one would be bound to kill poor Jacy. Or maybe it would be different a second time round . . . especially with a wife and children. He has been to hell and back so perhaps he has learned his lesson.

But Peaches' alarming phone call put most of this out of her mind as she hung around in the hall for the three stooges to present themselves. Hurry up, for God's sake, hurry! She imagines Peaches' terrified face, looking out for her. She's obviously worked herself up into believing something quite paranoid, God knows why or who put it into her silly little head. Belle wouldn't be at all surprised if it wasn't something to do with that smarmy, superior jerk she arrived with to view The Grange. She's often wondered since that short visit exactly what that relationship was. She'd nearly laughed out loud when Dougal called Peaches his fiancée. However, the sale of The Grange seems to be going through OK, according to the solicitors, so, baffling though it is, Peaches and her odd companion must have decided in its favour.

Jacy, of course, is now all mixed up as to whether they need to sell or not. 'What if I start bringing in the readies again? I need some-where to live in style. The last thing I want is for people to know that I live in a Close.'

That same old chestnut again. Belle had lost patience with it. 'You needn't tell anyone where you live.'

'They'll find out,' he said quickly, with his egotistical logic. 'They'll certainly want to know if we ever get huge like we were.'

Huge? 'Listen. You mustn't hope for too much this time, Jacy.'

He turned and looked at her with such withering scorn she kept her mouth shut after that.

So, he has decided to wear his boots with the snakes on. Fair enough; Belle's not going to comment. Even Cyd and Darcy have managed to make themselves look presentable, interesting anyway – especially the way Cyd is toting that leather handbag – a miracle of sorts thanks to decent haircuts, new outfits and a generous number of hot baths.

Belle chases to the station. In terms of the red Jeep she drives, that means reaching forty miles an hour on the long straight stretches of road. She hurries more from worry over Peaches' mental condition than to get the boys to the train on time. She was planning to go with them, for support, as usual – someone to find the carriage number, fetch the drinks from the buffet, grab a taxi at the other end – but as soon as Peaches phoned, all that went by the wayside and to be honest, Jacy hadn't seemed overly disappointed. Perhaps he's grown up now. Perhaps he feels he can cope without me, thought Belle, with a mixture of worry and relief.

She drops them off with cries of, 'Good Luck! Phone me!' parks the Jeep and hurries straight to the Ladies'. No sign of Peaches. People come and go, give Belle some strange looks – what's she doing loitering in here? She can't pretend to do her hair one more time. One cubicle remains locked, Belle notices. Either someone in there is very ill, or – no, surely not – it can't be Peaches?

Belle knocks on the door with some trepidation, and calls softly, in case it is a stranger. 'Peaches?'

A pause. Then a breathless, 'Tusker, is that you?'

'Of course it's me! Come on, let's go and get a drink. You must be in desperate need of one.'

'I've been here since I phoned you,' says Peaches, creeping nervously out, as if she's afraid that Belle is not Belle at all but some clever mimic determined to fool her. Her large blue eyes are terrified and, having assured herself that Belle is no impostor she flings herself into her friend's waiting arms and hangs there limply, like a frightened child after a nightmare.

'Oh Tusker, Tusker, thank God, I thought I wasn't going to make it.' And Belle can see in the mirror that Peaches is searching the white-tiled room over her shoulder with darting eyes. Peaches' heart is thudding hard. Belle takes her scared little friend's cold hand and she grips it. 'We can't stop here for a drink. We have to move on at once before their people spot me . . .'

'Their people? What is this?' Belle thought that Jacy was paranoid but this takes the biscuit. She tries to laugh it off. 'Have you got yourself involved in an espionage ring? Or are you laundering drugs for the Mafia?'

'Worse,' cries Peaches dramatically. 'Stop talking, we're wasting time. Quick, you go, I'll follow.'

So bemused is Belle by the overpowering fear of her friend that she doesn't stop to ask more questions. She sets off across the concourse, sympathetically keeping to the walls which she senses Peaches needs to do, and heads directly for the car park. 'I'll get in the back and lie down on the floor,' says Peaches, still wide-eyed and hysterical.

This is bizarre. Something is very wrong. Has Peaches flipped her lid? Does she need serious medical attention? Could she even be dangerous? Belle attempts to study her friend in the driving mirror but there's no sign of her.

'Don't speak, just drive,' commands Peaches. 'I'll try and put you in the picture, and then you tell me what you think.'

'Let me just ask one question first. Do Charlie and Mags know you're here?'

'Nobody knows,' says Peaches intriguingly. 'At least, I hope nobody knows. You didn't tell anyone, did you?'

Damn. So Belle is on her own with this. She had hoped Charlie and Mags might know what is going on. Perhaps Peaches' parents know, they were always a very close family, or has she cunningly concealed her mental condition from everyone? Perhaps there's some simple answer. Belle must reassure her, it's best to reassure the mad. 'Only Jacy, and he's far too concerned with his own self-importance to take anything in just now. He's probably already forgotten you're coming.'

'He's not here?' asks Peaches.

Belle attempts to sound firm and sensible. 'There's no one at home but me.'

'Thank God. Oh, thank God.'

Askance, Belle listens to Peaches' tale of love as she drives along. The voice from the floor at the back often breaks, and pauses while tears take over. *Bastard,* thinks Belle, when she realises the extent to which her gentle friend has been used and discarded. What the hell were Mags and Charlie doing, to let her get involved with such people in the first place? She is angry beyond belief, stabbed by pity and righteous indignation to discover that even now the foolish Peaches believes that James Henry Albert still wants her, in spite of the news of the royal engagement, in spite of the fact that he has not been in touch with her for weeks, or answered any of her letters or phone calls.

Some women are so sad, thinks Belle, unable to see herself in this bracket at all.

Peaches' sinister conclusions are a difficult and complicated matter. Yes, Belle can see that it does look odd to make an appointment at an expensive clinic under the circumstances, but then again, surely no one would dare to carry out such a foolhardy plan . . .

'That's exactly what I thought at first,' Peaches admits, her voice coming muffled from the back, almost lost by the revving of the Jeep's unhealthy engine. 'I thought I was going insane, probably affected by the shock of seeing them together like that. I sat and thought for ages, really I did, and then I started to get scared, knowing how powerful these people are, the things you read about Secret Services and what goes on behind the scenes, stuff ordinary people know absolutely nothing about. And then I thought, how easy it would be – just a prick in the arm and you're asleep, and you wake up not pregnant any more. Or worse, they could be planning even more ghastly things for me. What if they shut me up for good? They could inject me with powerful mind-bending drugs and get me certified . . .'

'Steady. I think that's probably going a bit over the top.'

'Why? There'd be very little risk when you think about it, and I've had loads of time to do that, all the way here in the train. Mummy and Daddy have no idea that I'm pregnant—'

'But Charlie and Mags . . . ?'

'They'd never dare make a fuss once they realised what had happened to me. They'd be terrified. And they didn't know about my appointment at the private clinic, either. All that would happen is that I'd lose my baby, a common enough event at this early stage, and if they locked me away, well, the doctors could say whatever they liked – that I'd made up the whole story about Jamie and me in my deluded state. Everyone would say how sad. And I'd be so befuddled with drugs I wouldn't even know what was going on.'

'Dear God,' says Belle. 'This is unbelievable. I just don't know what to think.' But Belle does realise the enormity of the threat to the Royals if the press should get hold of Arabella's story. Do such awful things as Arabella's imagining really go on in this country today? It's hard to tell. Perhaps they ought to go to the press, not for blackmail purposes but for immediate protection. At least the press, unlike the police or the services, are independent – *or are they?*

'The important thing is for me to see Jamie,' says Peaches stupidly, as they pull up and park outside The Grange. 'Whatever is happening I know that Jamie himself can't know anything about it. He'd never do anything cruel or unkind.' And then Peaches hesitates before she makes her staggering request. 'You live so much nearer, Tusker, I though you might be able to get me there.' As Belle alights from the Jeep, Peaches changes the subject again as if she's afraid she has gone too far too soon. The old terror is back in her voice. 'You get out and look round, and if the coast is clear I'll follow you.'

*

As the truth dawns, Belle listens to her old schoolfriend with mounting horror. It's good there's no one at home so they can sit on cushions as they did in the old days in Matron's sitting room, playing the old music . . . nothing of Jacy's for once . . . and eating sticky popcorn while Arabella goes on and on about the depths of her love for James, about the sinister Sir Hugh Mountjoy and his threats in the Brighton tea rooms, about the pressure she is under to move into The Grange. 'In spite of the fact that I consistently refused unless I could speak to Jamie first, they carried on with the purchase,' she moans. 'Dougal Rathbone is on the phone every day asking me what I've decided and telling me time is at a premium. Now, of course, I see why. All the time they were plotting to marry him off to this horsey creature just because it's convenient Establishment politics. And I can't bear it, Tusker. *I just can't bear it.*'

'And you expect me to run you up to Scotland so we can confront him? How on earth d'you think we could possibly achieve that?'

'Church,' answers Peaches swiftly, 'the Sunday ritual. Every Sunday morning They go to church. They don't bother with too much security there. All the locals worship Them – well, they would do, as most of them depend on Them for their bread and butter.'

'What would you do if you did get anywhere near him?'

'I'd make a scene,' says Peaches determinedly. She has obviously thought this all through. 'Then the press would see and the thing They are all so ashamed of would be out in the open. There'd be no more need for poor Jamie to play along with their stupid games. He would be free to choose and I know he would choose me – yes, Tusker, don't look at me like that. I am not mad, I have never had the slightest mental problems in my life, I have never seen a psychiatrist or even a psychotherapist. I am quite depressingly normal, in fact, and always have been. The only abnormal thing about me is my low IQ.'

'What about the fiancée?'

'I don't give a damn about her.'

'What if she really loves him?'

Peaches raises a silken eyebrow. 'Come on, Tusker, get real.'

Reason tells Belle not to touch this one with a bargepole. 'What if I refuse to help you?'

'Then I'd do it alone,' says Peaches defiantly. 'And you would have to live with the consequences if my plans broke down, if they caught me before I got there and the men in white coats—'

'That might happen anyway, once you'd made your first move

towards him.' Oh, this is quite ridiculous! Why are they sprawled here on the floor talking about this ludicrous fantasy and taking it all so seriously. 'Peaches, what do you hope to achieve?'

'Love and marriage, of course.' Such a pathetic answer, and Belle, knowing the feeling well, groans with some of her own anguish. 'I am determined, Tusker,' says Arabella, brushing the interruption aside with an obstinate look on her pretty, doll-like face. 'For the sake of my child. For the sake of Jamie's future happiness.'

Oh God, oh God. She is driven by some missionary zeal. Do it or die. Belle is shaken by Peaches' crazed resolution. She is clearly obsessed and suffering even more tortures than she shows. How the hell can she bring her to her senses? At the very best she'll end up in prison for a night. 'Let me get this perfectly straight. You absolutely refuse to consider that Jamie might not want you, despite all the signs that shout otherwise. Is that really how it is?'

Arabella Brightly-Smythe twists her nervous fingers. It is all she can do not to slap her friend. Hot and furiously stimulated she struggles to find the right words. 'Don't start sounding like Charlie and Mags – you don't know him like I do. He has been frightened and manipulated into taking this stand; he was probably afraid that something awful would happen to me if he fought to keep me. I see it all now, so clearly. Poor, poor Jamie, what chance did he ever stand against Them and their wickedness? I was such a fool not to understand what he was trying to tell me. But now, Tusker, with your help, I intend to take Them on and show Them up for what They really are.

'I intend to be there in church on Sunday with or without your help.'
Oh my God.

TWENTY-FIVE

No fixed abode

'Where the bloody hell is she?'
        'I haven't the vaguest clue.'
        'I thought Lovette was supposed to be watching.'
'I thought so, too, Sir Hugh. The man on duty clearly was not up to his job and Lovette assures me he will be severely reprimanded.'

'Let us hope so,' says Sir Hugh Mountjoy, pacing his sumptuous office, sipping from a glass of Andrews Salts every now and again because this is the very worst scenario he could possibly have imagined and it seems to have given him a peptic ulcer. In these dark waters even Sir Hugh is out of his depths. How he wishes, now, that he'd never taken Lovette's advice, that sinister little man with his crude devices, and it is quite apparent that Dougal, so clean-cut and dapper, standing so apologetically before him, feels this issue to be just as distasteful as he does.

But what else was Sir Hugh supposed to do, faced with the wretched girl's continued obstinacy? She couldn't be allowed to give birth to the child, that much was obvious once she refused to give up all claim to Prince James, and a quick and painless abortion disguised as a sad miscarriage would have alleviated much distress on all fronts, including her own in the long run. After that, well, it was merely a matter of branding the girl an hysterical fool given to delusions, and Lovette's tame doctor swore that a few visits to his private clinic, one little injection, would certainly achieve that with a minimum of fuss. There would be no proof, absolutely no come-back at all. The clinic's reputation was spotless. So Dougal might do well to take that look of disdain off his face. After all, it was he who advised that Arabella Brightly-Smythe was so dull-witted she would happily submit to private treatment, all expenses paid. 'She is easy to manipulate,' said Dougal, showing off to some extent, Sir Hugh is certain, eager to demonstrate his power over women although, of course, the cocky young fellow gets no satisfaction in that direction. 'And she is a fool.'

*

'Well, we know that already,' Sir Hugh had pointed out on the fatal day when they had Lovette in and discussed this option with him.

'She stubbornly insists on seeing Jamie and we're running out of time now. She's not going to change her mind, although I'll carry on with the house purchase in case we get some sudden alternative response.'

'Well, no one can say we haven't tried kindness,' mused Sir Hugh, reluctant to give Lovette his head even at this late stage. 'We have bent over backwards, and I'm still not convinced the wanton hussy isn't playing with us for what she can get.'

'She's not bright enough to do that,' Dougal annoyingly insisted. 'She'd have to have some larger brain guiding her from behind if she was intending to do that.'

'We don't know for certain that she hasn't,' argued Sir Hugh, at his wits' end, seeing his promotion going out of the window. 'How about those friends she shares that flat with? They must know what's going on, surely.'

'Apparently Arabella is playing all this business fairly close to the chest. According to her, these two friends initially urged her to have an abortion, just as James did. We all know her feelings on that subject. And because of that I believe Arabella is fairly careful with what she lets slip. I know she hasn't told them about The Grange, simply because I urged her that it would be better, at this stage, if she didn't.'

'Oh, and she does what you tell her without question, is that it?' asked Sir Hugh, disbelieving.

'She trusts me,' said Dougal with no shame. 'And why not? I am a trustworthy person. Or have been so far.' And he stared pointedly at Lovette.

The thin little man who wore a mac like a spy spoke up from his upright chair in the corner. Sir Hugh noticed with some horror that he was wearing the kind of white shoes gangsters in movies used to wear. 'Would she accept the idea that she should visit a private gynaecologist for further checks if you put this to her?'

'I'm sure she would.'

'And you would be prepared to go with her?'

'Of course he would,' put in Sir Hugh. 'It's his job.'

Lovette's voice was thin and sly. His predatory little eyes circled their sockets as he spoke. Both his superiors regretted the necessity of doing business with such a creature but he'd been reliable in the past, got them out of certain distressing scrapes concerning some Family members, particularly James. And he's tight as a clam. Ex-CIA. 'You think she would keep this matter to herself in the same way she took your advice over the purchase of The Grange?' he asked.

'I don't see why not, but I must make it clear at this stage that I am not entirely happy with—'

'We are not concerned with everyday morality here,' broke in Sir Hugh firmly. 'We are here to protect a great tradition and to ensure it goes forward from strength to strength in spite of all the little hiccups that sometimes beset it along the way. And may I remind you of your oath, young Rathbone?'

'I just feel—'

'And what makes your feelings so superior to everyone else's?' blustered an apoplectic Sir Hugh. 'God dammit, Dougal, I must say this is really most aggravating of you. We are all reluctant to take such a dire step, we're not monsters after all, but it seems there is no other way out. If you feel so strongly against it, then come up with something better why don't you. Put up or shut up! Hah!'

'I'm sorry my sincere opinions antagonise you so, Sir Hugh, but I really must ask Mr Lovette here, what sort of mental state would Miss Brightly-Smythe be in once she had succumbed to his friendly doctor's ministrations and miscarried? Would there be any longterm damage, for instance?'

Lovette laughed, not a pleasant sound, more like a rat scuttling along through watery gutters. 'No longterm damage, son. She'd get over it in the end, most women do.'

'Well, that doesn't sound too bad now, does it?' Sir Hugh looked at Dougal expectantly, tapping a polished shoe, waiting for a positive answer.

'And this drug, this little injection – it would merely induce a normal miscarriage?'

'Yes, although the miscarriage wouldn't start until some days later. She'd probably not even associate it with the clinic at all. But it has to be done quickly. The later the pregnancy, the more damage, psychologically as well as physically. That's just plain common sense.' Lovette fiddled with the cigarette wedged behind his ear. Sir Hugh had refused him permission to smoke, a decision he'd accepted with grumpy reluctance.

'So Arabella is going to be in safe hands,' Dougal stated uneasily, standing with his back to the others and staring out of the window.

'The end justifies the means in our job, dear boy, and it's time you started remembering that. Whatever happens to the girl it's hardly a fate worse than death. You're not here just to deal with garden parties, exercising the dogs and the launching of ships, you know. I'm afraid we have no choice.' Sir Hugh came and stood beside Dougal with his hands behind his back and his chin up belligerently high. He rose and came down on his smart black heels. 'It's time we made the decision.'

'Right,' Dougal capitulated reluctantly. 'I'll ring her up then and tell her that it's important she gets some top-rate maternity care. I'll say that the first appointment's for tomorrow then, shall I – tomorrow morning. Would that be convenient, Lovette, for your amenable doctor friend?'

'I think so, sir,' oiled Lovette from the corner, getting up to leave and picking up his scuffed little bowler.

'The only thing that's rather unfortunate,' Dougal added before Lovette could move, 'is the timing of all this. Pity we didn't do it earlier. The big engagement announcement is due to be made tonight and I do worry about Arabella's reaction.'

'We can't help that now,' said Sir Hugh crossly. 'There's even a chance the shock will make her more amenable.' He'd had enough of all this pussyfooting about. Problems, problems, they were ever beset by beastly problems and most of the time Sir Hugh, with his military background, derived the greatest satisfaction from solving them. But now they had to act; they'd explored other avenues and now there was only this. 'Carry on, Lovette, put a tail on the girl tonight in case she decides to do something silly. Let's get cracking and get it all over and done with. Make your arrangements, and Dougal, phone the girl from your office as quickly as possible. Tell her you'll pick her up at her flat at ten-thirty tomorrow morning and drive her to the clinic. She seems to enjoy your company, that might sway her, and give the idea you'll take her out somewhere nice for the afternoon – lunch etc. Give her some inducement, you know how to play it.'

'Right you are, Sir Hugh. Consider it done,' said Dougal as behind him Lovette crept from the room.

Damn. And now she has gone, decamped, flit, done a bunk and no one, it seems, saw her go. There's a loose canon on the deck of the Royal Yacht and it is imperative that she be found before she can fire and hole the ship and sink it to the deepest fathoms of the majestic ocean.

Dougal is forced to explain how he arrived at the flat in good time, only to find Arabella flown and her friend Charlie on the phone dressed in a vulgar jade-green nightie and in a state of excited concern. 'Disappeared – and in her condition,' cried Charlie. 'There's no note – nothing. She's not been in touch with home either. This is all so very worrying and not like Peaches at all. I knew we shouldn't have gone out without her last night. If we'd had the slightest idea that this blasted engagement was about to be announced – did you know, by the way? You must have – you're one of Them, aren't you! Well, we wouldn't have dreamed of going without her. None of her other friends have seen her either, and she's not been into work for days, ever since she gave in her notice. Oh God, oh God, and now I'm going to have to call her parents and tell them she was pregnant. They'll be so devastatingly upset I can't bear it! They'll probably blame my bad influence, and I suppose the police will have to be informed . . .'

Dougal was stunned. She couldn't have gone. She was expecting him at ten-thirty. She'd assured him she would be here waiting. 'Sit down and relax and let me make you a coffee,' he offers hurriedly. 'What makes you think she's gone? She could have popped out for a morning paper and lost track of the time . . .'

'No, no, it's not like that! Some of her things have gone – *Beppo has gone.*'

'Beppo?'

'Her old teddy bear. She'd never go anywhere without him. Her overnight bag has gone. Her brush, her comb, her make-up, her knickers – there's none left in the drawer, I looked. And Mags is at work and I can't contact her there.'

'I'll get in touch with Mags. She might well know where she is. Just leave all this to me. I will also inform Arabella's parents if necessary.'

'But I ought to. I am her friend and I am responsible.'

'I can do it much more effectively, and probably without filling them with gloom which you, in this hysterical state, are quite likely to do. I will also contact the police although they won't do much for twenty-four hours. After all, Arabella is a grown woman and can take care of herself.' Even as he said this Dougal found it hard to believe. She was an innocent, such a trusting, foolish creature. She'd be had by the first con man to pass her way.

Charlie, at her wits' end, and stung by terrible guilt, flung herself into the attack. 'This is all your friend Jamie's fault, playing around with feelings as if nobody's count but his own. He should be told. Jamie should be the one to feel responsible, should anything happen to poor little Peaches.'

'Hey, Charlie, sit down, calm down, and let you and me make a list of anywhere Peaches is likely to be, and I will get someone on to it right away.'

But Charlie, red-faced and fraught, eyed him with angry suspicion. 'You're trying to do a cover-up job, that's what all this is about, isn't it? You're not worried about Peaches at all. You're just shitting yourself in case the press get hold of this and your precious master is dragged through the dirt.'

'Charlie! Please don't.' He was trying to force his eyes off a mind-boggling display of Charlie's underparts, most upsetting. 'You can believe whatever you like but I am genuinely fond of Arabella and would do anything to make sure she was safe. I have the contacts to be able to take the necessary action, talk to her family, see the neighbours, get hold of her bank records and cash withdrawals and so follow up on where she might be. That's if your worst fears are confirmed and she's blundered out of here with no plan in her mind, just a deep unhappiness.'

Charlie sobbed, pushed back her tumble of hair. She lit a cigarette and drew on it deeply, tapping it nervously over the ashtray. 'I know that's what she's done. It would be just like her, to act without thinking – you know how soft and silly she is. Oh, how hurt she must have been when she saw Jamie and Frances posing together like that. We should have been here with her! Oh God, when Peaches needed us we weren't around. It's luck she didn't collapse from the shock. She really genuinely loves him, you know, and she's never been in love before.'

'I have to make a few telephone calls, so why don't you just lie back and drink your coffee while it's hot and leave everything to me for the moment.' And then, as an afterthought he added, 'I shall go and fetch you a dressing gown at the same time.'

'*Don't think you can pander to me!*' Charlie rose and faced him, her fists stiff at her sides. 'Who are you anyway? You're not one of Jamie's friends, are you? Some kind of shady minder? Working undercover for Them? The Government? Or are you from the police? Do you carry a gun? How come you can nose into somebody's bank account without their permission, and why were you always hanging around poor Peaches? What the hell did you want from her? Were you bullying her, is that it? Were you threatening her with what would happen if she didn't play by the rules? You disgust me, people like you, parasites, creepy crawlies, dressing up in your fancy robes and floating around with cushions and sticks. You're weird, Dougal, d'you know that? *You're so bloody weird.*' Charlie, exhausted, broke down and flung herself on the sofa in tears.

He let her give vent to her gathered fury and then gently, averting his eyes, Dougal covered her up modestly before making for the phone extension in Arabella's bedroom. He had to inform Sir Hugh at once, much as he dreaded the reaction.

No trace. No sign in any of the obvious places. Automatically security was increased around James Henry Albert but even his closest detectives were not given a reason why. Luckily he was up in Scotland where even a grouse stood out against a hill, not in the middle of crowded London, and he seemed to be behaving at the moment, not sloping off as yet to frequent his old haunts. Must be the influence of the managing Frances, or maybe he was at last aware of the mayhem he had left behind him down south.

Sir Hugh ponders in his restlessness. If this one went wrong it could badly affect his career. 'What is she likely to do, that's what we've got to try and discover.'

Dougal reminds him, as if he needs reminding: 'But she's never done anything like this before. This is quite out of character, according to all our information.'

'What about her old beau – Thomas the Tank, they call him. Has he been checked out?'

'Yes, all her friends have been checked. It was comparatively easy. They're a very tight bunch, you see, mostly old schoolchums who have kept in touch and go round being Sloaney together. Unless . . .' Dougal stops dead in his tracks. He whips round and stares at Sir Hugh, half-demented. 'Damn! Why the hell didn't I think of that to start with? Belinda Hutchins – the one she calls "Tusker" . . .'

'Do stop rambling, Dougal.'

'I told you about her, the girl at The Grange, with that has-been crooner, Jacy from Sugarshack! It's a long shot, and I'm probably totally wrong on this, but that meeting with Belle would have stuck in her mind. They seemed very close in the short time I saw them together.'

Sir Hugh proceeds slowly, stepping cautiously across the thickly carpeted floor as he speaks his thoughts out loud. 'If she has gone there, and it sounds as if you might have hit on something at last, Dougal, if she has gone to The Grange we can be *fairly* sure the secret is out. She wouldn't have fled all that way for nothing. Perhaps our little friend has more up there than we credited her for,' he looks at Dougal and taps his forehead, pausing briefly in his steady pacings, 'although I always suspected as much. Don't you see, Dougal, if she has gone to stay with her old friend, Belinda, she will have confided everything, and maybe, just maybe, she realised something was in the air with the clinic visit coinciding so unfortunately with the public announcement of James' engagement!'

'Damn,' says Dougal. 'That puts the cat among the pigeons.'

'It most certainly does. And it means that before proceeding further in that direction we must take extra care. We must ascertain whether or not our assumptions are right, and if they are we must find out all we can about this dude and his moll.'

'Leave that to me,' says Dougal.

'I already have,' replies Sir Hugh. 'This could be a sticky business and I cannot afford to dirty my hands. That's your job. You'd better not mess this one up though, or it's curtains as far as you are concerned. So for your own sake, my boy, I should jolly well remember that.'

TWENTY-SIX

Flat I, Albany Buildings, Swallowbridge, Devon

'Hurry up, Miss Benson, do. We haven't got all day.'

Miss Benson, with a handful of nails gripped between her teeth, the metal setting her nerves on edge, is going as fast as she possibly can. She is not used to manual labour even though she works with animals. She is a trained animal nurse, and a good one, and not given to doing odd handy jobs at the veterinary practice where she works; she leaves that to the trainees.

Mrs Peacock is pleased with herself this morning, not only because D Day has finally arrived, but also because when she entered her flat she found a sympathetic reply from the Queen waiting on the doormat.

However, Miss Benson, who has taken a fortnight off for this enterprise, is rightly concerned that if she makes too much noise with her hammering she will attract the attention of the neighbourhood. 'Don't worry about that, dear,' Mrs Peacock assures her, sitting watching her struggles from her comfortable chair, agitating with her stick while with the other eye she keeps watch by the far window. 'They'll think it's the new people moving in. You could set the place ablaze and no one would take any notice they're that wrapped up in their own affairs. Just keep going, you're doing very well.'

Miss Benson knows she is not, and that Mrs Peacock is merely being encouraging. The crisscross planks nailed against the windows could have fitted better, but there it is, there's no time to be finicky, just as long as they hold firm, which they do, nailed as they are to the wooden sills below and the solidly built pelmets above. Unfortunately the plastic surrounding the double glazing cannot be utilised for this purpose although that would have made a neater job. It is also a good thing that this is a compact little flat with only five windows because Miss Benson's arms and wrists are weakening fast.

Once these are done there is only the door to be barricaded when Miss Benson has gone, and Mrs Peacock reckons that if Emily starts

195

off the holes first, she will be able to manage that job herself, balanced on a chair. Once she has abandoned ship Miss Benson's work will not be over; as acting public relations person she will have her hands full, not only that but it's her job to make sure Mrs Peacock receives all necessary supplies via the secret floorboard connection they have worked on under the carpet in Miss Benson's lavatory. For who knows how long Mrs Peacock will have to hold out here until they finally capitulate and allow her to stay in her home, and die there if she wants to . . . Or what foul means will be employed by the shamed authorities to prise her from her sanctuary unless a supportive public is made fully aware of the situation first.

In this, surely, the Queen's letter is going to be a boon.

It said, *Dear Mrs Peacock, The Queen has asked me to pass on to you her sincere sympathies on hearing about your present plight. She has asked the local authorities and your local Member of Parliament to supply her with all relevant information and has requested to be kept informed as to your future circumstances.*
Yours sincerely,
L. M. Stokes, Lady in Waiting.

'That'll go nicely on the door once you've shut it behind you, and you're going to the stationer's down the road for photocopies, aren't you?' Irene Peacock fretted. 'Don't forget, in case they rip the original off.'

'I haven't forgotten. Just you stop worrying now and relax. Everything is in hand. You've got a good supply of ciggies and gin, and if you run out I'll send more down. Your glasses are mended and they're there on the table. There's magazines, all your favourites. And there's enough tinned food in that cupboard of yours to last six months.'

'If only I'd had a decent pantry here, like I had at the bungalow. I can't understand how they can be allowed to build anything without a pantry and an airing cupboard. So necessary. Almost as important as a bathroom, when you think about it. I never imagined that one day I would be reduced to a mere cupboard.'

Miss Benson is almost too weak to reply. She steps down off her little stool-ladder at last, trembling with exhaustion, and regards the last of the windows. 'That's done, thank goodness,' she says, pleased with her handiwork. 'They'll not break through there without making a hell of a racket.'

'Thank you so much, Miss Benson.' Mrs Peacock rises creakily to put the kettle on again. 'I really do appreciate everything you have done.'

'I was glad to help,' says her friend with feeling. 'You know I was. It's a way of relieving my own frustrations. I only wish I could have done something so simple in order to help my own mother.'

'Poor soul,' commiserates Mrs Peacock. 'The poor, poor soul.'

It hadn't taken long to convince Miss Benson to give her support to the plan, once they'd been out together a few times and Miss Benson realised how terribly unhappy Mrs Peacock was at Greylands. It came as a shock at first, well, of course it did, the very idea of a seventy-five-year-old woman blocking herself in her flat and refusing to come out until they agreed to her simple requirements.

'What if anything should happen to you while you're in there?' was Miss Benson's first alarmed reaction. 'I would be directly responsible.'

'There you go, just like the rest of them. Do I have to remind you, too, that *I am responsible for my own actions*. I might be forgetful at times, and I do behave oddly now and again, I know that, I admit it, but I am seventy-five and surely, at my age, there should be some leeway given for little eccentricities.'

'But you could die in there, nailed in, with nobody beside you.'

'Oh, honestly, Miss Benson! Haven't you learnt that lesson yet? When you are born and when you die and when you are ill and when you give birth, as you might do one day, you are alone of necessity. You are fighting life's battle alone, and it might be nice to die in friendly arms, but I'm really not too bothered where and how it happens as long as it's quick and relatively painless. At least I would be in my own home with my own beloved things around me. And, my dear, you must remember that you'll be constantly in touch.'

They'd had to act quickly or the 'beloved things' to which Mrs Peacock referred would have gone off to charities or been tipped into the nearest Council skip. They hadn't had long to sort out their plans, from the moment of conception a few days ago, to today's countdown which started at nine o'clock. 'Miss Benson and I are spending a day at the zoo,' Mrs Peacock informed Miss Blennerhasset. 'We want to leave early to get there in time to see the sealions and the penguins fed.'

'That's perfectly fine by me. Have a nice day,' said Miss Blennerhasset with her little smug smile, unhappily too easily affected by such colloquialisms from America. 'Ask the kitchens if they've got any old bread.'

'Oh no, you're not allowed to feed bread to the animals. Miss

Benson says they sell the correct food at the zoo shop. I'd have thought you'd have known that,' said Mrs Peacock, trying to sound casual while all the time her old heart banged against her chest and she was afraid it might give out before she could accomplish anything.

Miss Blennerhasset, who was only trying to be helpful, sighed and wondered if she ought to increase the dosage on the medication she was giving to Mrs Peacock. She seemed rather too lively and pleased with herself of late, not her old self at all, with a funny smell to her breath – gin? – and smoking far too much in that disgusting room of hers, swearing that she doesn't in spite of the stubs the cleaners find squashed down her washbasin sink. But then again, she'd rather have Mrs Peacock like this than the bad-tempered, evil-minded old crone she was when she first arrived, causing trouble and running away all the time. And her daughter, Frankie, feels much relieved about her, too. It's good to keep the relatives happy.

'When should we expect you back?'

'Same time as always,' sang Mrs Peacock, pushing her urgent way through the door with her stick to where Miss Benson's car sat waiting in the Greylands drive. Miss Blennerhasset waved to Miss Benson but she didn't think Miss Benson saw, or she deliberately ignored her – but why on earth would she do that?

The first thing they did was call at Safeways with a long list of essentials for the sit-in. Miss Benson gladly provided the funds. Then they collected the planks, hammer and nails from the DIY superstore next door. The wood, heavier than she'd expected, and awkward to handle, only just fitted in the back of Miss Benson's car, so that was rather a worry. From the store they also purchased a small camping stove, a battery radio and an oil lamp in case the authorities decided in their wisdom to cut off the electricity, although that wouldn't do too much for their image. The two-way radio from Mothercare had been purchased and tested a few days earlier and was already installed and working satisfactorily.

'What is Miss Blennerhasset going to say when she hears what we've done?' asked Miss Benson, giggling away like a naughty child. 'I wouldn't like to be around to hear her.'

'Well, I would,' said Mrs Peacock airily. 'It's poor Frankie who'll be most upset. I mean, it won't look too good for her, will it, even though she had little choice.'

'She did have a choice,' Miss Benson reminds her. 'She could have had you to stay with her. She could have done a lot more to help you, even though she's a busy woman. You are her mother, you know.'

'But I'd rather not upset anyone,' Mrs Peacock lamented. 'All I honestly want is to be allowed to stay in my own home and be carried out of it feet-first, if possible.'

'This is the only way to achieve that,' Miss Benson agreed. 'Sad but true, I'm afraid.'

'So let's get on with it,' said a determined Mrs Peacock, making herself comfortable while Miss Benson unpacked the supplies. She doesn't like to think about Frankie. Her daughter has been through the mill lately, with Michael defecting and money being at a premium and having to work so hard, suddenly becoming the main breadwinner. But Frankie should not have connived with the Council to sell her mother's flat, not in that underhand way, not without asking. She'd tricked her. Nor should she be so unwilling to support her mother's wish to remain at home. What Irene is doing might be mortally embarrassing for Frankie, but that's nothing like the suffering Irene herself has been put through.

No. The main worry is, have they thought of everything? Miss Benson spent one whole afternoon in the library studying lists of likely pressure groups who might assist Mrs Peacock in her plight, like the Council opposition parties, Age Concern, Amnesty and Liberty and many more who'd be likely to demonstrate an interest once the show got underway. She also made notes of the local media telephone numbers, including the local television. Miss Benson was used to campaigning because of her high-profile position in her various animal causes. She knew the sort of people to look for; she knew the best ways to approach them.

Nothing they are planning to do goes against the law. There is no compulsory stipulation that Mrs Peacock should be forced into an institution against her will and thereby have to sell her home. She hasn't been certified as mad. She hasn't been labelled as suffering from dementia, or any other mental condition apart from the natural process of aging. 'I did worry a great deal about you when you started wandering about at night. I thought you were sleepwalking. I felt quite frightened, nervous to come across you in the dark with your huge rosebud nightie and your old hot-water bottle,' confessed Miss Benson when they were on better terms. 'Now I realise you were merely unable to sleep, and couldn't be bothered to change your clothes. I thought you were going mad, and when I spoke to Mrs Rendell she said nothing to reassure me.'

'Typical Frankie,' said Mrs Peacock, rolling her aged eyes.

Miss Benson laughed with relief. 'And then there was the Morse

Code era. That's what I called it when you started tapping at night. I didn't know you were plagued by woodlice and were trying to kill them with your spatula. I though you'd lost your head and I told Mrs Rendell so, too.'

'Just because I was old,' said Mrs Peacock correctly.

Nothing states that it is unlawful to cover the inside of one's windows with planks, or bore a small hole from one lavatory to another directly below; no planning permission is required for that. No, the only unlawful action Mrs Peacock is planning to take is to refuse to obey the police if they tell her to open her door.

And that is hardly a hanging offence.

All the same, Frankie is going to be outraged. And Angus and Poppy won't be too happy either, their own grandmother behaving so badly, letting them down in front of their friends, a heinous offence according to Frankie who has even been asked to keep away from school concerts and sports days because of her hats and her loud voice. When Frankie told her mother that, Irene was flabbergasted. 'And you listened to that? You deliberately stayed away from school in case you embarrassed your own children?'

'Well, I was quite relieved, actually, not to have to go to some of the rubbish they put on.'

'Well, I wouldn't have had that from you. And your father would have been terribly upset to think you were ashamed of him.'

'I was, most of the time,' said Frankie. 'I was ashamed to see how you hovered round him, fuss fuss fuss, fetching him plates of food as if he couldn't get his own, finding his seat for him, spreading out a rug on the grass, buttering his bread for him, and even laying his own napkin on his lap. Ugh, Mother! Why did you do it?'

'I'm not going into that again, Frankie. You do have a knack of making such innocent things sound so unwholesome. It wasn't like that at all and you know it. Anyway, you never demanded we kept away from your school.'

'I would have done if I could,' said Frankie. 'And I think it's only natural for children to want to stop identifying with their parents at a certain age.'

'You might call it natural, I call it downright peculiar,' said Irene crossly.

All this pandering to the whims of spoilt teenagers, which is what Angus and Poppy undoubtedly are. No wonder they're such little tyrants – funny how Frankie seems to remember William in that role. Well, maybe the publicity from their grandmother's notoriety might do the little rotters some good, make them consider other people for a change. And if it doesn't, well, it won't make much difference – she rarely sees her grandchildren anyway. As for Frankie . . . it is only of late that Irene considers she has really started to know her daughter. Only since the Greylands episode have they started to deal with each other with any degree of honesty. And although Irene, like a martyr, knows she must do what is now required, she is loath to sacrifice that.

The efficient Miss Benson, with her strict eye for detail, is ticking the lists. Irene is grateful for her neighbour's help but if Miss Benson hadn't been there she would have attempted to do this by herself. What a blessing in disguise that the terrible death of Miss Benson's mother has affected her daughter in this heroic sort of way, turning her into a champion of the elderly, the despised and the helpless. What a boon that this colourless young woman with the wonderful compassionate nature happened to live upstairs, happened to befriend her old neighbour, visit her in Greylands and was willing to develop the relationship into a genuine friendship. Not that Irene ever bothered that much with friends. She didn't need them. She had always had William.

The undemonstrative Miss Benson had even insisted on buying a couple of bunches of flowers, a sweet little touch, but she said it might make all the difference during the long lonely hours to come.

On a more practical level Mrs Peacock is going to poke her washing and her litter up through the hole in the floorboards. And Miss Benson is going to poke the milk and the daily newspapers back. She doubts they'll allow the mail to get through, they will probably confiscate that. The most important thing is for Miss Benson to insist she knew nothing about the scheme, and had nothing whatsoever to do with it. In order to function competently, she can't have suspicion directed at her.

'I think that's it then,' says Mrs Peacock eventually. 'Shipshape and Bristol fashion. We'll just finish off the angel cake and then you can leave me here, go upstairs and get started.'

'Oh dear,' says Miss Benson. 'It's all happened so quickly I can hardly believe we're actually doing this. Are you sure you wouldn't rather reconsider?'

'And go back to that place for another night? Certainly not! I am utterly determined to do this and hold out to the bitter end if necessary.' Mrs Peacock tightens her lips with conviction. 'Don't forget to pin the Queen's letter to the door as soon as you come back with the copies. And make sure nobody sees you.'

'We've been lucky so far, no interruptions,' says a childishly excited Miss Benson.

'I didn't really expect any. Nobody calls here.'

'Well, what can I say?' asks Miss Benson shyly, finally rising to leave. 'Good luck, I suppose, and the next time I see you we'll know, one way or the other.' Her mouth works against her tears and she pats her eyes, much moved, so sensitive and highly-strung.

'I depend on you to keep me in touch . . .'

'Don't worry, I will,' says Miss Benson, quietly calling in a way you might use when waving a friend off at a station. 'And I admire you, I really do. I think you're being very, very brave . . .'

'Nonsense,' says Mrs Peacock, lighting a farewell cigarette and feeling gratified by the compliment. 'Just determined, that's all. I was always a determined woman, I always prided myself on my ability to pull through. Even William used to say . . .'

'Jolly good!' Miss Benson carefully opens the door and peers through to see if she's safe. 'I'm going now . . . take care . . . don't worry . . . keep faith, my dear. We'll win in the end.'

'We certainly will,' says Mrs Peacock exultantly, with her scrawny hand in the air, bestowing a smoky kind of blessing. 'Because we have right on our side.'

TWENTY-SEVEN

Joyvern, 11, The Blagdons, Milton, Devon

Now Vernon finds himself resisting the self-destructive urge to confess. In the past he has been victim to bouts of such masochistic whims, particularly at school when the compulsion to step forward and take the blame for something he had not done occasionally overwhelmed him. It was something to do with feeling guilty anyway, and knowing that he deserved punishment, if not for the crime in hand then for the secret thoughts in his head and the small misdemeanours he had successfully got away with in his past. Even before he committed the hideous murder of his wife, Vernon would feel a natural but inexplicable guilt when passing a policeman. He always hurried by wearing his most innocent expression.

Not that he had ever done anything for which to reproach himself, until his brush with bankruptcy, until he killed his wife. In his schooldays Vernon was a sturdy plodder who worked hard to the best of his ability and showed some talent on the games field which, lacking the necessary aggression, never blossomed.

Of course, it is the sturdy plodders, the ones who get stuck in the middle of the class, not through lack of trying, the reliable, the regular and the easy-to-please who annoy their masters so – unlike the bright and shining ones with their charm and promise who sit at the front, and the downright bad who sit at the back, able to command both sympathy and attention.

And therefore Mr Norman Mycroft regarded Vernon with distaste this morning as the offender sat down uneasily in the opposite chair while his case history was flashed up on the screen in front of the manager.

Vernon was early through nervousness, and had to wait twenty-five minutes, but as a branded failure he was well used to this treatment by now. In the chair at last he wanted to cry out, 'I have just buried my wife,' in order to save himself, but managed to refrain from doing so. 'It was my wife,' he said, instead. 'She has been suffering from depression just lately and took it into her head to go on a spending spree without my knowledge. When I got home after your telephone call yesterday I had it out with her and she became overwrought and depressed and could give me no logical explanation for her behaviour.'

Mr Mycroft sat back in his chair and stared blandly at Vernon. The hard sheen of the man showed in his smartly pressed suit, his tidy desk, his still fingers and his cold fish eyes. It was a varnish on a painting, you'd have to scratch hard to get it off. 'Ignorance is no defence in law,' he said in a jocular fashion, but not expecting a laugh. 'Naturally I am sorry that your wife is unwell, but I'm afraid that is not going to help us get to the root of this problem – which is how you are going to pay back the money you now appear to owe this branch.' At this point he pushed a statement across his desk which showed exactly how much Vernon owed, at an increased rate of interest because he had not discussed the matter first.

Vernon swallowed and his dry throat hurt. 'How could I discuss it? I didn't *know* . . .'

'That is beside the point, I'm afraid, Mr Marsh. Your account is a joint one. If you were worried about your wife's mental state you should have taken the appropriate action and removed any such temptations from her.'

Vernon glanced at the heavy glass paperweight beside Mr Mycroft's elbow and considered the pleasure it would bring to bash it down on the young man's dry and sandy head. The violence of his feelings disturbed him; perhaps his recent outbreak had uncorked a murderous genie which once released will not go back.

Humbly, and with penitence, which is what Mr Mycroft wanted to see, Vernon presented the latest documentation which showed a shortfall of just £2,000, taking into account solicitors' and estate agent's fees, stamp duty, removal costs, the money he owed and every penny of the accrued interest should the sale go through a month from today.

'Which it should,' said Vernon nervously. 'It all seems to be straightforward. Apparently there's only five in the chain and everyone is going ahead, according to our agent who has given the transaction five gold rings.'

'Five gold rings?' Mr Mycroft, mystified, made it sound like stars given to the less able at school.

Vernon hurried on to explain. He'd been rather taken by the agent's method himself, and much encouraged to hear it. In these uncertain times, estate agents made it their business to check a sale all the way down the line before recommending a deal to their clients. 'Apparently that's what he does if everything's looking good. If it's dodgy he rings the uncertain vendor in black, if it's fair he used an ordinary blue biro and as I said, if it's looking like a certainty he rings them all in gold.'

'A very unusual circumstance in today's depressed market,' said Mr Mycroft authoritatively, as if he considered Vernon's agent a fool with no clue as to what he was doing. 'I will give him a call later if I may.' Just in case Vernon was lying. 'Let us hope, for your sake, that everything does go well, because if not you seem to be in very deep trouble, I'm afraid, Mr Marsh. Inextricable, I would venture to add.'

Vernon hung his head and said nothing. He couldn't argue against that. If the sale failed to go through he was up the creek without a paddle and would have been, anyway, without Joy's little extra push. But Vernon has already decided exactly what he must do. He has no intention of going ahead with the purchase of Flat 1, Albany Buildings. Just before it is time to sign the contract he will pull out, let it be known that Joy has disappeared without trace, back out of the deal and go into rented accommodation. In other words – give up. He has no need for a permanent home now he's without a wife. He'd rather rent and keep the money; he just can't struggle on against this sort of tyranny any longer. All Vernon wants in the future is a shirt on his back and a little part-time job. Surely there are opportunities out there for a qualified electrician willing to work cheap?

But he can't let people know that Joy has disappeared yet. It is far too premature. He must allow a couple of weeks to go by before he starts fussing.

My Mycroft was flogging on, tugging at the matter like a dog with a festering bone. 'The two thousand pounds' shortfall, Mr Marsh. How do you intend to cover that?'

Vernon had his part carefully rehearsed. 'Gradually, with part-time earnings and a less expensive lifestyle, I would be able to repay a loan of two thousand pounds should you feel able to advance it,' he said obsequiously, almost bowing to the desk before him. He would say *anything* to be able to get out of there. 'And I am quite confident of that. The shop lease is up in three weeks' time and then I will be able to start looking for work at once.'

Mr Mycroft sighed and watched the offender narrowly. Never mind that the amount owed by Vernon at the end of the day was piddling compared to the vast sums he risked with the more self-assertive and charismatic of his clientèle. They, quite rightly, wouldn't put up with this demeaning treatment for a moment and so Mr Mycroft savoured to the full this opportunity to bully.

Home again, he can't face work after this morning's grilling which ended up with Mr Mycroft reluctantly agreeing to a two thousand pound loan a month from today, provided all other debts were cleared. Vernon can feel his blood pressure rising to boiling point; he badly needs to get indoors and sit down in the calm and familiar atmosphere of his house.

He is amazed at the depths of his disappointment. He always supposed he loved Joy, as you do when you've been married to someone for over twenty years, but he wasn't quite certain how much until now. As he sees the bedroom, the frilly bed with its apricot cover, the neat dressing table, the whole beige ambience, many strange thoughts struggle for birth but cannot live. Something – horror – is denying them life. But he must go on with this, he must, he can't turn back now. The publicity would destroy the children.

Typical. Just when he needs a diversion. He must not allow the dull conscienceless automaton which has taken control of him to allow him to feel. All the newspapers are bothered about is the engagement of that half-wit Prince, and some old fool who has barricaded herself in her flat in Swallowbridge. QUEEN IN SYMPATHY WITH SEVENTY-FIVE-YEAR-OLD PROTESTER, goes the headline which Vernon ignores. He throws the irritating newspaper down; he has far more important matters on his mind. It's funny, when these little issues count for you, you know that life is as good as it's going to get. It's refreshing to know, thinks Vernon, that life must be set fair for so many who at this very moment are busying themselves with crosswords, lotteries and the latest gossip about the soaps, surrounded by serenity and calm. The minute you're in deep trouble these become inconsequential. So anxious and preoccupied is poor Vernon that he can't even concentrate on the lunchtime television news.

He misses Joy with all his might. The house is so empty and quiet without her. He is surprised by a recurring and nagging urge to return to the ruined cottage to make sure that his wife is properly dead. Even in his short and sweat-drenched dreams this nightmare grips him, as if she might be alive and calling from the murky depths of the forgotten well, starving, wounded, terrified in just three foot of stagnant water with darkness all around her and only a pinprick of light pointing the way to life and hope. Almost as bad as being buried alive.

He talks to himself in the quiet house, trying to calm his illogical terrors. Nobody's going to find her there, nobody's going to open the well, and if, one day in the distant future, they find a skeleton at the bottom – well, Vernon will be long dead and gone.

And she can't be alive. There is no way she could live after the battering he gave her. Oh God oh God help me.

'Hello! Hello! Anyone home?'

Vernon jumps out of his skin. He was half-dozing; he feels sick and dazed as he answers the door. 'Ah, Adele, it's you.'

'I was looking for Joy,' says the brassy neighbour, moving too close to Vernon for comfort and peering in through dark sunglasses over his shoulder. 'She said she'd pop round today.'

After his sudden awakening Vernon is not at his best. 'She's not here.'

Adele waits for the explanation which Vernon seems to have forgotten to give. She cocks her head on one side and one great glassy earring touches her naked shoulder.

He rubs his eyes, 'Sorry, sorry, I've not been too well today.'

'No, I saw your car in the drive at lunchtime and I did wonder.'

'Didn't Joy tell you? She decided to go on earlier to the flat because we were worried about it being left empty. She is sleeping over there, sorting things out. Won't you come in, Adele?'

'No, Vernon, I won't, thank you. What? You mean she's there already, and not called to say goodbye first?'

Vernon pretends to laugh. 'Oh no, she'll be backwards and forwards from now on, for a few weeks anyway, until we move officially.'

'Into that temporary place? How inconvenient for you, Vernon. I must say, Ted and I think you're doing a terribly brave thing moving into a cottage in the middle of nowhere.'

'Cottage?' Vernon stands on his doorstep blinking stupidly, staring at his neighbour perlexed.

'Yes, that lovely old cottage with so much potential – what was it called, something bizarre. *Hacienda*, wasn't it, or something along those lines?'

Damn Joy and her big mouth, *damn her*! Vernon, with a shaking heart and confused head, had forgotten about the lie she'd spread around, so ashamed of people knowing they were moving into a flat. He puts his hand on the side of the door to hold himself up; he feels dizzy. 'Well yes, that was our idea to begin with, but we're still sorting that one out.'

'But I thought it was all in the bag, as it were. I thought it was all decided.'

'*Almost* decided,' says Vernon, clearing his throat, his brain racing like a jet engine searching for an answer. 'We're still getting builders' estimates.'

'Oh,' and Adele cocks her head the other way and the other earring strikes her bony shoulder and makes prisms in the afternoon light. 'I thought that was the whole idea. I thought you were going to do it, that was the whole point of this early retirement.'

He has inadvertently made Adele Mason's day; she has discovered some discrepancy in Joy's boastful stories and it won't be long before the news is all round the estate. Adele has good reason to besmirch Joy Marsh's name. Joy has always considered her common and said so in as many words to various other neighbours in the past. This rumour will run and leap like a spluttering flame along a fuse that twists in and out around the gardens and kitchens and back doors of The Blagdons. Well well well. *The Marshes are moving into a flat!* And what about the Frontiera Jeep? 'I suppose the new car will be arriving soon?' Adele enquires cheerily. 'It's all right for some! I wish Ted and I could retire and afford such luxuries.'

New car? What else has Joy been saying? 'Well yes,' says Vernon carefully, 'but not until we've actually sold the house. We're not made of money, Adele.'

'Really?' grins the buck-toothed Adele. 'You'll be telling me next all this is nothing to do with tax avoidance.'

'I'll tell Joy you called when I see her next,' says a flustered Vernon, desperate to get rid of the woman. But he cannot resist this first chance to spread the rumour around that Joy has not been herself of late. 'If she remembers where we live, of course,' and he gives a sad little smile to accompany the statement.

'*If she remembers?*' This is even more juicy. Adele stops in her tracks and gapes.

Vernon grasps the nettle. 'I wondered, Adele, if either you or Ted have noticed Joy behaving rather oddly lately? I am speaking to you now in absolute confidence, of course.'

'Of course, Vernon, naturally. You know me. And I *am* Joy's closest friend.'

'Forgetful? Unable to concentrate for long? Not listening to you when you are speaking?'

Adele has noticed none of this, she is far too self-centred to perceive much about any of her friends. 'Well, now you come to mention it, Vernon, I have found some of her behaviour a little strange just recently. Joy's been a little distracted, secretive almost, not her old self certainly, but I imagined it was because of all the changes going on. I know she loathed showing people round the house, and it's a big step, moving at her time of life. It's the third most stressful experience, apparently, after bereavement and divorce.'

'I just wondered, I hope you didn't mind me asking, only I am quite worried and wonder if I ought to encourage her to go to the doctor.'

'Oh *do*,' says Adele with alacrity, for this is one of her pet subjects. 'Don't delay, they have all sorts of pills for depression nowadays and it's only a matter of trying them all out until you find the right one for you.' She could have been talking about shoes. 'Ted is on Lithium and it's done absolute wonders for him. No one really knows why it works, that's what's so extraordinary. I will mention the idea to Joy, too, if you think that might help, next time I see her.'

'I would be most grateful, Adele,' says Vernon, forcing a certain unpleasant intimacy. 'But this is a delicate matter and we must tread carefully.'

'Trust me, Vernon,' says Adele, blinking delighted eyes as she hastens away with her fascinating news. If only Ted would show such gentle concern about her. Oh, it's true what everyone says – Vernon *is* a lovely man. Joy doesn't know she's been born.

Vernon sits heavily at the kitchen table. Had he looked out at this moment, it would have been possible to see a youth on a bicycle idling on the corner as if he was waiting for a friend, but with his face turned towards number eleven. But Vernon does not look out. It is impossible to settle to anything. Did he overdo it just now? In his terror, has he overreacted and caused nothing but suspicions to fester in the minds of his neighbour? Surely now she knows about the flat, Adele will forget about *Hacienda* and concentrate on the juicier gossip – Joy's worrying mental instability. It just shows you how complicated these things can get. Who else has Joy told about the ruined cottage? At least she didn't lie to the children; Suzie and Tom understand that they plan to buy the flat. He gets up and walks the floor with both hands gripped behind his back and a cigarette between his lips considering what other little flaws will be exposed in his plan as the next few weeks go by.

He is almost expecting it when he hears the next knock. It's probably more of the local carrion circling Joyvern for gossip, and he's half-relieved that it's all coming now so he can get it over and done with. He'd rather be talking to someone, rather be acting than sitting here musing alone and allowing his terrible thoughts to come through. How will he live the next thirty years without Joy, without a home he can call his own, without a career? His children have their own lives to get on with, they won't want to be bothered with him. Will he end up as one of those sad men on a bar stool, there waiting for the pub to open and still there when they shout Time? Walking the streets alone at night, unable to sleep and with no one to talk to? Living his life in a mean bedsit lit by the blue light of perpetual television.

Oh Joy oh Joy, let this be a dream. Come back, *come back and forgive me!*

It is a stranger. A lad with a bike parked at the gate beside the colourful mail box, painted a flamboyant purple by Joy last summer, before they knew they would have to move.

'Can I help you?' Vernon stutters, impatient to close the door on anything or anyone so unimportant in the vast scheme of his life today.

'I think you might be able to,' says the good-looking lad, who is tired round the eyes, weary, with messy fair hair, his arms burnt bright red by the sun. The boy's expression is embarrassed, strangely verging on fear. 'I came to look at the house which my family have just bought – we're the Middletons, from Preston – but I saw you talking to a woman a few moments ago and recognised you from somewhere else. So then I decided I'd better call in to see what else you and I have in common.'

What's this? Vernon can hardly be bothered to concentrate, but he doesn't like the youth's accusing tone of voice or the vague implications. 'In common?'

'If you let me come in I can put you in the picture and then we can decide between us exactly what you are going to do.'

TWENTY-EIGHT

Penmore House, Ribblestone Close, Preston, Lancs

The shock of it nearly finished him. Jody Middleton, once so spoilt and cherished, a child brought up on uncritical tenderness, the apple of his parents' eyes, could not believe his own. There he was, in all innocence, loitering to pass the time, spurred on by a harmless interest to see his new house, when lo and behold the monster appeared before him, the same sinister guy he had watched from the cottage bedroom only this morning dropping the body down the well. An ordinary, worried-looking, overweight, half-bald monster in shirtsleeves and glasses standing chatting, relaxed as you like at his own front door. And this is the house his family have bought. *This cannot be true.*

'You'd better come in,' says the fat guy, sweating profusely and that can't all be due to the heat.

'After you,' says Jody nervously, slipping his rucksack off his shoulders and onto the floor in one easy move. He takes a connoisseur's interest in all that he sees. Poor Mum. She'll hate living in this house with its rigid symmetry, its pokey kitchen, its prettified appearance on this estate of aspirations, quite different from their house in the Close which is old and rambling with high ceilings and lots of cupboards. A homely house, thinks Jody wistfully, full of mess and muddle and colour. What made them decide on this one? Weary, he understands just how desperate they must have been.

When they reach the kitchen the man swivels round and there are glints of fright behind his glasses. Jody steps back, equally terrified. He's dangerous, maybe a ruthless serial killer on the loose and prepared to do it again. The murderer's hands are shaking. 'Now I think it's time you explained to me exactly what you are doing here.'

He is quite safe. No one is looking for him here so Jody decides to jump straight in. 'I was there, and I saw what you did.'

'Marsh is my name,' says Vernon awkwardly. 'Vernon Marsh. And what do you mean, you were there?'

'At the cottage when you dumped the body. It was your wife, I suppose. Most murders stay in the family.' His voice is breaking, he must be firmer, put some authority behind his words. 'I was hiding in the bedroom.'

Vernon Marsh turns an ashen grey. He is struck almost speechless for a moment before he stutters, 'Please – sit down.'

Jody knows he must take immediate control of this situation and he wonders if he'll be up to it. Taking command of an adult is not so easy, nor is being in such close vicinity to someone who could be a vicious killer. Vernon must be made to believe that Jody knows what he's doing. 'I wouldn't mind a glass of milk if you've got one in the fridge, Vernon.' He's happy to hear that his voice sounds not flippant at all, but threatening.

Vernon, like a great big kid who's lost his mother, looks up at his visitor in horror.

'Milk, or a Coke will do. Or lemonade. I don't really mind which, it's just that I'm terribly thirsty.'

'Milk,' says Vernon, shaking his head, too bewildered to function on anything but the most basic level. 'We have two pints delivered a day. When Joy left I didn't cancel it. It's built up now, I don't know which are the fresh ones. Joy used to—'

'Joy was your wife?'

'Joy used to sometimes make milk puddi—'

'But she doesn't make them any more, Vernon, does she?' Jody sees Vernon's face drop. He is not a happy man in spite of the fact that, so far, he has got away with his heinous crime. 'I expect you miss her milk puddings, don't you?' Jody himself misses his mother's. His remark is not meant to be sarcastic but that's how it sounds. 'I even liked semolina, if it had lots of jam on.'

'It's not what you think,' quavers Vernon, seemingly unable to move from his chair, a heavy lump of guilty flesh gone to jelly. Something about his cravenness, that defeated look in his dry, aching eyes, reminds Jody of himself. They're victims, both victims, but this one has brought his fate on himself – unlike Jody, who is innocent. 'I didn't mean to kill her.'

'But you did kill her. Is that what you're saying?'

Vernon gives a silent dry sob. He sounds so hopeless, so empty as he implores beseechingly, 'What are you going to do?'

Jody, lean and tense, his hair a dry tangle, a most unlikely judge, strolls nervously round the kitchen, picking up odd bits and pieces, homely items that you miss in jail, inspecting them before putting them down. The curtains are drawn against the sun, it feels better than being exposed to the light. He stares at the row of photographs on the window-sill, the kids, he supposes, and they stare back at him like a cardboard audience in a toy circus he once had. There's a *Take a Break* magazine on the table. Someone is taking blood-pressure pills; by the look of him it's probably Vernon. 'I'm not going to do anything, not because I don't want to but because, at the moment, my needs are as great as yours. I must have somewhere to stay where I'll be safe for a while, as well as food and warmth and privacy.' He looks at Vernon to see how he's taking it. 'You'll have to let me stay here. You don't have much option when you think about it.'

Vernon rubs a limp hand over his crinkled forehead. 'There's no money,' he says tonelessly, meeting Jody's direct gaze, 'if that's what you're after. That's what caused it. Money. *Always money!*'

How crushed he looks.

Jody says nothing but opens the fridge door and pours himself a glass of milk. He downs it and pours another. 'It won't be for long.' He's surprised at his own reaction. He almost pities Vernon, he looks so lonely and pathetic and guilty. 'You're moving house soon, aren't you? You're probably moving anyway once they discover what you've gone and done.' He stares at Vernon as if he's a puzzle, trying to understand the man, to fit the complicated pieces together. He doesn't look like a murderer, doesn't sound like one either. 'To kill your own wife, that must really take some doing. You must have hated her for a very long time.'

But Vernon merely wipes his eyes and sighs in desolation.

It's fate. This refuge will suit Jody very well, just until Mum and Dad move in and then they'll have to play it by ear although he knows the police won't think of looking for him here. Mum's idea to come down south was inspired, but then she could never have dreamed something like this would happen. He's got Vernon just where he wants him and as long as he keeps his head down Jody's going to be safe and pretty comfortable for a good long while. Jody's interest is genuine, though fear and fascination play a large part. Is the man a psychopath, or just somebody driven right to the edge? He needs to know for his own protection, and in spite of Mum's ministrations his self-inflicted injury is hurting. 'When did you do it, Vernon? How long ago? And how did you kill your wife?'

'Please stop,' begs Vernon with dismay. 'Please, please leave me alone and go away and stop tormenting me like this. *I loved my wife.* Nothing was further from my mind than killing her. I've never touched her before in my life and I'd give anything to bring her back.'

'So how did it happen? We might as well talk to each other, Vernon, we can't just sit for hours in silence.' Does Vernon know what's in store for him, and does he care? All the vicious publicity, the loss of dignity, the descent into hell. A life sentence. Twenty years. But he looks like the sort who'd be let out for good behaviour, that's if he didn't lose his mind first. Jody, uneasy, still wanders round the kitchen looking restless.

Suddenly Vernon is struck by a thought. 'Listen, you're hiding from someone, too, I can tell. Well, let me warn you that someone might call here at any time. A neighbour. A friend. They are quite likely to pop in.'

'Well, don't show them into the sitting room, it's all perfectly simple. We keep the sitting-room door closed and you go and meet them in the hall.'

Vernon groans. 'They'll think that's odd.'

'Never mind. I'm sure you can think of a way to stop them going any further. Just keep in mind that it's in your interests as well as mine to keep me safe and out of sight because if I'm found I'm bound to tell the police what I know. I *will* tell them, Vernon, and I don't care what ideas you might have about why I'm hiding or what I've done but it's nothing like murder, Vernon, and I hope you understand that. You must realise that I mean exactly what I say.'

'I do,' cries Vernon breathlessly. 'I won't let anyone in. Just leave me alone. Please.'

Jody takes off his jacket and tries to relax. The courage of the young. The initial terror and distaste he had of Vernon fades by the minute and he is amazed to find himself feeling more pity than anything else. He almost wants to console the man, to offer him hope, some comfort, and maybe he would if his heart had not been replaced by a cold, empty space. Even in jail Jody rarely saw a man so defeated, so tortured as Vernon.

It's as if Vernon feels the sympathy; his wits are slowly returning. He looks at Jody properly for the very first time since he arrived. 'You said you were related to the people who are buying our house?'

'Yep. Jody Middleton, that's me.'

'Why were you camping on the moor?'

'Because I enjoy the moors.'

'How come you chose that particular house?'

'It was the first suitable place I came to. It was ideal, shelter if it rained and a ruined garden, off the beaten track which is what I wanted.'

'And then you decided you'd come to take a look at this house?'

'Because one day I am going to be living in it.'

Vernon shudders. 'And then you recognised me.'

'It was a shock, I can tell you. It took me some time to believe it.'

'But why aren't you contacting the police? Why do you need to do any of this? Why move in here? I don't understand.' Such searching questions. And Vernon's bemused eyes are still fixed on him.

Killer's eyes?

'You don't need to understand. I can't tell you, I can't talk about it. I'm just as vulnerable as you in a different kind of way and that's all you need to know for now.'

But Vernon is still perplexed. 'My wife never mentioned a son, only two daughters, when the family came round to look and they only came the once. Made up their minds immediately, the agent said. No need to view a second time, that was a relief for Joy.' This frightened man is rambling now. 'They didn't think much of the extension, I think that's what Joy said. And they wouldn't use the bar because they never drank. But I'm sure she never mentioned a son.'

'No,' says Jody sadly. 'They wouldn't mention me.' How he wishes Mum was here now. He's fed up of fighting the world on his own. All he wants to do is sleep, quietly and safely in his own bed, with her stroking his forehead and waking him up with a cup of tea. Will that ever happen again after this? Such innocent images yet Jody is forced to check them before he breaks out in tears.

If only they'd talk to Janice Plunket. If only she would tell them the truth. It's sod's law, isn't it? Here he is, on the run from the law, innocent of the charges, and here's Vernon in his own house getting away with murder.

Vernon scratches his aching head, incapable of clear thought, wrenching himself out of memories. He picks up a cigarette and lights it. 'How do I know you are who you say you are?'

Jody nearly laughs out loud. 'You don't know. But what does it matter? You can hardly ask for references.' Is Vernon a psycho? You're always astonished when the police finally produce their murderer; you can never believe they look so ordinary when they reach the dock. Is his wife his only victim, or has Vernon secretly been at it for years, stashing cadavers down the well? Perhaps his wife was a nag who drove him to it; or two-timing him, or an alcoholic. Vernon looks perfectly harmless. He's out of condition, not only overweight but breathless and abnormally red in the face. If it came to it, Jody could take him on with ease, but not if he's got the strength of a madman. Jody wishes he dare ring home and tell them where he is, but he fears the phone in the Close is bugged. No, what Jody needs to do now is thank God for this lucky break, take one day at a time and not think ahead at all. But how is he going to sleep tonight, knowing there's a murderer on the prowl in the next bedroom? He must remember to lock Vernon's door as well as his own.

Tucking into the egg fried rice that Vernon agreed to go and fetch because there was no other food in the house, Jody makes sure to keep an eye on Vernon's every move. The man's not hungry; so far he hasn't touched a thing or expressed the slightest interest in the programmes on the telly and who can blame him, there's nothing on in the summer. But when the local news comes on Vernon lurches forward in his chair with his ears pricked. It doesn't look all that riveting, just a nosy crowd in the road watching the police and ambulance people staking out a small block of flats . . . Some old woman has blocked herself in and everyone's going barmy about it.

Vernon drops his fork with a bang onto his plate and stutters, 'I don't believe this. I think that's the flat we're buying. Hang on, hang on, let me get another look. Yes, – it *is* the flat.' He turns round to where Jody sits slightly behind him on guard in the second chair, amazement in his voice. 'That's the one, that's Albany Buildings, and they're saying the Queen is somehow involved. What on earth is going on – and where does this leave us?'

'What do you mean?'

But Vernon, glued to the screen, ignores Jody's question. The journalist, keen-featured and well-tailored, is telling the tale in low reverent tones. Like a parrot, or someone under hypnosis, Vernon slowly repeats nearly everything he says. 'She's refusing to come out until they say she can stay there! Mrs Peacock, the old lady, is refusing to come out of her flat and her friend there is saying she has been treated abominably by the Council and the social workers and her own family, apparently. That must mean the woman who showed us round, that Mrs Rendell, the old lady's daughter. My God! Has the whole world gone mad?'

This means little to him. Jody is unimpressed. He shrugs his shoulders and carries on eating. Luckily Vernon remembered to bring some Cokes home, too. In a weird way Vernon appears to enjoy the lad's company, although he'd probably never admit it. 'They'll get her out in the end. It's one of those nine-day wonders, only local stuff so far. It shouldn't make any difference to you.'

'But there's helicopters on the scene, and arc-lights, as if it's a national emergency.'

'Well, I suppose it is, if she's that old. But you didn't know her so what does it matter?'

'But what's the Queen got to do with it?'

Funny. Vernon is really taken up with this, the first thing in which he has demonstrated any real interest since Jody arrived. Showing signs of life at last. Genuinely concerned about what he is seeing, and worried unduly. 'You'll have to wait and read about it when you get to work in the morning. They won't do anything more now. Come on, finish your bean sprouts or they'll go cold.'

It is just before they are settling for bed when the doorbell chimes. Jody stiffens and feels instantly sick. This is all he needs, and Mum, who likes her privacy, will go mad living here with neighbours visiting day or night. 'Who's this likely to be at this time?'

Vernon looks equally dumbfounded. Still pale and haggard with worry he resembles a terrified rabbit on guard, standing on the landing in his socks and underpants. 'What should I do?'

'You'll have to answer it. It might be some emergency. Go and tell them you were on your way to bed. Just remember, this is far more important to you than it is to me and don't panic, just be casual. I'll stay up here and look out of the window.'

Jody hears Vernon's heavy footsteps treading down the stairs. He clicks the hall light on, then opens the door as far as the chain will allow. 'Yes, who are you?' Vernon says.

'This is important, Mr Marsh,' says a confident male voice. 'I'd just like to have a few words—'

'But it's late,' argues Vernon, and Jody imagines him glancing at his watch.

'It won't take a moment, sir.'

And then Jody hears the chain click off the door.

'I'm just checking up on some information given to me today,' says the voice. 'Would I be correct in thinking that you are the punters who are proposing to buy number one, Albany Buildings, from a Mrs Frankie Rendell? Would that be right, mate?'

'Well yes, I am. I was . . .' starts Vernon. 'But this recent business has nothing to do with me.'

'Are you aware that this flat morally belongs to a seventy-five-year-old lady who is being forced to sell against her will?'

'No, of course we weren't aware of that. We weren't aware of anything. We just liked the flat, it suited our needs, and we just went along with it, like you do. Who are you, anyway?'

'When you say "we", Mr Marsh, is that your wife you're referring to?'

'My wife, Joy, yes. She's not here at the moment . . .' and Vernon tries to close the door.

'Pity. I would have preferred the two of you together.'

Jody listens from above, his gnawing anxiety growing. As they grew used to each other, as the evening wore on, Vernon had proved how desperately anxious he was to discuss his crime. He seemed relieved that Jody had come; he was able to unburden himself of something he found too heavy to carry. And Jody was interested. Jody listened. Let's hope that Vernon doesn't risk involving anyone else, some nosy parker who's come to the door to borrow a cupful of sugar. Vernon, with his dressing gown only half on, splutters, 'Sorry? What? Where did you say you were from? What did you want to know?'

'I'm Bob Simmonds from the *Daily Mirror* newspaper, Mr Marsh, and this is my photographer who would like to take—'

There's no time for choice. Before Vernon can step back inside, before he even realises what exactly is going on here, a shadow steps out of the flower beds and a brilliant light flashes in his face.

While directly above him, Jody Middleton shivers convulsively because he knows without any flicker of doubt that when they develop that photograph, they will be able to see his face staring between the curtains with frightened, hunted eyes . . .

TWENTY-NINE

The Grange, Dunsop, Nr Clitheroe, Lancs

'Hey, hey. Stand by for developments.' Jacy's excited voice barks over the answerphone. 'Make yourself ready. He likes us. *He loves us.* We're gonna be big. And what do you think of the name "Haze"?'

Arabella and Belle stare at each other, incredulous. So it worked! Against all the odds it actually worked! Sugarshack is dead and buried and Haze is about to rise from the ashes. 'I'm not so sure about the name. I thought it was a lavatory spray.' They can hear some kind of raucous celebration going on in the background and Cyd is trying to be crude in order to upset Belle. Jacy must have pushed him off because the message goes on, 'Can't stop now, more sessions to be getting on with. You can count on a quick wedding, my darlin', so get your glad rags on. I'll catch you later. Byeee.'

Peaches gives a rueful smile. 'You should have gone with them, shouldn't you, Tusker? I bet you wish you had. You could have been celebrating now, instead of being stuck here with me.'

'What nonsense you do talk sometimes, Peaches,' says Belle, meaning it, but interested to find herself back in her old role of protector of Peaches once again. It was a role Peaches seems to urge unconsciously on those around her, just like she did at school, as if she didn't possess the necessary weapons to defend herself. It is a useful trick which Belle, ever perceived as capable, would love to perfect. When does it come? In childhood, because of what you look like, petite and defenceless like Peaches, or dark and argumentative, a show-off, like herself and capable of anything, or is it triggered later as a result of a real failure to cope with the slings and arrows of life? She says, 'It would be worse than a nightmare to be around any of that lot at the moment. I'm quite happy to wait until they get home, when their bragging will be quite excruciating enough.'

'He says he's going to marry you, Tusker!' And Belle's pretty face is alight with joy. 'I think he means it.'

'He is going to marry me because this man Mathews must think it's a good idea as far as the new group's image goes and for no other reason. Believe me, I know him too well.'

'You're so cynical! You always were, even at school. You never looked on the positive side.'

'From where I stood there wasn't one.'

'Oh, Tusker! He really must love you – and I think you know that deep inside.'

'Hell's bells, Peaches, I wish you'd dry up with your silly little-girl romantic theories. Why must you always view the world through rose-coloured spectacles. Haven't you learned your lesson yet?'

'What if he comes home and needs you here?' Peaches is poring over the map of Scotland. She is stretched out on the floor chewing a pencil in the very same way she used to fidget over her scruffy prep at school. She fiddles with the silver chain round her neck as once she fiddled with her crucifix during the glorious religious phase they all went through together. 'Perhaps you should stay here and wait for Jacy's next call. If everything is so imminent, he might well need you . . .'

'He doesn't need me,' says Belle, listening to her own dry hopelessness with some surprise because she has always been so reluctant to admit this to herself, let alone to anyone else. 'No, and he never has. It was me who needed him. I got my kicks through him, I suppose, feeding off his energy but protected from the effects of the constant party by my self-assumed motherly role.' The capable one, the one with the mental First Aid box with the sticking plasters cut to size, forever up to date and handy. What she says is quite true. And when Peaches was called empty-headed at school, it had to be Belle who led the walkout and got sent home in disgrace. She must take up other people's issues and fight on their behalf, whether they want her to or not. She got expelled in the end for doing exactly that. 'I wanted excitement. I wanted notoriety, too. But I didn't dare go out and get them for myself. I knew jolly well I couldn't have put up with the grief. There was the other side of the coin, too: the worse he got, the more I felt needed. Listen to me, boring you to death with my woes – and I sound so disgusting, don't I? Like a leech. Like a parasite!'

'This is so weird,' Peaches says, 'because you could have all the excitement you wanted. Here you are, a top model, enough money for a good lifestyle, attention, publicity, open a magazine and there you are inside it, ride down the Tube and you're there basking beside the escalator, you had it all. I often saw you and thought that and envied you, Tusker.' She frowns, turns the map around as if she's been studying it upside down up till now, which knowing her she probably has. 'Tusker, you're miles from Scotland!'

'I told you that, you fool! At least five hundred to Aberdeen. Have you even found Aberdeen yet, Peaches? Come on, give it here.'

'I have found Aberdeen but I can't find Ballater anywhere, or Craithie Church. Whatever, it looks as if we're going to have to stay the night up there.'

'Well, of course we are, and we're going to have to leave now if you want to be there for the morning service. I still think it's the most reckless thing you could ever do and I'm not going to change my mind about that. This is not a sensible option, Peaches. Are you absolutely sure he'll be there? I couldn't stand to think we might make a journey like this for nothing. I would never, ever forgive you.'

'He'll be there. I checked in the Court circular they do in *The Times*. There was one opposite my seat on the train and he is definitely in Scotland although they don't put what they're doing when they're on holiday. And you're right, it's crazy, but crucial. It's something I *have* to do,' says Peaches, with that martyred Joan of Arc expression on her face again. Dammit, if Belle had known Joan of Arc she would have volunteered to burn for her. 'I don't care what happens to me after that. I have to confront Jamie and it's now or never.'

Yes. This whole thing is quite fantastic. Poor Peaches. But what in the name of heaven is Belle doing involving herself in this sort of madness? Why oh why does she always end up submerged in the dramas of other people? *What is the matter with her?* Why does she never have any battles of her own worth fighting? 'You could be walking straight into a trap. You could even end up losing your baby and I don't consider the Jeep much of a getaway car. That's if it gets us there in the first place, which I seriously doubt.'

'I've already answered that. How many times must I say this? If Jamie honestly doesn't want me then I really don't care. They can go ahead and kill me, if that would suit their purposes.'

'You don't really mean that.'

'Oh, but I do, I do,' says Peaches with a courageous smile.

'Clachan Keep. Bed and breakfast. H&C in all bedrooms.'

'And I should think so too. We are on the eve of the twenty-first century.'

A mile this side of the village and the Jeep splutters with an evil wind as they turn from the main road to follow the sign and take a steep track twisting between heather and bracken, bramble and thorn, up towards the wind-blown pines that stand out against the sky.

'My God,' Peaches exclaims, looking out with a shiver and gripping the edge of her seat. 'I thought The Grange was desolate.'

The worst part of the journey is over and if they can only endure just another few yards they will be safe, until morning anyway. Higher and higher they climb, the track becoming narrower and rougher and the woodlands stretching on either side, pale birches and dark firs amongst the crags and boulders. Apart from the roaring of the vehicle the air is filled with silence. They are high enough now, if they turn their heads, to see the long arc of the Grampian Mountains, dark and sombre, rising and disappearing into the ghostly mists of nowhere and an isolated rowing boat puts out on the lake below them, slight as a bug on a garden pond.

Belle is completely exhausted. It has taken them ten hours to get here with the minimum of stops and it is now eight o'clock. At least they are nearer than they expected to be, according to the map. The short morning journey to Craithie should take them less than an hour. They both agreed they'd be better staying somewhere out in the sticks just in case their invisible pursuers are on their trail. The bright red Jeep does tend to stand out in a crowd.

Oh dear God for an early night.

This place is ridiculous. Almost impenetrable and it's twenty degrees colder up here. Belle, her neck and her shoulders aching to a point of unbearable stiffness, is beginning to believe it doesn't exist when the track turns into a gravelled drive and they pull up in front of a domineering granite square covered with ivy. There are turrets on the four corners of the house and with all the evergreens and the sombre stonework it is hairy and dark.

Belle turns to her tired passenger and groans. 'It's like bloody Dracula's Castle. Shall we go back? I can't face this.'

'But it's getting dark and starting to rain. No, Belle, please. We'll have to stay here now. Come on, I'll go and knock and see what happens.'

A big nose overhanging a lank grey moustache peers out from under a checked peak cap. His knicker-bocker suit, the colour of gorse, hangs straight and loose on his tall and angular frame, and a hefty hound with a panting jaw and a pendulous tongue gazes at them with moderate interest over the Jeep door. 'By Jove, it's late to be out and about.' All in a broad Scottish accent which would have to be translated by sub-titles were he ever to appear on TV.

'I hope we're not too late for a room,' says Belle, nudging Peaches who is giggling helplessly beside her.

'*Down, Huntress, down!*' booms their host in a deep, commanding voice. And then, to them, in the same warlike tones, 'You'd better come on in as you're here. It's eighteen pounds the night for each of you and that's with a sturdy breakfast.'

'Stop it, Peaches,' hisses Belle. 'Don't upset him, for God's sake. I couldn't drive another inch. I don't care what it's like inside. Stop laughing NOW.'

'We don't see a lot of Them, to be honest,' says the little woman of the house in her button-through overall, pouring tea out of a fat brown teapot after her husband had padded off led by the straining Huntress with her gentle, pathetic eyes, not unlike those of her blustering master. Above the walk-in fireplace hang a pair of bagpipes with a coat of arms, and a vicious-looking tool with what looks like bloodstains on the handle. An entrenching tool, perhaps? Belle dare not look at Peaches. Above the twisted wooden stairs the long-dead heads of stags stared down on them with glassy nothingness when Belle and Peaches went to look at their bedroom. The same, almost-menacing look was echoed in the ancestors' eyes, imposing paintings in heavy oils in a line along the landing. 'Well, They keep to Themselves you know, it's best.' Their landlady serves them honey and hot scones. 'But They're sometimes seen in the village going about their business, and at church of course, and at the hunts. No different from the rest of us, you know, not really.' She turns to Peaches. 'Why do you ask, my dear? Are you a keen monarchist?'

'We want to see Them tomorrow if possible.' Peaches' cheeks are bright with excitement and her nervous eyes dart this way and that.

'They'll be in church, no doubt.'

'Do They mind strangers watching?'

'They're so used to it I don't think They notice. But you might have to prepare yourselves to be searched, as you're not known in the area.'

This is too close for comfort, no longer the far-fetched fantasy it seemed back at The Grange. Belle watches Peaches tuck into her high tea. They'll probably not search her at all, presuming her absolute innocence. It will be Belle who gets the treatment, the same way it happened at school when they got caught with the booze at the end of term. The next one was the A-level term. Peaches stood no chance of passing anything, she was merely there to pass the time before she went off to finishing school. It was Belle who had the high hopes.

Three A levels, all in the sciences, and she was predicted to get straight As in every subject. She'd been conditionally accepted at Oxford with a year out first, touring with a friend. It would be their proud contribution to her future, said her genial father, willing to fund the enterprise.

It was Charlie and Mags who had the idea of a wild, boozy party and everyone else agreed. Peaches tagged along, excited in her lispy, child-like way but no real practical help. She would provide the crisps. Belle, who was mixed up with a barman twice her age in a local pub at the time, was quite obsessed about him, took little interest apart from on the night itself when she helped to smuggle the boxes in. They all got caught because of Peaches' mindless giggling and larking about. When Belle stood forward and demanded to take the whole of the blame, she was dealt with quite without mercy, and expelled immediately, despite the A levels coming up next term.

What *is* this need to confess? Is it to do with wanting to be liked? Or a feeling of being more capable of taking the blame than anyone else? Belle has never fathomed it out. Apparently the others did eventually come forward and confess, but they dubbed her the ringleader although she'd had little to do with any of it. Her father was mortified; her mother devastated. You'd think Belle had committed murder rather than got caught in a piece of harmless boarding-school fun.

'Write to Mrs Coney-Wills, Daddy, please,' she pleaded in vain. 'She'd let me come back if you insisted, I know she would. She's just trying to make me a scapegoat.'

'I will certainly not write to Mrs Coney-Wills. She has made her decision with the good of the school at heart and I respect her for that.'

'Please, Mummy, make him listen! If I don't sit those exams my whole future will be affected.'

'You should have thought of that, Belinda, when you were behaving so badly. And in her letter to me Mrs Coney-Wills suggests that illegal drinking was not all you were up to either.'

Belle broke her heart, more over Alfie Jamieson, the barman, than the thought of lost exams, it's true, and Daddy refused to allow her the promised year out as a punishment. It seemed that the wrath of Allah descended and settled upon her head. Her mother would hardly speak to her. Belle heard her talking to her friends in hushed, disappointed tones on the phone. The local schools were doing a totally different examination syllabus so it was no good begging to be allowed to go there. Anywhere private was out of the question, as her furious father refused to pay.

And then she had answered the modelling advertisement and never really looked back since.

She had travelled the world in the end, to her parents' great disapproval. She had seen all she wanted to see, securely and safely, as part of Jacy's entourage.

And here she is again, in danger, and likely to be the one caught and punished.

She has brought her friend to the brink, so why doesn't Belle hold back now, stay here at Clachan Keep and have a good breakfast while Peaches goes on to fulfil her terrible destiny at Craithie Church in the morning? Because Belle knows that Peaches just couldn't cope without her. She would lose her way, or bungle the whole affair, or panic and end up in deeper trouble.

'You get the usual little crowd of supporters, there's not much fuss here,' goes on their busy little landlady, Mrs MacTaggard, clearing up after them and laying the kitchen table for the morning. 'Porridge and kedgeree all right for you? We always have that, it is MacTaggard's favourite. Security is important, of course. These days there are lunatics lurking behind every tree. But those craving personal attention, as most of these hooligans are, wouldn't choose Craithie as the ideal spot. They'd soon have the furious locals on their trails if they tried anything fishy round here. And on the whole the press are pretty good. They do try to give Them as much privacy when They come up here as possible.'

If the fierce MacTaggard only knew what he was harbouring under his roof tonight, he would no doubt steal in and finish them off with the ugly tool on the wall in the kitchen. Belle sighs and looks over at Peaches. Does she truly realise the enormity of the action she is so determined to take? Tonight, in the massive bedroom they share, she will try to change her friend's mind if she can stay awake long enough, if she can fight off this feeling of total and utter exhaustion, for her own sake, if not for Arabella's. Because Belle is beginning to realise that whatever happens tomorrow she is the one who will get the blame, as always, accused of being the instigator of the whole ghastly affair. Because everyone knows and understands that silly, soppy Peaches, the lovable, baby-faced Peaches, has no will of her own and is the sort to be easily led.

THIRTY

No fixed abode

Ten forty-five precisely.

The main security checks were completed early this morning. Now, granite-faced men with walkie-talkies and flinty eyes stand at the obvious bends and corners, bleeping to each other like baby chicks every so often to check that all is well.

As the majestic procession of big black Daimlers rolls into sight between the fir trees, a respectful little flutter of claps can be heard on the pine-filled summer air. Mostly regulars. Sir Hugh Mountjoy looks out of the last car and sighs to himself with relief. Beside him, Dougal Rathbone's eagle eyes scan the welcoming faces because if he slips up now, if this business should get any worse than it already is, he is out on his ear in disgrace with no pension, despite his noble family connections. Sir Hugh has made that quite clear. 'Because you've handled the whole thing with quite inordinate clumsiness,' he declares, 'when you knew very well how delicate it was.'

Sir Hugh did try to deter the Prince from attending church this morning, but his regal mother was with him at breakfast and so he could not pass on the fateful message which might well have been, 'Trouble brewing, stay home with your head well down.'

He did consider passing a note in with the toast, but concluded that would be far too risky.

And anyway, it does seem rather unlikely that Arabella Brightly-Smythe would dare to do anything foolish in the open, in front of the cameras. The little idiot, if she is so intent on seeing her lover, is far more likely to approach quite openly through the front gates of the castle and therefore be apprehended before she causes any unpleasantness. All Sir Hugh and Dougal Rathbone know, and this information came via one of Lovette's men, is that she was seen leaving The Grange in Belinda Hutchins' red Jeep at eight o'clock yesterday morning, but after that they lost them in the lanes.

On hearing this Sir Hugh was not pleased.

Security men lie in wait at The Grange to inform them if the women return.

In spite of a general alert put through the regular channels, nothing was seen of the Jeep after that, but that might well be because they couldn't give a reason for the apprehension of these two innocent women, and Special Branch haven't the facilities to watch all the roads except in high priority cases. The one helicopter employed for the task was greatly hampered by morning mists.

Nevertheless, as soon as they learned for certain that Arabella had fled the coop and found sanctuary with her friend, the two discreet Civil Servants felt duty-bound to fly at once to Scotland and form a warning presence beside the Prince in case the need should arise. This all based on nothing more than Dougal's intuition.

'She's always maintained that she won't rest easy until she has seen and spoken to James. In my opinion, and because I know the young lady to possess a simple and stubborn personality, I would venture to believe that—'

'Do get on with it, Dougal. You are not making a banquet speech now.'

'I think she will try to see him in Scotland, and church is just one of a number of regular activities which everyone knows takes place while the Family are resident here.'

Sir Hugh was nonplussed. He downed his third gin and tonic since take-off. 'But would her friend agree to such a flamboyant gesture, especially if she's been told of the danger Arabella believes she might be in? Of course we must hope and pray that this friend, Belinda, this dated pop-star's floozie, is a little more sophisticated and will assume at once that Arabella has let her imagination run riot this time.' He turned to Dougal with a worried look and the lines in his noble brow seemed more deeply etched than ever. 'Surely nobody in their right mind would believe such hysterical suggestions?'

'We don't even know for certain that Peaches suspected our plans. Perhaps she just ran away in despair after hearing about the engagement, fled to her friend for comfort and nothing more sinister than that. Perhaps they've gone away for a few days to take Peaches' mind off her present miseries. Shopping or something girlie.' Dougal eased off his shoes. His feet tended to swell in enclosed atmospheres, especially where there was also tension. 'That scenario is more than likely. We mustn't think the worst.'

A stewardess went by with a smile and Sir Hugh, after giving Dougal's socks a disgusted sniff, lowered his voice and murmured, 'We have to think the worst, that's our job.'

'But we can hardly warn anyone else without letting the cat out of the bag.'

'That is precisely why we are going up there ourselves. And you are the only one who can identify them both.'

'I feel like a spiv,' said Dougal, whose star, up until now, had been in speedy ascendancy. 'Somebody seedy out of the *Singing Detective*. I mean, what the hell do we think we are going to do if we see Arabella in the vicinity? We haven't the necessary powers to arrest her. We can only use persuasion and she's already turned her nose up at that.' They should never have messed with Lovette. With an inner emptiness that frightens him, Dougal knows he will take the blame for all this, although he considers himself not only the younger but the more dominant, the more capable man of the two even though he is only an assistant on probation. Sir Hugh is dutiful and competent but decidedly unremarkable and has risen to his present position by virtue of seniority and family influence rather than brilliance, just the sort of archaic type who does the Family no favours.

'Leave all that to me,' said Sir Hugh, inspecting his tray of plastic luncheon, that same old breast of chicken with the blob of hard bread sauce. And could this *really* be called fruit salad? 'You've caused enough trouble already. I, of course, have nothing to fear. My hands are perfectly clean.'

To which poor Dougal, with his smelly feet, said nothing.

The crowd murmur their disappointment. A romantic lot, they had hoped to see the new royal Princess-to-be this morning; they have brought special posies with which to mob her but word goes round that she is resting in Mustique and will be out of the country for a month until the excitement dies down. But it looks as if the Prince is here, and his two older brothers – a full hand, how wonderful, well worth turning out for.

There's a hush of wonder as the Queen steps from her car, that familiar little foot sticking out, so neat, so noble, so royal. And doesn't she look wonderful in that powder-blue hat, how it suits her, and look how reverently her gallant husband takes her arm. Oh, this is what it is all about, on a gentle, British summer morning with the birds singing sweetly in tune with the old church bells on the breeze.

Everyone smiles. Everyone waves; and the genuine happiness is infectious; even the policemen on duty wear smiles on their chiselled faces, every bit as catching as yawns. With equal solemnity the other Family members alight from their various cars and join Her Majesty in a little, familiar procession towards the old archway astride the doors of this unassuming church. The minister of Craithie himself, who is also a domestic chaplain, is at the door with a benevolent bow and a handshake and it is he who leads the way into the comparative dark of the church, down the aisle and towards the Family pew at the front.

The congregation plunge with great feeling into: *'Now thank we all our God, with hearts and hands and voices . . .'*

Doesn't the youngest Prince look handsome! Those left outside still call a soft, 'Congratulations, Your Highness,' remembering how sweetly shy his look seemed to be as he passed them, one more fleeting memory to take home and treasure for ever. How virile he looked, and how manly. There's bound to be children from *that* union even if his eldest brother, poor man, is finding it hard. How needlessly cruel the press have been. Why, any young man worth his salt needs to sow his oats. Pity his bride-to-be wasn't with him, but next time, perhaps, if they keep coming one day they are bound to be rewarded by a sighting of the grand Lady Frances herself. They will hang around and chat until the Family come out and cheer them on their way back to the castle and Sunday lunch.

The bell rings out a single knell as Communion is celebrated inside.

Some people take out their sandwiches and Thermos. Others, strangers, several Americans, take photographs while they are free to walk about. Some children make daisy chains sitting on the grass, or scratch pictures with sticks in the dust, whiling away the time as quietly as they can.

Sunlight and shade. Below them is a blanket of mist. Feet crunching on pine needles. The bright light glistens on the mountain crests. It is such a sleepy Sunday morning you can almost smell beef roasting. One hour later, as the crowd forms again, as the double doors start to open, a figure is seen flitting through the outer fringe of the woods. It's as much as the security men can do to contact each other, let alone move fast enough to stop her.

It is a stricken tableau.

'Jamie! Jamie! Help me, please,' the figure cries hysterically, hurtling down the pathway and immediately chaining her wrist by a bicycle padlock to the brass ring on the stout church door.

'Get back! Get back!' Somebody cries out frenziedly.

'There could be a gun!'

'Assassination!' calls an agitated member of the crowd who will be interrogated afterwards.

And suddenly there is action.

The chaplain pauses in his tracks and stands with his arms outstretched, warding off Satan himself, a crucifix in laundered white at the door of the church, mirroring the original behind him on the altar.

He is pushed to the ground and trampled on by the feet of a dozen security men trained in anti-terrorist tactics who desperately press their way past him. When they have gone he is left with the girl, his old head raised in astonishment capped with a floss of fuzzy white hair. 'What the hell . . . ?'

Peaches has peaked ten seconds too soon.

'*Where is he?*' she screams, doubled up with pain and fear. 'Where is Jamie? Oh dear God, tell him to come outside and talk to me, I beg you, I beg you!'

The chaplain, from his uncomfortable place on the ground, unavoidably in direct eye contact with this poor, misguided soul, can only look into her terrified eyes and murmur with feeling, 'God forgive you, my child, whatever it is you have done.'

The Royals are safely inside and the door banged shut.

Eyes are on stalks. Mouths hang open. Never has anyone seen anything as dramatic and unexpected as this. The nerve of the woman! And at church, too! Desecration! Cameras are whirring, not only the press, but every person in the crowd is hoping for a saleable picture, a good one might pay them thousands. So far, though, it is much too confusing to work out exactly what is happening.

The girl, still chained to the door, is now surrounded by plain-clothed men. Revolvers drawn, they form a ring round her and the fallen vicar. All that can be clearly heard, above the buzz of excited voices, is the clear, piercing cry of: 'JAMIE. JAMIE. JAMIE. *I am carrying our child.*'

Hello, hello. What can this mean? Then someone must have muffled her mouth because the sound peters out and is heard no more. From within the unholy scrum only the vicar's arm can be seen forming a wavering cross.

'You moved too soon,' says the girl they call Belinda Hutchins, sitting beside the saboteur's bed in a private room at the hospital. She's furious. 'You moved a good minute too soon. I told you to wait, but you would go. You wouldn't listen to my advice.'

'Would you mind leaving Miss Brightly-Smythe with us for a moment, Miss Hutchins?'

'And who might you be?' Belinda shouts at Sir Hugh, raising her fists as though to strike him. She is restrained by a waiting guard and taken away down the hospital corridor, still shouting absurdities behind her. 'I'll know exactly who is to blame if anything bad happens to Peaches! I'm warning you, I'll not keep quiet. I'll go to the press, I'll spread it around, I'll tell everyone what you did and you'll be hounded until you confess . . . I'm not without influence . . . Everyone knows my face, it's on the Tube, people will listen to me and I know all about you and your little ways,' she shrieks at the sheepish Dougal.

What fresh hell is this? Sir Hugh raises his eyebrows forlornly and shakes his head at Dougal.

'Miss Brightly-Smythe has been tranquillised in order to calm her down, and she *is* pregnant,' says a stiff-faced Sister, 'so if you would go easily with her. I'll be right outside the door should you need me,' she mouths to her patient.

In view of the mass of publicity it was imperative to bring the creature here, there was no other option. Requests for information about her condition are being faxed and telephoned every few minutes. The hospital switchboard has ground to a halt.

If only, if only the half-wit hadn't shouted out that damning phrase: '*I am carrying our child.*' A phrase quite likely to touch the heart of a nation. If only video cameras had never been invented. Until then she was merely another hysteric who could have been protesting about anything, from low wages to rail privatisation to cod wars. The Palace machine could have dealt with it, polished it, obliterated it.

Already she is public property.

This is quite dreadful. After they have spoken to the wench they have been summoned at once to the presence of the Queen's own Private Secretary, a Knight of the Bath and the most important person in the Household, in a meeting with the Press Secretary (who is flying to Scotland immediately), and various security chiefs. Naturally they will deny all plans to facilitate a miscarriage. Nobody must know about that little trick. The only people aware of that appalling truth, apart from Sir Hugh and Dougal, are Lovette and his blessed bent doctor.

But after they understand the unhappy situation, his superiors will be in agreement on two firm fronts. One, they have badly mishandled the issue and two, the truth must never come out.

The girl is tearful and still shaking. Lying in bed with the sheet at her chin she looks no more than a misused child only minus her teddy bear, Beppo. 'What does Jamie say? Is he coming to see me?'

Damn and blast. Turn the wretched record over! Dougal goes to sit beside her. He tries to take her hand but she jerks it away. 'I haven't spoken to Jamie,' Dougal admits sympathetically. 'So I don't know what he is going to do.'

'I made things worse, didn't I?' sobs the stupid Peaches.

'Well, you certainly haven't made matters any easier,' Dougal gently agrees.

'He must have heard me!'

'I am sure he did. Everyone heard you. But that's what you wanted, wasn't it?'

'No.' She looks at him surprised. 'I only wanted to speak to Jamie, and this seemed the only way. But I bungled it. I didn't even see him . . . five hundred miles and I never even saw his face.' She tries to sit up on her pillows but the drug has made her sleepy. She slips down in the bed again, limp, all energy gone. 'You should have let me speak to him earlier then none of this would have happened.'

Dougal tries to be reasonable. 'I knew it wouldn't do any good.'

'It wasn't that.' She looks at him oddly, bites her lip and glances at the door. 'You had other ideas, didn't you, Dougal? The private clinic, for example. You might think I'm stupid but I'm not that blind. What would have happened to me if I'd kept that appointment? After you had aborted my baby, what would you have done then? You pretended to be my friend and all you were doing was trying to harm me, you and your horrible friend.'

Sir Hugh stands back in the corner of the room, trying to hide, beside the ventilator.

Dougal laughs out loud. 'What an imagination, Peaches! You should have been a writer. What on earth put these ludicrous ideas in your head? You sounded pleased when I told you about the clinic . . .'

'I didn't know about the engagement then. And you didn't tell me either. You must have known all about it but you kept it from me—'

'Only because I was concer—'

'Rubbish! The only thing you two were ever concerned about was defending Jamie's reputation and saving your own skins and your office overlooking Constitution Hill! That's what you are paid for and that's what you were doing. You didn't give a damn about me, about how I felt or what I wanted. You must have been laughing at me all the time, and still are, especially now that I've played the only hand I had left and Jamie still hasn't come.'

'Nobody's laughing at you, Peaches. Least of all me and Sir Hugh. But they certainly will start laughing if you tell them those mad ideas of yours. They'll probably not believe you knew Jamie, either.'

Not the right thing to say. Arabella goes red in the face.

'They'll have to believe me if I go and have tests.' She tries to sit up again and this time she succeeds. She stares at Dougal with hate in her hard blue eyes. 'I am prepared to do everything now, everything my friends always said I should. Why should I suffer just to defend a way of life which is archaic and ridiculous anyway?'

'Be sensible, Arabella, please, before you do anything you might regret.'

'Ah, so you're threatening me now, are you, Dougal? Shall I call the Sister in and tell her what you are saying? You can't hurt me in here and I know that very well, not with everyone knowing about me, and aware of where I am. While I am here I am safe, quite different from that sinister clinic you were going to take me to. I can speak to who I like, even the press should I wish to do so. So this is my last request of you, and you either carry it out or I will take the necessary actions to defend myself and the future of my child. I want Jamie here, by my bedside, by ten o'clock tomorrow morning. I shall arrange to speak to the *Daily Mirror* reporter at eleven sharp. The only way I am prepared to cancel that is if I see Jamie. *Now do you finally understand?*'

Not quite so sweet, not quite so innocent, just as I thought, thinks Sir Hugh.

Dougal looks round at Sir Hugh, who nods reluctantly. Somehow they've got to try. Something has to be resolved or all hell will break loose and it will be instant dismissal for both of them. His doughty wife, Lady Constance, will leave him and his friends will stop phoning. He will lose his Grace and Favour residence and his future will be forever blighted. This doomed affair has turned into a living nightmare and may even get worse and descend into a fog of horror.

A blessing they've done away with Tower Hill.

Damn damn damn and damnation.

THIRTY-ONE

Flat I, Albany Buildings, Swallowbridge, Devon

Now Miss Benson knew there would be a fuss, but had absolutely no idea of the furore Mrs Peacock's simple act of protest would cause. Every so often, when the coast is clear, she sends gleeful reports to her neighbour by raising the floorboard under the carpet and kneeling down beside the bath.

Mrs Peacock also seems bemused by the national interest she has evoked, and the tremendous sympathy. She would be aware of most of this without Miss Benson's help because not only does she watch her flat on the local news quite regularly, but it is now featured on the national bulletins, too.

And everyone she has ever known appears to have an opinion.

It is Frankie she feels so sorry for. Frankie, who has been inadvertently turned into a caricature of the bad and negligent daughter. When this is all over, Frankie will never forgive her mother. The serious papers which Miss Benson kindly sends down the chute are sympathetic and rational; it is the tabloids that shout such cruel headlines with the high-minded, morally righteous bent. It is, Irene supposes, mostly the middle classes who do tend to dispose of their aged parents. Tabloid readers often haven't the wherewithal and thus get lumbered with them at home as the State is so reluctant to pay. Perhaps this section of the community have more of a right to be pious.

Irene cannot see out of her windows because of the heavy boarding, but she can hear the kerfuffle outside and the police are just one arm among a whole retinue of do-gooders who have already addressed her by loudspeaker. They cannot get through on the phone because Irene has taken it off the hook. Time passes more quickly than she can remember for years. It is all the excitement and fear and adrenalin; she thought she'd never experience such a rush of adrenalin ever again, but it must have been there, somewhere in her body, lying dormant under the Chilprufe vests.

'I feel exactly the same way when I go on some of my demos,' confirms Miss Benson from above. 'The thrill is hard to describe when you're lying down there in the road and the police are marching towards you with their batons and you know the risk you are taking is for such a jolly good cause.'

Oh dear, she makes it sound almost sexual. Irene changes the subject quickly. 'Who's out there at the moment, Miss Benson? Tell me what you can see.'

'Well, a moment ago Frankie was out there talking to the social workers and Miss Blennerhasset has obviously been called out for some reason. She didn't look too pleased to be anywhere in the vicinity, I must say, and can you blame her? I'm almost beginning to feel sorry for the woman. Greylands is taking one hell of a bashing.'

'Oh dear, and it's not that bad as far as Homes for the elderly go. I am very much afraid, Miss Benson, that the wrong people are getting the blame for all this. It really ought to be the Council, or the government with their heartless policies, but they are so faceless . . .'

There's a crackling on the loudspeaker outside and Miss Benson says, 'I must go. Someone else is about to speak. I'll report back to you later.'

'And I will turn the television down,' says Mrs Peacock hurriedly, scuttling back to her chair.

'Irene? Irene dear? Can you hear me?'

Behind the echo comes the unmistakable voice of Miss Blennerhasset.

'I will just assume that you can,' Matron goes on. 'Irene, please be sensible and let us come in to make sure you are all right. Everyone is so terribly worried about you. Do let us come in and discuss this whole situation. Surely there is a way we can make things right. We tried our very best at Greylands to make you feel welcome and at one point I thought we had succeeded. Obviously not. Obviously you were terribly unhappy and we didn't take your wishes seriously enough. Well, that will change, I promise you, if only you will agree to let Frankie or myself come in and talk to you, just for a moment . . .'

Mrs Peacock turns up the television again. Hah. A different tune all of a sudden. How very convenient. With the national media listening in, Matron is bound to sound benevolent but underneath the treacly words Irene detects a simmering anger. There's no two ways about it: Miss Blennerhasset must be absolutely furious.

It is all so fascinating – people and their priorities. There's a great debate in some of the papers about the involvement of the Queen, the monarch overstepping the mark and entering the world of politics.

However, a spokesman from Buckingham Palace assured a breathless nation that Her Majesty was merely responding humanely to the plight of one of her elderly subjects; anyone would have done the same in the unhappy circumstances. At a press conference last night Irene watched the reporters mob a Buckingham Palace spokesman who said the Queen was on holiday in Scotland, was being kept informed of the situation, and was unwilling to make any further comment at this time.

All the same, the suggestion was that Her Majesty's sympathy was entirely with Mrs Peacock and this, more than anything else, had goaded the nation into a voluble and often aggressive debate, so much so that Irene isn't sure whether to listen to the delicious arguments on Radio Four, or tune in to highly-charged discussions on the TV. The Prime Minister is naturally wiping his hands of the whole affair, saying the question of payment for old people's Homes lies with individual Councils.

Because of Mrs Peacock's age and vulnerable mental condition it is imperative to tread carefully, and this means the law cannot take any heavy-handed measures to force the old lady from her house 'for her own good'. Any sudden or violent action might well be the finish of her, and so, to a large degree, their hands are tied. This matter is one for kid gloves, and a regular psychiatrist trained to deal with hostages is brought over from Germany to try to defuse the situation and gain the confidence of the subject.

But Irene hasn't spent the whole of her life blindfold in the bottom of a barrel. She is wise to his cunning ways. She is not about to get into a discussion about her motivations or her inner self, least of all with someone shouting in a foreign accent on the end of a microphone. She is urged to pick up the phone, she need not dial, those outside are already connected. Just pick up the phone, they coo, and let us talk to you sensibly. What nonsense. These personal feelings should be kept private. The world would be a far better place if people kept quiet and dealt with their problems privately and with dignity instead of forever airing them.

Ragged people and anarchists, according to the authorities, have made attempts to join the circus surrounding Albany Buildings in order to protest in the road outside with their flags and banners. SET OUR PEOPLE FREE. WHAT NEXT, EUTHANASIA? The area has been cordoned off for this reason, and traffic re-directed. But still there are the odd scuffles every now and again, which feed the avidly waiting press photographers. It seems that just about every newspaper in the land has a representative here.

Irene watches another interview with poor, defensive Frankie, and it is painful to see what she has done to her own child. 'I had no other option,' argues Frankie tearfully. 'I wish you lot would understand! I have other responsibilities. How could I keep working with an old lady at home who needs constant care?'

'There are some who are saying that your mother does not need constant care! She is physically fit and only rather vague and difficult in her old age.'

'Well, that's easy for them to say. They don't know her like I do. Mother can be a very demanding woman, especially when she fails to get her own way, and I have teenage children at home whose needs are paramount.'

The interviewer went mercilessly on: 'Your former husband, Michael Rendell, says you were always an overly independent person afraid of commitment. You constantly blamed your mother, he says, for her blind devotion to your late father, and spent your life determined to make an alternative stand.'

Frankie snapped, 'Michael is still very bitter, I'm afraid, after a rather painful divorce. It might be more sensible if you people took a little more time to find a more independent source for the arguments you seem so eager to pursue.'

The interviewer persisted. 'But did you constantly criticise your mother for the way she seemed to idolise your father?'

'Honestly,' shouted Frankie, losing her cool and doing herself nothing but harm. 'This is nothing whatsoever to do with the issue! My mother is of a different generation. Attitudes change – of course I want to lead my life in my own way! And naturally I have criticisms of my mother – what daughter doesn't? But that doesn't mean I grasped the opportunity to dump her in a Home against her will—'

'But you must admit it looks as though your heartless behaviour might have something to do with petty revenge.'

'Oh, go away and leave me and my children alone! Stop pestering us! If I were a man, this subject would have no relevance at all.'

And then there were the fleeting comments made by young Angus and Poppy. Some media man must have caught Angus on his way to the Tech and shouted a question. The response was quick and prickly. 'My granny is nothing to do with me. Go away.'

And pretty little Poppy's response as she hopped on a passing bus. 'Go boil your head, you scrote.'

Oh dear, and what would dear William say if he could see her now?

William had firm beliefs and Irene never argued against them. She always voted the same way as he did, even in the local elections although she would have preferred to vote Liberal. She never learned to drive, or to change a plug, she had no need. After Frankie was born he decided one child was enough. He hated to see women 'making fools of themselves'. He hated to see them 'getting too big for their own boots', 'turning themselves into men', 'undermining the whole social structure by refusing to marry and choosing careers instead'. It was all right when Frankie was working part-time, when she and Michael were married. It was all right as long as Frankie was doing the shopping and cleaning and cooking. But a full-time career? Oh no. And he never believed one word of the television news after they brought in female newsreaders.

No, Irene supposes sadly that William would not approve of her actions, and if William had been alive he would have forbidden her to do this disgraceful thing. But then she would have missed so much. She would never have known how it felt to be really important.

When the whole procedure first began Miss Benson had difficulty in dissuading the police from using her flat as a Headquarters. Fatal. A desperately close shave. But she sensibly suggested that the neighbouring flat on the ground floor would be a far better location and so that poor Asian couple were forced to move out, God only knew for how long. They went to their children in Bristol.

She also had some persuading to do when they accused her of encouraging Mrs Peacock in her unfortunate venture, particularly when they found out she was responsible for contacting the press and the relevant pressure groups who were causing so much hassle outside. But Miss Benson told them, 'How would I know she had a key? When I brought her here for the odd day out I thought nothing of it when she set off for the odd little airing. I could hardly prevent her from leaving the premises, could I? And all along she must have been buying bits and pieces behind my back to help her withstand the siege.' And the planking across the windows? 'I know nothing about any planking. As far as I am concerned she could have used old floorboards.' The strength to pull them up? 'Who knows what a body can do when one is driven to extremes. And Mrs Peacock, contrary to reports, is a perfectly healthy old lady.

'But having said that, I am right behind her all the way. What they did was iniquitous!'

They believed her in the end, thank the Lord, gave up all ideas of a secret accomplice. Little, prim, inoffensive Miss Benson does not fit the part.

That night, Miss Benson calls down again.

'Ready for bed yet?'

'Only if you think I'll be safe.'

'They won't try anything tonight, don't worry. The issue is far too sensitive and there are too many people about. I will stay on watch. At the slightest sign of any hanky-panky I will call you, and phone the press immediately. They daren't do a thing! You've got them by the short and curlies.'

Oh? A rather crude expression for Miss Benson to use; funny how little you really ever know about people. 'Is it time to make my final demand, d'you think?'

'Another couple of days should do it, if you think you can hold out that long.'

'I can hold out here as long as I want. I am perfectly comfortable and enjoying the whole business. I must say I never thought I would. This is the most exciting thing I have ever done in my life. I have just finished a nice piece of plaice with some new potatoes and parsley sauce, one of those packets you just shove in the oven. I had a couple of welcome gins just before the six o'clock news so I feel lovely and relaxed and I might have another as a nightcap.'

'That all sounds very good. You must keep healthy. A couple more days and we'll throw in your request to the Queen. By then I think it will be quite hard for anyone to resist it. Public opinion is one hundred per cent behind you, and growing, if that were possible. It's all very well for the Royals to keep out of the political arena, but this goes further than politics. This touches the very heart of our civilisation and I am sure the Queen realises that.'

'I do hope you are right, Miss Benson. I so long to meet her.'

'Well, it shouldn't be much longer now. You go to bed and get a good eight hours. I will keep watch from my front window. I will contact you first thing in the morning and send the papers down. They are not bringing your post here, of course, but I was told there were sackloads of letters waiting at the Post Office. All, I imagine, from avid supporters.'

'Good night, Miss Benson. And once again, thank you so much for everything you are doing for me.'

'Good night, Mrs Peacock. And it's my pleasure. Really.'

It sounds a bit like the Waltons, all cosy and homely, thinks Irene as she changes into her dressing gown and prepares for an early bath.

Snake in the grass. Frankie Rendell is certain Miss Benson is behind all this, although there is no way to prove it. She comes across as far too naive and simple for belief and there is no way her mother could have prepared for an exercise as massive as this without somebody's help. My God, if she could only lay hands on her mother now, she would probably strangle her with her own bare hands. The children are going through torture at school through no fault of her own. And how typical that Michael should put his oar in, given the chance to besmirch her name in public, to make her sound like a hard-faced cow when she's not, not really.

There's nobody on her side! Perverse, really, when you consider how many families have managed to dump their elderly relatives, take power of attorney over them and get away with it without a murmur. Where are they now? Where are the hundreds of thousands of voices of support? So easy for those to criticise who have never been faced with the immediate problem of a doolally old woman who goes about forgetting to dress.

My God. Mother was ever a determined woman. Even while under the thumb of the dominating William, Mother would find a way to wheedle and persuade. So much for the helpless victim. But what a sick and humiliating way to have to behave! It's not as if the powers that be had not considered allowing Irene to stay in the flat with a home help and a nurse popping in at bedtime. They decided against it only because of a lack of funds.

Greylands was cheaper.

What could Frankie do, faced with such firm Council policy?

So why is everyone blaming her? Including her own miserable children! It's wretched and it's just not fair.

What does Mother intend to do now? she wonders. How long does she plan to stay barricaded in there while outside, the media await developments? They have discussed turning off the water, the gas and electricity, trying to flush her out in this way, but because of her age and the huge public concern, these obvious options are not available to them. Mother has got them exactly where she wants them, with that sly Miss Benson's help.

Frankie has spent hours standing outside pleading by megaphone, feeling like a fool, despised by the world, able to offer nothing for barter because there's just no way Mother can come and live at home, not that she'd even want to. As far as the flat is concerned, it is already sold to the Marshes from Milton; the contract is about to be signed. The Council cannot go back on their policy just in Mother's case. If they backed down now, all hell would be let loose. The aged and infirm would come crabbing out of all the Rest Homes in the land, intent on reclaiming all those lost properties once again.

And the Queen should know better. Frankie is furious with the Queen. It's all very well for her, her mother would have been put away long ago but for the army of servants employed to keep her going in the style she has been used to. And her kids would have probably gone into care, by the sounds of it. If only it were so sodding simple for everyone else. How dare the Queen take sides when she doesn't know what she's talking about?

One last try. The flustered Chief Constable insists upon it. 'Mother! *Mother!* I know you can hear me! Come out! Come out of there at once before this goes much too far. You have made your point, now let's all get together and talk about it, for goodness sake!'

'Dear me,' says the elderly reporter from *Woman's Own*, moving like a bat in her crocheted cape, snaking out from the shadows and into the limelight, adjusting her half-moon glasses and peering up at the harassed Frankie. 'Couldn't you try *a little more sympathy*, dear? I must say, you sound quite aggressive. No wonder your poor mother's gone to ground quite unable to face you. No wonder the poor soul has been forced into such harrowing devices.'

At her wit's end, Frankie grips the megaphone and rams it down on the silly woman's head. And this, of course, is the picture which will appear in the morning papers.

THIRTY-TWO

Joyvern, 11, The Blagdons, Milton, Devon

So.

Poor old Vernon.

He has failed in this, as in everything else he has ever attempted in his life, and it is with weary resignation that Vernon Marsh watches the police march up his garden path.

If Joy was alive today she would be screaming about the neighbours watching. It only takes a couple of police cars, an ambulance or a fire engine to bring all the residents of the cul-de-sac rushing to the front doors of their houses but, Vernon supposes, he mustn't be bitter. It's only that feeling of 'Thank God it's him and not us' that brings them that kick of pleasure.

He watches their approach with a shaking heart. What should he say? How should he play it? Will they caution him first? Will they lead him away in handcuffs with everyone watching? Does it matter any more? His life has been turned into a constant hell anyway. Since Jody Middleton arrived last night Vernon had known his time was limited but he never expected the young fellow to turn him in so quickly. A decent kind of lad in a way, he felt they had more in common than they knew. He'd been surprised to wake up and find him missing after the interesting conversations they'd got into last night – everything from football to the keeping of hamsters – but he must have got up early and decided to go straight to the law. And who can blame him for that? This morning started badly anyway, as soon as he opened the paper he saw himself on the front page highlighted there amongst the sensational pictures of the siege which has captured the nation. As soon as Vernon saw that, he knew it was going to be a bad day. And look, they even blame him for agreeing to buy the old woman's flat, as if there was something unkind behind it, as if he already knew she was being hassled into a Home by the authorities against her will. My God, they'll use every trick in the book to make an innocent person look guilty, he'd thought when he'd read it. How they would curse if they knew the truth.

By tomorrow the whole world will know. He might have the front page to himself and not even have to share it with that household name, Mrs Irene Peacock. *Ding, dong bell.* He can see the headlines now. How they will relish it when they hear he hid his dead wife in a well.

'Mr Vernon Marsh?'

Vernon stands at the open door and awaits his fate in a cloud of shame. 'Yes, I am Vernon Marsh.'

The policeman, not unfriendly, gets out his notebook and unravels a daily paper. 'I am here after our Lancashire branch faxed us over a message just now regarding the man at your window here who resembles an absconding prisoner.'

Vernon studies the paper as if it's the first time he's seen it, so astonished is he. And there is Jody's face at the window, staring, horrified. *'Wanted?'*

'Jody Middleton to be precise. He is wanted to stand trial for rape, Mr Marsh. This is very probably not he, but would you mind identifying the person who was standing above us last night when the photographer took this picture?'

So they're not here to take him away! They don't know anything about the murder! It's Jody Middleton they're after. Vernon is totally confused, almost speechless. His brain races madly in his head. 'There was a boy staying with me last night,' he agrees quickly. 'And yes, he did introduce himself as Jody Middleton, said he was a member of the family who were buying this house and asked if he could have a bed for the night as he was touring the West Country. Well, I thought it was rather odd, but felt I couldn't really refuse. I had a spare bed and my wife is away . . .'

'Where is Middleton now, sir?'

'I really don't know,' says Vernon truthfully, helplessly shrugging. 'When I got up this morning, he was gone. No word of explanation or thanks . . .'

'Would you mind, sir, if we came in to have a quick look around?'

'No,' says Vernon helpfully. 'Come in, do whatever you have to. I never imagined for a moment the boy was on the run.'

'It was a bit silly,' reproves the second policeman, removing his hat on the stairs, 'to invite a total stranger to stay overnight.'

Vernon scratches his head and readjusts his glasses. He goes on with studied carelessness, 'But he wasn't a total stranger, Inspector. As I said, he told me he was the son of the people who are buying our house.'

'Even so,' says the Inspector, moving on. 'These days . . .'

'I realise that now,' says Vernon, going back to his coffee and cigarettes at the kitchen table, only to find that he cannot sit down and is forced to wander to and fro. He longs for them to go so he can be alone with his crazy questions. Menace seems to be everywhere. If the lad is on the run and manages to keep going there's a good chance the police will never find out about Joy, but when they catch him, and they're bound to catch him, the murder will be the first thing the boy starts to blab about. What a malignant trick of fate that such a distasteful person should catch him about his gory task, then that the camera should catch *his* face at the window, that he should then disappear, so that even if he never gets caught, Vernon will never again feel easy. What has his life descended to now – dependent on a rapist to stay free?

This situation is almost worse than being charged and convicted. At least that way he would get it all over. But no, no, not when he thinks about Tom and Suzie. Anything rather than destroy his children's lives in misery and shame like that.

So this explains the strange behaviour of the couple who came with their nervous daughters to view Joyvern, it seems like years ago now. That explains why they never bothered to barter over the price of the house, and didn't seem particularly bothered about much anyway. Their son was on remand for rape. Having met Jody, Vernon is very surprised, but then he manages a wry little smile. How can you tell what people are capable of by their behaviour, by how they look? Nobody in their right mind would think him capable of a brutal murder. His awful circling thoughts go round and round again. Tick tick tick goes Joy's kitchen clock on the wall, designed to resemble a fresh green apple. Is it ticking his moments of freedom away?

'Coffee?' he asks the returning policemen, while trembling inside.

'We'd better not, sir. We'd better get back, thanks all the same. If this man is in the area it is imperative that we catch him, bearing in mind the sickening nature of the crime. Someone will be back to take a statement from you later.'

'Yes. Absolutely. That's fine,' agrees Vernon, his disloyal eyes straying to the place on the kitchen floor where Joy had fallen, where he had beaten her head to pulp.

The hours go by so slowly when you are expecting trouble, when every passing footstep might represent the end of your freedom for ever, every cruising car, every shadow on the wall. He hates being alone doing nothing, for this allows him to think too much. Driven by his need for action, any action, it no longer much matters what, Vernon is compelled to telephone the Middletons in Preston, half-wanting to discuss the matter of their absent son and his likely whereabouts, and half-wanting to know if the house sale is still going through according to plan. In spite of the fact that Vernon's world has gone all twisted and awry, everyday life must go on. Mr Mycroft at the bank must still be satisfied, the lease on the shop must be paid.

'Oh,' Mrs Middleton sounds most surprised to hear from him. 'Mr Marsh. Yes, certainly everything is going through on our side, and as far as we know some people called Smedley are still buying ours. The solicitors seem quite happy, anyway, there have been no snags that we know of. Why? Is everything all right your end?'

So Vernon proceeds to explain about last night's extraordinary visit.

'Jody actually called at your house? He insisted on staying the night? I must say it was good of you to have him.'

Vernon smiles at her little game. 'He would have stayed longer, I believe, but for the fact the newspapers sent their photographers round and the police picked up his trail.'

She is silent for a moment. 'You know?' she whispers with horror. 'You know about Jody?'

Vernon feels a spasm of pain. He's a sentimental man, a believer in mercy and forgiveness – how many times has he forgiven Joy her reckless behaviour in the past? He imagines how terrible this mother must feel in her innocence, not only her but her whole family.

'The police told me this morning.'

'But he'd gone?' She is desperate for reassurance. 'He'd gone before they arrived?'

'Yes, Mrs Middleton, he'd gone. I think he probably left some hours before.'

'And how was he? How was the cut in his poor chest?'

What can he tell her? That the lad was tired? Immature? Homesick? A young man of some intelligence with tousled hair and a couple of earrings? 'He never mentioned a cut to me. He seemed well. He ate a good supper. We shared a Chinese meal and watched the news. I am surprised the police haven't contacted you yet.'

'The police tell us nothing, nothing at all. It's a real eye-opener to be at the wrong end of the law, you soon stop saying how wonderful they are. And so this siege which is hogging the news at the moment is at the very flat which you were supposed to move into? That is why the press came round? How terrible for you and your wife.'

Vernon pauses for a planned few seconds. He might as well start the ball rolling. 'Actually,' and it's easier to start with a stranger, 'I haven't seen my wife for some days now. She walked out after an argument and she's never been back. I am quite worried, to be honest. She has been behaving rather oddly of late.'

'Oh no, how awful for you!' The woman's concern is genuine. Perhaps all women are naturally sympathetic when they hear about one of their number gone over the edge, although they say that these days men are quickly catching up, especially young men. And the suicide rate is growing. 'Have you informed Missing Persons?'

'Not yet. She would be most upset if I told them and she had just decided to go off for a while to cool down.'

'I suppose so, yes, but I know how worrying it is to have a relative missing and be unable to get in touch. I do wonder, Mr Marsh, if Jody is in the area, whether I might pop down that way to do some measuring for carpets and curtains, just in case . . .'

'I doubt that he'd come back here now.'

'No, but just to be in the area, just to know I was near him would make me feel better. Do you understand how I feel?'

Vernon, who fully understands, says kindly, 'Of course I do. Has he got friends around here?'

'No, it was my idea he went there, actually. Safer than hanging around his old home.'

Vernon the murderer cannot help but feel shocked. 'You helped him? He evaded the law and you helped him do it?'

'I am his mother, Mr Marsh. I might be foolish, but I believe my boy when he swears to me that what he did to that girl was not rape at all, and I hope you realise he hasn't even been tried yet. But when you're suddenly accused of something as sickening as rape, I'm afraid that no matter what sort of person you were everyone believes the worst of you.'

Vernon silently thinks about this. He must discover as much about Jody as he can and this is his only chance. 'A good boy, was he?'

'A son to be proud of. This has broken his sisters' hearts, and mine, and his dad's.'

Overindulged, most likely. 'I understand. It would be unendurable if something like this ever happened to our two children.'

'They must be terribly concerned about their mother's disappearance.'

'Oh they are, they are.' His next job, and one that he's dreading, is to tell them. 'So you have no idea at all where Jody might be now?'

'None, but I do feel the urge to come down there. I need to take these measurements anyway, and have some discussions with you about what you are prepared to leave. I take it you are still intending to go, even though your flat, at the moment, seems to belong to the media? I'm sure the whole business will soon blow over, and hopefully your wife will be back.'

'Oh, I'm still leaving,' says Vernon, 'don't worry about that. If necessary I will put our things into storage. And if my wife doesn't return I don't think I'll bother to buy, I'll rent . . .'

'Don't dwell on the black side, Mr Marsh. I know how easy that is, to let that darkness take you. You *must* believe that all will be well. You must have faith . . .'

But Vernon is no longer listening. Fear and cunning have taken him over, and self-preservation is all he can see. He liked Jody. He doubts if that boy would rape anyone and yet they share one terrible secret. Life is hard and life is unfair and if opportunity drops into your lap you'd be a fool not to take it. He is shocked to discover how easy it is to betray a stranger. To save your own skin. Since the murder, what does it matter how shabby his conscience or his behaviour? He's doomed to hell anyway, the flames are already licking his ankles and he's loathsome in the sight of God. He is already working out in his mind how he can implicate Jody. From what he can gather, the boy is finished anyway, and probably he is guilty of rape and the mother can't bring herself to see it. That's perfectly natural, he would be the same. How simple it would be for the police to get hold of the wrong end of the stick. If the boy is going to be locked up for the rest of his life, then he might as well take the can for Joy's murder, too. He can deny it as much as he likes. Nobody will believe him.

When the police return that afternoon Vernon emphasises in his statement just how peculiar Jody was. 'Very twitchy. Of course, I understand why, now that I know he was on the run. Very interested in my wife, which was odd. Kept asking questions about her – and the strangest part of all was that the boy turned up here on my doorstep soon after Joy went missing. He gave me no other reason than that his family were about to move in here. I sensed there was something wrong with him. I was nervous, quite frankly, suspecting he might be one of those young schizophrenics let loose from hospital. That's why I allowed him to stay. I was concerned what his reaction might be if I sent him packing.'

'That's interesting, sir,' says the policeman, scribbling. 'But you had no idea that he had escaped from remand, accused of rape?'

Vernon shakes his head. 'Of course not, no. I would have found a way to inform you if I had suspected anything like that. I have always been a most law-abiding man.'

'Quite so.'

'To tell you the truth, Jody Middleton terrified me. There was something sinister about him.'

'He is a thoroughly bad lot, according to my information from Lancashire.'

'Capable of anything, I would have said.'

'You are probably right. A bad apple.'

'It's his family I feel sorry for.'

'I wouldn't waste your sympathy,' said the tall lanky policeman, bending almost double on the sofa to prop his pad on his long bony lap. 'It's normally the parents' fault. Too damn soft.'

'I agree with you absolutely,' says Vernon. 'You see enough of it round here.'

'You see it everywhere these days, I'm afraid, sir.'

Vernon hesitates slightly. He looks up sadly at the lean man in blue. 'At what point would you advise me to report the disappearance of my wife?'

'How long has she been missing now, sir?'

'Five days. I dropped her off at the shops after a slight argument and haven't seen her since.'

'Might I ask what the argument was about?'

'Yes, it was about which property we ought to buy. She favoured an old ruin out on the moor, I tried to persuade her that the flat would be more sensible. Funnily enough it's the self-same flat in Swallowbridge which is featuring so highly in the public eye at the moment. The siege.'

'Oh? Of course, I think you mentioned that earlier. That's what brought the photographer round.'

Vernon nods. 'Exactly. But Joy had her heart set on a cottage called *Hacienda*. I did wonder, actually, if she might have called there . . . She's been behaving so strangely lately.'

The policeman nods knowingly. 'We can certainly check that out, Mr Marsh, if you would give me the directions.'

'I can do better than that.' Vernon gets up and retrieves the estate agent's particulars from the drawer. 'It looks quite nice in that picture but really it would have cost a fortune to make it habitable, and my wife—'

'I know what they're like, women – romantics, most of them. I see it's even got its own well.'

'A hole in the ground, no more than that, probably. Character, they call it.'

To Vernon's relief the policeman finally gets up to go. 'Well, you leave this all with me and as I said, someone will check it out just in case Mrs Marsh decided to pay the cottage a visit, although how she would reach it in the middle of nowhere is quite another matter.'

'A lift?' queries Vernon. 'Not difficult at this time of year when you've got all the holidaymakers crisscrossing all over the place.'

'That's always possible,' says the constable, straightening his helmet in the mirror by the door. 'Or there's probably even an odd bus once or twice a week. The driver would probably remember.'

The driver will not remember. Nobody will remember giving Joy a lift to *Hacienda* five days hence but that won't matter; given the other evidence, that won't be of vital importance. But sure as eggs are eggs, fugitive or not, Jody Middleton will have left clues back at that cottage – discarded Coke cans, packaging, footprints and fingerprints, advertising the fact that he was there. Whereas Vernon himself left no sign at all. Any tyre-marks the car might have left can be passed off as those they made the first time they visited *Hacienda* together. The offending iron has been sold on in the shop, cleaned and done up as new, and an excellent second-hand one now sits on the shelf in Joy's cleaning cupboard.

She came upon him while he was hiding there, didn't she? He acted out of sheer panic.

No, Vernon rubs his hands. Not such a failure after all. Joy would have been proud of him. Soon they will not only be after the unfortunate Jody Middleton for rape, *but for murder as well.*

THIRTY-THREE

Penmore House, Ribblestone Close, Preston, Lancs

Never mind about Jody, Babs Middleton feels like she's on the run from something herself. Speaking on the telephone to Vernon Marsh who has seen Jody so recently, even had him staying in his house, has lit the feverish flame of protective motherhood once again at the thought of her child reduced to begging for food and sanctuary at the door of total strangers. They should never have turned him away from home when he needed them most. Although she was in agreement at the time, Babs blames Len for that, and the attitude of Dawn and Cindy. If they were more sympathetic towards their persecuted brother she herself would not have felt the need to defend him against them.

Babs is angry. She is angry towards the police who are out to get him, the judicial system which is out to stitch him up, Janice Plunket and her unimaginative family who are determined to exact an unjust revenge, but most of all she is angry at Len and the girls who seem relieved to be shot of him.

The only real sympathy she has been given of late has been from an unexpected source, Vernon Marsh at Joyvern. He seemed to understand a degree of the sort of despair she is going through. He might have more news of Jody than he was willing to give on the telephone. He has seen her beloved son, spoken with him, spent time with him – perhaps there is something more he can tell her? She knows these cravings are quite illogical but she feels compelled to go down to Milton in Devon, just in case something might happen. Jody might get in touch with Vernon again, and Babs wants to be there in case. She fights the great hope within her, knowing how unlikely it is.

She shivers and suffers not knowing his whereabouts.

'Don't be silly, pet.' Len sees right through her arguments into the neurosis within. 'There's no need for you to be down there. There'll be plenty of time to measure and match once we move; we're in no hurry for that sort of thing.' And then he looks at her sadly, in the patronising way she is getting used to. 'You won't find him, you know. And what would be the use if you did?'

'I'm not discussing the matter with you any more, Lenny. You don't understand a mother's feelings and that's all there is to it. I am going down there for a couple of days to stay at the Old Mill and I've already booked so don't try to dissuade me.'

'Dawn and Cindy might quite like to come. It'd give them something different to do, choosing some colour schemes for their new bed-rooms. Why don't you ask them? You could have fun with some company, go round the shops, eat out, a day on the beach, take some time off for yourself.'

Babs looks at him sharply, her brain almost too disorganised to find the appropriate words. 'I do not want Dawn and Cindy with me just in case Jody should get in contact. You know that, Len, so what are you really trying to do? Keep Jody from me, that's the truth, isn't it?'

His is a heavier sigh than hers had been. He pities her; but he finds it increasingly difficult to resist the longing to shake her. In a score of ways Lenny has tried to protect Babs from these debilitating hopes of hers, tried to help her accept the reality that Jody is probably lost to her for a long, long time, soothing her in her nervousness, ministering to her physical needs but he knows he has lost the battle. She seems intent on self-torture. None of them are enough for her. The sunshine has gone out of her life. Dawn and Cindy have tried in their own ways, too, helping round the house, bringing back videos they thought might distract her, using the recipe book to make interesting meals, all to no avail. Babs is possessed with the image of her son as an innocent, much-maligned little boy who still needs her in the way that he used to. And although this is true, she will not see that it must be left to the process of law and that by interfering she can only damage his chances further. Jody might be temporarily free but Babs is imprisoned and driven. There seems to be some sickness in her that only Jody's need can cure. Take it away and it starts afresh, the buried conflicts, draining all energy. It is awful. *Awful.* There is now a wide gulf between him and his daughters and the restless Babs, so often overwrought with worry, dominated by an all-pervasive urge to find and protect the missing Jody, hungry, lonely, unloved and unsatisfied.

Their life of persecution goes on in the Close, more intermittent now, but bad enough all the same. The odd anonymous letter comes with horrible regularity through the door, as well as the occasional abusive phone call; the standoffishness of the neighbours and the nasty whispering in the street goes on. Dawn and Cindy dare not return to school and a teacher comes in twice a week to give them work. But at least the police have relaxed their vigilance now they know that Jody has left the area, and the Middletons don't feel quite so much like fish in a bowl. The sooner they move house the better, and thank God everything seems to be working to plan. The Smedleys, although hard to contact according to their solicitor, are still pressing ahead with the purchase of Penmore House. Len will be sad to leave it, although since Jody's arrest there has been a shadow cast over it. No matter how hard Babs and he try to make a happy home again, nothing they do can override the unjust fate of their first-born child.

If there was anything to be done to help Jody, anything in this world, Len would be doing it. How many more times can he try to convince Babs of this simple fact?

Babs flees to Devon, in pursuit of wholeness and fulfilment.

She has never really thought about her new home before. She hardly took it in when she came to view with Lenny, Dawn and Cindy. Now she must take notes of the details and concentrate, make out she is interested when she is not. It's a small house, and lacking in character, with an empty feel about it although it is full of matching furniture, mix and match, and the neighbours are very close. There's not much protection or natural cover in the form of fully grown trees or hedges; it seems that some people prefer the open-plan idea. How on earth will she manage to fit everything into this minute but squeaky clean kitchen?

'It is good of you to let me come. It must be a nuisance, especially when you are so concerned about your wife.'

'No problem,' says the courteous and helpful Vernon Marsh, with a bright unconcern. Such a nice, gentle man, rather red-faced and overweight, but quite prepared to hold the other end of the tape when she needs him to. 'These things have to be done.'

She smiles at him disarmingly. 'Did Jody say anything else?'

He must be getting fed up with her unending questions by now.

Vernon thinks harder. 'No, as I told you already, he really didn't say much. He asked lots of questions about my wife, looked at all the photographs with very great interest – that surprised me, I must say. But I am absolutely positive he made no mention of where he was going. I didn't even know he was leaving, you see. He left some time in the night after the photograph had been taken.'

'And you don't know where he was staying before he decided to come here?'

'No, well, he'd only just arrived down here. He can only have spent one night in the open, camping, I suppose. His legs and arms were burnt. That would be the effect of the cycling.'

They are sitting discussing Jody's visit, nibbling biscuits and drinking coffee, when a serious knock which is obviously not just a chatty neighbour popping in, sounds at the door. Vernon jumps up to answer it.

He shows the two official-looking men, who are wearing jackets and ties on this warm day, into the kitchen where Babs is sitting. She knows at once they are police. She's had enough dealings with them recently to know a policeman, plain-clothed or not, when she sees one.

Neither visitor enquires as to her identity; clearly they have more important matters on their minds. 'We have some very sad and rather shocking news, I'm afraid, Mr Marsh,' says the front one grimly. 'Perhaps you might like to sit down.'

Vernon sits down heavily at the kitchen table. With his cuff he clumsily knocks the teaspoon from his saucer on to the cloth and even at this crucial moment he is trained well enough to pick it up and wipe it.

'I think we have found the body of your wife.'

An unnatural hush. And that short statement wraps the room in a freezing blanket.

Vernon jerks, props himself up on one arm. The other hand is clenched beside him. 'The body of my wife?'

'Yes. I am afraid she is dead, Mr Marsh.'

'She can't be dead! We were moving house—'

'And when you feel able, we would like you to come and identify the body.'

Vernon looks like a man who has just been told he is dying of cancer. His skin turns grey. He pants for breath. He removes his glasses and shakes his head. The loose flesh under his chin shakes like the jowls of a dog and the only expression in his soft brown eyes is a total bewilderment. 'You must have got the wrong person.'

'I doubt it. I wish I could say otherwise.' The policeman, used to delivering such news, is sympathetic yet necessarily distanced.

Vernon looks at Babs and gives her a sickly smile, blunted by perplexity. 'Would you believe it? They are telling me that my wife is dead.'

Babs, dazed and nauseated by such sudden horror, sits there in hopeless silence. She experiences the most blistering pity, but what words can you give in this situation? What possible gestures can you make?

And then the final blow, delivered in a decently sombre tone. 'I have to tell you, it looks as if she has been murdered, Mr Marsh.'

The shock is so great that Vernon falls back in his chair, his mouth wide open so his bottom teeth show as if he has suffered a physical blow and the pain of it is too much to take. A great shiver runs through him. His head begins to roll in an agony of realisation. His despair seems too complete for tears. The first policeman puts a supportive hand on his shoulder while the second gazes out of the window, absent-mindedly folding and re-folding a piece of paper. Babs wishes she'd never come; she wishes she was miles away. This is the sort of thing that ought to stay on the television. You should never have to experience it in real life.

Eventually, and his words are so slurred it sounds as if he is gibbering. *'But who would want to kill Joy?'*

'At the moment it looks as if it was one of those sickening coincidences.' The policeman speaks as if he knows his words are wasted, but he speaks all the same. 'A man who the police are seeking quite urgently was hiding out at a cottage on the moor and your wife must have made her way there and surprised him.'

'You've got him? *You've got the man who did it?*' A sudden stab of life appears in what seemed, only a moment before, to be dead man's eyes.

'We haven't found him yet, I'm afraid, Mr Marsh. But we think we know who he is. It won't take us long to apprehend him.'

'Who? Tell me? Who? Who would do such a terrible thing?'

'His name is Jody Middleton, sir, the boy I believe you allowed to stay here three nights ago. The one who acted so strangely and showed such a peculiar interest in your wife.'

Slowly, slowly, it seems to take a lifetime, Vernon turns his heavy eyes towards Babs. She doesn't see. She faints completely away and slides off her chair onto the spotless and brightly polished floor.

Three hours later, Jody Middleton, pedalling away and feeling healthier than he has felt in a long time, wonders vaguely why the police car is following so slowly and deliberately behind him. He has seen so many in his hours on the road he no longer suffers that stab of fear every time one passes. His confidence grows by the mile, and he has found a reasonable place to stay – an old, disused Army hut where he has spent the last two nights and managed to light a fire. He even began to enjoy it as he lay out on the short moor grass on a midnight that felt as warm as noon and only the dark hills rolled beneath the stars. As he watched the rosy tint of morning flush the tor tips, and the sky, his hope started to grow. Perhaps, after all, if he is caught he will be able to fight the ludicrous charge against him. Perhaps Janice Plunket will speak out and defend him. She loves him, or she used to say that she did. And then he can go home, take up his university place and start all over again. Life's not so bad after all. Today he ventured into a shop for the first time, a supermarket where he'd less easily be recognised. He managed to refill his rucksack and buy a couple of good paperbacks while he was at it.

He even has the confidence to gesture them past with a wide arm signal.

Hey. They are driving him right off the road and into the verge!

'Get in!'

'What?'

'I said get in!'

'But what about my bike?'

'I'll deal with your bike.'

'How did you find me?'

'A description, a good description, given by the bloke you skived off the other night.'

Jody cannot believe this. '*Vernon Marsh?* Vernon Marsh gave you a description of me? But why would he do that?'

'Because he knew who you were and what you have done. What other reason would anyone need?'

Jody's lips go tight; his jaw sets in a tense line. He sits numbly in the back of the car between two policemen, breathing harshly and fanning himself. He is suddenly conscious of a feeling of alarm. There's something wrong here, unless Vernon has given himself up and been overcome by the need to confess.

Back at the station in a spartan interview room he is surprised at the interest his arrest is causing. OK, so his case is a big one back in Preston, but he hadn't realised he'd made those sort of headlines here. *What's going on?* Why all the kerfuffle? The maddening pressure of another locked door begins to unnerve him. Where is everyone?

'Your mum's here, Jody.'

He almost cries with relief. 'Mum? That was quick!'

'She was down here anyway. She came to take another look at the new house – you know, the one at the Blagdons, number eleven, where you stayed with Vernon Marsh, and where you had your photograph taken.'

'Yes. I know the house.'

There are two detectives at the table and a uniformed policeman by the door. He can feel that man's eyes boring into the back of his neck. What's all this about?

'You knew the wife, too, didn't you, Jody?'

Jody's eyes widen. Every nerve in his body goes taut. 'What's Vernon told you? Has he confessed – is that it?'

Jody's interviewer smiles, but it's a cold one as he delivers the official warning. The tape recorder goes on and he introduces everyone in the room. 'Charged with the murder—'

'Hey! Wait a minute! What did you say? What's this about? *Murder?* How come you're charging *me* with murder? Mrs Joy Marsh! Vernon's wife? You're way out, this can't be true. I watched him get rid of the body, down the well. I was there, upstairs, and I watched him.'

They listen to him with placid, plastic faces, not believing a word he is saying, acting as if this is just everyday tedious business. The first interrogator, the hairy guy with the permanently knitted brows, moves towards the tape and states clearly, 'The accused's mother is at present outside arranging for a solicitor, so until the accused has representation, we will interrupt this interview.' But Jody isn't listening. His heart deadens. This is astounding. He can't cope with this. Good God, is this some sort of nightmare? Surely he's going to wake up in a minute. He feels that old terror that comes when disaster knocks on your door. He sees his whole future laid waste before him.

'Where's my mum? I want to talk to my mum.'

Pathetic little prat. His eyes flash and his voice rises as the detective throws down his papers. He's seen so many of these cringing creeps in his life, and Detective Inspector Martin Lane firmly believes they ought to be put down. No good to man nor beast, nor ever will be, while decent upstanding citizens like Vernon Marsh have their lives torn in half by the scrotes. He is going to do his damnable best to make sure this little wanker goes down for the rest of his life. Only for the sake of his future career must he force himself to be reasonable. 'Later, when we're through with all this. When you tell us what's been going on, you creepy little bastard!'

Sobbing as if her heart's going to break, faced with such blinding desolation . . .

'Please, I beg of you, *listen to me!* I know my boy, I know him better than myself. Jody would never harm a fly let alone murder anyone, let alone beat them to death and then throw them down a well. Can't you see it for yourselves? You must have some experience of the criminal mind, of the thug and the brutal psychopath? Where does my Jody come into that? Can't you use your eyes, your common sense? Does he look that type? There's been another awful mistake, just like the rape was a terrible misunderstanding, and I know they shouldn't have escaped and hit that poor prison officer, but wouldn't you feel desperate if you had been held in custody for something you hadn't done, if you'd been deprived of your freedom, despised by the whole community, threatened by your peers, seen your family forced out of their home and when all's said and done Jody is only eighteen years old, *a mere child*, and if he's saying Vernon Marsh did it then I'm afraid he probably did, OK he doesn't seem like a murderer and he's having treatment for shock, I know, but Jody doesn't tell lies . . .'

'Now why don't you just sit down, Mrs Middleton, drink your tea and wait for your son's solicitor to arrive. You can talk to him. He is paid to listen. Quite frankly, we have neither the time nor the inclination.'

Gawd. Why doesn't somebody get that daft bat out of here?

THIRTY-FOUR

The Grange, Dunsop, Nr Clitheroe, Lancs

Hey hey hey! How different everything suddenly looks, rose-coloured and glorious, and Jacy raises his eyes to the sky and it's almost a prayer. He could almost fall to his knees and worship himself with his arms outstretched in supplication to the powerful, greater being he knew has been merely resting inside him.

Piercingly sweet, it is like returning from the dead, wiser, and with a brand new chance of fulfilment, thanks to the bluff and outspoken Walter Mathews who knows damn well what he's talking about, knows exactly what he wants and is keen to re-launch the new group, Haze, with Jacy in front as lead singer. It's an appeal, not to the kids any more, but the new young adults who are looking for something familiar to latch onto, something with class, something with which they, with all their hopes and fears in this crazy world, can identify. He's got hold of this new song-writer – Jacy was slightly miffed about that because he used to write all the songs in the balmy days of Sugarshack – and Walt is eager to try this new guy out. There's almost too much going on so you don't know what to talk about first, but as it goes they don't talk much on the train on the way home. Instead, Jacy, Cyd and Darcy get through three packs of lager between them and upset the rest of the carriage with their lewd and dirty jokes and smoke themselves into a yellowy nicotine sickness.

Celebration!!! But how? How do you celebrate something too big to put a name to? It's a case of silent ecstasy. The joy is almost intolerable.

That's part of the reason he hasn't told Belle the true enormity of their expectations. Right to the top, is what Walt believes, and he's got the charisma to make everyone else believe it, too. Oh sweet Jesus, this must be like climbing the highest mountain in the world and catching sight of the summit again. Golden and glorious amongst the clouds . . .

There's one small, slightly worrying condition. Walter's made this quite clear: the launch is to coincide with Jacy's wedding to the could-be-Supermodel Belinda Hutchins, at The Grange. Walt is going to lay on a publicity celebration to outdo all others, ferrying the various influential journalists and DJs backwards and forwards from London by helicopter, and the revels under the monster Union Jack marquee are to last a day and a night. 'By which time the bastards'll be so damn sozzled they won't know their microphones from their dicks,' says Walt. Tickets will be given to celebrities, TV and newspaper moguls, the young nobility and even the minor Royals – 'and those blue arseholes could do with a few stiff lunges of positive publicity for a change, by God,' says Walt.

A man of action, and expansively stylish, he has already hired a specialist firm from the States to organise the whole mega-event. Walt is like the charismatic Minister of some sort of weirdo church, bowers and arbours, palaces and forests included. It's going to cost him an arm and a leg. *A Midsummer Night's Dream* is the title of the group's first expected smash-hit CD, which will take another couple of months to complete to Walt's satisfaction. 'We're gonna need a few fairies when you think of who's coming.' He has even booked the couple in at the Register Office – merely an irritating formality: 'Get the sordid business over and done with first thing in the morning to make way for the main event,' says Walt, belching upon his fierce cigar.

After their long spell in the gutters of London, Darcy and Cyd seem more bewildered than anything else, hardly able to believe their good luck. But Jacy, who has been waiting and hoping and dreaming for this day with an aching and unending hunger, casually reassures them: 'We're good. We were always good. OK so we cocked up last time. We're not going to cock up again.'

'Yeah, and Walt thinks if you're safely hitched to Belle it'll increase your chances of staying straight. Christ, I don't envy you man, chained to that vicious hag bag.'

Jacy snorts. 'Belle doesn't have any influence on me. Hell, I tried to explain that to good old Walt but he just wouldn't have it. Still, when you think about it, the kind of nuptial feast Walt has in mind is kind of romantic – just what the punters want these days. Hey – a wedding to outdo the Royals.' He rubs his hands with delight as the train pulls into the station. Wait till he tells Belle how it is. He hasn't told her he's on his way home; he thought he'd surprise her and get a taxi. Well, he'll soon be able to afford a fleet of taxis, won't he?

Jeez! Hey! *Get a look at this!*

Walter is a man of his word. A team of men are already at work in the grounds of The Grange; the gardens have been cleared and cut, the marquee is laid out flat on the lawns, vans belonging to carpet-layers and caterers, lighting and sound-systems engineers, florists, musicians and decorators are packed around the entrance.

'Walt doesn't hang about.'

But annoyance shows in Jacy's eyes. 'Where's Belle?'

You'd think she'd be out here watching, in her element, loving all this!

Life, intolerable last week, is now an ecstasy. Filled with an easy flowing energy Jacy leaps the stairs three at a time and almost rips his pants. Belle is upstairs in the bedroom, hiding. She creeps out when she hears him calling. 'You rotten beast! Why didn't you say? I've done nothing but answer the door since I've been back and they had to tell me what was happening. I didn't have a clue what to say. They have taken over the whole place and there's nowhere private inside or out. Peaches is in a terrible state . . .'

Thus she dampens the white light of exultation filling his head. 'Who the hell is Peaches?'

'Jacy, wake up! Haven't you looked at the papers since you've been gone? How could you have missed them?'

Jacy, who hasn't had time to look at anything except the music magazines, and that only fleetingly in between sessions, is taken aback by this mixed reception. He'd imagined it otherwise. He had imagined a chastened Belle, proved wrong yet again, running into his arms with a beautiful worship in her eyes. In his heart he had seen them acting out a Cathy-cum-Heathcliffe scene, the lovers reuniting, together again against all the odds, and he the strong, proud one, she the adoring fool. That would have looked good in front of the army of workers outside. But no, as usual she lets him down; as usual it is him who has to come and find her.

'When the Siege of Swallowbridge isn't grabbing the headlines, it's Peaches and the Prince – where've you been? The whole world is reading about it. And we come creeping back here to find the biggest publicity campaign in living memory being acted out on our own doorstep.'

'*My* doorstep,' Jacy reminds her, irritated beyond endurance to be faced, at this psychologically crucial stage of his come-back, with a contender for Belle's attention.

'Poor Peaches is a nervous wreck.'

Peaches? He vaguely remembers now. Wasn't she some old schoolfriend of Belle's, suffering from some sort of breakdown?

'She is pregnant,' Belle is angrily forced to explain. 'She is pregnant by that ass, that stuck-up oaf Prince James. We are only just back from the most gruelling experience imaginable. But everyone's after her story, so we thought we'd be safe back here. As it was I had to rescue her from the hospital at dead of night and ever since she's been holed up here. It was only a matter of time before the press ran us to earth, despite the Palace attempts to distract them, and the police have been very helpful, but now, dear God, the Lord only knows who is loose in the grounds. You're not even safe going to the lav.'

Jacy taps his steel-capped toe, he folds impatient arms. 'Aren't you even slightly interested to know what's been happening to us?'

Belle is so distressed and uneasy she can hardly bother to reassure him. He always behaves so like a spoilt child. 'Of course I am, *of course*, but this is a dire emergency!'

'I don't see why,' Jacy sulks. 'She can stay up here, can't she? Nobody's going to come up here.'

'If they discover where she is they will probably pull her to pieces in their efforts to reach her. Jacy – this is the biggest story ever! And bang in the middle of the Silly Season, too. This is likely to rock the Crown at its roots. The press have employed hundreds of extra reporters to find her.' She thrusts a newspaper in front of his face. 'Read that! Look at those pictures! That's poor Arabella, chained to the church door with a bicycle lock, that's the Prince's shocked face when he eventually came out of the church, that's the black look the Queen gave the flashing cameras and those are the guns which were actually pointed at us! *Guns*, Jacy, imagine it!' Belle is actually sobbing with fright. She gestures towards the windows and all the activity going on outside. 'We've been through hell and now this!'

Jacy hands the newspaper back. 'She's a stupid fool to try this on,' he sneers, totally without sympathy.

'Of course she's a fool. Everyone has always known Arabella was a fool.'

'Why did you play any part in it?'

Tension stalks like a presence in the room. 'Because she is my friend, and she was in trouble. If I hadn't gone with her she'd have gone alone, and God knows what might have happened to her. They were about to abort the child, anyway – some sinister mandarins from some obscure Palace department. Jacy, you just wouldn't believe what's been happening!'

Aggrievement rankles within him. Jacy says quietly and slowly, 'You're not suggesting, surely, that we turn all these people away?'

Belle scratches her messy, bird's nest hair. The normally beautifully coiffured ringlets spiral hysterically anywhere. 'Turn them away? I suppose not. I just wish I'd been given some warning, that's all, so that me and Peaches could have gone somewhere else. Now Peaches says she daren't leave the house. Poor thing. She spends most of the time in your dressing room where there aren't any windows.'

'Look! I need you here, Belle. These are our wedding preparations.'

'Don't you think I know that, Jacy? I've been told by total strangers enough times!'

'So you couldn't go off with Peaches. I'm the one who needs you now.'

'Oh hell, what a mess!'

'Of your own making.'

'Huh! You're a fine one to talk.'

Resentment storms in Jacy's head. 'And you can cancel that miserable little house in that godforsaken Close for a start.'

Belle stands her ground, too exhausted to budge. 'No way, Jacy. No way. If you want to stay here, you damn well can. I've had enough, I'm going. And if you don't want to buy that house then I will.'

'You've no confidence in me, have you? Even now! You think this is a flash in the pan, you don't think I've got the guts to make it. That's what you're thinking, isn't it, Belle? *And you'd rather I stayed a failure.* You really hope this doesn't work out, don't you? Be honest – why don't you tell me the truth?' And Jacy's eyes are aflame with rage.

'Jacy! Why do you never listen to me? I've got quite a lot else on my mind just now, although you would never be able to understand concepts like loyalty and caring and responsibility . . .'

Jacy stalks from the room and heads for the whisky locked in the library.

A feeble voice from the dressing room. 'Oh God help me. What are we going to do?'

'It's OK, Peaches, it's OK.'

'What if he did come to see me as I demanded, and I wasn't there?'

'Peaches, please, I'm begging you now, listen to me! There is no way he would come. Not with the hospital swarming with photographers and a reporter lurking round every corner. We were incredibly lucky to smuggle you out, and that's only because that Sister agreed to help and show us all those underground passages along by the morgue and the Path. Lab. Dear God,' and Belle shivers, 'we even travelled down in the lift with a corpse.'

'But the Queen knows now – the very situation poor James was so keen to avoid. He'll hate me so much for causing all this trouble. All I wanted was to speak to him!'

'I know, I know, please try to stop crying, Peaches. Your skin's gone all blotchy and your eyes . . .'

'Why should I care what I look like?' Her voice is hardly above a whisper. 'I only want to die.'

What can you say to that? Well, nothing really, nothing that will do any good. Belle spreads her hands and sighs. Peaches sits silent for hours, staring at nothing with hopeless sorrow in her eyes. Her beautiful memories are poisoned and slain and surely there can be no experience so awful as this destruction of the past. The muscles of Peaches' face are tautened with the pain of it and her head is made of wood that aches. All she needs now is for the man-hunting press to get hold of her.

And all the while Belle is supposed to be concentrating on her own marriage. The marriage she has yearned for, for so many years, has come, at last, to fruition. Typical that it should turn out to be a wedding like this, done for publicity, done to promote the group, Haze, with none of her friends in attendance, only useful people in the media and the music world. She hasn't even been proposed to properly. Jacy just always rightly assumed she'd say yes and jump at the chance.

But Peaches' sad and doomed infatuation has opened Belle's eyes. She would never have compared herself to her foolish friend. Even weeks ago she would have sworn she was a fiercely independent woman, needful of no one, but happy to be with Jacy for as long as he needed her. But just like Peaches, she thought she needed this man to be father to her children. Husband equals hearth, home and happiness, which is what Belle truly wants, although she would find this political incorrectness embarrassing to admit to her friends.

And what about the house in the Close? Why would she want to spend her savings on an ordinary Victorian family house in a place so unglamorous, so far from the buzz of the capital? Perhaps Penmore House is a statement of her hopes and dreams: solid, ordinary, homely, dependable, an untidy old place with interesting corridors and corners and attics and fireplaces that would burn red in the winter.

Or horror of horrors, could this be a description of the kind of man she subconsciously wants? Not Jacy at all?

Does she want to cook cakes and stews? Could it be time to remove the rings from her nose, her navel and the other place?

But how can she possibly, at this late and essential stage, let Jacy down? She can't.

And she loves him.

A few days ago all was hope, now all is horror. *Exposure*. The newspapers running round with the news and everyone knowing –her friends, her parents, her little brothers doing so well at school, both sets of grannies and grandpas . . . but she cannot bear to contact them yet, she wants to be alone. Peaches has now been publicly spurned, vilified, and is branded, mostly by other women of course, as a vicious bitch out for any revenge she can get. This, as we know, couldn't be further from the truth. She did what she did in the honest belief that if her Royal lover was outed, he might opt to do the decent thing and return to the person he really loved. And they would live happily ever after.

So, she was wrong. She was dim. Peaches is used to being loved, not hated.

But if only that was the end of the matter. If only she could be left alone with her sickness.

She reads the papers, she listens to the news, she bites her nails to the quick, but she dare not leave the bedroom.

The world now makes it its business to heap all its spite and self-righteousness upon the head of the Queen's third son. *DEGENERATE. DEBAUCHED. DOWNRIGHT DISGUSTING. She might well be a money-grabbing little hussy but James should not have discarded her like an old polo shirt. He has his responsibilities like any other young man. There are too many unmarried mothers in this country today, parasites on the rest of us. These men must be made to take the consequences, and pay for their indiscretions for the rest of their lives.*

What does his mother say about this?

'The Palace has no comment to make.'

But the hordes are restless, grumbling on street corners. Decency and common humanity have jetted out of the window, when a little old lady is forced to barricade herself in her humble home, when a rapist is allowed to escape to go and kill an innocent person, and when a foolish young woman is reduced to chaining herself to a church, go begging, cap in hand, to her privileged and supercilious lover.

'An offer was made,' states the Palace eventually, with tremendous caution, like feeding a morsel of meat to a lion.

'Bought off,' growls the predictable response. And never has public support for the Crown been so low.

'I forgive him,' goes Lady Frances Loughborough from her island retreat. The original statement was too foul-mouthed to reveal. 'We all make mistakes, after all. We're none of us perfect.'

Chuck 'em out, goes the *Sun* with contempt.

Leave 'em alone. They're human and we love 'em, goes the *Telegraph* reverently.

A dazzling mist of words.

But what is happening out there now?

Downstairs, in the gardens of The Grange, preparations are in hand for the biggest publicity stunt ever mounted, while timidly hiding in the windowless dressing room upstairs sits the world's most wanted woman, weeping for her lost love, wondering where she went wrong, and rocking her unborn child.

THIRTY-FIVE

No fixed abode

Hubble bubble, toil and trouble.

Revolution? Civil unrest? Something must be done to raise the positive profile of The Family, and soon. The mutterings and grumblings up and down the streets of the land are growing into marches and meetings, and fanatical people are appearing on the TV ranting and raving about Republics and saying it is high time Great Britain grew up.

Vive la république is a favourite theme on student T-shirts, and flutters of serious articles appear in the national press.

Only ten people turn up to watch Prince George open the new visitors' centre in Aviemore, and they are all female and over sixty with hats on. Dangerous times. Worst of all, it looks as if Sir Hugh Mountjoy and Dougal Rathbone are going to have to carry the can. They might even go down in the record books as the pair who finally pulled the plug on centuries of venerable Royal history.

O me miserum.

It is no good denying the whole ghastly mess and endeavouring to label Arabella as a silly little infatuated fool driven to revenge by lost love. Because of the public nature of her protest, because the whole hellish incident was captured by two dozen cameras, the follow-up took a natural course and Sir Hugh was compelled to watch the whole charade unfolding with his hands tied behind his back. She had posed no serious threat to The Family, a search had revealed nothing more dangerous than a charm bracelet on her wrist, all she could be accused of was disturbing the peace, and if they made too much of that, as the Monarch's Private Secretary pointed out with a sneer, they would only make matters worse. 'If that is possible,' he added. The main thing, of course, was that it was blatantly obvious that Arabella Brightly-Smythe had a grievance as old as time. Hussy or not, she was quite justified in making a fuss.

If the press get hold of her, they swear they will take her for tests and prove the paternity of the baby.

So there's absolutely no point in denying it. 'No comment' is the favourite official response, but that only seems to inflame the people more.

Although the security services suspect that Arabella has gone to ground at The Grange, they know that to pursue her there would be far too publicly insensitive. They cannot be seen to be hounding her now.

The Scottish holiday has been ruined for The Family, although they put a brave face on it and keep potting deer and stalking and fishing and golfing and picnicking with hampers and tartan rugs. It is hard to ignore the furore going on outside the castle grounds; you cannot turn the television on or pick up a newspaper without being struck by the enormity of the scandal. Typically, a number of other young women have come forward with babies in their arms, swearing the Prince put them up the duff, but their stories are soon disproved.

The Prince himself eyes up the contenders. 'I wouldn't touch those with a barge-pole, give me some credit,' he sniggers. The rest of The Family just frown, look away and say nothing. There but for the grace of God . . .

There are meetings almost every day with the Press Secretaries, the Private Secretaries and their secretaries, the Equerries, and even the Lord Chamberlain comes back from his holiday on the Nile so great is the fuss and so dangerous the threat to the Throne. And all because of this chit of a girl . . .

Conceited men of all shapes and sizes, each as loquacious as the other, some stout and lively, some thin, bespectacled and earnest, meet with their coffees at a chosen hour after breakfast. 'We must make contact with the wench somehow,' says Sir Hugh gravely, trying to ignore the critical stares as he sits at the end of the long oak table, sick with shame and disappointment. The carpets and curtains in this room are all of bright green tartan. Twigs and enormous fircones fill the silent fireplaces which, in the winter, crackle and burn so merrily with gigantic logs collected from the estate. But now the French windows are open and a grey squirrel, frightened by something, scurries off down the russet path and dives into the thyme. Sheep nibble the tufty turf on the slopes. In the distance the mountains lie in shawls of purple and pale mauve. Protected by the castle's vast stone walls they are on the edge of an uninhabitable world where civilisation dwindles away. If only Sir Hugh was out there with a stout ash-stick in his hand and not in here trying to defend his perilous position. 'We have to communicate in order to know what she intends her next move to be.

Perhaps we can increase our offer in exchange for her future silence . . .'

'From all I've heard,' says one of his supercilious superiors, making some notes on a sheet of foolscap, 'she wouldn't give you or young Dougal here the time of day. Some fellow rang me this morning to say he was bribed by a Harley Street quack to take part in a decidedly fishy business at the exclusive clinic where he works as a nurse. Unfortunately this blasted character has also been in touch with the newspapers.'

'I can't think to what he might be referring,' says Sir Hugh quickly, his vanity pricked and his worst fears surfacing. 'I hope you are not suggesting—'

'I am suggesting nothing,' the speaker snaps back impatiently, 'merely stating, Sir Hugh, that you and your friend have already done enough. It might be better if, from now on, you take a back seat.'

'It might be preferable to kick them out of the bus altogether,' chuckles Lord Tickle, the Crown Equerry, a thin and active little man. 'Unless they pull their socks up. Silly asses, both of them, overreacting like that.'

'Gentlemen, please.' The Lord Chamberlain's quavering voice brings the meeting once more to order. His wrinkled, bejewelled finger wags in the air. 'Let us remember why we are here and bear in mind the grave responsibilities now resting on our shoulders. I have to agree with Sir Hugh, I'm afraid. Contact must be made with the lass before the press get hold of her and exploit her for all she is worth.'

An elderly gentleman in the corner of the room brandishes a rolled up copy of *The Times* as though, like the conch, it will enable him to speak uninterrupted. A high-pitched wind whistles down his nose as he warns the exclusive group, 'Word has it that there's to be a high-society wedding at The Grange with every blooming newspaper in the land well represented. And the television. And the radio. And the satellite channels . . .'

'Thank you, Sir Godfrey,' someone retorts with hostility. 'We all know that without you rubbing it in.'

'We'll just have to hope the friend she is with, a Miss Belinda Hutchins, will manage to smuggle her off the premises before the fireworks begin.'

'Or that she manages to remain *incognito*.'

'That would be quite impossible. Her face is known throughout the land.'

And so the arguments pass to and fro, and all because Sir Hugh has mishandled the situation. Anxious and preoccupied, his exhausted brain twisting and burrowing, how he would love, for the sake of his career, for the sake of Lady Constance, for the sake of his Grace and Favour home, for the sake of his crippled father, oh how Sir Hugh would love to be able to redeem himself and thus find favour once again. On the fact-sheet before him he re-reads the name of the promoter of the hideous musical event – Walter Mathews. Could it be the same Walter Mathews who shared Sir Hugh's dorm at school? That spotty little fat boy with the moneyed American folks? Nobody approved of him, naturally; he was a foreigner, ever the outsider. Sir Hugh had influence over him then, so why not today? *Could it be the same chappie?* There's always the remotest chance; it's worth a try. He daren't mention anything yet in case he trips up again, but he will corner Dougal after the meeting (how quiet the normally precocious Dougal is, all of a sudden), and have a word. Maybe Lovette could do some digging but time is quickly passing and whatever needs doing needs doing fast. In the meantime Sir Hugh decides he finds Dougal's silence impertinent.

There are other topics which must be discussed at this most delicate time, like Her Majesty's untimely involvement in the political life of the State regarding a certain personage, one Mrs Irene Peacock, who seems to have shut herself in her home and to whom the Monarch sent a somewhat foolhardy reply. That particular Lady-in-Waiting wants a good slap on the wrist. Lindsey Marigold Stokes really ought to know better by now.

Unfortunately, the letter in question has been exploited to the hilt, nailed to the door of the dwelling in question and photocopies of the document circulated most generously. Every member of the meeting reads the Queen's reply thoroughly.

'Apart from the few bumptious old fools who always take up the cudgel, this seems to have met with an almost euphoric response on the part of the general public,' says the Equerry with a brave smile. 'Not to be sneezed at in the present circumstances, I would suggest, and certainly not a matter to be regretted. Indeed, so concerned is the country in general with the fate of this stubborn old woman that this impetuous reply is probably the best thing that could possibly have happened. Or so the polls are telling us.'

'Out of order,' gasps the Lord Chamberlain, once more raising his palsied hand.

The Chief Press Officer takes up the argument. 'It might well be out of order but it's a jolly good thing it happened. Without it we might well have seen a revolution by now, the people are so angry at the way things are moving.'

'Not a subject for jest, old boy.'

'I assure you I am *not* jesting,' says the Chief Press Officer severely. 'They are lining up to ask questions when Parliament returns.'

'And what do you suggest?'

The bald man with the red bow tie pauses for effect, pleased to have the attention of the room. 'Another letter has been received from the old lady in question, gentlemen. Apparently she left it with a friend before she took her outrageous action. The instructions she gave were that the letter should only be posted seven days after the siege began. I have copies of the letter here; if I pass them round, perhaps you will read them.'

Bloodthirsty pictures of stags and crags and otters and rivers, various prey in their killing grounds, frown down upon them as they read. A few stuffed and speckled fish peep out between the reeds of their glassy coffins.

Eventually – 'She's a cunning old bird, that's obvious, putting forward such an absurd notion.'

'Read it again, please, gentlemen, and then tell me if you think the notion quite so absurd. Read and bear in mind the public reaction to this little drama, and ask yourselves if this might not be a good way to restore faith in a system which most people now, as the result of Prince James' unfortunate behaviour, seem to consider to be overprivileged, immoral and distanced.'

There's another brief silence and a rustling of papers and then Sir Hugh speaks up. 'You're not trying to suggest, I sincerely hope, that the Queen should respond to this blackmail threat and go and knock at this woman's door like a neighbour in slippers and headscarf? Good God, man! Where will it end?'

'That is the question we are all trying to answer, Sir Hugh,' says the Press Officer quickly. 'Please consider the idea carefully before you dismiss it out of hand.'

'The thin end of the wedge,' warns the Equerry.

'Not necessarily,' answers the PR expert. 'This particular incident is quite unique.'

'Never! There'd be demands sprouting out for Regal visits to every Tom, Dick and Harry who happened to find themselves in trouble. By Jove, everyone would start blocking themselves in and making threats and before we knew it—'

'But couldn't we make it clear that this was an exception to the rule, unlikely ever to be repeated? Merely a private visit by Her Majesty, who happened to be moved by this one most upsetting circumstance.'

'What about the political implications?' somebody comments significantly.

'You have just pointed out yourself that Parliament is in recess. If we're going to do it, now's the time, when anyone who's anyone is out of the country. There would be the most tremendous public response.'

There comes an unpleasant wheezing sound from the corner of the room. 'One hell of a risk.'

'The time has come, I'm afraid Sir Godfrey, where risks are inevitable.'

'Hell, man, it is County Council policy to advise the elderly to sell their homes in order to pay for care,' says a flurried Sir Hugh, slipping into the pause. 'There's no money in the bloody kitty. The blighters have run out, squandered it on the feckless poor and the work-shy instead of on wars and weapons and Windsor Castle and other essential expenditure . . .'

'Oh, do be quiet, Sir Hugh, and let the rest of us think! This does seem a most dangerous precedent to set, but I realise the circumstances are unusual, and bearing in mind this latest unfortunate scandal, it could well be a way of minimising the damage.'

Sir Hugh sits back and straightens his tie. Is Dougal daring to smirk beside him?

And so the argument goes on, with some talking and some slumped in thought, listening and changing their minds, then changing them back again . . . A servant in black with a bright white apron brings in fresh coffee and a welcome plate of shortbread biscuits.

After a communal lunch of shepherd's pie and rice pudding with blackberry jam, the meeting breaks up and Sir Hugh and Dougal retire to their apartment, a small suite of rooms devoid of luxury and comfort as are most of the rooms in the castle. Sharing a suite with Dougal is upsetting for Sir Hugh, but there it is, he is on his way down in the world and this is one way They are making his new and lowly position clear to him. Suddenly he feels very tired, and would love to take an afternoon snooze, but at least he has bagged the best bedroom. All now hangs on the slim hope that the fat boy at Eton who called himself Mathews is the same fellow who's running this tasteless show at The Grange. He's some pop promoter, apparently. Big in the USA.

'But can you trust him?' asks Dougal, magically finding his voice again.

'Of course I can trust him,' snaps Sir Hugh, sitting on his spartan bed with its predictable tartan counterpane. 'We were at school together, weren't we? The horrible Mathews was my fag.'

'But you didn't particularly get on?'

'That is quite beside the point.'

'You can't possibly take the risk of confiding—'

'I shall do what I think fit,' says Sir Hugh, cutting him off and unscrewing the cap from his newly purchased bottle of Scotch. He won't offer a snort to Dougal: let him buy his own. You would think, in the circumstances, it might be provided but no, all that's on offer beside the bed is spring water and ginger biscuits.

Enquiries are being instigated by a confident Lovette even as they speak. They await with interest the result of his investigations. Lovette's computer lists are extensive. There are many businesses and organisations who would die for a glance at the information stored in that micro-chip brain; to the right people it would be worth millions.

'How will you find out if it is him?' asks Dougal somewhat peevishly. Talk about deserting a man when he's down, thinks Sir Hugh. He's going to remember this.

'I will ring the man up – what else?'

'You don't think a more cautious approach might be safer? After all, it has been years since—'

'I know what I'm doing,' says Sir Hugh impatiently. With a bit of luck, Arabella Brightly-Smythe will be delivered to him on a plate and Sir Hugh's career will be back on its glittering course again. And if Mathews is not the man . . . No, no, he can't think that way! His heart dies within him at the dreadful thought of perpetual banishment.

A piper below their window suddenly bursts into life with a gasp like a tortured soul from hell. The hairs on the back of Sir Hugh's neck bristle. How in the name of buggery can he deal with an important phone call above this tumult of agonised sound? Dammit, he won't hear a word Lovette says. He leaps up and closes the window but the wistful sound of the piper rides in waves through the thick stone walls, washes against the windows, passes, untrammelled through Sir Hugh's aching head and on towards the wastes of the valleys and mountains and over the surface of the whole world as far as Sir Hugh is concerned, so that when the phone finally rings his nerves are knotted with raucous tension.

It's not Lovette after all. Blow me down. On the phone is the weedy Mathews himself.

'Mathews? Is that you? Mountjoy Minor here, old bean. You remember me, surely?'

THIRTY-SIX

Flat 1, Albany Buildings, Swallowbridge, Devon

The matter is attracting worldwide interest and there is just no let-up. The authorities are at their wits' end. If anything, the pressure gets greater as supportive crowds move in with their tents and their sleeping bags. Neighbours provide coffee and charge the press for good vantage points. Unwittingly, Irene Peacock has been turned into a national symbol, a symbol of the good old days when people cared, little boys could go fishing in riverside pools and little girls could safely visit the ice-cream man, when valued grannies sat on steps smoking pipes, telling tales and rocking the family babies and everywhere there were poppies and bluebells. Ahh. Dream on . . .

The campaign headquarters has moved to Emily Benson's tiny flat, where extra phones and faxes have been installed, along with an instant soup machine. Naturally the police tried to prevent the world and his wife strolling into the very building which was the centre of operations, but the police were too busy, at that stage, trying to present a sympathetic image, eager not to upset the mob. They would rather capitulate than force any confrontation which might cause the ever-present fuse to spark and flare. Anyway, it's too hot for any sort of conflagration. If only the weather would break, if only it would rain. That would wash most of the camping fraternity away but they'd still be left with the hard core of troublemakers – long-haired weirdoes who make it their business to fan the flames wherever there's a likely crisis.

So here we have it. Two lead stories side by side each as strong as the other and both hanging on issues of morality and responsibility to those weaker than ourselves. And everyone is perfectly entitled to give an opinion; from the youngest to the oldest, chins are wagging, from early morning till the last news comes on at night. Miss Benson is now overwhelmed by mail every day and it is mounting up, unanswered, in her small bedroom. She certainly needed this fortnight's holiday. The vet, where she usually works, has kindly allowed her to use his storeroom at the back of the surgery for the excess mail. His customers are suitably impressed, and likewise, all sorts of companies have offered aid and sustenance out of the kindness of their hearts and also for publicity purposes because supporters of the siege are perceived to be GOOD; anyone else is BAD. The County Council is bad, the government who caused all this because of their mean mentality, is bad, the Social Services are bad for not sorting the matter out before poor Mrs Peacock was driven to take such extreme action, her uncaring family are bad, Greylands Rest Home and all who work within it are bad . . .

In spite of her promiscuous youngest son, the Queen did the decent thing by responding to a desperate old lady's plea for help, but is that all she is prepared to do – send a letter of commiseration? The cautious statements issuing from the Palace do not seem to support that initial goodwill, and loyal subjects are becoming restless and uneasy. What is the point of paying out all those millions every year merely for ceremonial purposes designed to bring in the tourists? Is that what the Royal Family have now been reduced to, apart from screwing the odd infatuated subject and leaving her in the lurch? Some predictable old codgers rant on about the role of the Monarch and the dangers of interference, while some folks remember how the old Prince of Wales went round decrying the poverty of the miners and then hopped off to a life of luxury in the Bahamas with his American moll.

No wonder the country is in the state it is.

Everyone's got their snout in the trough. Some folks are earning fifty grand while others cope on seven.

The Health Service is on its knees and turning away children with cancer and animals are disappearing off the face of the earth.

The sun is even strange, these days; it doesn't feel like it used to, and that's because of the hole in the ozone layer – and yet they're fighting over oil at the North Pole. They give grants for home improvements to people with Listed houses, while thousands haven't even got one.

Teachers get beaten up regularly in their classrooms and there's never anything on the telly.

Something is badly wrong.

Hooray for Irene Peacock. Someone, at last, has made a stand.

Ambulances stand ominously by. The Fire Service is well represented in case a ladder might be required, or cutting devices. Stalls selling baked potatoes, doughnuts, flags and hand-made jewellery have been set up.

At night, in the well-lit street which, with its boarding, has turned the area into a forum, people link arms and sing *Land of Hope and Glory*, and *He's Got the Whole World in His Hands*. Yes, religion has moved in, albeit rather late in the day, and Bishops and Archbishops appear regularly on the news giving their guarded support and leading prayers for the little old lady behind the walls.

Jesus cares.

The whisper goes round that a startlingly new development can be expected at any moment. The fax machines are jumpy. The mobile telephones bleep. Miss Benson is besieged in her flat as she waits for the appropriate moment and she chooses to make her announcement from the window like the Pope addressing the crowds in St Peter's Square.

Miss Benson's window is a balcony which is not a balcony, in other words you can open two French windows but you cannot step out, there is nothing there but a window box surrounded by safety bars. It is possible to hang your washing to dry over the edge of the little mock-balcony but residents are requested not to do so for aesthetic reasons. She is a timid but dignified figure as she stands there with a note in her hands, then turns to accept the megaphone passed over by a gentleman of the press.

Below her, all heads are turned up towards her. The crowd is hushed and waiting.

She clears her throat in readiness to proceed. She hopes Mrs Peacock can hear her. They discussed how this should be done last night. 'This is a letter which was given to me by Irene Peacock before she was forced to board up her home. I have no idea what it says, and still don't know,' she lies. 'It was she who wrote it. I was required to open it and read it seven days after it was given to me and I have kept my word. Now I intend to share it with you – *with all Irene's good friends*.'

A roar of approval goes up from the crowd. Miss Benson trembles; she is understandably terribly nervous. She has never spoken in public before, only in elocution at school when she stood on the stage and chanted, after thirty others before her, and using exactly the same inflections, *The Lake Isle of Innisfree*.

'This letter,' she starts, 'is addressed to the Queen, and I sent off a copy to Her Majesty this morning. Tomorrow she should receive it.'

The crowd crows with delight. They are part of this, and this is undoubtedly revolution. History is being made tonight.

'*Your Highness!*'

Below her comes a pleased flutter of anticipation.

'Thank you so much for your kind reply to my letter. As you will probably have heard, I have been forced to resort to extreme measures in order to protect my freedom and my property. By now, hopefully, everything will have been solved and this letter might never need to be posted. I regret having to bother you again with my little problems and hope I may not need to do so. However, in the event that I am still stuck in my flat, negotiations having come to nought, I now beg you to intervene on my behalf and on the behalf of all elderly people at present in this same plight.'

Miss Benson pauses for a breath and for effect. That initial palpitating fear has left her. 'Can you hear me all right at the back?' she calls.

A roar of, 'Yes!' comes drifting back. And a few shouts of, 'Get on with it.'

'I would not normally presume to make any request of my Sovereign, but my present shattered circumstances mean that I am having to behave in all sorts of abnormal ways and I hope you will find it in your heart to forgive me. I am not merely requesting now, I am begging at this tragic hour. I know you have an elderly mother of your own, I know how fond you are of that very frail and lovely lady. I know too how caring you are about your family and relations, so that is why I am begging you please to intervene in this dilemma which affects so many of your most vulnerable subjects, and come to speak to me personally. Come and knock on my door so the whole world can see how much you care, and I will open it and accept my fate whatever it might be.'

Some yob sets off a firework. It spirals into the night sky leaving a trail of stars behind it and starting a frenzied wave of stamping and clapping which grows so thunderous and threatening that those few security men who are armed put their hands on their hidden guns and stand to immediate attention.

'Damn,' says the Police Superintendent, hiding in the back of a reinforced security van. 'That's put the cat among the pigeons.'

'You don't think the Queen will come?'

'Of course she won't. You can't blackmail your Royals like that. You can't start off on that slippery slope, God knows where it might lead.'

Miss Benson has to visit the lavatory. She fights her way through her little sitting room, locks the door behind her and kneels on the floor with a beating heart. She pushes back the carpet and raises the floorboard.

'*Mrs Peacock?*'

A short pause while Irene Peacock positions herself to answer. 'You were wonderful, Miss Benson! *Absolutely wonderful!*'

'Oh, thank goodness you think so. I was so afraid I might muff it.'

'Now we can only wait and see. I have played my last card.'

'And if there is no response from the Queen?'

'Well, let's face it, I can't stay down here for ever. There's nothing else for it; if there is no response I shall have to creep out and suffer the humiliation of a complete U-turn. At least we have brought this wicked practice to public attention. At least people have been able to talk about it and get angry and be listened to by those few folks in London who are only interested in wars and foreign lands and the Common Market and such like. We've kept those issues out of the news for a few days anyway, those and all the devious sex practices nobody wants to know about. MPs and their silly wives.'

'You have bravely defied them all,' says Miss Benson from her bathroom floor. 'You ought to be very proud of yourself.'

'I couldn't have done it without your help, Miss Benson. You have been my inspiration and my right hand. Heaven only knows how you are coping with all those newspaper people in that small flat. It will want complete redecoration when they have gone. And what about the carpets with all that wear?'

'Now is not the time to worry about such insignificant matters,' Miss Benson reassures her neighbour. 'I will contact you at seven-thirty in the morning and we will decide on our next course of action. Have you got everything you need? Cigarettes? Gin? How about lime juice?'

'I'm fine, thank you, Miss Benson. In some ways I shall regret having to come out at all. It's so cosy living like this and never having to see anyone. I could go on quite happily like this for weeks. My only real regret, of course, is that Frankie has been so upset.'

'That was unavoidable. She'll get over it, you wait and see. And perhaps it will make her think a bit harder about her attitude towards you.'

It's so nice being waited on hand and foot and yet comfortable in your own home without having to get up and face the everyday turmoil of life. Irene can only compare this strange lifestyle to being ill in bed when she was little and let off school and having her favourite meals brought up on a tray to tempt her. Those were the only times she was allowed to read uninterrupted, listen to the radio, go to sleep when she wanted, presented with little treats like comics and jigsaws and ice cream for her sore throat. The only times she was ever totally approved of. After all, you can't misbehave when you're ill. Whatever your behaviour, you can't help it.

You get to be a monster by the time you are better, calling down with impatient demands, sulking and desperate to get out of the house. Quarrelling. Hot and scratchy.

William. How she misses him still. But now she gets to thinking that William was treated as if he was ill all his married life. Did she treat him like that because he was a man, and whatever his behaviour might be she secretly believed he couldn't help it? She knows how angry her relationship with William always made poor Frankie. 'He's nothing but a bad-tempered old misery and you are the one who made him like this. There's no one to blame but yourself if he doesn't lift a finger to help you. Hell, Mum, he's even jealous of the kids! And they don't like coming to the bungalow because Dad is so spoilt and unpleasant.'

Well? Was William spoilt and unpleasant? For the first time in her life she has the space, the peace and quiet to consider the whole matter. William was a self-centred man, everything and everyone revolved around him, much as the world is revolving round her today. It makes a change for Irene to attract this sort of attention, any sort of attention.

And she is thoroughly enjoying it. *She has never seen life from William's angle before.*

It is an excellent angle. She looks round her safe and cosy flat with the planks nailed across the windows, all this: her cupboard full of good things, enough gin and fags to last her, the television on in the corner, Miss Benson upstairs, the great provider . . . This comfortable life she is living today, this protected, peculiar existence, is what William enjoyed all the time. There was Irene keeping the rest of the world at bay, answering the telephone, dealing with the letters and cards, entertaining the grandchildren, going to bed when he went to bed, watching the programmes he chose to watch and eating the food which was always his favourite. Except when he was out at work William conveniently barricaded himself off from the world while she fed him all his necessities down through a chute and felt just as satisfied as Miss Benson does, poor Miss Benson, racked by a guilt which is her undoing.

But Irene had never minded.

She enjoyed taking care of William.

Oh, William.

Well, now it is my turn, and I'm only sorry you're not here to see it.

Irene Peacock once again readies herself for bed. It's all such a struggle these days. She eases herself up off the chair and pauses, resting on her stick for a moment, wondering if it is possible that she might need the sort of permanent care that a Retirement Home could give her. She would find it difficult, now, to cope at home without a great deal of help with the shopping, the cooking, the laundry. Sometimes, and she admits this only to herself, she can scarcely walk for the pain in her legs. For a long time now she has avoided looking in her mirror because the person she sees there is not the person she wants to be. Inside herself she is still sixteen with the whole of her life ahead of her; she has all the passion, all the silliness, still there under the grey hair and wrinkled skin, the scraggy chest and varicose veins. When she eventually pulls herself into the bedroom, moving slowly, putting one foot in front of another and using the table and chairs for support, she feels like a toddler learning to walk. It is as if she has made no progress at all in the long years in between.

What is the point?

What is the point of all this fuss?

Perhaps she should have just let them sell the flat after all.

So many people have been hurt in the process – Frankie, the children, Miss Blennerhasset, and now the poor dear Queen herself has been put in an embarrassing quandary because of it. And will Mrs Peacock feel any better at the end of the day? At best she will be allowed to remain in her flat, but for how long? Six months? One year? Perhaps two if she's lucky?

We shall see.

THIRTY-SEVEN

Joyvern, 11, The Blagdons, Milton, Devon

'That's the flat,' shouts Vernon above the hubbub and clamour. 'The one with the spotlight right on it.'

'Gosh, Dad, how awful,' and Suzie shields her eyes from the glare. 'How awful' seems to be Suzie's stock phrase ever since she came home for Joy's funeral.

Joy would have been proud of her children, Vernon thought vaguely on the day, as he stood there, numbed, in the crematorium chapel, when everyone's eyes were tranced in thought, manners subdued and voices low. There had been a post mortem, of course. The undertakers were so sympathetic, the very oil of sympathy, the distilled essence of courtesy, understanding and consideration, given the terrible circumstances. Vernon's muddled thoughts rambled over the last few days. Everything assured him that he was perfectly safe. He wondered if there was a God, or a Devil to whom he had sold his soul, and if this meant he would be unable to enter Heaven. No, surely not, he reasoned with himself. The idea was preposterous and only a prop for those who find the need to worship, a similar role to that of the Royals, who were under threat at that moment. And Vernon, nursing his guilty secret, knows what it's like to be under threat.

He went through tortures choosing a suitable coffin, knowing how much prestige and style meant to Joy, and how important it was that she went off in style, even into the fiery furnace. Vernon shuddered. For not only has he murdered his wife but he has shifted the blame to an innocent man and so is doubly damned, if, in fact, God is in his Heaven and all's right with the world.

Which it's not.

He was given Joy back in a jar and wondered what to do with the ashes. Ideally, Joy would have enjoyed being scattered in the city centre arcade, or in Monsoon or Next, but of course Vernon couldn't do that. After leaving her on the mantelpiece for a day or two he went and sprinkled her down the end of the garden where she'd enjoyed so many happy gossips.

And at the house afterwards he chose the most expensive finger buffet on the caterers' list just as Joy would have wanted, hang the expense. He can only trust that the Middletons are still going ahead with the purchase. He made a point of assuring them that he'd rather the deal went through, in spite of the tragic situation, but they hadn't seemed able to take it in. Too harrowing, he supposed. He was surprised at how many people came to the funeral. Since Joy's tragic and terrible death Norman Mycroft at the bank has changed his tune entirely. Well, nobody could continue attacking a man who has suffered as Vernon has suffered, and Vernon has an idea that someone had a strict word with him from above. At any rate the terrible fellow has been moved from overdrafts to mortgages – *not* a promotion, he was pleased to note – and replaced by the young woman with a bob and sensitive eyes who used to deal with travellers' cheques. Mrs Eccles insists on wearing ill-fitting suits like female weather forecasters, a silly mistake which makes Vernon warm towards her, and her name was on the bottom of the note of sympathy sent to him by the bank.

And now here they are, drawn, as so many people are, to the siege of the century, the very flat which Joy and Vernon intended to make their last home.

'You told us she'd moved here early because you were afraid we would overreact if we knew she'd gone missing,' Suzie shouts back, hanging on to her father's jacket for fear of being lost in the crowd, just as she used to in her chidhood. 'Poor, poor Dad, how awful for you! Having to cope with all that as well as the shop going down the pan. It's incredible that Mum wouldn't tell us the truth. We both honestly believed all was well and that you were only moving because it would be more convenient. And to think it was just a façade!'

'What about all those lies she told Adele next door,' Tom calls from the crush. 'I spoke to her at the funeral, she was very sympathetic, but nobody really believed Mum and you were moving into that cottage. Everyone knew exactly what was happening. All she was doing was making a fool of herself. Poor Mum, she must have been very sick at the end.'

'Perhaps, who knows. Could be it was a happy release after all,' says Suzie thoughtlessly.

Tom is appalled. 'How can you possibly think that, Suzie, after the horrible way that she died?'

'Thank God they've got him, that's all I can think about now,' says Vernon, leading the way to a hole in the crowd beside the police security van.

They have come here this evening because none of them could bear the thought of another sad evening at home playing rummy. Apart from the horror of the latest events, the three of them have little in common. Tom and Suzie are their mother's children, and dressed accordingly – Suzie in a neat navy outfit with large white high heels and Tom in a linen jacket, smart striped shirt and tie. Suzie's cooking is the sort of clean, sterile affair her mother's had been, nothing sloppy, everything undercooked as is the vogue these days, raw vegetables and even the lamb she did last night was served pink with some sort of herb sprinkled on it. During the day, of course, they picked at the funeral fare which seemed to taste of sawdust and ashes or perhaps that was just Vernon's guilty taste buds joining all the other rebellious parts of his body.

For Vernon is not a well man. The doctor has increased his blood-pressure pills and he is on tranquillisers and sleeping pills at night to cope with the shock. In fact, the shock, which was so apparent to all who saw him, was one of the most convincing aspects of his innocence, not that the police believed for one minute the ravings of Jody Middleton who is still being held at the station. They applied for several extensions to hold him in custody until their enquiries were completed and the lad appears before the Exeter magistrates tomorrow. No, the shock which genuinely came upon Vernon, was caused, he knows, by the sudden and complete change of character which crept over him the minute he started accusing somebody else for his crime and actually believing that to be true.

Never before in his whole life, until now, has Vernon done anything shoddy or mean. He has always owned up to his misdeeds, he has been kind and gentle, thoughtful and caring to those about him, never forgetting to shut field gates behind him, never dreaming of emptying his car ashtray in lay-bys as some downright ignorant people do, and happily hurrying to the police if ever he found a purse or a ten-pound note or a stray dog. The same as most other people of his generation really, but now he has committed two ghastly crimes and he's not even certain which is the worst, Joy's death or his wicked denouncement of that poor boy Jody Middleton.

If, at first, Vernon suffered from fear of exposure, it diminished with every day. Not in a living face anywhere could he see a trace of doubt or questioning. He cannot believe that having committed such a brutal murder, life can go on so quietly and unremarkably. That one memory anaesthetised, all is amazingly peaceful even though they are only one week away from that bloody afternoon which he has shut away in a locked cupboard of memory. Poor Jody hadn't a leg to stand on. Just as Vernon suspected he would, the youth left an assortment of clues behind him at *Hacienda* – fingerprints lay everywhere, and even shoeprints leading to the well made by his trainers, while no clue to Vernon's visit existed. Vernon, schooled for so long by Joy and his houseproud mother before her, is always careful to clean up behind him. The police haven't even tested the car in which Joy took her final ride – to the shops, he said, and they had no reason to disbelieve him.

'And she never returned?'

'No, she never did,' said Vernon sadly.

'And so you told the story about her moving into the flat in order to protect your children?'

'I did, yes,' admitted Vernon, 'although I know now I should have confided in them. It was just that Joy was always covering up for herself, for me, for the plight we were in, and I suppose I automatically did the same thing.'

'That's understandable, Mr Marsh. You have nothing to blame yourself for.'

'Perhaps if I'd been honest with myself and gone to you people earlier . . .'

'There was nothing you could have done, sir. Your wife was probably killed quite quickly after her disappearance. You must not be so hard on yourself.'

Everyone is so kind. Everyone has always perceived Vernon as a nice, gentle man; all the neighbours in the cul-de-sac, all his fellow sufferers in the arcade, they all told the police what a lovely person he was. Happily, they can't see into his head.

And he is, really.

It's just that he was pushed right over the edge, lost his marbles for a hellish few seconds, reached the end of his tether and Joy happened to be in the way when he picked up that iron. The police have not found the murder weapon although they have scoured the area, and of course poor Jody can't help them out although they spend hours interrogating him.

All around Swallowbridge is an atmosphere of excitement and carnival, with the savoury smells of food wafting from the stalls, the arc lights, the sense of expectation and the comforting feeling of so many people uniting as one against the enemy. What will happen next? Will the Queen put in an appearance? In spite of their mother's tragic death, both Suzie and Tom have flushed faces and delighted eyes tonight. Joy, of course, would have rebuked them for joining in with the rabble: 'What's the matter with staying at home and watching it on TV? You don't need to go there in person in order to show your support. You can phone it in, look, there's special phone-lines set up for the purpose.' No, Joy wouldn't be seen dead at a public event such as this. 'Making a spectacle of yourself,' she would have told Vernon, 'among the hoi-polloi.'

Much as he is loath to admit it, Vernon is gradually finding life without Joy a happy release himself. A blessing. He had always believed that he loved her, and maybe he did, but being without her has its plusses which he is beginning to appreciate, and it is rather like a rebirth. He is looking forward to selling the house if it all goes through, eager to rid himself of all those expensive and, he suspects, tasteless knick knacks. Naturally he offered her clothes to Suzie and she rummaged through them with alacrity. Vernon hopes she will take them with her when she goes because they are just too irritating to have cluttering up his bedroom cupboards. He has already pulled out of the deal to buy Flat 1, Albany Buildings, and under the circumstances everyone understands. Even the estate agent with his five gold rings managed to be courteous. The press were trying to pull him to pieces for his perfectly innocent behaviour, but these days anyone who is not 100 per cent behind Mrs Peacock is against her. Vernon was relieved to pull out. The prospect of a rented room to keep as spartan or as messy as he likes appeals to him greatly after his life of furniture polish, lavatory fresheners and plastic sheeting on new suite covers. He will furnish his new home with old chairs from junk shops, comfortable chairs you can pick up for a song, and a homely old bed with a creaking mattress.

'Oh Dad, how awful,' declared Suzie when he shared his new plans. 'Just because Mum's dead you still need a home to call your own.'

'No, I don't,' said Vernon decisively. 'That is just what I *don't* need. I intend to make my new life free of possessions and responsibilities.'

'That's just the shock talking.'

'No, Suzie, it's not. I have worked for a lifetime to accumulate the things that I have, and they bring me no pleasure. They brought your mother pleasure, yes, but now she is gone there's no point in cluttering my life with stuff I no longer need. I am opting out of the consumer society, Suzie, I am turning my back on it for good. I shall pick up the dole if necessary and go for long walks every day by the river, or play cards with friends, or sit in the pub and put the world to rights. I might even get myself a dog if my landlord will allow it.'

'Oh God, how awful, Dad,' proclaimed Suzie sadly.

And Tom is as bad, accumulating, consuming, borrowing, worrying, working all hours to provide for his wife and baby. They have long discussions about cars and washing machines and microwaves and personal computers, the best models, the state of the art, and have you read the latest report from *Which?*.

'If you're not careful you'll end up like me, working my guts out and making yourself ill, and for what, Tom – *for what?*'

'I would be proud to end up like you, Dad,' said Tom, trained in politeness as well as in neatness and good manners. 'These strange ideas of yours are just a natural reaction to the trauma you have suffered. Don't do anything rash, Dad, take things one day at a time, and you really should try to give up smoking. It's not going to help your health and it is so disgusting and off-putting these days.'

'We'll help you find another place to buy, Dad,' said Suzie. 'You might need to go into temporary lodgings just while you're looking round, but we'll come down again and help you look for somewhere permanent when everything's sorted, won't we, Tom?'

'Well, it's quite hard for me, actually,' said Tom apologetically. 'What with work and Sally finds it hard to cope with Baby alone at home for very long . . .'

'I'll come, any time,' said Suzie kindly. 'You and Mum wouldn't have wanted to live in the middle of the town anyway. I don't know what you were thinking of after this lovely house.'

'I wonder if Miss Benson will come out and speak while we're here,' asks Tom, excited as a schoolboy.

'I doubt there's anything left to say. Now they seem to be waiting for the Queen. The ball is in Her court.'

They mingle with the crowds; it's a cross between the old VE Day newsreels and the miners' strike. Discarded newspapers and litter flutter around like fallen petals. Some people are here for the fun of it and some to make trouble, and an odd camaraderie, a certain mutual respect, has developed between the two. People have come with their whole families, children of all ages and old people carrying banners and flags. All their differing colours in the bright night-lights are like sequins on ballgowns. Bodies move restlessly, arms wave, faces shine and one trumpet blares occasionally from the centre of the throng, the type of sound you hear from the terraces at a football match. Only a few hisses and boos are directed towards the police by a party of hooligans eager for mischief at the back of the crowd, drunk of course and a newsvendor cries, '*Read the latest news on the Siege,*' or '*Sensational Royal scandal brims over.*' There's a sense of something extraordinary about to happen.

'What if the Queen does come tonight?' shouts Suzie. 'I've never seen her. I'd *love* to see her. Shall we stay and have a baked potato?'

'We don't want to eat here in the street,' Tom admonishes quickly. 'For goodness sake, Suzie. You never know what germs are about, and those potatoes don't look too healthy to me. Look at the state of the man's filthy hands.'

Suzie persists. 'But do you think she might actually come?'

'I doubt it,' says Vernon, 'not tonight. Give her a chance. She only got the letter this morning.'

'Oh, I do think you are wonderful, Dad,' says Suzie, infected by the exciting atmosphere and kissing him impulsively on his cheek. 'We both think so, don't we, Tom? Coping like you have. And with Mum being so difficult.'

'Poor Mum,' says Tom.

'Yes, poor old Joy,' agrees Vernon softly, and wishes he was innocent. He wishes that Jody *had* killed his wife, and then he could feel completely happy.

THIRTY-EIGHT

Penmore House, Ribblestone Close, Preston, Lancs

Babs and Lenny Middleton are possibly the only couple in the land who are unaware of the dramas unfolding around them. They and their two persecuted daughters, Dawn and Cindy, are rigidly focused upon their own dire situation, faced not only with a rape charge but with murder, too. It feels as if it is they who have committed the crime; Jody, the perpetrator, is only one step further along the line of communal disgust. The excess flows over and drowns them.

It is now quite out of the question that they should purchase Joyvern, totally unthinkable that they should move into the very home which has been shattered by the alleged murderous behaviour of their son. Vernon, unhinged by the whole affair, suggested foolishly that all should continue as if nothing had happened, but that is quite impossible. They must find somewhere else while hoping against hope that their own house-sale goes through. They are down in Devon for the committal proceedings tomorrow morning, staying at the Old Mill Hotel where Babs has remained since Jody's arrest last week. Dawn and Cindy are with them although they have no intention of attending the court tomorrow. They will look round the shops, go to the cinema, take a trip down the river instead, anything rather than associate themselves with their contagious brother. At least, down here, nobody recognises them as they do up in Preston. At least here they do not suffer the slings and arrows of outraged locals.

Plans have been drastically changed. Lenny has informed the estate agent that he no longer wishes to go through with the purchase of Joyvern, and, owing to the extraordinary circumstances the agent quite understood. He has so far, however, been unable to contact the vendor, Vernon Marsh, who, he understands, has abominable problems of his own just now. 'What a ghastly mess,' he says to his secretary Miss Bevan after Lenny leaves the office looking deathly. 'You just don't realise how lucky you are until you meet some of these poor souls.'

But despite the fact they have nowhere to go, the Middletons have no intention of returning to Preston where they will now be hounded from pillar to post. They like this area, and Lenny is keen to take up his new job as store manager, so they have decided to look around for somewhere else. They will enrol Dawn and Cindy in a school with a good reputation (their education has suffered enough through no fault of their own), and rent a house while they wait for a suitable property to come on the market. This time they are decided on a house in the middle of nowhere, where nobody need know their name, and the excruciating stain of poor Jody will eventually, given time, given patience, be removed.

Lenny has almost been converted. He now half-believes in the guilt of his son and is resigned to face the appalling truth. Dawn and Cindy are Don't Knows, and they don't care what their mother feels, they are not prepared to pussy-foot around the subject any longer. Jody should be denounced and disowned, eliminated even from memory. It would be better if he had never been born, and if he's found innocent – well . . .

'I want to change my name by deed poll,' Dawn declared.

'Don't be silly,' Lenny said firmly. 'There are thousands of Middletons in the country. Nobody is going automatically to associate you with our Jody.'

Dawn sulked and said nothing. How could she explain to her father that she secretly believed that some lingering scent, some inflection of the voice, some unconscious mannerisms would always give her away as the sister of the so-called rapist, the kin of the possible murderer? She and Cindy were tarred with the same brush, leapt from the same womb, nurtured by the same breast that succoured the 'Beast of Preston'.

Yes, that's what the press are calling him now. And she hates him.

If approached, she is not even certain that she would stand up and support him any longer. She knows it's awful. She knows she's disloyal. But she hasn't the courage, she hasn't the strength to be despised and she no longer has the conviction that her brother is innocent. And perhaps, if they turned publicly against him, people would start to like them again.

When their mother enters a room they both look away, they lower their eyes, they turn their faces, no longer prepared to share the communal suffering, to listen to her wailing protests, to endure the agony of a parent who is demented with grief. The sooner Jody is dead, dead to her and the rest of the world, freed or behind bars, the better.

They are in the dining room at the Old Mill which is crowded with journalists. Every hotel and guest house, with vacancies limited anyway because of the season, is full to overflowing because of the Siege of Swallowbridge. Babs hasn't bothered to tidy herself up; she looks as if she's got straight out of bed with her clothes still on after a long and feverish sleep. But she hasn't come from her bed, she has come from the police station.

'That evil man, Vernon Marsh,' Babs rants on, and nobody else is interested. 'To think I trusted him, to think I went to his house and talked non-stop about Jody, giving him all the ammunition he needed to spring his wicked trap.'

'Shut up, Mum, and let's order some food. We've already been waiting for half an hour.'

'Don't say shut up to your mother, Cindy, please. That sort of attitude isn't going to help. You know we must all pull together.'

'I'm not pulling on her side, not any longer, and I don't care what I say to her any more,' says Cindy loudly.

'*Shussh,*' whispers Dawn. 'People are staring.'

No, they're not, it's you who's paranoid and no wonder,' says Cindy, but she keeps her voice lower all the same.

'Aren't you even going to ask me how he was this afternoon?' Babs, all twitchy and nervous, wraps her napkin round one hand as if to bandage a part of her which is hurting.

Her daughters look away. Lenny consults the menu. Eventually he asks her politely, 'Would you like some wine?'

Babs looks bemused. 'Would I like some wine? What sort of a question is that?'

'Oh Mum, *don't start!* Just answer, will you! Why must you always cause a scene.'

'Oh!' Babs sits up stiffly. 'I'm so sorry. I didn't realise I was. I must try to behave better in future.'

'*Oh Mum!*'

'It's just that whether I would like wine or not doesn't happen to feature very highly in my list of priorities at present. You,' and she stares glitteringly hard at all three of them, 'would not understand.'

'Forget it, pet,' says Len. 'It was only a thought.'

'*I* would like some wine,' says Dawn.

'So would I,' says Cindy. 'As an anti-depressant.'

'If you two can't be more tolerant then I think you'd better go upstairs and I'll have something sent up to your room,' says Lenny distractedly.

'If Jody was innocent they would set him free,' states Dawn suddenly.

'And compensate him with millions of pounds for the damage they have done. Not just to him, but to us as well,' said Cindy, just as coldly.

'I know how you feel, pet, I know,' said Lenny, lost for any more useless words. His daughters have been damaged, and it's understandable they feel as they do. In addition, Babs' almost fanatical behaviour since the murder is not making life any easier for any of them.

So the girls stalk out of the hotel dining room and one more evening is ruined. *How much more of this can any of the Middletons take?*

Babs is gradually losing her mind. Jody continues to protest his innocence and only she can tell that he is speaking the truth. Nobody will listen to her, either; she has defended him too violently and too often.

'But this time I know beyond any doubt that he is telling the truth!'

This afternoon even their solicitor Mr Goodyear looked at her strangely. 'The odds are against him this time, I'm afraid.'

'When haven't they been against him? The odds have been against Jody since this whole nightmare started.'

'I didn't do it, Mum', says Jody from the opposite chair in the mean little room assigned to him while he waits for his fate in the morning.

'I know, love, I know. It's not me you have to convince.'

'*I saw him!*' How many times has Jody said this, shouted this, shrieked this – and all to no avail? How many more times must he say it? 'I saw Vernon Marsh drag the black bag up the front path, through the house and into the garden. It was wrapped in a tartan rug! I sat up there and watched him drop the body down the well. I kept quiet because I was frightened, terrified. He might have been mad for all I knew, I was hardly likely to go down and confront him. What was I meant to say – "What are you doing, Mister"?'

'But Mr Marsh is a small, fat man with glasses. You are young and strong and athletic. What on earth did you think he would do if you did go down and face him?'

Jody's face turned puce. 'I thought he might have a weapon, a gun or something. I was shocked. I didn't want to be seen. I was on the run, if you remember. Why would I leap out of my hiding place just to find out what was going on and risk being caught?'

'If Mr Marsh was doing what you thought he was doing, he would hardly be likely to inform on you . . .'

'You don't believe me either, do you?' howled Jody in despair. 'My own defence doesn't believe me so where does that leave me?'

'Don't shout, Jody, it doesn't help.'

'Be quiet, Mum.'

'And nor will it help you tomorrow if you are heard addressing your mother like that.'

'Dear God! Here I am accused of rape and a brutal murder and you're rattling on about being polite.' Jody covers his face with his hands. *'Somebody help me, PLEASE!'*

'I just need to get this perfectly straight in my own mind,' said Mr Goodyear patiently. 'The prosecution will want to know why you didn't tackle Mr Marsh, and they will also want to know why you went round to his house after you'd seen what he'd done. Why didn't you go to the police? Why not make an anonymous phone call?'

Jody sighed for the hundredth time. 'I went round to his house not knowing it was him who lived there. I was shocked when I recognised him. All I could think of was finding somewhere safe to stay and I thought that if I confronted Mr Marsh with what he'd done I'd be in a good position to hide out there for a while.' Jody closed his eyes and slumped hopelessly in his chair. 'And it worked. It would have kept on working if that photographer hadn't come creeping round, if my mugshot hadn't got published, if Vernon Marsh hadn't known who I was. The moment he found out who I was he decided to implicate me.'

'So all of a sudden you ceased to be afraid of him, did you?' asked Mr Goodyear. 'You daren't confront him at the cottage, but you changed your tune when you saw him talking to a neighbour in his front garden. Isn't that rather odd?'

Jody shook his head and groaned. 'On the moor I was taken by surprise, and horrified when I saw what he was doing. He didn't look so sinister in his front garden, he just looked like anyone else, and I suppose I'd had more time to think logically. OK, I was stronger and fitter than him, but I still kept a wary eye on him, I can tell you. I didn't turn my back for a second.'

'But you lied to the police, Jody, didn't you? You told them you went to the Blagdons because your parents were buying a house there and you wanted to take a look at it. Now that has to be a lie. The coincidence that Joyvern was the very house where the murdered woman just happened to live is totally unbelievable! You must have met Joy Marsh at *Hacienda* and she must have told you where she lived . . .'

'Hey! Hey! You're mixing me up! Stop! I never met Joy Marsh at *Hacienda* or anywhere else. When I first saw her she was well and truly dead and I only saw her hand anyway. *I never knew Vernon Marsh lived at that house.* Why d'you keep twisting things?'

'Because that is what they will eventually do when you come to court!'

'But not tomorrow?'

'No, not tomorrow. Tomorrow you just agree to your name and address.'

'So why go through all this now?'

'For my own benefit, Jody. I want to have a clear picture in my head of what you say happened.'

Jody got up and slammed his fists down on the table between them. 'You're just the same as the rest and I'm up to here with all this. If you don't believe a word I say, why don't you find someone who does! Why don't you all just go away and leave me alone.'

'Jody! Don't!' pleaded Babs, in tears.

'You let me down at the rape committal . . .'

'Jody, be quiet. Sit down and control yourself, please,' said Mr Goodyear quietly.

But Jody was lost to reason. He hammered against the door, shouting and kicking and demanding to be returned to his cell.

Babs and Mr Goodyear sat side by side, Babs shaking and Mr Goodyear calmly making notes.

'He didn't do it, you know, Mr Goodyear,' said Babs.

'Well, he's got a funny way of proving it,' sighed Mr Goodyear, getting up stiffly to go.

So Babs has quite a few things she would have liked to discuss with her family, but the girls have gone upstairs in a huff and Lenny has clearly had enough and doesn't want to talk about it tonight.

'Let's go out and see what's happening at Swallowbridge.' He tries valiantly to change the subject, tries to distract her for her own sake. He cares. At least Len still seems to care. 'People are talking about nothing else. Half the guests here are from the press.'

'Oh no! Don't tell me that,' is Babs' immediate reaction.

'No, Babs, they're not here for Jody's committal. They are here because some old lady has locked herself away from the world . . .'

'I don't blame her,' says Babs. 'I'd love to do that. Even Jody was saying how much he admired her and her friend. It was quite pathetic, Len, to hear him. He said how he'd love to do something brave and noble like that. It was that little Miss Benson who seemed to have captured Jody's imagination, as if to say – if she can stick it out and succeed, then so can I.'

'They say the Queen is involved, that unless she does something to please the protesters the Royals have well and truly had it. Curtains. Finito. Apparently the hanky panky at the top has gone too far this time.'

'Oh Len, I find it so strange how life goes on and how people get involved in things which are nothing to do with them as if their own lives aren't hard enough.'

'Most people don't have the sort of problems we've had to put up with for so long,' Lenny says gently. 'Come on, you're not hungry. Sitting here is a waste of time. You won't taste anything if you do order it. Let's fetch the girls and go out and join the throng. At least if you're doing something, pet, you stand a chance of forgetting about Jody for a second or two. If we don't do anything you'll get more and more depressed and weary and you won't sleep again and we've got all that to get through tomorrow.'

Babs smiles at him weakly. 'I don't think he's going to get off, Len.' A little shudder runs through her as she wanders round in her loneliness. 'I think they've got him this time.'

Len stands up and helps his exhausted wife from her chair. 'Come on, love, let's go and get Dawn and Cindy and give them something else to think about, too.'

'How could that evil man do this to Jody?'

'Give over, Babs. I said, let's try and forget it just for a while.'

'Jody gets done for this and a murderer walks free.'

'I know, Babs, I know. But we can't be sure of anything yet.'

'Jody's a good boy. He is our son.' She pauses and turns to face him. 'But you think he is guilty this time, I can tell. Don't you, Len?'

He is so very tired of lying to protect her. His final betrayal is said with sad reluctance. 'Yes, I'm afraid I do.'

A total stranger, a little boy with big brown eyes travels up in the lift to the first floor. He gives Babs a bashful smile as he gets out and she and Len are left to continue alone. She stands stock still with her hand to her mouth, like a child with a difficult problem. They have nearly arrived at their floor when Babs collapses in Len's strong arms, trembling, shaking, heartbroken. He notes with alarm the despair in her eyes but what she says is the best thing he has heard since she first told him she loved him all those years ago.

'Oh Len, Len, I'm beginning to think so, too.'

THIRTY-NINE

The Grange, Dunsop, Nr Clitheroe, Lancs

Hah!

Since Walter Mathews was eleven years old he has been waiting for this moment. In the early days – not recently, recently it's become just an aching fantasy – he used to dream about paying that wretched arsehole Mountjoy Minor back. For never has Walter forgotten one moment of his most miserable childhood, when he was bullied, taunted, mocked, humiliated, hounded and beaten by the very man he spoke to so casually yesterday afternoon.

And the jerk had the gall to ask for a favour! Walter almost messed it up and laughed out loud. Good grief, the English public-school set are way beyond the pale, smugly secure in the warped belief that old school connections will get them anywhere, all they have to do is wear the tie and mention a few memorable cricket matches.

To start with, he couldn't believe it was him Lovette was rambling on about. He was checking Mountjoy's antecedents for a book, the abominable Lovette lied on the phone, but once Walter sussed that Mountjoy was after a favour he leapt at the chance and suggested that he ring him himself. The nerd was at the Sovereign's Scottish retreat and Walter thought, how typical, ever the brown-nose, ever the snob.

It is crucial for Walter to get this promotion over quickly, to launch his new group, Haze, in the vacant August slot, this group which is far more of a curio piece than a serious enterprise with worthwhile expectations, sad sods. One freaky CD, rather dated, most of it sentimental rubbish which will appeal to the young married fogies, and their come-back will be over, but of course their puffed up egos blind them to this simple truth. There isn't the scope for a follow-up; their talents are far too limited. Walter is using them to make a quick buck. The finances for this cranky fun-day will soon be recouped – the man's a wizard with money, and unbeaten in his record for spotting tomorrow's chart-toppers. One week at the top for *A Midsummer Night's Dream* – which is exactly what it will be as far as the performers are concerned, a round of crazy interviews and it'll be good night for the three of them. Fair enough. A week to remember is better than nothing at all, and on the strength of the one-off earnings, Walter should be well set-up for his next serious project.

Because of his glittering reputation, the wedding launch at The Grange is not an event those precariously balanced at the top of the music tree can afford to turn down. They'll all be there, the short notice won't mean a thing. They will do anything, pay the earth for last-minute flights, cancel previous engagements just to be where it matters, in the right place at the right time. Nobody in the business is going to risk a turn-down which might slight the influential Walter. Already there are fights going on over the invitations, carefully designed to cause a fuss and upset those who are not invited. The wounded feelings over the guest-list at the last Royal Wedding was never a patch on this.

A sprinkling of blue-blood is always essential and Walter knows that against all the wishes of their hapless advisers, especially in these dodgy times, James Henry Albert and his older brother, Rupert, the baton-dropping member of the next Olympic relay team, are bound to put in an appearance under the names of Wayne and Derek. Such an old and tiresome joke. For this is how the brothers get their kicks, one of those few occasions on which they can let their hair down, away from the stuffy confines of the rest of their lives.

The press are normally sympathetic. There's an unwritten law at times like these, to which most people who know which side their bread is buttered, adhere.

Walter rubs his fat and heavily ringed hands. Everything's looking good. It is a Hollywood film set, and just as temporary, like the fame of Haze, easily achieved if you've got the dosh and the know-how. The morning dawns with a perfectly soft summer light, the sun's orange beams slant on the vast red white and blue expanse of the main marquee which straddles the daisied lawns, the romantic rose-strewn bowers, the patterned pathways, the waterfalls, the discreetly breezy bunting, all reminiscent of the Chelsea Flower Show and surprisingly similar. Here, amid the fantasy, is where the wedding will take place. The altar is like a night sky ablaze with silver-white, virginal flowers. A few carpeted paces away and the Hawaiian bar with its thatched umbrellas is set around the deep blue pool, and the dining area, under imported palm trees, is riotous in a tasteless and gaudy Calypso style.

The wedding itself is scheduled to take place at noon. During the morning the helipad will be constantly busy and the sky overhead nothing short of a buzzing hive as everyone who is anyone hastens to the place where it's at. The field below the drive has been designated as a car park and by half-past eleven it will be filled with the world's most desirable speed machines. Waitresses dressed in nymph-like tunics of gold and wearing dainty thonged sandals, the fairies of Shakespeare's *Dream*, will circulate balancing trays of exotic and mind-blowing cocktails. Nothing has been overlooked. Walter has checked and checked again with his expert and highly-paid generals who assure him that nothing can possibly go wrong.

At ten o'clock precisely, because Walter likes to time his operations carefully, he makes his way into The Grange itself and marvels at the changes money can make. A quick lick-over, a few expensive and sumptuous rugs, pictures, soft-footed uniformed servants and floral displays – all to be returned – and, apart from the unfortuante changes undertaken by Jacy during his short residence, like the removal of the leaded windows and their replacement with double-glazing, the house has taken on an entirely different ambience. The style of the place has returned. Walter Mathews grins with pleasure and puffs on a fat cigar.

Jacy, the bridegroom, comes from the dining room wearing a look of exultation and a white linen suit with knee-length cowboy boots. His arms are covered in bracelets. The jerk still doesn't seem to realise that he is being exploited as a time-warp freak. Cyd and Darcy, dressed in identical costumes of black, have clearly been indulging their habit already. Darcy's eyes are partially glazed and Walter must remember to put a minder on him at least until the main ceremony is over.

'Wow, man, you're amazing,' says Walter, slapping Jacy's outstretched hand in a manly yet youthful greeting. 'And how's Mrs Smedley, the beautiful bride this morning?'

'Gone back to bed to have breakfast there,' says Jacy grumpily. He's been disappointed by Belle's half-hearted reaction to the hasty Register Office marriage at nine this morning, and now to this crazy hyped-up wedding reception, all done without consultation and with none of her family or friends invited. Walter has been informed of all this and is interested to note that Jacy defensively fails to tell him.

'I'll pop up and have a quick word,' says Walter, and before Jacy can stop him he's off up the stairs, nimble, as heavy men often are, and striding straight into the main bedroom without bothering to knock. He had half-expected to have to wheedle Arabella's whereabouts out of the saucy Belle, but luckily the fugitive is draped on the bed pulling apart a piece of toast, sharing her hostess's breakfast. Both women look up in alarm as the large, undisguisedly American, imposing presence of Walter Mathews himself steps through the door and closes it firmly behind him.

Back outside in the sunshine again, and just one hour later the unmistakable vintage Packard convertible belonging to the much-maligned James Henry Albert rattles up to take its place in the car park. Beside him is his brother, Rupert, both of them relieved to escape, albeit briefly, from the heavy tension of life at home at the moment. It was hell to slip their minders but they'd bested them in the end. The holiday has been ruined by the scandal and it's all James' fault. People are going tediously round with long faces, saying it might be the end. But James Henry Albert laughs it off, and puts it down to the periodic hysteria of the masses. What would they be talking about if they weren't talking about him? He vaguely remembers that this is the place where Arabella holed out before her disgraceful performance. It is also the place that oaf Sir Hugh was pressing him to buy, but he has no idea that Peaches is still here. His advisers considered it wisest to keep the unpredictable Prince in ignorance of that piece of information.

This is a fun day out as far as the two Princes are concerned, and they are dressed accordingly, in the costume of Elizabethan nobility – jerkins, leggings, cod-pieces and big hats with feathers, to complement the theme of the day.

They stroll towards the marquee at a regal, unhurried pace, their eyes turning neither to right nor left because they know very well that all the faces they pass instantly swing to recognise them. Immediately they arrive, one of the sprites in a wispy dress which hides nothing makes it her business to offer them champagne cocktails, and ply them with more and more as they circulate. These two handsome swells are naturally two of the most popular guests.

Walter Mathews sidles up and a fawning crowd gathers immediately. The cameras flash, but everyone knows these pictures will circulate harmlessly among the in-crowd, there's no real danger at a bash like this. The principal players, Jacy, Darcy and Cyd, whose day this is, are introduced to the Royal brothers and Jacy, already on a high, hits it off immediately, gooning and clowning around and slapping the backs of perfect strangers.

Talk naturally moves towards wedding bells and lack of future freedom. 'At least I've done the decent thing,' says Jacy, euphorically, 'and Belle's not the sort of woman you see every day.'

'Belle is amazing,' Walter chips in. 'She's going to do more for your popularity with the punters than any amount of songs you might sing.

She's got class, she's a real little honey . . . It says a lot for your prowess in bed, getting hooked to a looker like that.'

'Yeah,' says Jacy happily, surrounded by the great and good. 'And she thinks the sun shines out of my arse. Always has.'

'That's the kind of woman you want,' says fat-cat Walter, nudging Jamie, familiar enough with the young man jovially to slap his brown leather cod-piece. 'So how's the horsy Lady Frances going to take to this overworked equipment?'

From the crowd comes a nervous snigger but the Prince knows the roguish Walter; he graciously takes it all in his stride. Splendidly self-confident and fighting fit, the ornament of the day, he takes another drink from the cutie with the tray and the tempting cleavage.

Walter points to the house. 'There's one little stunner in there who's got the hots for you. She thinks it's the best thing she's ever tasted.'

There's so many, the Prince looks confused.

'Does the name Peaches ring any bells?'

'I say! Not Arabella?'

'You've got it in one.'

'There? Inside this house?'

'Yep, a real little doll.'

The Prince frowns and his regal nostrils flare. 'She's caused me some real aggro.'

'She's a woman in love, for Christ's sake. She's blooming and broody and she's still swearing to God that you are the one and only love of her life.' Walter cracks a tasteless joke. 'If you were a real man, you'd be taking her up the aisle today, side by side, with old Jacy here.'

'What a laugh,' giggles the little girl with the huge breasts and the colourful cocktails. 'Wouldn't they all go mad if they knew?'

'Jamie daren't even think about that,' says his older brother, smiling grimly. 'Even for a laugh, if it ever got out . . . And her people are nothing, really.'

'Yeah, it's a dream, that's all it is,' goads Walter, 'much too risky to try even here.'

'What a wheeze, though,' says Jamie in the best of spirits, his nose rather red at the tip and his words slightly slurred. One of the worst criticisms of himself he had ever read was when some stupid columnist said he had a schoolboy humour, for Jamie prides himself on his humour and wit. 'To do the real thing and then follow up with an out-take of me and Peaches . . . so wonderfully vulgar.'

'The sad thing is that the little idiot would probably believe it was true!' roars Walter, highly amused by this new thought. 'She wouldn't have the nous to know the thing was a set-up, a stunt!'

'It would be mildly amusing,' smiles the Prince, glancing with glazed eyes at his elder brother, defying him to interfere with his hard-won independence. In his fuddled, alcohol-fuming mind he senses that his pride is at stake and his vanity is wounded. 'But far too risky. And anyway, she probably wouldn't have the right sort of clothes to wear.'

He has said enough. So Walter smiles to himself and leaves the topic alone.

'You're married, Belle, and I still can't believe it.'

'But only so I can take him for all he's got when we divorce.'

'That doesn't sound like you.'

'Why not? I've always been a cynic, and now you're going the same way. No longer the sweet and biddable Peaches and I don't know if I can take the change. It's far too extreme.'

'These are extreme times,' says Peaches. 'You only have to read the papers.'

'But can we do it? Are we strong enough to do as we promised? Walter was absolutely right, you know. We have both been used abominably, although we both went begging for it. This would be the perfect revenge. I can see his point, but oh God, *it's so cruel*. And I never thought of myself as cruel.'

'Think of the fun we're going to have after it's all over. Just keep your mind fixed on that. Back to the flat with Mags and Charlie until we can find somewhere bigger and posher, and I don't think that's going to take too long. We'll be richer than we ever dreamed! And we'll be together in the marquee, we won't have to brave it alone, that long walk under the roses with the cameras flashing and the music playing. Jamie and Jacy think life's a game and people exist to be used and dumped when they feel like it. They deserve all they're going to get, both of them. Walter is quite right.'

'You're more determined than me!' says Belle, bewildered by the sudden change in the gentle, kindly Peaches, no longer cowering in the closet but pulling out all the stops in preparation for her wedding day. And she looks nothing short of a princess, Walter has seen to that, in a magical dress like that of the Disney Cinderella, as outrageous and as over-the-top and as classic as her lover's disgraceful behaviour.

'Can you blame me? After hearing that the man I love is prepared to take me down the aisle for a joke?'

'Poor Peaches.'

'No, I'm *not* Poor Peaches,' she says, settling the sparkling tiara in her hair and adding the final touches to her glamorous appearance.

'Not any more, not ever again. And that's exactly why I'm perfectly happy to do it. At least the child will be recognised. There's no way the randy idiot is going to get out of that!'

Belle, already dressed for what she now regards as the sacrifice, watches Peaches fiddling around with her curls, and sighs. 'By the time my ordeal is over, I bet you'll have changed your mind. I bet you don't follow on down the aisle like Walter says you should, arm in arm with the Prince of your dreams. I bet you collapse in tears at his feet before the ceremony even begins.'

'Well, you'll have to wait and see then, won't you.'

'I'm longing to see Jamie's face when he realises that the marriage certificate is perfectly legal.'

'What about his mother's face, then? And Sir Hugh's, and Dougal's, and the whole damn lot of them!'

'Trust Walter to find a willing priest. Trust him to cut straight through all the red tape. If you want anything done in your life, Walter's your man. He'll do it.'

'He must have had one hell of a grievance against that slimy Sir Hugh.'

'He did. That terrible man fouled up his whole time at school, poisoned his entire adolescence.'

It's a scene straight from a magical setting. The world's cameras follow the progress of Jacy, lead singer of Haze, and his enchanting bride, two beautiful people both decked in bridal white as they glide towards the dreamy altar.

And after that is all over there's a breathless pause as Prince James takes his intended Princess on his arm and bows low, if unsteadily, before proceeding down the golden carpet of flowers towards the floral cross.

Smiling broadly and winking to his knowing friends.

You could almost believe the priest was a real one, with his *'In the name of the Father and of the Son and of the Holy Ghost,'* and with all his genuflections. He reads the service so beautifully, like an expert, not merely some old actor who has found himself on the glitzy American circuit. Choristers from the Cathedral, crystalline and sugary as if off a Christmas cake, sing with their sweetly-cold little-boy voices; not a wrong note is struck.

Two perfect weddings. Two perfect brides.

Almost before the two new wives have left the stage, shrieking with laughter and heading, still in their outlandish gowns, straight for the helipad where a jubilant Walter is waiting, the priceless pictures of the day's events are well on their way to Fleet Street.

FORTY

No fixed abode

Miss Benson can hardly speak for excitement and jubilation. 'She's on her way, my dear, I just heard the news two minutes ago and thought I ought to give you due warning so you could spruce yourself up, choose something special to wear.'

'Oh, Miss Benson,' cries Irene, flabbergasted. 'I have to admit I never truly believed any of this would come to pass. My hair is a mess, I can't reach to do it myself . . .'

'Just push it all up under a net and it'll be fine. And why don't you wear that blue dress with the daisies, the one you wore at the Shire Horse Centre. It suits you so well – and don't bother with any make-up, Mrs Peacock, you really do look so much better without.'

'Just a touch of powder perhaps,' calls Irene, now in a total panic, wondering if she'll even manage to dress herself at all she is so overwrought. 'How long have I got?'

'The official announcement was made this morning and apparently She is flying down from Scotland as we speak.'

'Miss Benson, answer me truthfully. Have I done the right thing, causing all this dreadful trouble?'

Should Miss Benson share her suspicions, and the suspicions of the very well-informed people around her, busily faxing and mumbling into their phones, that the reason the Queen has agreed to do this is more to do with desperate measures than any personal empathy she might feel towards the old lady? The incredible pictures of the Prince's shotgun marriage have been flashed all over the world and nobody's talking about anything else. In Mustique, his former fiancée, the stalwart Lady Frances Loughborough, is stiffening her large upper lip and saying nothing. Nothing that could possibly be reported. Her humiliation might well be horrendous but it is a transitory thing, and her short engagement to the Queen's youngest son will do her prospects nothing but good in the long run. Her parents rush to her side in order to console her, and one of the Queen's best friends, the

Countess of Loughborough, is a friend no more. Sad – but there we are. Such is life.

The general and immediate view is, 'Gawd blessim, he's done the right thing.' Agony Aunts from across the land are rushed into television studios to give their opinions of the likely success, or otherwise, of the unexpected union. Is throwing yourself at the feet of the man you love a sensible and profitable course of action, bearing in mind that it certainly worked for Arabella Brightly-Smythe, now elevated to the position of Princess of the Royal House? There are mixed opinions on the subject, lack of pride being the main objection, but others speak up and say to hell with pride when you've got a kid to bring up on your own, and if you're madly in love why not go for it?

Staunch monarchists hold a different view. They see the outcome of this as pandering to blackmail and media pressure. After all, Arabella's family, while perfectly respectable middle-class people are certainly not out of the top drawer. Hell, not even titled. Although, of course, they soon will be.

The thing that really sticks in the craw, is the tasteless type of ceremony, and the sight of the Prince, his curls springing under his feathered hat like a latterday Robin Hood, in that ridiculous outfit! That, and his secrecy, and the fact that this 'Royal Wedding' followed on behind a hyped-up piece of advertising for a degenerate trio of pop musicians, Jacy Smedley of Haze getting hitched to his artful piece. *A Midsummer Night's Dream* my foot. The affair was a pretentious sham, held in the gardens of some country house in the middle of Lancashire, not a cathedral spire in sight, not one tasselled robe, just a congregation of publicity-seekers and a questionable old priest to lead the service.

So far there has been no comment from The Palace.

So far no statement has been made by either the Prince or his bride. In fact, there is a rumour that the new Princess left in a hurry straight after the ceremony, roaring with laughter. In spite of early attempts to trace her, and vast offers of money in exchange for a tip-off, Peaches' whereabouts remain a mystifying secret.

Although most people seem to think the Prince was right to marry the mother of his unborn child, the opinion polls are still giving the Royals their worst showing ever.

Under these circumstances it is obvious that the Queen's advisers will feel a public response to the Siege of Swallowbridge is the necessary, indeed the only move to make. Thus the official announcement that Her Majesty is on her way. Thus the confused excitement of the old woman at the centre of the whole controversy. Irene Peacock's liver-spotted hand shakes as she struggles to put her teeth in. She cannot possibly meet her Sovereign with grinning pink gums.

'Sir, your mother is absolutely livid.'

'I know, Hugh, I know. No need to rub it in.'

'What on earth did you think you were playing at?' the other man groaned.

'It seemed like a good idea at the time. Quite a jolly jape, actually. How was I to know that the whole bally thing was a set-up – and all because you bullied some wretched toady at school. Instead of venting your spleen at me, perhaps it would be better if you wised up to a few simple facts. Wouldn't it have been sensible to quiz this character, Mathews, before opening your heart to him? Didn't that even occur to you? Had you forgotten about the time you hung the poor fellow over the school parapet minus his trousers?'

'I had forgotten about that, actually,' confesses the broken Sir Hugh.

'Well, he hadn't, unfortunately for us,' says Jamie, enjoying the upper hand for once, but with angry flecks of amber sparking round the pupils of his eyes.

'I have to inform you that your mother now knows all the ghastly ins and outs surrounding the whole affair. She has decided to continue with the purchase of The Grange rather than cause unnecessary inconvenience to all those innocent people involved in the chain.'

'Come on – she's no need to do that!'

'She has her reasons, but is not prepared to discuss them with us.'

'I didn't like the house anyway,' Jamie sulks.

'That is beside the point. The main problem facing us now is how to extricate yourself from this latest mess. A message has already been received from the Princess to say that she wants an instant divorce. The only reason she married you was to legitimise her child.'

'Bitch from hell.'

Sir Hugh cannot but agree. 'It has been decided by those in authority over you that you must make every attempt to change the Princess' mind. Now the business has come to this, eventually the public will accept it, and this instant divorce she is demanding would be quite unacceptable to anyone.'

'Peaches has us over a barrel.'

'You could well put it like that.'

'So what must I do?' Prince James must indeed be suffering to display such abject obedience.

'You must court her, sir, in a gentlemanly manner, surreptitiously, of course, and try to get her to agree to move into your apartments at Kensington Palace.'

'She'd laugh in my face. Just as she did straight after the wedding.'

'Nevertheless, somehow this attitude must be overcome. And no more gadding about and whoring. Arabella is clearly not another Lady Frances. She has her pride.'

Jamie is not quite so self-confident this morning. He answers with a new and rather attractive humility. 'And if this course of action fails?'

'It must not fail, sir. You must pull yourself together and try to behave like a gentleman. Already you have made a public spectacle of yourself and the spin-off has fatally tainted the reputation of The Family. Matters are at their direst for years. Your poor mother is doing her best by flying down south to sort out another unpleasant little matter, and while she's away it is up to you to play your part unless you want to be greeted with jeers and brickbats wherever you go.' And although glory lies no longer in the downward path of Sir Hugh, he is an Englishman after all and determined to do his best and not end his career parked in some Palace corridor.

Poor Dougal has already been demoted and will soon be selling wickedly expensive cardboard clocks and picture frames four months a year at the Palace gift shop.

'Look at this! Read this! Granny is going to be meeting The Queen!'

'Lucky old Granny.'

'Poppy, please don't talk about my mother in that sneering voice!'

'Why not, Mum? You do.'

'Not any more I don't.'

'Only because everyone hates you. They all think you are hard and horrid.'

Yes, Frankie has to agree, that is all part of it. She thought her divorce was painful enough but never did she imagine she would have to face the fury of the whole British public, defending her decision to put her mother away. My God, the sort of spiteful twaddle they have written about her! She'd never recognise herself as the unfeeling and acquisitive cow they painted her in print. But over the last few terrible days she has been forced to rethink her position and yes, she admits, she could have been more supportive when Mother begged to stay in the flat, on those various terrible occasions when she ran away from

Greylands and they dragged her back against her will. Just like a child.

It hadn't seemed so dreadful then; it had seemed like the only sensible option. How would they have paid for daily care when the local authority refused to help, when the experts said she should go into Greylands because of the expense? 'I don't need daily care,' Frankie remembers her mother insisting. 'Just leave me to get on with it. If I fall down and there's no one around, so what? I've got to die of something, Frankie. If I set fire to myself with a fag the fire alarms will go off long before the fire can spread, and if I get burnt alive then there's no need for you to feel guilty! If I get knocked over crossing the road, tiddly or not, then so be it. I like my gin and I'm not afraid, and whoever knocks me over can be reassured by knowing it was probably all my fault. I'll even buy an alarm so that if I get ill all of a sudden I can contact someone and they can take me to hospital. What I want is to make my own decisions! Not have them torn out of my hands like this as if my opinion is suddenly not worth anything. There might well come a time when I need to go into a home, *but let me decide*, Frankie, please!'

It's all down to guilt in the end, because what would everyone have said if something awful had happened to Mother and Frankie had ignored the advice of the experts? They would all have blamed her, wouldn't they, would have said she was uncaring. Hah, that's a laugh, they're all blaming her anyway. How can you win? How the hell can anyone win these days, whatever they do?

She has been amazed by Irene's courage. Mother is a far cry from the humble fool Frankie thought her. Mother is a powerful and independent woman. And after her brave protest, after she's won the support of the world, how can Frankie continue to despise her feeble relationship with Dad? Quite clearly, that was Mother's decision. She was not betraying her independence, she probably regrets it now, now she knows she can cope without him, but at the time there was possibly no other way. We all have to cope however we can – and how can you blame anyone else for choosing a different road?

Let's face it, Frankie has to admit that her way hasn't worked too well.

Frankie, so embarrassed, so mortified at first, as if Irene had come to school wearing an outlandish hat, has gradually come to feel proud of her mother. She's a heroine. She's a fighter. The children, Poppy and Angus, have been infected by Frankie's attitude. If Frankie had been less critical of Irene over the years, the children would have followed her lead as children mostly do. Now that the sale of the flat has fallen through there is the chance of starting afresh, of getting to know each other again if Mother is prepared to do so. In future the experts can say what they like; in future Frankie is determined to try and listen to Mother.

'We're going to be there when The Queen comes, we're going to be there to support her.'

'They'll only slag you off again, Mum.'

'Well, I can put up with that – if you can.'

They pick up all the litter.

They erect barricades. They move the crowd behind them.

The large police presence in the small town of Swallowbridge is massively reinforced.

They clear the rest of Albany Buildings and Miss Benson and her press associates are forced to pack up and go. 'For security purposes.' Miss Benson regrets that all this excitement will soon be over and life will resume its boring old routines again. Although not quite . . . Her expertise has been recognised by several leading charities and Animal Aid have invited her to act as their Chief Press Officer, an opportunity she cannot turn down. Think of all the good she can do. She might, in the end, even make enough money to buy her own piece of land and start a small animal sanctuary – something she has dreamed of doing since childhood. She longs to tell Mrs Peacock about that. She hopes her old friend will survive this ordeal. Miss Benson stands at the front of the crowd and keeps her small fingers firmly crossed.

As the black, shiny motorcade makes its dignified way through the pressing crowds, a dainty gloved hand can be seen raised at the window of the second car. Some people give the occasional small shout of appreciation, but most are mute and waiting, watchful, for this is a tense and dramatic moment. Will Mrs Peacock be all right after this period of incarceration? Will she agree to come out? Will The Queen actually get out of the car and go and knock on her door, or will a hireling do it for her? Communal anxiety stirs. And what will happen to poor Mrs Peacock if she consents to be released? Will they haul her off to hospital like an astronaut returning to earth, for medical tests? And mental ones? And what if she should fail either?

At this, his proudest moment, the Mayor of Swallowbridge stands before the entrance of Albany Buildings resplendent in his golden chain. His wife made him wear white gloves, fearing The Queen might be concerned about picking up germs, as she herself is. The rest of the Council dignitaries have been advised to stay away, as it was their policies which caused the furore in the first place, and the security people are concerned that nothing should inflame the unpredictable crowd at this most sensitive stage. The few men beside the Mayor are either policemen or involved in Palace security.

The cars draw to a halt. Someone with experience steps forward and opens the door of the Queen's car. She climbs out, her handbag on her arm, and surveys the scene with a mild look of interest. Journalists jabber over their phones and television cameramen jostle for position for this is quite unprecedented. Accompanied by two officials – one is a doctor in disguise – she walks calmly and purposefully towards the entrance of Albany Buildings and disappears inside.

The crowd leans forward and holds its breath; it hasn't long to wait. In less than five minutes the Queen is on her way back, arm-in-arm with a wildish-looking Mrs Peacock. So she hadn't stayed for a cup of tea. The Queen stands by as Mrs Peacock, her hair all over the place and stains down her cardigan, is helped into the limo and then She gets in beside her. The bullet-proof window on the crowd's side rolls slowly down and out comes the stick with a hound's-head handle which is waved triumphantly at all her loyal supporters.

A sigh passes over the people like a sharp shudder of wind in a wheatfield before cheers begin to break out and catch on until there's a great roaring of approval. Flags, hidden away up jumpers just in case things should go wrong, come out and are waved energetically. *Somebody cares.* Somebody cares enough to go to the rescue of poor Mrs Peacock and take sides against the faceless men at the top. And that somebody is their Queen and Sovereign, the very spirit of the nation. Nobody cares much about the motive; all must be well because The Queen Herself has answered their prayers.

Mrs Peacock, and anyone else of that respectful, cap-doffing generation, would be the very last person to divulge what was said in that short journey by Daimler, so the press clamour for her secrets in vain. She has agreed to go to live at a very luxurious Home for the Elderly near Clitheroe, purchased by The Queen herself, to be run by a Trust along with several other large country houses planned for the same purpose. Here, the vulnerable elderly will be allowed to behave as eccentrically as they wish, to smoke, to drink, to dance, to sing, to make merry, to keep as many pets as they like – and good luck to them. Nobody will mention Meals-on-Wheels, nobody will mention Bingo, no schoolchildren will sing there at Christmas-time and no blanket squares will be allowed over the threshold. It is whispered that The Queen is planning to send some of her own elderly relatives there, but this could well be nothing more than gossip and rumour.

EPILOGUE

Anyway.

Here we are then, bidding a final farewell to them all as our little company save one, RIP, trip along to their next encounter, promenading, circling and quickstepping across that embarrassing, slippery and overcrowded dance-floor of life. The next time we see the small, trim, unassuming person of Miss Benson will be on our television screens six months hence when she is called in to speak on behalf of Animal Aid, or raising funds in the short slot before the news on a Sunday. Still something of a national celebrity after her handling of the Swallowbridge Siege, and greatly praised for her managerial skills, she is in her element, organising, encouraging, beavering away on behalf of the animals she loves. Nobody is afraid of her and that is how she achieves so much. Nobody bothers to raise their defences while in Miss Benson's unthreatening company and that is their undoing. She has found her rightful niche in life. She was born to be a moral crusader.

No more cautious shopping at C&A for Miss Benson, whose salary has risen a hundredfold since her straitened years with the vet. She would now be the envy of poor Joy Marsh, had she lived. But some people don't care what they look like. Miss Benson could choose to buy her clothes from any boutique in London, and indeed she has a flat there, but her interests do not lie in self-promotion. A country girl at heart, she has her eye on a cottage with fifty acres on the Somerset border, a cottage with barns she can turn into cosy homes for animals in distress.

Of course she invited her friend, Mrs Peacock, to move there with her, should she go ahead with the deal, but Miss Benson already guessed the old lady would turn her down. However, an interesting approach has been made to her, completely out of the blue, by the probation services dealing with Jody Middleton. A Mr Jerome Tigley contacted her by letter after reading an article about Miss Benson in the *Mail on Sunday Magazine*.

I have heard so much about you, this letter read, *as has my client who followed with interest and admiration all your activities during the summer.*

As you might already know, the charge of rape was dropped against him after the girl in question admitted that no coercion had been involved.

In fact, poor Janice Plunket, threatened by her father that she would no longer be allowed to live at the Centre away from home, confided in Mrs Maddison, a part-time worker at the Centre, that if only Jody was set free she would be willing to marry him straight away.

'Marry him, Janice, dear?' exclaimed that good woman. 'How could you possibly agree to marry such an animal, after everything he did to you?'

Perhaps Janice was not as clever as was suspected on her various reports.

Janice sobbed, knowing that life at home would be constricted and dull, no freedom allowed, not even a trip to the shop. After the rape Daddy was naturally even more protective of her than normal. 'But he didn't do anything I didn't want him to do,' she cried, wiping her nose on her cardigan sleeve, 'and I could have followed him home only I didn't want to.'

'But you never said this to anyone, Janice, not the police, not the counsellors, not the social workers,' said a bewildered Mrs Maddison, wanting to shake the girl hard, 'and you must have known, Janice, the trouble Jody was in.'

'I wanted him to be in trouble,' the girl snuffled on.

'But why on earth would you want that, dear?'

'Because I knew he didn't really love me.'

'Well, causing him all this harassment was hardly the way to change that, was it, Janice, surely?' Mrs Maddison could hardly believe her ears. Janice's surprise confession was so awful she was in two minds as to whether to pass it on, but eventually common decency got the better of her and she reported Janice's last-minute retraction to the friendly Constable on the beat.

The lovelorn lass was interviewed at the Centre rather than at the station, the thinking being that at the Centre with all its primary colours she would be under less stress. Another change in circumstance was that, this time when she gave her statement, her intimidating father was not present and so she felt able to tell something closer to the truth. If the victim was no longer a victim, nothing could be done and the charge of rape was reluctantly dropped.

Jody the murderer, angry and frightened in his cell, broke down completely when he heard the news and was instantly persuaded to sue for colossal damages by his surprised solicitor. His mother, Babs, was over the moon. 'I knew it!' she cried triumphantly. 'I always knew it. Jody could never do a thing like that.'

The probation officer's letter went on, *Much has happened to Jody since all this started, and it is now looking increasingly as if he was innocent of both crimes with which he was originally charged.*

The murder case, at first so successfully solved, was unravelling bit by bit. The first man to throw in a cog was Constable Ryan Bodie, who happened to come upon an innocuous roll of black dustbin liners under Vernon Marsh's sink. These dustbin liners came on a long, industrial roll from B&Q, and had yellow draw-string handles – the very same kind of liner which was wrapped round the body in the well.

'Funny,' said the detective in charge. 'Funny,' as he scratched his head. Why would young Middleton be carrying such a dustbin liner around with him in the first place? There were no such rolls at his parents' house and that was the last place he visited.

Another concern was that no weapon had yet been discovered although the area had been combed. But even more confusingly, the weapon in question was believed to be an ordinary household iron because the imprints left on parts of the skin were of a rounded triangle shape that perfectly resembled the bottom of a Tefal lightweight 20S steam, along with the pattern of holes that were found on the body here and there. The iron in Vernon's house, albeit the same brand and not new, was ever so slightly different.

'So where would the wretched Middleton get his hands on a steam iron somewhere in the middle of Dartmoor?' the detective in charge was forced to enquire, though much against his will.

There were far too many loose ends to proceed with the charges, but not enough, unfortunately, to point them firmly in Vernon's direction. This case was clearly not as open and shut as had first appeared. It would take time and careful investigation, further questions and more statements – and that meant more men and less financial resources left for the already fully stretched Devon and Cornwall Force.

In these complicated circumstances it is difficult to know the best course to take with Jody's immediate welfare in mind after his release. The publicity used against him has been so unfairly damning. This is a young man who, through fear and trauma, has suffered greatly and does not feel ready to take up his university place yet.

Miss Benson, so concerned with justice for all, had read on with interest. Apparently the traumatised Jody, so badly done to like her own dear mother, needed a quiet and private place to go well away from the public eye, and he himself, having read the article in the *Mail on Sunday*, and having seen the place on which Miss Benson had her eye, suggested he might go and work for her. 'If she'll have me.'

It is always heartening to be able to help the needy.

Miss Benson, in her thorough way, went to visit his parents still residing in their lovely old house in Preston.

'No, I understand that he can't come home for a while, not until things have died down, and now our purchase has fallen through we are going to have to think again. It would be very kind of you, Miss Benson, if you would agree to take Jody on in the meantime. There are always the few vicious people out there who will continue to believe my son to be guilty no matter what happens.' Thus Babs Middleton conveniently ignored the fact that in the end, when the pressures seemed too great to bear, torn by doubt, she too, had faltered. 'Because this is what they want to believe.'

The two Middleton daughters sat on the sofa in silence.

And Babs, who can afford to open her eyes again now that her wounded cub is about to be freed, at dear last gets up off the sofa and hugs her two damaged daughters as she hasn't managed to hug them in months. Their mingled tears are not for Jody, at last they are for each other. Some new understanding is born as Miss Benson sits there feeling as gratified as a guardian angel, and smiles.

Emily Benson's one concession to her new and advantaged lifestyle is that she shops for food at Marks & Spencer, although still with her tartan shopping trolley. Naturally, as a person who likes to keep her finger on the pulse, she takes a keen interest in the other newsworthy event that was taking place at the same time as the Siege of Swallowbridge. She picks up a glossy magazine from the newsagents on the way home and reads avidly about the fate of the new Princess of the Royal House.

Such a scandal. And so remarkable how her little story had linked to that which rocked the nation.

They couldn't have done it without the Queen and that was Mrs Peacock's idea, bless her.

The last time Emily visited, she was escorted by the pleasant receptionist in the hall into a sumptuous room on the ground floor which opened out onto the grounds of The Grange. The only nuisance was the kilted piper marching up and down on the terrace outside. There, holding court as usual beside her own log fire and surrounded by her many little treasures, was her friend Mrs Peacock, sipping a gin and tonic and smoking a cheroot, before preparing to go into the wood-panelled dining room for smoked salmon and duck and lemon meringue pie. No mince or cauliflower cheese here, or soft ice cream with tinned peaches, unless specifically requested, of course.

Flat 1, Albany Buildings is up for sale again.

The mortified Frankie had invited her mother to move in with her and the children. This request, at one time so impossible, proved to be simple in the end, extraordinarily so, and the children, Poppy and Angus, after their uncomfortable persecution experiences, were quite in accord. Their grandmother was a star, after all. But Mrs Peacock kindly refused – and who wouldn't, given a chance to live at The Grange with all its luxuries and all the interesting people there. But mother and daughter were reunited, however, and Miss Benson was happy to see they were both more comfortable in each other's presence than she had ever seen them before. The battling of these two generations had ceased at dear last.

The Queen herself takes an interest in the progress of the newly named Royal Grange, putting an exalted Civil Servant, a previous aide to Prince James himself, in charge. Quite a violent career change for Sir Hugh, although not quite so humiliating as being parked in a Palace corridor or behind the counter in the Palace gift shop all summer long like the hapless Dougal. Grace and Favour. Sir Hugh Mountjoy and his wife live quietly in the lodge in the grounds, although there is talk that Lady Constance is seldom there; she prefers the London high-life. Sir Hugh goes for long walks alone, and fishes for hours in the river, and is often seen and even heard talking to himself in the strangely formal and mostly indecipherable language of his kind.

The magazines and journals so fascinating to Emily Benson (she would pass them on to the residents of the Royal Grange except they have them all delivered on the day of publication) leave nothing out in their telling of the progress of the new Royal couple. Princess Peaches, as the media insist on calling her, resides stubbornly in a Knightsbridge flat with her friends and is leading the life of Riley. The birth is now imminent and it remains to be seen if the profligate Prince can win back his blossoming wife in time.

There is nothing he will not do to woo her, and the fickle public are now right behind him, happy to see the mighty humbled and the straying sheep returned to the fold. He has even attempted to improve his mind by going to concerts and ballets, by giving up all those childish sports and enrolling part-time in a university course, reading Psychology and Sociology. He was last spotted with a group of friends coming out of a fathers-to-be session run by one of his own charities, and the rat-pack discovered that the recalcitrant Prince had put his name down for all five one-hourly workshops.

The nation's heart was instantly warmed.

But will she have him? Is there a faint renewal of hope? Nobody knows. Only time will tell.

Oh, it's all so fascinating, following the fortunes of the rich and the famous. Belinda Hutchins, the Supermodel who once lived at The Grange and now shares a flat with her Royal friend, is involved in good works down the East End, helping to run a Centre for down-and-outs and piss-heads, one of whom appears to be Jacy, the has-been singer from SugarShack, who made a feeble come-back before flopping gutlessly back to the shadows with his two dubious friends. Apparently they turn up from time to time at the Centre, when it's cold or when it's raining or when they have been turned out of their squat. The little trio play sad songs to the men and women who huddle over the plastic tables in the canteen, adding a little warmth to the patched overcoats and the sweet teas. Sometimes the more vigorous join in with the words and it sounds like wolves howling in some desperate night.

But it is reassuring for the public to know that the new Princess is cohabiting with the caring.

The only character in the chain whose fortunes evade Miss Benson is the husband of the murdered woman, Vernon Marsh. She would be sorry to hear that the bank foreclosed on Vernon Marsh after giving him adequate time to mourn the tragic loss of his wife. The bank foreclosed and Joyvern was immediately put up for auction. He ended up with a few thousand pounds and moved, with only one shabby suitcase, into a bedsit in Plymouth.

'Come to us, Dad,' urged his polite daughter Suzie, speaking on behalf of herself and her lover. Vernon knew she didn't mean it.

Tom didn't even ask.

And anyway, after a life struggling with Joy, Vernon would rather be his own man. What's more, he's nervous, horrified to hear that the police in their wisdom have finally let Jody go without telling him why. They ought to have told him why. Hell, he is as much the victim as poor Joy herself. Vernon believes Jody did it – well, he couldn't have done such a thing himself. *Not him*. Not gentle Vernon. Could he?

And they won't leave him alone, either. Irritating detectives keep calling, cornering him, asking questions, seeking answers, buzzing round him like blowflies on bacon, and the single bulb in his room gives no hiding place. His self-control is threatened. His inward terror flourishes. For consolation he has taken to spending his evenings down at the local, an unprepossessing place where drunks and the lonely keep company at the long wooden bar. But at least he can lie in bed in the mornings and trace pictures across the broken ceiling. He doesn't have to get up and head for Marsh Electronics in that damn depressing arcade in the rain.

Miss Benson will be tickled pink to give a home to Jody, a refuge for a boy who, like her rescued animals, has done nothing to cause his own distress. Animals are renowned for their remarkable healing powers, so there's hope for Jody's quick recovery and the renewal of his education. He will make a very good lawyer after his own hair-raising experiences.

It seems appropriate that Faith Steadfast, the poet and thinker who gave such comfort to Irene Peacock and other house-bound mothers of that era, should have the last word.

> *Why feel alone, why feel abandoned*
> *As down life's highway on you go?*
> *Smile and see that chain reaction.*
> *See how people's faces glow.*